BOOKWRIGHT

BOOKWRIGHT
Book One of the Vanir Trilogy

George R. Dasher

BOOKWRIGHT
BOOK ONE OF THE VANIR TRILOGY

This is a work of fiction. All of the characters, names, incidents, organizations, and dialogue in this novel are either the products of the author's imagination or are used fictitiously.

iUniverse books may be ordered through booksellers or by contacting:

iUniverse
1663 Liberty Drive
Bloomington, IN 47403
www.iuniverse.com
1-800-Authors (1-800-288-4677)

Because of the dynamic nature of the Internet, any web addresses or links contained in this book may have changed since publication and may no longer be valid. The views expressed in this work are solely those of the author and do not necessarily reflect the views of the publisher, and the publisher hereby disclaims any responsibility for them.

Any people depicted in stock imagery provided by Thinkstock are models, and such images are being used for illustrative purposes only. Certain stock imagery © Thinkstock.

ISBN: 978-1-4917-5336-1 (sc)
ISBN: 978-1-4917-5338-5 (hc)
ISBN: 978-1-4917-5337-8 (e)

Library of Congress Control Number: 2014920875

Printed in the United States of America.

iUniverse rev. date: 12/05/2014

THE OLD MAN

One of the flood lights he had placed near the door flickered, and Jarl knew someone—someone deadly silent—had entered the room. He moved to his left, just as quietly, and placed his wrench on the floor and picked up his blaster pistol. He knew he had no time for this, not with what little air there was escaping, but he also knew—with all probability—that whoever had entered the room so silently had most likely come to kill him.

Jarl was desperate. With one exception, everyone else on board the ship was dead, killed by the *Mjollnir*'s two attacks or the CEP's assault force. His head hurt, his knuckles hurt, his right knee hurt, and he was terrified. Deathly terrified. Twice now, the dying *Cassiopeia*'s artificial gravity had failed. The first time had been brief, only two seconds, but the second time had lasted a full Earth minute, long enough for Jarl to float more than a meter into the air, and then—when the gravity came back on—slam him hard back onto the steel deck, hurting his right knee, and bouncing his tools all over the transport bay.

And there was no time. Three times he had injected foam into the damaged hull of the spaceship, hoping to stop the escape of the air. But that had not worked, and now the duct behind him automatically vented air into the room again. That made four times in the past hour, and Jarl knew there were other holes in the hull, holes he could not find, and holes he had no more foam to plug.

He rubbed his arm across his face, wiping away the sweat, and feeling the roughness of an old scar. And he waited, silently, listening to the rapid, terribly loud beating of his heart, waiting for the other person to make the first move. But that person did not. He was clearly a hunter, patient and also waiting.

Jarl had been trying to bolt the last hatch onto the last life pod, and then inject himself into space. *But then what?* He knew that no one, other than the *Mjollnir*, would hear his distress beacon, and—without power—he had no hope of descending to the planet below or traveling to the great golden ship they had seen in orbit. And, more than likely, the *Mjollnir* would return and destroy the pod—or capture him. And his capture, Jarl knew, would lead to a very public, very humiliating trial, and he would be tortured for the secrets he knew. Suicide, he knew—and dreaded—was the best choice of all.

He risked a quick glance at the yeoman on the table behind him. He could hear the faint rasp of her breathing, which was good, but with no medical supplies there was little he could do other than stop the bleeding. She had been shot in one shoulder with a blaster rifle, and was now struggling with fluid in her lungs. If he could get to the medical supplies, maybe then she would have a chance.

But that was another lost hope. The *Cassiopeia* was dying. No one—Jarl had thought—had survived the pitched battle that followed the assault of the CEP's landing party's on the ship. The sick bay and bridge were cut off by the automatic air locks, and there was no way to get to the medical supplies, no way to send a distress signal, and no good way to get off the wrecked ship. Not that, Jarl knew, abandoning the ship in this remote corner of the universe was any kind of solution—the best it would bring would be a slow death trapped in a powerless life pod.

Damn that Sharon Hindman anyway! What right did she have to knock him out? And why, with dozens of drugs on board, did she hit him over the head with an electronic clipboard? What had she hoped to gain? Had she hoped to somehow get him to the golden ship they had seen orbiting the green-blue planet below? And why couldn't she have organized a simple ambush for the CEP storm troopers? Jarl had seen the results, and it was obvious that she, her crew, and all the Space Marines had walked blindly into a firefight, into what had become a slug match, where both sides threw reinforcements piecemeal into the battle, and where everyone on both sides had been killed.

Jarl rubbed his forehead again. High above him, the vent released another hiss of air. The noisy air stopped, and Jarl held his breath and listened with all his being. And then he heard it, the faint scrape of a shoe on the floor. He moved a little more to his left, and more behind the escape pod. There he waited, still listening. There were no other sounds. But still he waited, trying to hold his breath so he could hear better. And then a shadow passed in front of one of the lights.

Jarl was careful to make no noise. He moved slowly backwards, so that he was now behind a crooked stack of discarded equipment.

There was another person in the transport bay. That person stopped in front of the pod, then quietly started to circle it. Jarl, on cat feet, moved further left and hid behind the broken remains of a large radio transponder. The other person reached the front of the escape pod and stepped toward the bright lamp under which Jarl had been working.

Slowly, ever so cautiously, Jarl edged his head around the side of the transponder. There, bending to look inside the pod, was an old man. He was wearing neither the black uniform of the CEP nor the brown of the Space Marines. Instead he wore heavy gray robes, and he carried not an assault-blaster—but rather a long, wide sword. The man's boots were leather, not plastic and Velcro, and his hair was long and gray.

Jarl blinked, once and then again. He felt his breath catch in his throat and his jaw go slack with surprise. He risked a glance around the bay. He and the old man were alone. The door was now open a score of centimeters, but he could see no one on the other side.

The old man lifted his robes with one hand. He ducked his head, preparing to enter the escape pod. Jarl took a small step, so that he would be partly visible to the old man, and he softly whistled. The old man turned, at the same time whirling his sword in a graceful arch, and looked up. When he saw Jarl with his pistol leveled, one thick, white eyebrow arched upward, but he said nothing. His eyes were gray, and they were calm and unafraid.

Jarl stared at the man. Nothing—*nothing!*—about him made any sense. He had worn boots and was dressed in tattered archaic woolen robes. He carried a long obsolete weapon. His hair hung down to his shoulders, and his face was weathered with what seemed to be several lifetimes of experiences. His great, brushy eyebrows almost met above his large nose, and his eyes—those gray eyes—were amazingly calm.

Jarl moved more to his left, so he could better see through the open doorway, and the old man moved in the opposite direction. He now held his great sword with both hands, with an easy grace, and with its tip pointing at Jarl.

They stared at each other in silence for most of a minute, then Jarl asked a single question, "Do you speak English?"

One of the old man's gray eyebrows again arched upward. He spoke one word, "Yes."

That too was surprising. Jarl paused, considering what to say, then he asked, "Are you from the *Mjollnir*?"

The old, white-haired man shook his head no.

Jarl was confused. "Are you a stowaway?": he asked.

The old man spoke slowly and softly. "I am not a stowaway. My name is Kvasir Haroldson." He paused, then spoke again. "I am from the nation of Vanir, on the planet of Vanir." He had a strange accent, but his words were easy to comprehend.

"Is that the planet we orbit?"

Kvasir paused, considering the question. "The answer is yes... if I understand the concept correctly." He paused again. "And who are you?"

Jarl was not willing to answer this question. Kvasir repeated it, but not verbally—this time telepathically.

Jarl was again surprised—so surprised, in fact, he took a step backward. He answered slowly, but also telepathically. *Few, if any, of my enemies are telepathic.* He hesitated, then lowered his pistol so that it was pointing somewhat toward the floor.

After a moment of hesitation, Kvasir made the next move, and dropped the point of his sword toward the floor.

Jarl spoke aloud, "Your orbiting ship came as a surprise. I presume you saw our battle." The old man did not speak, and—finally—Jarl asked, "You are from that golden ship, aren't you?"

"No."

"Are you from a shuttle?"

"No."

"Then how did you get here?"

Kvasir said nothing.

Jarl did not know what to do next. He moved to the open door and glanced into the empty corridor beyond. He looked at the young woman laying on the table. It required only a second to see that she had died. He forced a mask onto his face and made his thoughts neutral, then he turned back to the old man. "My name is Jarl Hawkins," he said. "I am from Earth."

Both of Kvasir's eyebrows shot upward in surprise. "Earth!" he exclaimed. "Where is that?"

Jarl was also amazed. "Earth is the planet where all human life originated...," he began.

"I know that. But Earth has become a myth to us. We are not sure it exists..."

The deck underfoot shuddered, reminding Jarl of their need to hurry—and to focus on their problem. "It you are not from the *Mjollnir* or the golden ship, then where are you from? And how did you get here?"

Kvasir looked at his clothes, as if he was seeing them for the first time. "I understand your dilemma... my clothes... my sword... They are not what you are used to... And your dress is equally strange to me. I can travel through the void that surrounds this ship, but not in the manner you are used to." The old man's voice was soft and strong, and somehow reassuring. The gray eyes had never changed. They were still calm—and confident.

The air vent hissed again, then became silent. With the quiet, the ship felt even colder and more tomb-like. "We need to go," Jarl said. "This ship is dying. Can you get us out of here?"

"I can take you to the planet...," Kvasir said. His eyes flickered to the dead yeoman. "Are you the only one left alive? I saw many other bodies. Many were torn apart..." His words were now soft, and with a hint of pain. Jarl knew, without asking, that this man had seen death before. Perhaps a lot of death.

Jarl spoke quickly, "I'm the only person left alive." He momentarily fingered the bruise on his forehead, but decided he did not want to go into the details. "The escape pods have been damaged, and I can't get this one to hold air. I cannot get off this ship. It is your way or no way."

Kvasir still waited. It was clear he was hesitant about something.

"And," Jarl added, "the *Mjollnir* might come back at any moment. That's the ship that attacked us."

"That ship will not be back." There was a dry finality to Kvasir's voice.

"How do you know?"

"Because it is hanging out there in the void, not moving. It is a wreck, and as bad as this ship is. I saw it through one of this ship's round windows. Clearly you were not defenseless..."

"We fought the battle as best we could," Jarl murmured. "How did you get on board?" His questions were becoming insistent.

Kvasir nodded suddenly to himself, and it was clear he had made some kind of decision. He sheathed his long sword, stepped forward, and—before Jarl could back up—placed a strong hand on his shoulder. "Please have no fear. I will help you." He paused, and then added, "How long will it take you to gather your things?"

As if on cue, the ship shuddered again. There was an instant when Jarl felt heavier, then there was a second of being too light. "I have very little," Jarl said quickly. "Everything I had was on the upper deck, which is no longer accessible."

"How long do we have...?"

"It could be only seconds." Jarl had no options, and he knew it. He holstered his pistol, moved to the other side of the room, and quickly retrieved a blue pack and began stuffing it with a considerable number of odds and ends.

"What is this room?" Kvasir asked, watching.

"It is the port transport bay, right now filled with one hell of a lot of useless junk and one broken auxiliary life pod. The *Mjollnir* destroyed the starboard transport bay. That contained two anti-grav shuttles." Jarl moved to a cabinet and opened a metal door. He took out a camouflage jacket and slipped into it. It was too small. He dropped it, and produced a second coat from the cabinet. This one was larger, and Jarl put it on and began filling its pockets with various items, including a small projectile pistol. Finally, he found a wide-rimmed black hat, slung the pack over one shoulder, picked up an assault-blaster, and declared, "I'm ready."

The ship shuddered yet again. Kvasir reached into a deep pocket and produced a small, smoky quartz crystal, which was a little longer than the width of his hand. Jarl stared at it, his confidence gone and suddenly terribly frightened again. He wondered if the old man was insane, and he had no idea what he was going to do.

"I don't know if this has a name," Kvasir said quietly. "It is something I have inherited. I have discovered that, by utilizing a mental process I do not completely understand, I can move myself to a different geographic location."

Jarl's right hand began to tremble with fear, and he hid it under his jacket. "*This will not work!,*" he thought. But he did not voice his concerns, in part because Kvasir was very serious, and in part because he had no choice but to trust the man.

Something in the older man's manner made him ask, "You are a teacher?"

Kvasir smiled. "Yes, I taught at Vor for more than a decade."

"Vor?"

"It is a city of wizard-teachers on the Western Ocean."

Jarl was perplexed, and astounded. "The Western Ocean? Wizards? You used this crystal to come here?"

"Yes."

"And you knew somehow to come to this ship?"

"No. I was traveling to the *Western Star.*"

"The what?"

"That, I think, is the ship you are calling the golden ship. It is still far away. We had thought it was a star, but we recently developed a device for making things far away appear closer."

Jarl's confusion was so great that he actually lost his balance, and he had to put out a hand to steady himself. "A telescope," he said slowly. "But if you have just invented the telescope, then how did you build this *Western Star*?"

"We did not build it. We observed that it is a great palace floating above our planet."

Jarl was even more confused. "And all of your people travel using these crystals?"

"No." Kvasir's voice was very stern. "This crystal and the power that comes with it are very, very secret. No one knows of them but a very select few of my order."

Jarl did not ask about this order. Instead he said, "And how did you end up on this ship?"

"I don't know." Kvasir paused. "You will have to be very careful when we get to Vanir. Such inquisitiveness will be not liked, and you will be labeled a sorcerer. You will be imprisoned... or worse." The old man smiled again, obviously now trying to be reassuring. He added, "Now, let's get started."

The smile was not lost on Jarl, but he was leaving his only link to his home. Emotion crept into his voice. "All right..."

The older man held up one hand. "When I distance-jumped I was with the King's army. I will take us to a hill near the army, then I will take my leave and we will travel to Vor. Is that satisfactory?"

Jarl was even more hesitant. "Are you sure arriving so near this army is a good thing?"

"Aye. Too many people know I was with the army. Disappearing and then being seen at Vor could cause problems. Big problems."

Jarl nodded his understanding, and Kvasir asked, "Are you ready?"

"Yes."

There was a brass cylinder attached to the base of the crystal, and while Jarl watched, Kvasir—his face a mask of concentration—adjusted a small ring on this base. Then he said, "We have to touch," and he again placed his left hand on Jarl's shoulder.

The last thing Jarl remembered was the interior of the *Cassiopeia* shimmering around him. Then the ship vanished forever.

CHAPTER ONE:

THE NIGHT BATTLE

For a brief second, Jarl's feet touched a slippery slope. Then his boots slid out from under him and he tumbled onto a hillside of wet grass. Beside him, the old man had also fallen. He was muttering under his breath, but did not appear to be hurt.

It was dusk, and the air had a clean feel, as if it had just rained. Nearby, a tiny stream of muddy water hurried down the hillside and into the gathering darkness. A short way up the hill, a row of tall trees formed a broken line across the skyline.

Jarl took a tentative breath. He could smell nothing but the wet grass and woods. He could hear nothing but the quiet of the impending night. The air was heavy with moisture and Jarl could feel the sweat already forming on his forehead. The atmosphere seemed correct for his lungs, and the gravity also seemed like what he was used to. He took a another breath and peered around, but saw nothing but the deeper darkness near the bottom of the hill.

Then one of the trees along the skyline moved. Both men had been getting to their feet. Now they both tensed and stooped, to make themselves less obvious. Jarl rotated his assault-blaster forward. Kvasir, caught securing the crystal, slowly removed his right hand from his deep pocket and silently withdrew his long sword from its scabbard. Another shadow on the ridge line followed the first and the movements became several people, then a line of soldiers, climbing toward the top of the hill. Silhouetted against the last bit of daylight were bayonets or pikes, pointing every which way, and a limp banner hung, all of its energy spent. As his senses cleared, Jarl could suddenly hear quiet cursing and the soft clank of equipment.

Kvasir reached out and touched Jarl on the shoulder. It was a statement of support, but it was also a gesture for silence. Together, they listened as the line of toiling men climbed up the hill. Then, in a voice almost too faint to hear, Kvasir whispered, "They are friends, soldiers of the King." He stood upright and began to climb toward the trees.

The old man moved silently and quickly on the wet grass. Jarl followed. He rotated his rifle behind him and under his coat, but he maintained his hold near the trigger.

The soldiers were exhausted. Jarl could see it in their movements and hear it in their tired voices. He could smell their dirty uniforms. They held what appeared to be muskets and wore dark jackets. Behind them, a cluster of artillerymen—wearing large, floppy hats—struggled to push and pull a heavy iron cannon with high wooden wheels up the hill.

There were also swordsmen, who appeared to have no standard uniform, holding all manner of shields. Some, like Kvasir, carried long broadswords. And there were pikemen, with short pikes and rectangular shields, wearing leather helmets. Only Kvasir wore a long woolen robe that almost touched the ground.

A short man stepped away from the main body of soldiers and approached the two men. He wore a huge, floppy hat and carried a curved sword at his side. Jarl heard the sharp intake of breath as the soldier saw Kvasir's face, and then the man spoke in a reverent, hushed whisper, "We heard you was dead."

"Not yet," the old man replied. "Not yet..." Even in the dim light, Jarl could see the bright sparks of Kvasir's eyes travel down the long line of soldiers. Then the eyes dropped back to the shorter man, and Jarl could see one of the bushy eyebrows arch upward in an unspoken question.

The short man answered, "I'm Sergeant Schad Shofstal. I was stationed in Tyr when you tutored the Prince." There was a pause. "Now I'm with the 14th Foot."

"What happened?" Kvasir whispered.

Shofstal let out a long breath. "Late this afternoon, Hisson and his cavalry encountered some Glassey pikemen on the main Foord Road near Bryan Creek. They drove 'em back a ways, or so we heard. Goran, his ownself, showed up, and sent in some pikemen and militia. They shoved good, and the Glasseys gave way and it looked like we might shove them clean out of Kettlewand." The sergeant paused and instinctively ducked as first one—then two more—screaming yellow streaks arched over their heads and exploded, with bright flashes and dull blasts, onto the empty hillside above them.

No one had been hurt by the cannon fire. In the stillness that followed, Kvasir spoke, "I was there. The Glassey cavalry came out of the woods on our left and stopped our attack. But there was a regiment of the King's Rifle behind us. Didn't they come forward and help?"

If the sergeant thought it strange that Kvasir did not know what had happened, he did not show it. "Aye, they came forward. And for a moment things looked good. Damn good."

Shofstal snorted, then continued, "But those Glasseys had a bunch more cavalry in that woods. There were cannon too. They laid down a terrible fire. Hisson got all tangled up with some of our pikemen, and then suddenly the King's Rifle was giving ground. Some of our artillery opened up, but damn if the shells didn't fall short and into our own people. Goran couldn't get the mess straightened out and we've been retreating since then. Goran is probably halfway back..."

The sergeant cut himself short as two riflemen and a pikeman joined their small group. One of the soldiers was a fair-haired girl, no more than a teenager, holding a musket with a long, thin bayonet and wearing a practical wide-brimmed hat. Her face was tired, dirty, and anxious. Not wanting to draw attention to himself, Jarl slid his own weapon a little more behind him. Other soldiers trudged by, and he could hear whispers of "Kvasir" and "There's Kvasir." But he also heard another word too, one that sounded as if it was spoken with fear, "Wizard!"

Shofstal continued, his voice full of irony, "'Course on top of it all, it poured buckets of rain for about an hour." Another pause. "Anyway, this here ridge runs clear down to the road. We are going to try to hold it until morning and then try to straighten this mess out." He turned and waved a hand toward the confusion of troops behind him, and continued, "This is supposed to be our left flank."

The sergeant then said something about food and officers up on the hill. Kvasir thanked him, and the small group of soldiers moved up the hill and melted into the darkness. Below, a second column of men and women staggered up the hill in a parallel direction. Jarl had been relieved and comforted by Shofstal's friendly and down-to-earth manner, and he realized suddenly that Kvasir was whispering to him.

"When I left this afternoon, it appeared the Empire was routed. I thought we had stopped the counterattack that left me surrounded and almost captured." Kvasir ended his sentence with a curse, one uttered so intensely it came like a physical blow.

This made no sense to Jarl. "You decided to travel to this *Western Star* in the middle of a battle?" he asked.

"Yes," the old man admitted, sounding tired. "My decision was totally made at the spur of the moment. I had been knocked down and left behind for dead. The battlefield was covered by heavy smoke, and the rain was threatening. There were Glasseys everywhere. They hadn't found me yet, but when they did... and saw who I was... Well, let's just say I didn't want to be captured."

"And?"

"I was lying on my back, and I could see the *Western Star* hanging far above my head, and somehow it didn't seem that the risk of traveling to the star was as great as it had been, at least when I had thought about it in weeks past. And at least not compared to being captured. The Glasseys do not like my kind..."

Jarl wondered why a person would take such an incredible risk, even in such terrible circumstances. Perhaps Kvasir had been that desperate. He did not voice that concern, but instead asked, "Your kind? What do you mean?"

The old man's eyes twinkled, and then abruptly dimmed. "I may have the reputation of being a wizard...," he softly said.

Jarl let a long breath slide between his teeth. He was badly frightened again, but he knew he had no choice but to trust this old man. "What do we do now?" he asked.

Kvasir was thoughtful. "Go up the hill. There might be food and there might be someone who knows what is going on."

"I thought we were leaving for this Vor place?"

"We will. Soon."

With one smooth move, Kvasir sheathed his heavy sword and the two men began to climb the hill. Then the old wizard stopped abruptly and said, "Say nothing of your ability to mindbeam. Do not even do it. Many don't like it and Church will jail you. There are rewards and many slight mind talkers will turn you in as a sorcerer."

"Is it illegal? This mindbeaming?"

"Not officially, but the Church is a law unto itself and they can imprison you." The old man then smiled, but it was a smile with sad eyes. "Personally, you could have done better in your choice of company."

"I do not understand..."

"I have powerful enemies. And there is no other wizard in all of Vanir that the Church would more like to have in their dungeons."

Jarl grimaced. "Will my clothing cause problems?" he asked.

Kvasir thought for a second. "I think not. There are many uniforms in the King's army, and your English is closer to ours than the Glassey gutter talk."

The old man started to turn away, but Jarl caught his sleeve. "That crystal," he whispered, "it is very important."

"I know," the old man replied. "*Say nothing of it!* It is far more dangerous than the mindbeaming. We will talk of it later." He again turned and started up the hill.

Jarl followed, but with each stride up the hill, his apprehension of this strange place became worse and worse, until finally his fear swept over him like a cold rain and settled into a hard knot in his stomach, leaving him both chilly and sweating.

He fought to control his emotions, to remember other deadly circumstances that he had survived, but he felt so out of place and alone, and in surroundings that were so different from what he was used to, that there was no fighting the fear. In the end, he peered at the old man striding purposely up the hill at his side. This was an individual who could be trusted, Jarl decided, despite the Church's opinion. And whatever fires drove the old wizard, Jarl thought, they burned bright and intense, deep inside.

There was no officers or food at the top of the hill, but the soldiers, expecting their enemy from the dark forest in the valley on the other side, began to move fence rails, stones, and fallen trees to construct a battle line along the ridge. Kvasir moved among the men and women, offering occasional words of encouragement. Despite the old man's words concerning the bad company of wizards, a surprisingly large number of the soldiers were friendly and seemed to take courage from his presence. The night was strangely quiet, even more so with the growing number of soldiers, and—other than the three cannon shots—there had been no sign of any enemy. A full moon rose through a hole in the mist. It was a bloody red orb, with black streaks across its face, about half the size of Earth's bright, pock-marked moon.

Someone handed Kvasir a biscuit, and he broke it in half and shared it with Jarl. It was hard, and very salty and dry. The old man pointed down the ridge line and said, "The road runs more or less west and east here. The ridge we're on runs downhill to the road, and it climbs up to the higher hills to the south." Jarl peered down the ridge, toward what he thought was the north. He could just barely make out a white, thin essence far below. Kvasir produced something from one of his pockets and shoved it into Jarl's hand. It proved to be an apple, identical to an Earth apple, and it was fresh and juicy after the dry biscuit.

Kvasir was also eating an apple, and he continued to talk, "About 200 kilometers west of here is the Kettlewand border; however, the Glasseys have broken past the border forts there and are coming down the road into the heart of Kettlewand. The Vanir army, commanded by the great and noble General Sir Kevin Goran," Jarl could hear the sarcasm, "was supposed to stop and otherwise detain the Glasseys." Kvasir took a long look at the moon. "That is Mytos," he said. "It is the small moon of Vanir. The other is Kmir."

"And Vanir is the name of the planet?" Jarl whispered.

"I think so... It is also the name of our nation." Kvasir took a thoughtful bite of his apple. "The old legends say that it was once the name of all the peoples who lived here."

Jarl too was thinking. "Then Vanir must have been the name the colonists chose for their new home, and this particular people have retained it. I wonder, did your ancestors come on the *Western Star*?"

Even in the darkness, Jarl could see one of Kvasir's bushy eyebrows arch upward. The surprise was mirrored in his voice. "I always assumed someone else built the *Western* and *Eastern Stars*. We have never had that capability."

Jarl said nothing more about that. Instead he asked, "Who are these Glasseys? And why are they invading Kettlewand?"

Kvasir took a long time to answer the question, and—when he did—his voice was full of pain. "The Glasseys are pure in the old religion and seek to convert the rest of us poor heathens. That, and they want our land."

The old man took another bite of his apple. "To the south are the Blue Hills, which rise to the great, snow-covered Sabre Mountains. That highland protects most of Vanir's eastern and southern borders, as does the Cimarron Sea. To the west are the Plains of Cimarron. To the north are the White Plains, which are the home to the Ghost Raiders."

There was a sudden coldness in Kvasir's voice, and Jarl asked, "These raiders and the Vanir don't get along?"

"The Ghost Raiders used to be a part of the Vanir, but there was a parting of the ways long, long ago. It was over religion... and pride." Now the old man sounded tired.

"What is to the east?"

"To the east lie the rest of the Kettlewand lands and the Forests of Atrobee. Both are a part of the Kettlewand Plateau. Beyond that is the Land of Nowell and the capital of Vanir, Tyr." The old man tossed the core of his apple into a vacant area between the soldiers. Now, from another of his bottomless pockets, he produced a large, wide-brimmed floppy hat, which he carefully fitted to his head.

Then he continued, "The Glasseys, or the Royal and Most Holy Empire of Glassitron, inhabit a tropical land south of the Cimarron Sea. Within the past fifty years or so, they've crossed that sea and taken most of the Province of Cimarron and the port city, Horst. Now they want Kettlewand."

"Are they crowded for land in their Empire?"

"No, they just want to make the Empire larger. And they want to convert all of Vanir to the one true religion. Lately, the Vanir have been straying and marrying out of their social classes." The old man's voice again sounded worn, and he suddenly added, "And we have too many books."

"The Glasseys don't like books?"

"We have far too many. And few are pure in the old religion."

Jarl finished his apple and tossed the core aside. He let out a sad, long sigh. "It sounds like there are many similarities between our two worlds. And many of the same troubles."

"It is a sad thing indeed," Kvasir admitted.

"How big are the two respective armies?" Jarl asked.

"Goran has about 10,000 soldiers, about a third of which are Kettlewand militia. Kivlor, the Glassey commander, has about half that many again, but many of those were left to guard the six western border forts he captured."

"Are there problems with the quality of the militia?"

"Sometimes, but less so with the Kettlewand. These people lead harder lives than most, caught between the wind, the cold, and the Ghost Raiders." Kvasir paused, then asked, "Tell me... are you a military man?"

"Not by choice. I was a civilian in the wrong place at the wrong time. I had to pick up some training on the run."

"Surely your wars are not this primitive?"

Jarl took a long time to reply, wondering how to describe a ruthless, no-quarter partisan conflict. His words were quiet and painful, "Actually, they can be a great deal worse." He could feel Kvasir's unasked questions weighing down on him.

"You saw the dead on our ship," Jarl continued. "My people are the United Colonized Planets, or the UCP. We are for the most part republics. Our enemy is the Consolidated Empire of Planets. Or the CEP for short. They want *control*, they want our planets, and they want our peoples in their Empire." Jarl had long since given up clutching his blaster, and now he shoved his hands deeper into his coat pockets. "I was a neutral civilian, but ours is a war where sooner or later you have to join one side or the other."

Kvasir looked thoughtful, then asked, "How does a large republic function? It has been theorized that..." He was interrupted by several running horses approaching the ridge top from the direction of the red moon.

The riders came though the first line of soldiers and drew up near a cannon. Several officers appeared and there was a brief discussion. The horsemen then spurred their lathered animals down the ridge and toward the center of the long Vanir battle line. One officer began barking instructions and, despite the late hour, two lines of Vanir soldiers started their final preparations for a battle. Jarl looked at Mytos; it was only a few degrees above the horizon, moving slowly. The first stars were appearing.

Then, in the bottom of the valley below them, a long, ragged volley of white and yellow musket fire erupted. It was the Glasseys, beginning their attack. All along the Vanir battle line, men and women shouted and cursed, but no one fired back. There was a second irregular line of gunfire from below, but still the Vanir held their fire. Above them, up the hill, a large body of archers hurriedly moved into position among a grove of dead trees that appeared to be the remains of an old orchard.

Kvasir motioned Jarl forward, and together they walked to a point near one of the trees, where they could see down the hill and into the woods. To their right was a gigantic cannon. The evening was warm and Jarl whispered, "Do you have seasons? Is this summer?"

The old man was consigning his hat back into a pocket. His patience seemed endless, "Yes. Late summer." In many ways, Jarl thought, he was like an old college professor. Except that this professor, he had noticed, always kept his right hand—his sword hand—free, like an old-time Western gunfighter.

To their front, a Vanir officer gave an order and the first line of soldiers fired their muskets. There was a ragged line of yellow and white fire that lasted almost three seconds, and dense clouds of heavy gray smoke drifted toward the old orchard. From below and to their left, the flash of a longer ragged volley broke the dark night. It seemed that the Glasseys were moving up the hill. Behind him, Jarl suddenly heard the twangs of many bowstrings, and arrows, humming like angry bees, flew over his head.

Jarl reached behind him and pulled his long weapon to his shoulder. Ignoring Kvasir's sudden and intense interest, he touched a button, and the night sight glowed to life. Below him, through a large cloud of billowing smoke, Jarl could see that the first line of Vanir soldiers were frantically struggling to reload, a slow process that necessitated ramming a power charge and ball down the barrels of their muskets. Groups of Glassey soldiers were moving up the hill, not as a single orchestrated line, but as large, tightly packed clusters of men. Behind them, in the forest, Jarl could see more movement. Suddenly, there were three Glassey cannon blasts, one sounding on top of the other. Jarl flinched, and waited for the shock of the impact. There was none; the volley whistled overhead with an evil whine and exploded in the valley behind them.

Jarl turned off his night sight and lowered his weapon. He looked to his right. The Vanir artillerymen were unloading ball and powder from the backs of a half dozen twisting and kicking mules. Men were shouting and holding tightly to the reins, but one mule suddenly broke free and ran down the ridge, away from the battle. Then a young boy began ramming the first charge down the mouth of one of the huge weapons.

Kvasir tensed forward, grasping his unsheathed sword. The Vanir front line was now preparing to meet the Glasseys with their bayonets. An officer, wielding a saber, was behind them, shouting commands. Something smacked the tree beside Jarl, throwing a wood splinter in his face, causing him to duck and flinch.

The Glassey onslaught suddenly surged up the hill and struck the Vanir front line. The two masses of soldiers writhed and twisted like two snakes fighting for most of a minute. Then a Vanir sword unit suddenly sprang to its feet and raced down the hill, screaming some battle cry that only they could understand. The enemy did not fall back; instead—incredibly—they began to push the confused mass of Vanir further up the hill.

Immediately in front of Jarl and Kvasir, the Vanir riflemen gave ground and suddenly there was a hole in their battle line. Jarl caught a brief glimpse of a young girl turning and falling, and then a tangled group of fighting men surged over her body. There was a sudden, nearby roar of an explosion, and the cannon next to Jarl belched bright fire and jumped like a living monster. Before the smoke cleared, dozens of Vanir pikemen rushed forward. The Glassey onrush seemed to pause, then suddenly it was flowing back down the slope, as if someone had pulled the plug on a giant bathtub of soldiers.

There was no slack in the noise, and the Vanir cannon fired and fired again. Jarl's mouth filled with the taste of spent black powder, and he could see confused masses of men running down the hill and away from the Vanir line. He could also see the bright streaks of cannon fire in the far-off woods, and the ground to Jarl's left—and a little down the ridge—exploded in a flash of fire. Dirt, equipment, fence rails, and the silhouettes of broken men were thrown into the air.

Jarl let out a long breath, wondering what was next. He did not have long to wait long: Even as the Vanir officers were repairing their front line, the next charge of Glasseys started up the hill. Again there was the buzz of arrows overhead, and again the Vanir cannon belched their throaty roar. The reformed Vanir front line opened fire with a bright, orchestrated volley of musket fire, and dark clouds of billowing smoke hid the desperate action. Then the smoke cleared. The Glassey onslaught hung for a long, timeless moment in the beginning of a fall, then it evaporated back down the hill.

Once more the Glasseys came up the hill, and once more they were met by Vanir arrows, cannon fire, and musket fire. Then the night became quiet. Kvasir moved off down the hill to help with the wounded, and Jarl, hiding his rifle behind him and under his coat, followed the old man. He was terrified and knew he had to find something to do, or his fear and anxiety would overwhelm him, plus he wanted to stay close to Kvasir. As the night wore on, the two men carried unknown numbers of wounded back and over the ridge to where a large tent had been set up in the bottom of that valley. Jarl lost count of how many times the Glasseys attempted to breach the Vanir defenses. Twice Kvasir lent a hand with his long sword, but Jarl never so much as reached for one of his weapons. Fresh Vanir units came up, replacing those who were tired. Other reserves waited on the ridge above the battlefield. Fresh ammunition and water for the parched throats arrived, and—through it all—the large iron cannon roared out more of their terrible flame and smoke.

To Jarl it seemed as if the battle went on forever, but in fact the night was only half spent when the Glasseys gave up their futile attacks. Then, as the battlefield became quiet, the cries and moans of the wounded could be better heard, becoming one continuous wail. Patrols of Glasseys and Vanir roamed the night, ignoring each other and carrying their wounded back to their lines.

It was in the Vanir aid station that Jarl came into his own. He cached his pack, hat, and weapons in a corner of the large tent, hiding them under his coat, and then—with Kvasir's assistance—began to open, clean, and bandage the lesser wounds. He was one of a dozen people who helped carry the wounded to the surgeons' tables, and he helped carry away those who had been worked on—with their bound-up middles and heads and their amputated legs and arms—to the long line of high-sided ox carts that waited behind the tents.

He also helped move dead bodies—soldiers who had died in and near the tent—off to another side of the aid station, and he carried buckets of drinking water to the large group of men and women who sat in the dark, waiting—silently and without complaint—to be put under the surgeon's knife. And through it all, the surgeons worked, tirelessly and endlessly, using the same tools and tables, cutting people open, removing shrapnel and spent lead, and amputating limbs. It was a gruesome—yet somehow fascinating—sight, that was lit by the bright spots of lanterns, and seemed to go on forever.

But, sometime and somehow, in the deep dark before sunrise, the eternity came to an end and there were no more wounded. They washed their hands and cleaned their bodies as best they could. Kvasir offered Jarl food and water from an unknown source. Neither man spoke. The night became quiet as the doctors and nurses moved off to sleep, or lay on the water-washed surfaces that had so recently served as their operating tables.

Jarl was exhausted. Above the ridge to the west, still close to the horizon, Mytos continued its slow rise. But now there was another, larger, pale blue moon beside it. This was the moon Kvasir had called Kmir, and it was about twice the size of red Mytos. It was a bright, unblemished giant, surrounded by a wide ring of yellow dust, and moving at a much faster speed than the red, black-streaked Mytos.

To the east were the faint, red beginnings of a new day. Soon overhead, the stars would begin to wink out. Jarl wondered if there was a morning star, and—if there was—would it be one of the seven planets in this solar system, or would it be his own ship, the *Cassiopeia*; the CEP's hammerhead ship, *Mjollnir*; or the great golden giant ship that he had seen only from afar.

He expelled a long, drawn-out breath. It did not matter. Even with Kvasir's ability to distance-jump, it would be far too dangerous to return to any abandoned and wrecked spaceship without an environment suit.

With the rising sun, Jarl's old life was gone forever, and—like Kvasir—he was now a part of Vanir, the nation and the planet. He turned, head down and despondent, and began to search for a bed among the bloody tables and planks of the battered and littered aid station.

CHAPTER TWO:

THE BATTLE ON THE MOUNTAIN

An incessant shaking woke Jarl. He painfully rolled over, moaned, and opened his eyes. It was full daylight. He pushed himself off his pack and leaned against the bed of the wrecked wagon next to where he had slept. He rubbed his face with one hand and muttered, "What?"

Kvasir shook his head in exasperation. Behind the old man stood a tall, handsome, well-dressed Vanir officer, who was slapping a set of heavy leather gloves against one hand, and staring impatiently at Jarl. Kvasir spoke quickly, "Come. We are needed."

Without waiting for a reply, Kvasir turned and started toward the top of the hill. The officer stared at Jarl for a moment longer, then followed.

Jarl, feeling tired and old, had to work to stand up. Once on his feet, he gathered his pack and rifle, adjusted them painfully on his shoulder, put on his hat, and began to trudge slowly after the two tall figures striding toward the top of the hill. He felt lost, an empty man without a purpose, and a soldier in the wrong war. He slung his pack higher onto his back by one strap, slid his modern rifle behind him and under his coat, and then began to hurry up the hill.

Clustered over the grassy hillside were small and large groups of men and women, sleeping, resting, eating breakfast, cleaning weapons, and dressing small wounds. All were exhausted and dirty, worn out from the long night. They formed two crooked and muddled battle lines, one on the ridge top, and a second—the front line—on the opposite, downward slope. Scattered here and there were corpses, lying in the mindless confusion that only sudden death can bring. One was a black-haired man in a gaudy, pea-green jacket, who had a broken, black arrow driven through his chest.

Jarl suddenly realized that this was one of the enemy, a Glassey, who had somehow reached the top of the ridge the night before.

On his left and above him, the battered limbs of the old orchard were outlined against a blue Vanir sky. To his right, the ridge dropped in a long, gentle slope to the thin, white line of a road, located almost a kilometer to the north. Beyond that, a flat steppe stretched an infinite distance in the clear morning air. As he approached the top of the hill, Jarl could see that the ridge—from his present position to the far-off highway—was lined with the massed troops of the Vanir army, waiting for the day to begin. Here and there were the gray smudges of smoke from wood fires and the occasional movements of horsemen. Nearby, a tattered banner fluttered in the slight morning breeze, and shirtless artillerymen labored to unload shot and powder from two sets of limbers and caissons.

There were only a few soldiers to his left, and—beyond and above the apple trees—Jarl could see the crest of a barren, rocky slope. Above that were the rounded peaks of a higher massif. This mountain was forested, and the many greens of the trees formed a long wall all across the entire southern skyline.

Kvasir gestured for Jarl to join a group of officers who were standing between the two Vanir lines. Conscious of his strange pack and clothing, Jarl moved toward the tight cluster of men. They were uncaring of his dress, as they had other, more important matters to discuss.

The tall officer was leaning against the top of a broken fence, oblivious to the artillery crew cleaning a cannon a few meters behind him. He was arguing, in a friendly manner, with Kvasir. He wanted to attack, but the old wizard wanted to let the Glasseys come to them. Two other officers took Kvasir's side of the argument, and the tall officer listened intently for several minutes, rubbing his chin with an ungloved hand. Suddenly he looked up, his brown eyes bright and hard, and nodded to himself—his decision was made. Kvasir had made his point; they would wait.

The tall officer turned to a subordinate and ordered him to move a unit of swordsmen from the apple grove. To his surprise, Jarl found himself suddenly speaking, "Leave them there, or move in other troops to replace them."

Faces—suspicious faces—turned toward him. "Why?" someone asked.

"If the Glasseys take the orchard or the steep ground above it, they could sweep your entire line from there."

The tall Vanir officer's scrutiny became suddenly very intense, and Jarl wished that he had said nothing. The man pointed to the slope near the apple orchard. "That ground is too steep and too rocky to be attacked successfully."

The man was only pointing out what he felt was obvious, and his manner was stern, but not antagonistic. Jarl hesitated. The conversation was now aimed at him, but he no longer wished to be a part of it.

"Perhaps it is," Jarl began, "but if they do attack there and win that hill, then..." He again hesitated, then spoke with more confidence. "In fact, it would be better to move more companies up there. Even if there is no attack, you can use them as reserves down here, because they can sure move faster down that hill than up."

The tall officer continued to stare at Jarl. A tall, lanky man who had been squatting nearby suddenly stood and spoke, "That's a good idea. If the damn Glasseys get above us in that orchard, then this here position is doomed. It might even pay to put some people on the mountainside above. If the Glasseys get up there, it's going to be big trouble." The man wore a wide felt hat and was dressed in the faded green of a woodsman, and he carried a long, narrow rifle easily in the nook of one arm.

The tall officer suddenly chuckled. "Always looking for a way to get into the mountains, aren't you, Teague?" He spoke to one of his junior officers, "Leave the sword company where it is, and move a company of Rifle up there too." He glanced at Jarl and nodded his approval, then he looked back at Teague, "And get your company of Rangers up and onto that rock slope. We have nothing to lose by putting you there, and—as you say—we might have a lot to gain." He paused, thought for a second, and then said, "The meeting's over!" He turned and moved to a courier who knelt next to a mouse-colored horse.

Kvasir took Jarl by one arm and led him away. "You seem to have learned quite a bit about war when you were trapped as an innocent civilian..." he whispered.

Jarl suddenly felt old and tired. "That's a very long story and not a happy one." He paused, then added, "I hope I didn't make matters worst by speaking just then."

"No," Kvasir said. "You didn't, and your advice was sound. You did, however, make yourself noticed, and that may not be a good thing."

"I know... I should have said nothing...," Jarl muttered to himself. Then he spoke in a slightly louder voice, "Last night, you said you weren't in good graces with the Church..."

"I did."

"Well, you seemed to have neglected to mention that the Army comes to you early in the morning for advice."

Kvasir's bright gray eyes burned with a new light, and he suddenly laughed. He clapped Jarl on one shoulder and said, "Come, my friend, let's see if we can find some breakfast. I don't think the Empire is ready to attack just yet."

Jarl was pleased, and his mind hung on the words, 'my friend.' The two of them walked a short distance to where a small group of artillerymen were eating breakfast under a mutilated apple tree. There, a wide, powerful man in a loose, faded orange blouse offered them cold sausage, bread, and cheese. While the man and Kvasir spoke of old campaigns, Jarl ate in silence, listening, glad to be a part of the man's easy generosity.

Jarl stared around him, and looked at the world he was now in. Many questions came to his mind. First, the resemblance of this planet's flora to Earth's was incredible. But what had happened to the technology and science that had brought the Vanir ancestors to this place? Their descendants apparently had neither steam power nor electricity. And was the great golden spaceship from this culture or from something entirely different? Had these people—like himself—been marooned here? A new line of thought, one that he did not like, abruptly occurred to him: perhaps the people who had built the great golden ship were still there, and watching this deadly battle for their entertainment. Jarl found himself suddenly staring skyward, trying to see that golden ship. He had no answers, but he vowed to watch for anyone else with any kind of advanced technology.

Kvasir had finished eating. He stood and wiped his hands upon his robes. Then he turned to Jarl and said, "Let's go up into the old orchard. Perhaps we can be of some use there." They started to climb upward and, as they did, a distance clamor began near the bottom of the ridge. They turned, and they could see ordered lines of soldiers crossing the road. Then the road and the bottom of the ridge disappeared in a dirty, white cloud of battle smoke. The day's combat had begun.

The far-off noise continued for the next hour or more, unabated. In the orchard, the swordsmen were joined by two rifle companies. The place became crowded and Kvasir suggested they climb higher on the ridge, onto a steep, barren slope. For the first time—and not without some embarrassment—Jarl noticed green-clad Rangers sitting and resting, waiting on the hillside above.

The two men slowly climbed up toward the Rangers, walking around smooth outcrops of limestone. Teague stood and joined them. Then they all climbed up onto a flat, grassy meadow above a small spring. There, the Rangers stacked their packs. Without speaking, Jarl—tired from the fast climb up the steep hillside—added his own blue pack to their cache. Then, after a short conversation with Teague, a dozen Rangers loped off through the knee-high grass toward the forest at the base of the high mountain. They were scouts to guard against a high-mountain attack.

The conflict on the road far below had stopped, and, as near as anyone could tell, there were no changes in the battle lines. Kvasir and Jarl wasted the morning away, eating a second breakfast with the Rangers. Then, sometime in the warm midday, Jarl fell asleep.

It was again Kvasir's hand that woke him. The day was nearly spent, and all the Rangers—with the exception of a few who were dozing—were lined along the rim of the meadow, intently peering at some scene below.

This time, Jarl woke immediately. "What's happening?" he asked.

Kvasir jerked his head toward the Rangers. "The Glasseys are preparing to attack the main lines below us. And they have been spotted on the mountain above us."

Jarl rolled to his feet. While Teague was giving orders, Jarl and Kvasir moved to the edge of the meadow and looked at the scene below. Directly below them, in the old orchard, Vanir officers were forming their companies for battle. Below these soldiers, at the site of the previous night's battle, the two Vanir lines were also preparing for an attack. On the ridge to the west, across the valley with the trees, a long line of green-coated Glasseys were readying an immense attack. Jarl attempted to count their men and their companies, but he soon gave up—there were far too many to count.

Behind them, the Rangers were checking their weapons. Teague gave an order and the entire company, Kvasir and Jarl included, tore themselves from the scene below and moved up the hill, across the meadow, and into a hardwood forest of huge oak and chestnut trees. There was a floor of leaves underfoot and little undergrowth, and scattered through the forest were lichen-covered sandstone boulders that had rolled down from the heights above.

The Rangers formed into a thin skirmish line and, in a remarkably short time, began to move westward across the mountain slope. One squad, under the command of a man named Aaron, climbed up the mountain to protect them from a high attack. Kvasir went with them, but Jarl stayed near the middle of the line with the tall Ranger captain.

The woodsmen did not all move at once. Some moved quickly; others moved more slowly. They held their long weapons at the ready, careful to make little noise. Each stopped often, pausing only near cover, their eyes roaming the mountainside. Jarl moved behind a large, flat-topped rock and squatted there, listening and watching, and memorizing his surroundings.

The hillside was broken into shallow gullies and low ridges that ran perpendicular to the main mountain, and some of the Rangers had climbed onto one such ridge just past where Jarl stood. There the original scouts waited, led by an ancient woodsman. Below them, on the steep mountain slope, other Rangers moved onto the tiny ridge. They hid themselves in the deep-green summer foliage.

To their front was a shallow gully and then another small ridge of sandstone boulders. Downslope of the largest boulder, which was more than three meters high, a clutch of green-coated soldiers suddenly appeared, moving toward the Rangers, and each holding a musket with a bayonet. Even as Jarl and the last of the Rangers slid into their positions, a gesturing Glassey officer appeared and motioned more of his soldiers into view.

The Rangers waited. The Empire's soldiers moved slowly and appeared confused. Finally, a score of Glassey swordsmen moved past the rock. Only then did the men with the muskets lurch forward, led by the officer. Other greencoats filled the position by the large rock. The enemy was struggling forward in tight groups, and there appeared to be no manner of organization. Their bayonets were pointed in every direction, catching on vines and small trees; their feet seemed to tangle in the forest litter; and they moved in a strange stop-and-go fashion.

Teague slid his rifle silently forward, and rested the butt against his shoulder. His men quietly followed his example. There was a slight hesitation as the captain aimed, then he fired. The Glassey officer abruptly jerked backward, and dust flew off his coat. The man then sat abruptly down. The remaining Rangers fired a ragged volley, and other green-coated soldiers tumbled onto the forest floor. The remainder turned and stumbled back up the hill, leaving their dead and wounded and a few of their weapons.

The smoke from the small battle drifted down the mountain. The Rangers reloaded, first fitting a paper cartridge containing powder and lead ball into the barrels of their rifles, then ramming the ball down those barrels with a practiced efficiency.

A tall Glassey officer had appeared at the large rock and began to organize his men. Teague slowly slid his long weapon forward again and said, quietly and without emotion, "Fire."

Once more a ragged Ranger volley cut into the enemy soldiers, still milling on the opposite ridge. Some were quick to drop down and hide among the rocks; others sank to the ground, holding wounds.

There were now three score greencoats at the rock, opposed by less than thirty Rangers. Teague turned and bellowed down the mountain, "To me! Rangers to me!" There were more minutes of confusion among the Glasseys, but the tall, officer, now hatless, managed to coerce a small number of soldiers with muskets up across the slope, past the large boulder. The officer halted his men on a low, flat rock about seventy meters from the Vanir, but a good deal higher. More Rangers arrived from down below and, after sending a long-legged runner racing downhill to the Vanir command, Teague moved himself and most of his group—including Jarl—up the mountain, being careful to stay on the low ridge and behind the sandstone boulders.

More greencoats moved to the large sandstone boulder, and still others joined the tight cluster at the flat rock, where the hatless Glassey officer was attempting to organize an attack. Teague had seen enough; he directed his own squad to fire on the would-be attackers, and he ordered a lower group of Rangers to fire at the greencoats at the sandstone boulder.

The woodsmen opened fire. Immediately, the enemy soldiers at the boulder returned it. Jarl ducked at the wince of a ricochet, and—for the first time—he brought his modern rifle forward. The greencoats at the flat rock became a panicked, confused mass as each man attempted to hide himself in the middle of the cluster of soldiers. Then, abruptly, a young officer charged downhill, racing toward the Vanir position. One Glassey soldier followed, then another and another. Suddenly, the entire mass of men lurched forward, chasing the young officer downhill.

Below, on their small ridge, the Rangers hurried to load their weapons. The Glassey charge picked up speed, but they ran as a mob, with bayonets pointing in every direction. The young officer was still in front when the first Ranger fired; the officer continued running, but his legs collapsed and he grabbed at a small tree. He hung there for a second, then slid to the ground. A short, ragged Ranger volley followed the first shot, and other Glassey soldiers stumbled and fell, plowing into the rocks and leaves on the forest floor. But the main group continued to run forward, propelled on by the slope of the mountain. They fell into the bottom of the gully, and tried to hide themselves among the sandstone boulders there. One man's rear end protruded into the air, and there was the dull sound of a black-powder explosion as a Ranger fired. There was the whomp of a bullet striking home, and the green bottom disappeared with a yelp of pain.

The day was waning, but there was still enough light to pick out individual targets through thick clouds of spent black powder. Each Ranger reloaded, then fired carefully aiming at a target. Greencoats fell near the large boulder, and others—climbing toward the hatless officer—stumbled and dropped to the forest floor. Men cried in pain, and staggered and crawled back toward the safety of the boulder. From there, enemy riflemen peppered the Vanir Rangers with a covering fire. Jarl caught a glimpse of the hatless officer peering around a small tree—then a rifle ball struck the tree at head height, exploding bark out in all directions, and Hatless scurried to a larger tree.

Amid the heavy, swirling smoke, the scene was fascinating to watch. The Rangers, most of whom were down the mountain from Jarl, were crouching among the sandstone boulders, meticulously aiming and firing, or purposely sliding ramrods up and down their rifle barrels. Some struggled to push the pre-packaged paper cartridges down the throats of their long weapons. Others poured a small amount of black powder into flash pans or eared back the heavy hammers of their flintlocks. A few of the woodsmen were climbing behind the ridge to a position above Teague, and an occasional Ranger—like Jarl—simply watched and waited.

More Glasseys continued to stagger toward Hatless. Jarl realized, with a start, that many of these soldiers held short pikes—this meant there was another Glassey company joining the fight. He checked the ready button on his blaster. Now the Ranger line became quiet. The woodsmen were reloading, or waiting for the imminent assault.

It took several minutes for Hatless to organize the confused knot of frightened men milling around him. More greencoats moved into a position below the boulder while he did so, and still more hid among the smaller sandstone rocks. Jarl gave up trying to count the enemy—the Rangers were outnumbered at least three to one.

Finally, someone barked a short command, and then Hatless and the milling knot of riflemen charged downslope, toward the Vanir position. The greencoats at the large sandstone boulder shouted and joined in the rush. Both groups met near the head of the gully, where, after the briefest of pauses, they resumed their downward rush. The Glassey riflemen hidden in the gully bottom clawed their way to their feet and joined in the onslaught.

The attack had become a confused mob. Individual soldiers outdistanced the main group. Pikemen, riflemen, and swordsmen were all mixed together. Some fell on the slippery leaves, and others bumped into trees. Most struggled back to their feet and rushed forward again. The Glassey riflemen who had remained at the large boulder began a sporadic peppering of covering fire.

Then, in a ragged volley, the Rangers opened fire. Three running greencoats staggered together and one fell, clutching his head. Others tumbled to the ground in front of the mob. One soldier grabbed and hung onto a small tree, and another man threw his musket high in the air and fell backwards down the mountain. But the main group came on.

Jarl watched, unwilling to join the battle with his modern blaster, yet unwilling to watch his newfound friends die. Then, to his left, a Glassey officer jumped over a sandstone rock, and ran crouching toward him, his sword pointed forward. Jarl knew he had no choice—the man was that close. He touched his trigger, and a super-slow pulse of red light chewed into the man's chest. The man fell forward, throwing sticks and dead leaves into the air. Behind him was a rifleman. Jarl shot that soldier and then the one behind him.

A group of greencoats crossed his sight. A long burst of red pulses cut into them. They stumbled, dying as they fell. A man behind them stopped and stared at Jarl, and Jarl shot him too. Then a noise on his right distracted him. Two Glassey swordsmen were almost to Jarl's position. A quick burst of the blaster, held chest high, knocked the first man down, but the second man was on him. Jarl tried to block the sword with his weapon, but could not. Suddenly, a thrown knife slammed into his attacker's throat. The man fell, and skidded to a stop against the sandstone boulder behind Jarl.

A thrown pike flashed over Jarl's head. Three Glassey swordsmen surged up on his right, only two meters away. A green-coated rifleman was also running toward him, screaming, his bayonet down and aimed for Jarl's middle. Jarl swung his blaster in a tight arc. The rifleman fell over backwards, his feet flying in the air, his chest shot away. One of the swordsmen also went down, shot in the shoulder. But the second shoved forward, grabbed the blaster, and muscled the muzzle skyward.

Jarl fell over backwards on the steep slope, losing his hat, but holding his weapon. A rock ground into his back, and leaves and twigs swept across his face. The Glassey was a big man; he continued to hold the blaster in one hand while his other arm arced high, sword in hand. The other swordsman moved in from one side, trying to position himself for a quick saber thrust. Jarl managed to tangle his feet in the legs of the Glassey struggling with the rifle, and that man fell sideways—but he pulled Jarl with him, exposing him to the second attacker. That man now raised his sword high, and brought it down with a terrifying speed.

But another sword intervened! Sparks flew, and there was the loud clank of metal on metal. The new swordsman shoved his blade and the Glassey's up and into the air. The greencoat fell backwards and onto the ground, and for an instant the other man towered above him, in a whirl of gray robes and white hair. It was Kvasir!

The old wizard's sword flashed and Jarl felt the warm flood of blood cascading down on him—Kvasir had cut the big Glassey's throat. He then turned to the greencoat on the ground. But that man threw his sword up, blocked the first cut, and then crawled frantically away. Another green-coated swordsman jumped over the rock, but Kvasir's sword knocked that man's weapon out of the way and cut deep into his belly. More Glasseys were below the sandstone boulders, but they now hesitated, wary of this new gray menace. Kvasir hurdled the rock, and moved toward them, his sword swinging.

Jarl struggled to his feet, his breath coming in ragged gasps. Down over the hillside, away from Kvasir, a large greencoat was banging a smaller Ranger in the head with the broken end of a pike. Jarl raised his blaster and shot the Glassey full in the back.

Kvasir was caught in a whirl of flashing swords and enemy soldiers. Jarl moved toward that fight, and shot one man on the edge of the melee. A Glassey jumped up from behind a boulder and threw a rock. Jarl jerked his head to one side, and fired his weapon again. His off-the-hip shot missed, and the red pulse exploded in a bright, white light against a sandstone boulder. The Glassey turned and raced away.

Then, suddenly, the battle was over. Kvasir was standing still, breathing heavily, holding his great sword with both hands, but there were no more greencoats. Jarl sighted his weapon across the mountainside, but the only Glasseys he could see were racing back toward the large sandstone boulder. Below, Rangers were disentangling themselves from hand-to-hand confrontations. Occasional rifle balls whistled overhead, but none came close. Black powder smoke drifted everywhere.

Jarl increased the magnification on his blaster's scope and looked across the narrow valley toward the sandstone boulder. The hatless Glassey officer was standing there, staring directly at him. Jarl touched his trigger, but did not fire. The battle was over and the greencoats were retreating, and he did not want to make everyone more aware of his modern weapon. The officer turned and disappeared into the dark forest. The Rangers had the forest battlefield to themselves.

Jarl clicked his blaster's safety on. He started to move off down the mountain toward Kvasir, but he tripped over a moaning Ranger, the young man whose life he had saved. There was a wide, flat sandstone boulder below him, and Teague and a thin woman with a narrow face were treating four wounded Rangers there. Jarl pulled the young woodsman to his feet and, with Kvasir's assistance, helped the man down to the rock. Then, using an old shirt someone produced, he assisted with the bandaging.

Teague, with a long hop, jumped off the flat rock and began to inspect his company. The woman, who said her name was Mylea Orlando, began tending to the young Ranger. For a moment, Jarl watched—with intense fascination—the deft, quick movements of her long, strong fingers. Above them, Kvasir's figure was unmistakable in the growing twilight; he and Aaron were carrying a hurt Ranger down the mountain toward the small group of wounded. From down the mountain there was a long "hello" and, after several minutes, a white-haired Vanir officer climbed up the slope. He was followed by a rifle company, who climbed with slow, dispirited movements. Jarl realized, with a start, that these men—like the Glasseys—were afraid of the deep woods.

Teague slid down the steep mountainside, throwing leaves and sticks in the air and grabbing a small tree to stop. He handed Jarl his lost hat. Decisions were made quickly, and the two officers began to form the two companies into a long skirmish line. One small group was left behind to tend the wounded, but the main body began moving westward. They threaded their way past the Glassey dead in the gully, and—when they arrived at the large boulder—found a half-dozen wounded greencoats, all with their hands held high. Teague ordered a Ranger to herd these prisoners back down the mountain. Then the long, loose Vanir line moved forward again.

They traveled about a kilometer to the west, but they found no one other than two small groups who wanted to surrender. Teague finally ordered Aaron to take a small reconnaissance squadron further west, and the main Vanir force turned back.

Jarl and Kvasir went with them.

CHAPTER THREE:

THE CRISIS

Jarl slipped twice while climbing down the steep limestone hill to the apple orchard. He had traded his lightweight boots for a good pair of leather Kettlewand boots, given to him by Teague, but still it made no difference—he was exhausted.

Overhead, red Mytos hung in the twilight sky, its deep black streaks an omen of events to come. Below, in the orchard, long locust rails had been stacked around one cannon, boxing it into a corner, and there men and women waited. Far to his right, down off the ridge, Jarl could see the yellow lights of the aid station. Underfoot, the ground was torn up from uncounted boots, and corpses lay everywhere. Some wore the gaudy green of the Empire of Glassitron, but most were dressed in the faded gray, blue, and green woolens of Vanir. And everywhere were scattered the broken and lost articles of battle—muskets, canteens, clothing, swords, shields, and pikes.

He was part of a group of five, including Kvasir and Teague, and they now approached a larger cluster of officers waiting near the cannon. That group appeared exhausted and dejected, and some were sitting on the ground.

There were no introductions. The tall officer from the morning's briefing spoke, mostly for the newcomers' benefit. "Goran ran!" There was a heavy quiet, and then he said, "With him went most of the High Ejliteta, several companies of Rifle, and a godly mess of the supply train."

Jarl was confused. It was only when Kvasir spoke that he remembered that Goran was the overall commander of the Vanir army. The old wizard's words were very serious, "When did this happen, Enrick?"

"About the time the attacks up here were at their worst. Late afternoon." Enrick looked at Jarl with a fierce expression, "Had we not listened to you this morning, we would have lost it all here. The Glasseys attacked with more than five regiments, a third of which were assigned to take the old orchard. The reserves high on the ridge were the only thing that saved us."

There was a long pause that Jarl recognized as a silent thanks, then the tall officer spoke again, "The word about Goran hasn't gotten around yet, except for the cavalry. Once the word gets out, this army is going to be hard on its heels. And then we will be dog meat for Kivlor's wolves."

"He left while we were winning?" Kvasir asked. It was obvious the old wizard was having trouble comprehending what the tall officer was saying.

"A report went back that our line was broken and that the Glasseys were sweeping the ridge of all opposition. Goran's morning briefing wasn't all that good, and I'm not certain he knew we had moved extra troops high onto the ridge. Anyway, he thought the battle was lost."

There was more quiet all around. In the distance near the aid station, Jarl could hear someone screaming in pain.

Kvasir spoke, "What happens now?"

"Now...," Enrick paused, considering the options. "Now, I guess we break at the next Glassey attack. No one is going to stay once they know the commanding general has run for home."

There was another long silence, and finally Jarl could stand it no longer. "How much of the battle did Goran direct?" he asked. When no one answered, he continued, "From what I've seen, you've got a good army. Your soldiers held their positions, and they held them well. Last night they filled a break in the line damn fast, and your officers have been very good about keeping your reserves handy, and switching out the tired troops with fresh ones. Plus, you've got a good ridge here. You've stopped the Glasseys today. You could do it again tomorrow."

Someone had lit a lamp, and Enrick spoke with anger, "Tell us something we don't know. If we retreat, the Glasseys are going to hurt us bad. There aren't many who are going to make it to Atrobee."

The tall officer hesitated, then looked directly at Jarl. "Damn it! They're good troops. They are damn good troops, but there isn't a soldier around who has the heart to stay and fight when his leaders have deserted him."

The silence was becoming tense when Enrick spoke again, "Best we can hope for is an organized retreat, beginning tonight under the cover of darkness." He paused again, exhausted from the day's fighting, thinking unbearable thoughts. "We'll have to leave the wounded and most of the cannon, and four or five regiments to man the lines."

Jarl's imagination ran quickly through such a night. He could see the Vanir army, exhausted from the day's battle, trying to fight and retreat. The road was probably narrow, dirt, and badly rutted. Soon—if not already—it would be jammed with traffic. Quite likely there was also a large camp following that would get in the way and impede travel. Units would become confused, and any battle would probably degrade into a long series of small running fights. The Glassey cavalry would sweep in off the plains, no one would be able to tell friend from foe, and equipment, cannon, soldiers, and even entire units would be left behind. It would be a slaughter. He found himself asking, "Have you lost to the Glasseys before?"

The question irked Enrick, and Kvasir quickly interceded. "This war has been going on for three years, ever since the Empire first tried to take the Kettle. We've not really lost much of the Kettle, but we haven't kicked the Glasseys out either. Goran is the fourth..."

Someone behind Enrick, a new voice in the darkness, interrupted, "Fifth!"

Kvasir continued, "Fifth general in three years. There have been almost as many campaigns. No one can win a clear victory."

"And in all of these campaigns," Jarl asked, "you were on the defensive."

"We started out on the offensive this spring, but Kivlor changed that. He is a competent general with a capable army, and he quickly forced us onto the defense. So far, we have managed to survive."

Enrick's unwavering gaze was cold and gave Jarl no respite, and the dark night surrounding them seemed to mirror that icy feeling. Jarl looked up, but all he saw was the terrible red eye of Mytos. But then, on the eastern skyline, he saw another light—the pale, blue orb of ringed Kmir. "Can you take to the hills? The Blue Mountains?" he asked.

Kvasir spoke, "You mean the Blue Hills. You could and I could. The Kettle Rangers could. But everyone else thinks those hills and the mountains behind them are haunted and full of evil witches and wizards. You saw how the Glasseys and the King's soldiers moved once in the forest."

"But to retreat and to take to the road is sure death. Your army would not survive."

"That much is certain," Enrick said bitterly.

"Then your only choice is to fight, here, on the high ground."

"But our leaders have run..."

Jarl shook his head. "You've survived for three years, and I'd be willing to bet you've stopped the Glasseys each time they've come up the road."

Enrick nodded, and Jarl continued, "You still have your officers and your non-coms, and you said yourself that they are damn good ones too. The Vanir soldiers I saw today have been well trained. They know what they are doing. You stopped the Glasseys. You can do it again!" Jarl stopped speaking. No one appeared to be listening. He switched to a new topic. "How many of your troops to have left?"

Enrick shrugged. "About four-fifths, and most all of the cavalry."

"Will the cavalry leave?"

Enrick almost smiled. "Wherever you are from, you sure don't know Hisson. He'll stay. If there is any chance of a fight, he'll stay." The tall man paused, then continued, "It's true no one has run for Atrobee yet, but when the first man runs, then the first company breaks. And as soon as that happens, then no one is going to stay and hold this ridge."

Jarl asked, "Did you have much faith in Goran?"

The voice in the darkness snorted, then said, "Damn no!"

"Then your troops sure weren't staying here and fighting because of him. Why should they leave now that he is gone?"

The voice started, "It won't be..." but Enrick's sharp glance brought silence. The tall officer looked back at Jarl. "Do you really think we can do this thing, just *talk* our people into staying?"

"*You have no choice.* To retreat is to die." Jarl paused. "But yes, I think they'll stay, because they are experienced troops and because they too know what awaits them on the road. And I think, with good leadership, that victory is possible. Or at least enough of a victory to get your army out intact."

Kvasir interjected, "Will Hisson stay?"

Enrick shrugged again."I suspect so," he said. "At least until we are routed. Then he'll get his cavalry out as intact as he can."

Jarl was intense. "If he doesn't... or if he can't keep their cavalry off your right flank..."

Enrick was suddenly more positive. He had made a difficult decision. "If anyone can do it, Hisson can." The tall officer glanced sharply at Jarl. "How do we do this?" he asked.

Jarl felt empty all over, but he repeated all his arguments again, realizing—as he did—that Enrick and his officers were listening, not so much to his words, but rather to his manner and confidence. He ended by saying, "This ridge is your best bet. You can always try the retreat later if you have a mind to..."

Enrick nodded. He looked up at Jarl and Kvasir. His manner hesitant, and he asked, "I know you two are civilians, but will you help?"

The old wizard answered for the both of them. "Of course."

The tall officer said a quiet, "Thanks." Then he stood and marched off purposely into the night, giving orders, sending men back to their units, telling the senior commanders to brief their junior officers. Jarl was surprised to discover how large the group had become during their meeting. Many of the listeners were common soldiers, holding pikes or muskets, their butts on the ground.

Jarl let out a long sigh. He was suddenly left without a purpose, wondering if perhaps retreat was, after all, the best option. As if hearing his silent anxieties, Kvasir placed a strong hand on his shoulder and, for the first time since their planet fall, mindbeamed a tight, soothing message *"We would have been chopped up like rabbits on the Foord Road. This ridge is by far the best choice."* He then spoke aloud, "You did well. I could not have convinced them. They know too well my shortcomings and faults."

The two men climbed the hill to their artilleryman friend in the orange blouse. He waited there, expecting them with two steaming mugs, which surprisingly contained hot soup, and good soup at that. After eating, Kvasir and Jarl began a scenario that they repeated over and over throughout the long night, talking to the common soldiers of the Vanir army, trying to build their morale, and telling them they could stop the Glasseys, with or without their general.

Some of the Vanir troops cursed when they heard Goran had abandoned them; others winced and moaned. A few cried, and there was even occasional hysteria. But all listened to Kvasir's deep baritone voice as if it were the essence of strength itself, and they paid close attention to Jarl as he described in calm detail their excellence under the fire and pressure of the Glasseys' attacks.

It was a long, tiring night, full of lengthy, identical arguments, and plaintive appeals. Kvasir and Jarl visited artillery units, campfires, groups of riflemen, and companies of swordsmen and archers. They walked the picket lines in front of the main battle line and climbed back up above the apple orchard to the Kettle Rangers. And at each place they gave their calm speeches, repeating the same sentences over and over again, listening to identical arguments, and sometimes just standing in silence while tiny groups of officers on the same mission talked to and rallied the soldiers. They were all fortunate in one aspect—it seemed that no one had had much confidence in Goran to begin with, and much less now that he was gone.

Finally, they returned to the aid station, where Kvasir talked in his confident voice to the two or three companies of Rifle that crowded into the light and got in the way of the surgeons. It was a memory that stayed with Jarl long afterwards: the quiet, serious faces shining bright in the yellow lamps, the intense silence that seemed to have infected even the wounded and those on the operating table, and the surgeons working quietly in the background.

Sometime later, under the full moons of Mytos and Kmir, the tall Vanir officer—whose full name was Enrick von Rhinehart—Jarl, Kvasir, and a dozen other officers met with General Liebs Hisson, a tall, craggy, gray-haired gentleman who reminded Jarl of Kvasir. The senior cavalry officer needed no words of encouragement—he was well aware of how crucial his role was. And, although a few of his companies had joined Goran, most had stayed, and the old man promised they would keep the Glassey horsemen from crossing the plains and encircling the Vanir.

Afterwards, Kvasir and Jarl rode a springless farm wagon up the pot-holed track that followed the valley bottom east of the Vanir's battle position. Intact companies were asleep or preparing to sleep. There was no sign of panic. Many of the soldiers who were still awake waved at the two exhausted men. Rather than climb high to the Ranger position above the apple orchard, Kvasir and Jarl slept the remainder of the night side by side in the same place they had spent the previous night, next to the overturned wagon below the aid station.

CHAPTER FOUR:

THE FIGHT FOR THE ORCHARD

As he had on his first morning on Vanir, Jarl was again awakened by someone shaking his shoulder. This time, however, the hand belonged not to Kvasir, but to a teenaged, baby-faced Vanir officer. Jarl sat up, rubbing his eyes. The young man was abrupt and almost arrogant. He waved his hand in the general direction of the crest of the battle ridge and spurted out, "Staff meeting." Then he started climbing quickly toward the top of the hill.

Jarl looked around. Kvasir was already gone. Somehow, the aid station, which had been a scene of frantic activity when he and Kvasir had fallen asleep, had caught up with the seemingly endless supply of wounded. Now, although littered with debris, overturned tables, and a huge pile of amputated limbs, the place was quiet and no one was in sight. Jarl stood. For a long moment, he fought an urge to mindbeam Kvasir, but then, bruised and tired, he pulled his blue pack onto his shoulder, put on his hat, and began to climb the hill, walking like an old man, following the teenaged officer.

Jarl was the last to arrive at the meeting, which consisted of the same exhausted group of Vanir officers, gathered by the fenced-in cannon. Nearby stood the young officer who had awakened him, impatiently waiting for Jarl to climb the hill. And next to the officer—Jarl thought at first his eyes were deceiving him—was the artillery man with the orange shirt, who someone called Wolff, waiting for him with bread and a large mug of water.

Jarl dropped his pack and appropriated both, then he joined the meeting, receiving a brief nod from Teague and an easy smile from Kvasir.

Von Rhinehart was doing the talking, and everyone listened, saying little. The orders for the day were identical to yesterday—they would hold the ridge and let the Glasseys attack. The 7th Kettlewand Rangers—Jarl took that to be Teague's company—had been reinforced with more Rangers, who should be unafraid of the deep forest and who would hold the end of the high left flank. Kvasir would go with them. Jarl thought that would include him, but von Rhinehart shook his head no. "You," he ordered, "will stay here and help coordinate the defense." The tall commander was unshaven and exhausted, and it appeared as if he had been up all night, so Jarl did not argue, but he was not happy to see Kvasir climb the limestone hill with Teague and disappear from sight. His loneliness came back, and he was once again terrified of this strange planet.

Jarl whiled away most of the morning talking to individual soldiers, napping, speaking with a few of the officers, and trying to remain calm. The officer in charge of this area was a man of about Jarl's own age who hailed from a place called Desjhan. He had little to say, perhaps disliking Jarl's outlander clothing or his friendship with the most famous wizard in Vanir. Twice Jarl overheard very hushed talk about his magic rifle that fired red shots and never needed loading. Afterwards, he kept his strange weapon hidden behind him and covered by his camouflage jacket.

Somehow, the previous day spent with the Kettle Rangers had been reminiscent of Jarl's own rural friends on Earth and Jubal, but now—for the first time—he noticed the men and women of the Vanir army as individuals. They were, as near as he could tell, mostly farmers, although a good number were from villages and cities. They were ruled by an upper caste, the High Ejliteta, and they all seemed to have the same god and religion. He heard talk of a new steam technology, of new factories, of some vague wizardry, and of ancient traditions and old kings.

Most of the soldiers wore clothing woven from heavy wools. Most had fair to dark complexions, but there were a few more brightly-dressed, blond-haired men and women, with light-colored eyes and feathers braided into their hair, who served in the sword companies. Many of the swordsmen used sabers or broadswords, which they carried in wide scabbards, strapped to their sides; but these blond people—as well as a tight-knit group of sour-faced soldiers—carried curved swords. From what Jarl could see, these weapons, which had angled points and long hilts braided with string, were identical to the weapons of Earth's ancient Japanese Samurai.

A tiny group of pikemen talked freely, enjoying Jarl's company. They said that the sour-faced men and women were E'landota, or special soldiers, trained from childhood in the arts of close warfare. Some of the regular Vanir troops admired the E'landota, but others distrusted warriors who fought by stealth and guile. But when Jarl asked about the blond people, the easy conversation came to an abrupt halt. One frightened trooper turned away and another gave him an angry stare, and Jarl knew his friendship with the pikemen was over.

The morning wore on. The only battle sounds were a cavalry engagement far out on the plains. Then, past mid-morning, the Glasseys directly across the wide valley began massing for an assault, causing a sudden commotion in the Vanir ranks.

The Vanir officers formed their men and women into three battle lines, the last of which had the six cannon, commanded by Wolff. Jarl was highly apprehensive—partly from having little do to, but also because he knew so little about the Vanir army. Wolff was absent-mindedly smiling, as if waiting for a band to begin to play; and—as if called to life for the battle—a breeze stirred the nearby banners.

Jarl climbed to a high point next to a dead apple tree, to the left of Wolff's cannon. Formed lines of greencoats had begun to march down the opposite ridge. Jarl counted the flags of seven regiments, the first of which had muskets. A Glassey drum began a slow beat from somewhere on the opposite hillside. Close by, Vanir drummers joined the cadence. Vanir officers walked the ranks, talking to their soldiers, trying to instill in them the sureness of victory. Jarl could see Glassey leaders moving among their men, and he knew that they were doing the exact same thing.

Several Vanir reserve companies, with banners dancing in the breeze, moved up the ridge behind the cannon. Small groups of sweating, gray-coated riflemen—the Vanir pickets—rejoined the line at various points, often running to jump over makeshift breastworks. A tall, pale officer, worn from the previous day's battle, with jet-black hair and wire-rimmed glasses, joined Jarl at the apple tree. The man was in his early twenties, and had a dirty bandage on his lower right arm. Jarl said a polite hello.

This startled the young officer, but after a moment's hesitation, he nodded back, staring wide-eyed at Jarl's strange clothing.

A sudden burst of Glassey cannon fire distracted them both. Immediately that noise was lost in the roar of the nearby Vanir artillery, firing over the heads of the front two lines. The ground shook from the noise of their explosions, and men ran back to their limbers for more powder and shot. Officers shouted orders above the swell of noise. Banners jerked like living things caught in some painful moment.

The smoke was already thick. Wolff's cannon crews were racing to reload. Jarl caught a brief glimpse of a lead canister, shoved into the cannon mouth by a young girl, then rammed down the barrel by an equally young boy. There was more shouting and yelling on the ridge to the west, and suddenly the enemy came charging, racing down their hill.

Jarl found himself fighting an urge to run as far away from this terrible scene as he could. The physical emotion was so powerful that he found himself facing the bandaged young Vanir officer. The young man's face was dirty, wide-eyed, and strained. Behind the glass lens, the brown eyes mirrored Jarl's own terror. For an instant the two men stared at each other; then, with great effort, they both turned back toward the fearsome battle.

In front of them, an officer's saber flashed down and there was the roar of a Vanir musket volley. Through a drifting gap in the heavy smoke, Jarl saw the first Vanir battle line working its way back through the second line. There was another downstroke of the same sword and another flash of fire, this time from the second battle line. A company of swordsmen was moving though the smoke and into position on Jarl's other side, his left, and one of these was a tall woman, feathers braided into her long, light-blond hair and her face streaked with wide, bright swaths of paint. She held a samurai sword in her right hand and, at the sight of Jarl, she grinned, displaying a set of dirty yellow teeth.

To Jarl's right, Wolff touched the end of a long flaming pole to the touch hole of his cannon. There was a moment's pause and then the great cannon jumped into the air and disgorged another load of flame, smoke, and shot. The Glassey onslaught had crossed the narrow valley bottom and was climbing up the Vanir hill. It struck the forward Vanir line, and—once again—the smoke and noise became an all-encompassing thing.

The forward Vanir line took on a life of its own, twisting back and forth and adding to the confusion. Then it separated, becoming knots of fighting, advancing, and retreating soldiers. Two or three men ran, weaponless, up the hill and past Jarl. In front of the cannon, a knot of Vanir riflemen fired a long volley of smoke and flame. At first Jarl could see nothing, because of the smoke, but then it parted and he saw that the Glasseys were still advancing up the slope. With a series of flashing swords, these greencoats overwhelmed the riflemen who had fired the volley, and suddenly there was a wide opening in the front two Vanir lines. The Vanir commander moved forward, shouting orders. Someone was holding a flag near the officer, but a Glassey cannon shell knocked that soldier to the ground. The officer managed to duck and survive, but a mounted greencoat jumped his horse over the remnants of a fence and impaled him with a long cavalry sword.

Suddenly, the air was alive with the smell of Glassey victory and Vanir fear. Gray- and blue-coated men and women paused, unsure what to do, terrified of what could happen next. Green-coated foot soldiers began pouring into a gap between the Vanir swordsmen and the Vanir cannon. An advancing company of Vanir riflemen stopped and condensed into a hesitant mass of soldiers, withering before the greencoat onslaught.

The mounted greencoat reined his horse, waving his bloody sword, urging his men to follow. Glassey infantry swarmed around him, pushing the Vanir swordsmen aside. The remaining Vanir riflemen began to fall back. Then the greencoats, led by their mounted officer, lurched forward.

A red pulse of light from an assault-blaster lifted the officer from his saddle and threw him bodily onto the foot soldiers. Other light bursts tore into the now surprised company of greencoats. It was only when a Glassey swordsman ran from the mob and began to attack him that Jarl realized it was he who was firing the blaster. He had left the tree and had run forward into the fight. He shot down the swordsman, and turned and looked up the slope. The young, pale officer with the eyeglasses was staring at him with wide eyes and an open mouth. Jarl shouted at him to order the stalled Vanir reserves into the battle. Somehow, in spite of the noise, that man heard him—or knew what to do. He turned and waved his sword, and the reserves surged forward. Someone knocked Jarl down, but he was instantly on his feet, blasting randomly into a confused knot of oncoming Glassey pikemen.

Then there was a musket volley on his right—black smoke and spent paper wads seemed to be everywhere—and the company of Vanir riflemen charged, bayonets forward, into the Glassey pikemen, who gave way and started to retreat. From the corner of his eye, Jarl caught a brief glimpse of his pale friend, his sword held high in the air, trying to rally the Vanir.

Jarl glanced down the slope, and saw that more companies of green-coated pikemen were coming up the hill. These men carried short pikes, with long iron tips, and long rectangular shields. Jarl picked up a dropped saber, and still holding his blaster in his right hand, waved the sword above his head, and then—with a do-or-die determination—bellowed at the top of his lungs, "Forward! To me! Forward!"

The Vanir reserve heard him and surged down the hill, stumbling over the dead, the battle-dumb, and the wounded. The Glassey pikemen drew nearer. A Vanir officer shouted and the Vanir riflemen raised their weapons, aiming them into the battle. As Jarl scrambled to get out of the way, they fired a volley point blank into the greencoats. Hoarse throats screamed Vanir battle cries, and the riflemen rushed forward with their bayonets, toward the decimated Glasseys.

Suddenly—unbelievably suddenly—the battle was over. The greencoats were washing back down the slope. None of the Vanir stood as organized companies; they were all now disorganized knots of dumfounded men and women.

A Vanir cannon bellowed a final blast, and Jarl looked up the slope for Wolff. He instead saw the tall, pale officer, who was still holding his saber in the air, his face and glasses covered with black smoke. Cheering and shouting broke out from the Vanir soldiers, and Jarl found himself glad to join in. Someone handed him a canteen of warm water that tasted of black powder. Medical orderlies swarmed down the hill and began helping the wounded.

Then the cheering slowed and stopped. Men pointed down the hill with apprehensive faces. Jarl tried to peer downslope at the danger, but the thick smoke obscured his view. Someone was pulling on his sleeve, and Jarl turned to discover the pale officer. Behind his glasses, his brown eyes were dark and fearful. The man was gasping, "Sir, sir, you have to take over."

Jarl was reeling, "Why? Where are your commanders?"

"Wounded, sir. Dead, sir. You will have to take over. The Glasseys are attacking again."

This time, down the ridge, Jarl could see through a drifting gap in the smoke. Glassey officers were once again lining up their men, and one company of pikemen was already marching up the hill toward the Vanir. Jarl looked around him. Many officers and soldiers, including Wolff, his orange blouse in rags, were staring at him. Groups of men were beginning to move up the hill, and he knew the panic could come quickly.

Jarl looked back downslope and let out a violent breath of air. A second greencoat company was starting up the slope, directly behind the first. To his right, a confused mass of Vanir riflemen were moving backward, beginning a retreat. Jarl pushed the young officer off his shoulder and shouted, "Form the men into ranks!"

The pale officer jumped as if shocked. He ran toward the Vanir riflemen, yelling, "Form up! Form up!"

Jarl screamed the same words to a disorganized company of swordsmen. He turned and shouted a loud order for Wolff to get his cannon loaded. The man also jumped, then he turned and began readying his artillery pieces. A Vanir officer stood above the dead apple tree, staring down at the confusion. Jarl yelled at him to go find some more reserves. The man turned and sprinted over the ridge top. The two companies of Glassey pikemen still marched toward the Vanir. Then, as the tall, pale officer yelled, "Ready! Ready!" the Vanir riflemen raised their weapons. The greencoats suddenly broke into a run, trying to sprint up the debris-covered slope, shouting their battle cries. Fired from somewhere far down the ridge, a Vanir cannon shot tore a huge hole in the attackers' lines. A few Vanir pikemen rushed to join the waiting mob of swordsmen, but no fresh companies arrived to strengthen the tired battle line.

The charging Glasseys were within fifteen meters, but the Vanir riflemen did not fire. Then, suddenly, Jarl realized the pale officer was shouting at him, "Should we fire, sir? Should we fire?"

Jarl bellowed a loud, "Yes!" and the Vanir riflemen fired a broken volley. For a second—amid fresh clouds of billowing smoke and floating paper wads—the bloody onslaught paused. From behind Jarl, one of Wolff's cannon roared, cutting down more of their enemy.

Jarl waved his sword and shouted a loud "Charge!" and all the Vanir rushed down the ridge in a desperate counterattack. There was a sudden clash as they ran headlong into the greencoats. A long moment of hand-to-hand fighting followed, but the Glasseys were badly outnumbered. Soon the greencoat survivors were running back down the hill. Jarl and the pale officer shouted orders and the exhausted Vanir men and women began stumbling back up the hill. With them came small groups of green-coated prisoners.

In the bottom of the wide valley, Jarl could see more companies of enemy pikemen, standing in near-straight lines, waiting for some unknown order. A mounted officer moved among them, forming them for yet another assault. Another company of greencoats stepped out of the smoke and the officer directed them into place.

There were still no Vanir reinforcements. Jarl climbed, stepping over and around the many corpses, toward an injured woman who was holding a horse by the reins. He searched the top of the ridge for the badly needed reserves. All he saw was the pale officer, staring at him with wide expectant eyes, and he knew that the man—in fact, all the Vanir men and women—was expecting him to do something.

Someone spoke to him, and Jarl turned to see the woman with the horse. It was a young animal, a light-gray horse flecked with uncountable spots of darker gray. Jarl rotated his blaster behind him on its strap. He grabbed the horse's mane with his left hand, put his left foot in the stirrup, and—with a practiced ease—swung his right leg over the horse's back. He hit the saddle with a satisfying thud. The woman let go of the reins and the horse danced sideways, but Jarl was used to horses, and he soon quieted the animal—or as much as was possible on the battlefield full of smoke and the smell of blood.

Jarl walked the horse up the slope. There he turned the animal, so that he was facing downslope. He sat there, forcing himself to appear calm and in control of the situation, knowing that there were many Vanir eyes upon him, looking to him for support. The pale officer's riflemen had formed into two lines. Behind them, the large artillery pieces were now silent, loaded and waiting for the next Glassey attack. But now there were only four cannon—a fifth lay in a heap of wheels and iron, and another had been knocked off its carriage.

But the Glassey attack did not come. They waited, and the day grew strangely quiet. Finally, after a long twenty minutes, a company of Vanir pikemen came running up the backside of the Vanir ridge. They were followed by a company of swordsmen and then von Rhinehart himself, riding a black horse.

Three companies of gray-coated Vanir riflemen were next to arrive. Jarl ordered them down in front of the cannon and moved the tired rifle companies up behind the cannon. Von Rhinehart sent two mounted couriers racing downslope. A small group of E'landota arrived, strutting with stiff-legged arrogance, their sword scabbards thrust through wide waist sashes, along with another company of Rifle. The greencoats had waited too long.

Then there was the beat of a drum and the sound of a trumpet. Below, the Glasseys started marching forward, led by a mounted officer. Two more companies of Vanir reserves arrived, and Jarl was glad to see the long spikes of the bayonets. He stationed them in front of the cannon, next to the tired riflemen. Jarl's fear was gone and all he felt now—deep inside— was a terrible urge to drive the Glasseys from the field.

The Vanir waited. The Glasseys came closer, across the narrow bottom, stepping forward with an unnerving calm; their precision unbelievable. At thirty meters, just after they had started up the slope, the Glassey horseman shouted for his troops to halt, and Jarl waved his hat and screamed for his own soldiers to fire. There was the roar of Vanir cannon and rifle, and in brief second before the thick smoke obscured the battlefield, Jarl saw the enemy officer fall from his horse and the Glassey line disintegrate.

Jarl's horse was frightened by the sudden onslaught of noise and began to dance across the battlefield. He fought to control it, and he waved his hat again and shouted for the rifle companies to attack. The Vanir riflemen leaped up and—screaming their battle cries—rushed down the slope, bayonets to the fore. Jarl yelled for the officers by the apple tree to bring their companies down. Everyone but the E'landota charged down the slope.

The Vanir riflemen ran headlong into the Glassey pikemen. Although there were more greencoats than Vanir, the Empire's troops were disorganized from the concentrated rifle and cannon fire. There was an intense moment of confused hand-to-hand fighting, and then the first Glassey companies begin to fall back. One of Wolff's cannon blasted a hole in what remained of the enemy battle line, and the greencoats stumbled backwards and began to retreat. Banners jerked back and forth, and suddenly all the Glasseys were retreating.

The smoke was thick, but perhaps the breeze had become stronger, and Jarl could see that the greencoats in the valley beyond were beginning a long climb back up the ridge to the west, their weapons and banners drooping toward the ground. Just below the top of that ridge, organized greencoat companies stood watching, their flags proudly floating in the breeze. But, after many long minutes, these soldiers too turned and slowly started to climb back up the hill.

The battle for the old orchard was over.

CHAPTER FIVE:

THE WIZARD LOST

During the remainder of the morning, while the greencoats carried their attack to other parts of the Vanir battle line, Jarl and the tall, pale officer, whose name was Will James, redressed the nearby battered companies, oversaw the transfer of the wounded to the aid station, and made sure their battle-weary troops had plenty of food and water.

Those Vanir soldiers with minor wounds were treated in the battle lines, usually with a dirty, white bandage wrapped around a leg or arm. The dead were moved—as much as was possible—so that they were out of the way of the living. Ammunition and powder were brought forward for the riflemen and the artillery. The depleted companies that had fought so determinedly were marched off to a rest area behind the lines. With them went Enrick von Rhinehart, a hundred or so Glassey prisoners, and the tiny squad of E'landota.

Behind the ridge, the aid station had been expanded. Surgeons were now operating—in reality, amputating and searing—not only inside the sagging gray tent, but also on makeshift operating tables set up under the blue Vanir sky. Still, long, congested lines had developed, where men and women cried for water and help, prayed to their god, and died from neglect. Orderlies scurried back and forth—Jarl sent down part of a company to help—bringing water to the injured, assisting soldiers with temporary bandages, and carrying men and women to the operating tables. The screams and moans became the wail of a continuous chorus, one that sounded like the spectators at a sporting game, and one that Jarl fought not to hear.

Von Rhinehart sent up a major to take command of Jarl's section of line sometime in the early afternoon. With the man came the news that all up and down the long Vanir ridge, wherever the greencoats had attacked, they had been stopped, usually in fierce and bitterly contested confrontations. On the northern plains, the two armies' cavalries had fought each other to a standstill, with neither side achieving the upper hand. But this was to the Vanir's favor, because it meant that for the moment, their army's right flank was protected from the fast-moving Glassey horsemen.

Jarl, after leaving the dapple gray with the horses assigned to Wolff's artillery, walked among the Vanir soldiers, joking with them and sharing a small meal. But, in a moment of sadness, he discovered the body of the blond woman who had grinned at him during the battle. With some distaste, he unbuckled her sheath and took her sword, which Will James wiped off with a dirty rag. As she had before she died, Jarl hung the curved sword and its scabbard across his back.

The two men crossed the ridge and climbed down to the aid station in the middle of the afternoon, passing an immense pile of discarded equipment. There, they spotted a tall woman bending over a wounded swordsman, tightening a leather tourniquet with long, strong fingers. The tight bun of her black hair was beginning to fall apart and, as she moved one hand to brush the hair from her eyes, she caught sight of the two men standing just outside the tent. For some reason she jumped, ever so slightly, catching her breath as she did so. As she slowly straightened, Will James gasped and his pale face turned a lighter shade of white. The two stared at each other for a long moment, astonishment written on their faces, then the young woman wound her way carefully through the wounded lying on the ground, and moved to where the two men were standing.

Her manner was shy and hesitant. Despite her fatigue, she spoke in a musical voice, and said her name was Stori Hrafkel. Even as she spoke, Will James was introducing himself and Jarl. For a few seconds, while Will James' face changed from nervous anticipation to excitement, the three of them shared a moment of relative quiet, discussing the battle that had taken place that morning on the ridge above. Then Jarl walked out of the tent and into the bright sunshine, leaving Will James and Stori to a hushed and serious conversation.

A balding, portly surgeon saw Jarl standing outside the tent. The man glared his way, then moved determinedly toward him. Jarl turned, expecting another polite conversation, but instead the man growled and said, "I want you out of this area! Leave!"

Jarl was taken aback. The surgeon stepped forward, and shoved his face into Jarl's face. "Leave!" he ordered, raising his voice. "Get out!! Leave! Now!" Will James suddenly appeared at Jarl's side, grabbed his arm, and escorted him up the hill. Behind him, the surgeon was standing under the edge of the tent, with hands on hips, feet spread apart, his face an intense red, and a look of undisguised satisfaction on his face, watching Jarl's hasty retreat.

The two men climbed back up the ridge toward the battle lines. Jarl was unnerved. He took a long breath and looked at his new friend. Quietly he asked, "What was that about?"

For a few moments Will James said nothing, then he blurted out, "I think it was because of your strange clothing. Or your witch weapon. Or maybe it is because you are a great wizard, and some people don't like wizards."

Jarl managed a short, surprised grunt, and the younger man continued, his words rushing out all at once, "The witch weapon shoots red rays. There is no explosion or fire, and it never needs reloading. A lot of people are afraid of that, even if you do fight with us."

Jarl was slow in replying, "I am not a wizard." At his side, Will James stared, saying nothing. Jarl asked, "Do you believe me?"

Will James did not answer. Jarl met his eyes, but the young man looked away. Jarl repeated, "I am not a wizard," but his words sounded weak and without truth.

Will James stared southward for a long time, toward the green mountains. Then he looked back at Jarl and spoke again, slowly, "This is my first big battle... it... it... it was like nothing I imagined." There was a long pause—then, "It was... Were you afraid?"

Jarl was glad to change the subject. His answer was short, "I was terrified. At least when the battle stared. I almost took off running."

Will James was shocked. His brown eyes were wide behind his glasses. "So did I. Is it always like that?"

Jarl answered truthfully, "This is my first time in this kind of a battle." He paused, and shivered, thinking of the countless small partisan ambushes where no advantage or quarter was given to the enemy, and where the fights usually lasted only minutes; of the massed battles where the soldiers groveled on the ground, hiding behind any and all conceivable cover, firing hundreds of thousands of projectiles, rockets, and energy bolts at an unseen enemy; and of the space battles, which were so impersonal and cold, but terribly frightening because of the power of the weapons and the lack of defenses of the ships involved.

"I have been in other fights...." Jarl continued, "and most were very frightening." He stopped, knowing he had lied, because he had seen people, after losing their friends and family, with no emotion other than the satisfaction of killing their enemy; and he knew that some people, long attuned to war, live only for the excitement of being in a battle. But then he took a long, deep breath, remembering that this planet was a long way from the pain and death on Jubal.

Will James spoke again, "I thought it would be... different. The men who speak to my father... talk of the glory and the honor... of grand deeds." He paused, as if admitting an unforgivable sin, "I almost ran..." He repeated the three words in a hushed and almost reverent whisper, "I almost ran."

"So did I."

"But, for you it is different... I am... supposed to be brave in battle... Men are supposed to follow me into battle..."

There was something the young Vanir officer was not saying; perhaps his family or caste had a long military tradition. Jarl looked at the mountains, searching for the right words to say, "I don't know what to tell you... Someone once said that a man who says he has never been afraid is a man who has never traveled or done anything... or is a liar. Even leaders are afraid, and a situation is always worse the first time." He paused, thinking, remembering. "Fear is a companion I have had for a long time, and it has become like an old friend in some ways. Perhaps other people are luckier and not afraid, but I am not one of them..."

Will James was staring at him, listening intently. Something in his manner made Jarl feel that the young man had many acquaintances, but few friends. "I thought I was the only one who was afraid," the young man said. "I thought I was a coward. I thought I had failed in my duty."

Jarl smiled, "I think you would have been hard pressed to find someone on that battlefield who was not frightened, including the Glasseys. And I thought you did damn good during the battle. You kept your head, you helped bring up our reinforcements, you helped me get the companies reorganized. I appreciate that. I don't think we would have won without your help."

Will James looked down at the ground, then back at Jarl. It was obvious he was taken aback by the compliment, and it was clear he appreciated Jarl's words. "This morning," he said quietly, as if he was afraid of being overheard, "my commander dismissed me. He was very angry. He said I was too slow in organizing the company. He said I was incompetent. He called me some names that..."

Jarl suddenly realized that Will James was being very open, and that he was an extremely hurt young man. Once again, he had the feeling that he had very few friends. "What rank are you?" he asked.

Will James was surprised, as much at the question as well as Jarl's inability to read his insignia. "First Lieutenant."

"Well, you did damn good up on this ridge. If you had been slower getting those riflemen organized, we both would probably be dead or captured by now. Maybe your commander had a problem... like that surgeon." Jarl allowed himself a tired, sad smile. "But from what I saw of you on the battlefield, you have nothing to be ashamed of."

Will James started to speak again, but at that moment a young man ran the last few steps down the hillside and slid to a sudden stop. It took this man several seconds to catch his breath, and in that moment Jarl recognized him as one of Teague's woodsmen.

The Ranger faced Jarl and sputtered out a brief message: "Aaron Walker thinks you should come up on the mountain."

It took Jarl a second to realize who Aaron Walker was. Then he asked, "What happened?"

"The Glasseys ambushed the Captain. He is hurt bad. Real bad." The young man paused. "Some are dead. I was sent for a doctor, but they are...." Jarl did not have to look back at the aid station to understand the man's hesitation—the lines there were still impossibly long. "Someone said you patched up some hurt soldiers the other night. The Captain is hurt bad."

Jarl reply was quick, "I am not a doctor, but I'll do what I can." The three men turned and climbed toward the apple orchard. As they passed the cannon, Jarl noticed that both Wolff and the new commander were silently watching them. He didn't know if that was a good thing—or a bad thing. "What of Kvasir?" he asked.

"Kvasir? The old wizard? I don't know."

Jarl considered that for a moment, but he knew that Kvasir could take care of himself. He looked at Will James. "You don't have to come if you don't want to."

He had made a mistake—a bad mistake. The young officer was startled, and his new-found confidence shaken, "If you don't want me..."

Jarl interjected, "I thought you might want to stay here."

"I am not needed here."

The fast uphill walk was leaving Jarl breathless and he did not want to sound abrupt, "Come on then," he said, as kind and honest as he could. "We can use your help."

They continued climbing. After a moment Will James asked, "Have you known Kvasir long?" There was a pause to breathe. "I have heard so much about him... a lot bad. But some... say nothing but... good."

"I have known him two days."

Will James stopped. "I thought you and he were old friends," he gasped.

"We are. But only for two days!" Jarl looked back, sucked in a deep breath, and shouted, "Come on!" The young officer hurried to catch up.

Their young guide introduced himself as Stefan Ker. With a long, distance-eating stride, he led Will James and Jarl up the steep limestone hillside—they had to rest twice—and across the meadow and into the forest. Once in the woods, Will James immediately became nervous, but at Jarl's anxious glance, he became angry and shouted, "I'm coming!" For twenty minutes they wove through the trees, following the steep slope west along the side of the mountain, climbing over sandstone boulders and fallen timber. Will James clutched his saber, but he did not remove the cumbersome blade from its sheath. Jarl rotated his blaster so that it was in a ready position. Ahead of them, Stefan moved easily, unafraid of the deep woods, carrying his long rifle in the nook of his arm, as if it was a part of his body.

Finally, among a cluster of flat sandstone boulders, Jarl saw a half dozen men kneeling or standing. As they approached, a second group of Rangers, numbering no more than the first, descended the final meters to the first group. Even at a distance, Jarl identified the tall Aaron Walker. There was no sign of Kvasir. Away from the group of standing men, several Rangers lay on the ground, face up, dead. A half dozen dead green-coated Glasseys lay in less arranged positions, with arms and legs twisted in every conceivable position, as if they had fallen from the sky. Jarl scanned the surrounding forest. He saw no other sign of life.

The Rangers' faces were long and somber. They were gathered around one man, who was lying supine on the ground, a small pack for a pillow. Aaron knelt at the man's head. As they walked the last few meters into the group, Jarl could see that the man on the ground was Teague. The Ranger captain's face was an ashen gray and a large bandage that had been the same color was wrapped around his abdomen. Now the bandage was almost entirely red. The tall Ranger captain was clearly beyond the help of any doctor.

Stefan, his face suddenly tear-streaked, grounded his rifle butt-first on the forest floor. Aaron looked up at Jarl, his expression rock-hard. Jarl muttered a weak, "I'm sorry." Teague had been a competent and caring leader, and Jarl had truly liked him. Plus he had given him his boots.

The Rangers were quiet, paying their last respects. Several were openly crying. Jarl quietly asked Aaron what had happened.

"Teague, Kvasir, and about a dozen Rangers bumped into a large squad of greencoats west of here. There was a brief fight and then the Rangers retreated in this direction, across the side of the mountain. They took turns firing and running. Well, they ran into a big group of Glasseys right about here. The damn greencoats waited till Teague and his boys got close, then they opened fire. The Rangers never knew what hit them. The first volley wounded Teague. The rest... English and Grayson were able to scoot downhill and get away."

"And Kvasir?"

"The rest surrendered... Kvasir too. There wasn't much else they could do..."

Dangerous or not, Jarl immediately sent out his strongest mindbeam, calling Kvasir, asking where he was. He directed it west, along the side of the mountain. There was no answer.

One of the Rangers was a thin, old man who squatted next to the body, his arms wrapped around his long rifle, chewing a plug of tobacco. This man spoke with a dry voice, "I was hid-out up-slope. The son-of-a-bitch greencoats knew who Kvasir was... They knocked him around some right off... They knocked him clean to the ground once. Then they marched 'em all off to the west. All told, they took seven prisoners, counting the wizard. I counted twenty-five Glasseys."

Aaron abruptly stood up. "Let's go get them.."

Stefan asked, "What about him?" He pointed to Teague. "We can't just leave him." The young man's voice was plaintive.

Aaron was brisk, "We can and we will; our first priority is to the living."

"But he was our Captain!"

"And my cousin... But staying with him ain't doing anyone any good. Our people need our help. We are leaving Captain Walker."

"And him?" the old man asked, pointing with one finger. For the first time Jarl noticed one of the Rangers was sitting on a small boulder, blood oozing from a leg wound. Someone had tied a red handkerchief above the wound. Jarl moved to the man's side and examined the leg. The wound was ugly, but the bullet had passed completely through, hitting no bones. When he gently loosened the tourniquet, the Ranger, who was a little more than a boy, gave a small gasp of pain. The wound began to bleed more profusely. Almost absently, Jarl heard another young Ranger say he could get the wounded man back to the meadow. Jarl looked around for a bandage, and someone handed him the inevitable dirty white cloth. He tore it in half, and using the cleanest portion as the bandage and the remainder as the wrapping, tightly covered the wound. The bleeding slowed and then stopped.

Then he looked up at the wounded man's companion. There was a good deal of similarity in the two men's faces. Jarl asked, "You brothers?"

The second Ranger nodded yes.

Jarl continued, "Go slow. If it starts bleeding bad again, rest for a while and tighten the wrapping around the bandage. Don't tighten the tourniquet. A little blood loss won't kill him and that tourniquet might cause him to lose the leg, so don't use it unless the bleeding gets real bad."

The second Ranger nodded again.

"When you get back to that limestone spring, you wash the wound. I could see unfired powder in it, so you wash it real good. Use a lot of water, and wash your hands before you work on him. Wash your hands good. Try to get the powder out. Then put a fresh bandage on it. The cleanest bandage you can find. Use pressure directly over the wound to stop the bleeding, and use the tourniquet only as a last resort. And unless the bleeding will not stop or the wound gets infected, don't take him down to the aid station.."

The hurt man visually paled at Jarl's last words. "Will I lose the leg?" he asked.

Jarl did not know the answer. "Maybe not, wash it well and bandage it again. Use a clean bandage and lots of water. The clean bandage is real important." He stood, wiping his bloody hands on his pants.

Aaron asked, "You want somebody to go with you?" The tall Ranger glanced at Will James, who was clutching his sheathed saber and looking nervously at the forest.

Unaware that Aaron had been trying to offer Will James an honorable way off the mountain, the unhurt brother answered, "No, we can make it."

Aaron looked uncomfortable. He glanced back at Will James. The young officer suddenly realized Aaron's intent and sputtered, "Don't worry about me, I can keep up." The old, thin Ranger punctuated Will James' statement by spitting a stream of tobacco onto the forest floor.

Aaron looked Will James over, "Leave the sword and take this." He offered Teague's long rifle.

Will James' nervousness increased. For an instant, light reflected off his glasses. "I can't... my father gave me this sword..."

Earlier on the battlefield, Jarl had noticed the fancy engraving down the length of Will James' blade. It was an expensive, perhaps priceless, sword. "Maybe..." Aaron said, "but it is going to be damn noisy in the trees and it will slow you down. It might get someone killed."

The old man added, "Best take the rifle, boy. It's a good 'un and it will do you more good in a far fight." He spat again. The old man was clearly no respecter of rank, and his words were sound advice.

For a moment Jarl thought Will James was going to make an argument of it. But then, he moved his hands to his belt buckle and, after a moment's hesitation, removed the sword from his waist. He handed it to Jarl. Gold and silver had been intertwined to form the hilt, from which a short, expensive red sash hung. Together with his newly acquired samurai blade, Jarl hung the saber in the fork of a small tree. Aaron handed Will James his cousin's rifle. "It's loaded. Teague was killed by the first shots and never got a chance to shoot back. Can you handle it?"

Will James nodded yes.

Jarl bent over and started to pick up one of the flintlock rifles. He wanted to carry something less conspicuous than his blaster. But the old man stopped him. "A man would be a fool not to use the best weapon he could lay his hands on." Then he spit again.

Aaron had been taking a long, last look at his dead cousin. Now he turned and moved off to the west, following the trail of the greencoats. After a few steps he asked, "And so speaks the wise and reverent Otis Gottress?"

The old man made no reply, but Jarl noticed Aaron did a quick step to avoid a brown stream of flying tobacco.

There were nine Rangers, all men. For the most part they moved single file, rifles at the ready. Otis moved to the front, Aaron was behind him, and Jarl followed Aaron. The remainder of the woodsmen strung out behind. And they moved fast; the old man half limped and half ran in a cat-like crouch, jumping lightly over trees and rocks. The way on was obvious—there were churned-up leaves, broken sticks, and overturned rocks—but Jarl got the impression that Otis was following a specific portion of the trail, not the wide, general track. Twice the old man paused, and once he stepped several paces to one side. With each westward step, Jarl's fear for the old wizard increased. Twice he sent out strong mindbeamed messages. But no one answered.

The risk of encountering Glasseys increased as the Rangers moved west. Nevertheless, they held to their fast pace. There were no pauses to search out the enemy, and no scouts were sent ahead to locate possible trouble. Twice, they heard voices higher on the mountain. Once, through the trees, they spotted the bright flash of gaudy green high above them. They halted and waited, but the greencoats did not move off. After no more than a minute, Aaron made a small hand motion to Otis, and the old man silently moved off to the west, staying low and keeping behind rocks and fallen trees. The rest of them followed, as quietly as possible.

For several more minutes they moved west, then Otis led the Rangers to the top of a wide, flat sandstone boulder. There he paused, as the path had turned downhill. As the trailing Rangers climbed onto the massive rock, Jarl and Aaron moved to the outward edge. Here, the boulder was three or four meters above the floor of the forest—and here they surprised two dozen Glassey riflemen.

The greencoats had been carrying two of their dead down off the mountain. Tired, they had rested behind the rock without posting a guard. Although startled, a few of them moved with lightning speed. A young lieutenant reached for his saber. Behind him, two of his men started to bring up their muskets, one dropping an upturned boot to do so. But most of the Glasseys simply stared, and one soldier let his weapon fall into the leaves at his feet. Both Aaron and Jarl—as quickly as possible—swung their rifles into a firing position.

This was a fight the Vanir could ill afford—not only were they outnumbered by this small group of greencoats, but the first shots would bring additional Glasseys at a run, trapping the Rangers behind their enemy's lines. Even as his blaster leveled on the young Glassey officer, Jarl felt a dread settle in his stomach. And the young officer was quick—his sword was half out of its sheath and his mouth opening to shout for help.

But they were all too slow, the officer, Aaron, Jarl, and the green-coated soldiers. A squirt of tobacco smacked the young officer square in the forehead and a hard, cold voice growled, "Hands up! You're captured!"

The Glassey officer stopped, frozen in time. The other greencoats also paused. Jarl repeated the command, "Hands up!" More Rangers crested the rock, skylined against the forest sky, rifles at the ready.

Aaron spoke, in a low but commanding voice, "You are our prisoners! Drop your weapons!"

The young lieutenant remained unmoving for a long, tense second. Then, with a loud click, he slammed his saber back into its scabbard. Behind him, the other greencoats began to drop their weapons. One rifle chattered off a rock and Jarl held his breath, afraid it would fire. Fortunately, it did not. The Glassey lieutenant unbuckled his sword belt and dropped it and the scabbard to the ground. Another man allowed his saber to fall from his fingers. The Rangers arranged themselves along the top of the rock. Jarl counted twenty-three Glasseys. The Rangers' position was still precarious, but thanks to Otis, they had some breathing room.

Aaron motioned for the Glasseys to leave their weapons and climb above the rock. Once there, he had them sit, cross-legged, with their hands on their heads. Otis and Jarl hopped down and quickly inspected the two dead greencoats. Both were high-ranking officers. Jarl rolled one over and shucked him out of his coat. Three Glasseys, including the young lieutenant, who looked more ridiculous than dangerous with a tobacco smear running down his face, abruptly jumped to their feet, but the stern looks and menacing rifles of Aaron and his woodsmen eased the greencoats back into their sitting position.

Jarl climbed back up onto the rock, carrying the coat. "What now?" someone asked.

Aaron said, "We can't go on, not with these prisoners. And we can't leave them, because then they'll holler for help."

"Are we near where they descended to their camp?" Jarl asked.

Aaron shrugged, but Otis spoke, "Might be. The trail turns down here, and Kvasir is still with them." The old man sounded sure of his facts.

Jarl looked at Aaron, "Stay here and guard these prisoners. Let me go take a look." Aaron was somewhat uncertain, but he nodded a tentative yes. Jarl stepped up to within a few centimeters of Aaron and lowered his voice to a whisper, "If there is trouble, run west and then uphill. They will be expecting you to go east."

Aaron again nodded, then he whispered, "Be careful. I don't want to lose you too."

Jarl turned and, still carrying the Glassey's greatcoat, hopped off the boulder's low side and continued down the mountain. He had only gone a few steps when he realized Will James was following. Jarl stopped, turned, and put a hand on the young man's shoulder—it was a gesture that brought pain when he remembered that Kvasir had done the same thing to him less than two days ago on board the *Cassiopeia*. "No offense, Will James, but two feet are quieter than four. And besides, I've spent a lot of time in the woods. Plus, you are badly needed here to help guard the prisoners."

The young officer nodded, and it was obvious he was relieved to remain with the small squadron of Rangers. Jarl again turned and started down the hill, and—once more—a second set of feet followed. Just as he was going to turn and argue with Will James a second time, Jarl heard a splat of tobacco hit the leafy forest floor. It was a comforting sound. Perhaps four feet could be as quiet as two, and Otis was a proven asset in an emergency.

The two men eased down the mountain, following the wide path to the edge of the cliff located a hundred meters below the other Rangers. Here, there was no meadow, but a single greencoated soldier guarded a small clearing and a narrow break in the limestone rim rock. Below them was the Glassey encampment. The day seemed to have turned quiet—there was no smoke of battle, no troop movements, and no loud noise of any combat. Jarl mindbeamed Kvasir once more, and again there was no answer.

Jarl slid out of his camouflage jacket and dropped it and his hat onto the ground. While Otis watched, he slipped into the gaudy Glassey coat and buttoned it. He started to show Otis how to use his blaster, but the old Ranger merely waved him off, whispering he preferred his long rifle. Jarl nodded and, pocketing his small projectile pistol, moved out into the open. He walked, with some arrogance, directly up to the sentry. He was frightened and he knew his impersonation might not work. But, with Otis behind him with his long rifle, he knew it was the sentry who was in the most danger.

The greencoat spoke first, in a heavy accent, and said he was surprised to see an officer alone.

Jarl answered, his voice full of authority, "That is not your concern." He paused, clasped his hands behind his back, and inspected the man's uniform. The sentry abruptly snapped to attention, his eyes staring straight ahead and his musket and bayonet pointing skyward. That gave Jarl the chance to examine the limestone hillside and the nearby forest. The nearest greencoats were a full thirty meters down the steep slope toward the main Glassey army. There, three men were sitting and enjoying the panoramic view. One smoked a long pipe from which bluish smoke rose.

Jarl turned his gaze back to the sentry. After a few seconds, the man spurted out a loud, "Sir?"

Jarl waited another long moment, then he spoke, his voice contemptuous, "We captured a small group of Vanir, one of them in heavy robes, reputed to be a wizard. Have they been taken this way?"

"Yes, sir!"

Jarl's heart sank. "When?" he asked, still using this voice of command.

"More than an hour ago, sir!"

Jarl let his face show his disapproval. "What kind of condition were they in?"

"Don't know, sir! I only just came on duty."

The sentry was shaking with fear, and Jarl thought that the discipline in the Empire's army must be a fearful thing. He continued staring at the man, and he pressed his question, "You have no idea what kind of condition any of those prisoners were in, soldier?"

"I think they might have been helping the wizard, sir."

Jarl was angry, thinking of Kvasir. "What do you mean, 'think they might'? Was the wizard injured?"

"Yes, sir! Ojimar... the man I relieved... said two other prisoners were supporting the wizard, sir!"

"Where did they take the prisoners?" This question, Jarl knew, might give away his masquerade.

"I do not know, sir!"

"What unit took them?"

"I do not know, sir!"

Jarl stepped past the man and looked down onto the Glassey's ridge. His only option was to carry this charade into the greencoat camp, pretending to be an officer of the Empire, searching for Kvasir and the captured Kettle Rangers, and then—if he found them—somehow walking them right out of the camp. But he knew the impersonation would never work—his pants were the wrong color, he had no sword or hat, and his knowledge of the Glassey army was virtually non-existent. And even if no one suspected that he was not a greencoat, the chances of finding Kvasir in such a large camp and then successfully rescuing him were infinitely small.

That unsavory decision made, Jarl unhurriedly searched the Glassey positions for troops preparing to attack the Vanir. There were none.

Then, in spite of the danger, Jarl tried one last long, strong mindbeam. Again, there was no response. *Were there no telepaths in the entire Glassey camp?*' he wondered.

He had no idea how strong Kvasir's ability was—perhaps the old wizard was attempting to answer and Jarl was beyond his range. Perhaps he was already beyond Jarl's range, or perhaps he had used his secret crystal to escape. Or perhaps Kvasir was beaten and unconscious. Or dead.

Jarl turned back to the sentry and gave him a long, last look. He then walked back along the path that he had come, well aware that the greencoat was still standing at rigid attention. Jarl's back was to the guard, but he trusted Otis to shoot the greencoat if it became necessary. He walked past the old Ranger and deeper into the forest until he was sure his gaudy green greatcoat could not be seen from below. Otis soon arrived, limping, carrying two rifles and Jarl's jacket and hat.

The old man spoke first, clearly impressed, "He's still standing at attention. Did it look like they have an attack planned?"

"Not that I could tell." Jarl took off the green coat and replaced it with his own. He then pocketed his small projectile pistol in his own coat, and he put on his hat.

"Damnest thing I've ever seen! You goin' and askin' them where they took Kvasir and the boys..." The old man paused, shaking his head, thoughtful, "Damn shame though, that the Glasseys have already taken 'em down to their camp."

Jarl, now that the tension was over, was so tired he could hardly stand. Even so, he managed to grin at the Ranger. He turned and began climbing up the mountain. Behind him, the old man spit again and then followed.

Within minutes, the two men rejoined Aaron's group. The Rangers herded their prisoners east, once hiding in a shallow hollow while other Glasseys moved about up the mountain. The sunlight was fading when the mixed group arrived at the spot where Teague Walker had died. There, Mylea Orlando waited, alone and with a tear-streaked face. As Will James and Jarl gathered their respective swords, the Rangers forced the captured greencoats to become litter-bearers, and they carried the Vanir dead along the side of the mountain.

Once a large owl erupted from a dead tree and flew silently down the mountain. This frightened the Glassey prisoners, and one group dropped their corpse, muttering among themselves. But the Rangers forced their prisoners to pick their burden up, and soon the quiet procession was again staggering east, often falling on the steep, leaf-covered slope. It was dusk when they arrived at the Vanir positions in the meadow. Here, Kettle riflemen took up the chore of herding the prisoners.

Jarl felt old, afraid, utterly exhausted, and lonely, and he was deeply worried for Kvasir's safety. Will James' face was also etched with concern, and twice he had tried, with words and gestures, to express his sympathy. As the night began to darken, Jarl began to prepare for one more inevitable staff meeting, but—without warning—he tripped and fell. He forced an arm under his body and attempted to lever himself into a sitting position, but he only collapsed back onto the dry summer grass of the mountain meadow.

CHAPTER SIX:

THE LAST BATTLE

Jarl spent the next two hours sleeping beside a small fire on the edge of the mountain clearing. Mylea then woke him and held him in a sitting position while he drank a full canteen of cold spring water. When he was finished, she said Enrick von Rhinehart had climbed the steep hill expressly to speak to him. Jarl rose and, shivering, allowed the thin woman to help him to a larger campfire at the edge of the limestone escarpment.

The Vanir colonel shook Jarl's hand and helped him to a seat on a nearby log, at the same time inquiring about his health. The tall man was full of smiles, his face was clean-shaven, and he freely admitted he had slept half of the late afternoon away. He said that the soldiers—of all ranks and castes—were proud and confident, well aware they had succeeded after their commanding general had deserted them. Most of the Rangers crowded in close and listened to the colonel's words. They were keenly interested, and their faces were bright, reflecting the light of the campfire. Von Rhinehart told of the day's actions, and said the worst crisis had been the defense Jarl had commanded—an onslaught that, if successful, would have swept down the long ridge and beaten the entire Vanir army.

Afterwards, the two men discussed Kvasir's capture. Von Rhinehart's voice was quiet, almost a whisper, "The Rangers will be treated as prisoners of war and exchanged back to the Vanir. Kvasir, on the other hand, is not only a known sorcerer, but the most famous wizard in all of Vanir and Glassitron. He was Sovereign of the High Council of Vor for more than a decade and a half. And, in case you have forgotten, Vor is a city the Empire has vowed to burn to the ground..."

Jarl nodded. He did not say that this was news to him.

Von Rhinehart sadly shook his head, "Some time ago, long before Kvasir was the Sovereign at Vor, he was found guilty of sorcery by the Regnant Court of the Royal and Most Holy Empire of Glassitron. On that occasion, he escaped in a bloody fight that sorely tested the Empire's honor and integrity. They say the Emperor himself carries wounds from that battle."

The tall officer thought for several moments, and then added, "The outlook for the old wizard's survival is not good. Glassitron law requires that sorcerers be executed. Kvasir's only chance might come if the greencoats transport him back to the Empire for a second long and well-publicized trial."

"Why?" someone asked. "Wasn't he present for the first trial?"

"No," von Rhinehart said, shaking his head. "Somehow he missed his first trial."

Von Rhinehart paused again, then said, "A journey to Glassitron will involve a trip by land to the inland Cimarron Sea, then by ship to the coast of the Empire, and a wagon journey to a principal city or perhaps the capital of Ottosand. In that interval, in spite of the fact Kvasir is currently enduring the King's disfavor, perhaps some agreement could be achieved by the Vanir ambassador to the Empire. More likely, something can be arranged privately or by Kvasir himself. That old wizard has as many friends as he has enemies, and I know of no one who has done so many favors, often at great personal sacrifice."

"Why is Kvasir in the King's disfavor?" Jarl asked. "Didn't he tutor the Prince?"

The tall officer smiled a painful smile, "That is precisely the reason... Or, at least, the latest reason. Although Kvasir is undoubtedly the finest tutor in all of Vanir, it is usually his liberal views that get him into trouble. A year or more ago, Kvasir and King William fell out over what the Prince was learning. At the same time, the High Ejliteta pressured the king into allowing the Church to arrest the old wizard. Somehow, in spite of the fact Kvasir had been beaten by street thugs, he worked some magic on the Church's guards in Tyr and they accidentally jailed Killeap, one of the high priests there. Kvasir got out of Tyr in a hurry, and he took all the imprisoned sorcerers with him. The Church was not happy, to say the least."

Von Rhinehart's brown eyes were sad. "It is not my business to say," he continued, "but I think it may have been the final straw that ended a long friendship between the King and Kvasir."

"And there is nothing we can do now?" Jarl asked. He had already weighed all the possibilities, and he already knew the answer to his question, but he wanted von Rhinehart's opinion—and he desperately hoped he was wrong.

It was obvious the tall commander did not like his next words. "Unfortunately, at present, there is precious little that can be done now by our army."

Jarl nodded his understanding. He did not press his argument, because he knew that von Rhinehart was right, but also because he hoped that Kvasir would use his quartz crystal and distance-jump to safety, making any rescue mission unnecessary.

Von Rhinehart expressed his sympathy. "Although many in the Vanir command and virtually all the High Ejliteta distrust and dislike Kvasir, I have a certain respect for the old wizard. This is a feeling, in spite of the old superstitions, that I believe is common to many of the Vanir soldiers. As I said, Kvsair has helped a great many people over the years, and people know that and remember it." The Vanir commander then stood, said his goodbyes, and carefully began to descend the steep mountainside, leaving to confer with Hisson.

The bright, pale blue face of Kmir was rising to meet the reddish-black orb of Mytos. Again, with Mylea's much-needed assistance, Jarl returned to the edge of the forest. Someone had retrieved his blue pack, and he curled up next to it and attempted to sleep. The woman Ranger covered him with two—then three—heavy wool blankets and brought him another full canteen of cold water. Will James arrived from somewhere and gave him two large, cold sausages for supper. Jarl ate and drank the water, and then he lay still for a long time, tired and sick, and—as each tall figure approached the fire—he expected to see Kvasir's bushy gray features. But no one proved to be the old wizard, and finally he drifted off to sleep.

Jarl woke just before dawn, feeling no better and discovering that his blankets were wet from a late night rain. Around him were the clustered, prone bodies of the sleeping Rangers, outlined by the soft morning light. One sour-faced sentry—Otis—sat on a nearby sandstone boulder, hunched over his long rifle, silhouetted by the sunrise and guarding a long-dead fire. From nowhere, Mylea appeared with more water. With her and Will James' help, Jarl staggered over to the edge of the plateau. There, he hunched over another, larger fire, shivering, and wrapped in a wool blanket.

The day was breaking into a clear, cloudless morning. To the west, the pale moon of Kmir was setting. Mytos had still not reached its zenith. On the ridge below the high mountain meadow lay the left flank of the Vanir army, and in the narrow bottom to the west, amid the broken and abandoned weapons and artifacts of war, lay hundreds of dead soldiers.

The day passed slowly, but all during that long morning the Glasseys massed cannon on their ridge to the west. In front of them, green-coated regiment after regiment marched and then stood in perfect formation. All these movements were obvious from their high position, and Aaron sent a runner racing to find von Rhinehart. Then, within a half hour, teams of horses began moving Vanir cannon onto the ridge below. These were followed by Vanir regiments. Some positioned themselves on the western side of the ridge, others on the top, and yet more on the backside, the eastern side of the ridge. These were out of sight of the Glasseys. Mylea brought Jarl his blaster scope, and he spent the middle of the day counting the enemy's soldiers, making maps of their deployment, and sending more runners racing down the hill to find von Rhinehart.

Far to the north, on the edge of the flat White Plains, a dust cloud was growing. Jarl increased the magnification on his scope, and the dust became large groups of running cavalry units, but he could see nothing else of the battle there.

Then Glassey officers began riding back and forth through their lines, and the Rangers could hear the far-off shouts of their commands. Next, all at once, a hundred Glassey cannon roared, beginning a bombardment of the Vanir battle lines. Vanir soldiers hunkered down and hid, and their artillery answered. The artillery duel raged for more than an hour. Cannon, caissons, and limbers were destroyed in fiery explosions and, later in the bombardment, huge holes were blown into the long lines of waiting soldiers on both sides of the ridge. Once, Jarl saw a post of the aid station clipped by a cannon ball, and on another occasion, he saw a Glassey cannonball kill a mounted Vanir officer. Huge clouds of black smoke whirled upward along the mountainside, often obscuring the bombardment, and Jarl worried for both von Rhinehart and Wolff. Will James was also nervous, and his pale face was white with concern.

The cannon duel ended in a quiet that was church like—and, in fact, the silence seemed abnormal, after the long artillery bombardment. Then, the greencoats dressed their units into long lines and began to march down the fore slope of their ridge. Banners fluttered in the small breeze, here and there a drum beat, and green-coated officers walked and rode between the lines. The Vanir waited, cannon and rifles readied. The orchard was now crowded with companies of riflemen and swordsmen. The Vanir reserve, behind the ridge, stood up from where they had been hiding, and began to form into their companies.

There was some unheard order and the Vanir cannon belched fire, smoke, and death. Before the smoke obscured that position, Jarl could see men and women racing to reload. The Glassey artillery again joined the battle. A Vanir cannon exploded from a direct hit. Artillery tore huge holes in the lines of soldiers, and officers rushed others forward to fill the gaps. Companies of Vanir archers fired their arrows over their own troops and into the advancing greencoats. The Glassey banners wavered and some fell, but always they were jerked back upright. Greencoats died and fell, and others stumbled, but—always—they kept marching onward.

Then the long lines of greencoats reached the bottom and began climbing the opposite slope. The Vanir cannon, now firing grapeshot, cut huge swaths from their lines. An almost endless, long line of smoke and white flashes erupted from the Vanir rifle companies. The noise was intense, and the ground—even high on the mountain—shook from the barrage. Vanir companies surged down the hill, usually as tight knots of soldiers, and Glassey units moved forward to meet them. Individuals ran this way and that, often falling, and riderless horses raced away from the battle. The Vanir reserves climbed to the top of the ridge and, shouting battle cries, charged down the western side of the hill. Then, heavy gray powder smoke obliterated the scene below and Jarl could see nothing more. He listened, trying to hear the sound of more musketry, but the roar of the cannon was too loud.

Suddenly there was a loud argument nearby, and Jarl turned to see Aaron and Will James shouting at each other. Before anyone could intervene, Will James vaulted a limestone rock and bounded downhill toward the battle. Two thirds of the way down the steep slope, he slipped and tumbled end over end, falling over a limestone outcrop. But then he bounced back to his feet. The last Jarl saw of the young lieutenant, the lanky officer was sprinting toward the battle, hatless, his sword held high above his head, the blade flashing in the sunlight. Then the billowing smoke engulfed him.

Long minutes passed. The Glassey artillery had ceased firing—they too had been blinded by the heavy smoke. A Ranger shouted he had spotted a Vanir battle flag near their cannon, but no one could see for sure. It seemed as if lifetimes were passing, then—all at once—there was loud cheering and shouting. The battle was over, but still the smoke was too thick for the men and women in the high meadow to see who had won. The cheering continued and grew. It came from a thousand hoarse voices.

Then the smoke cleared, just a little. It was Vanir who were cheering. They still held their ridge. First they could see part of the ridge below, then a banner. Now the riflemen and the Rangers in the high meadow began to shout and throw their hats in the air. More and more Vanir banners appeared below through the smoke, and more and more of the Vanir troops could be seen. Jarl, shivering inside his blanket, remained silent.

The smoke cleared and more troops became visible. Residue from the black powder hung everywhere. Large clusters of dirty greencoats were sliding and walking back down the ridge, their bayonets at all angles and their uniforms more black than pea-green. Their battle flags hung limp and exhausted, and they too were black with powder.

The cheering stopped as more of the battlefield became visible. The number of dead was appalling. Jarl attempted to see the aid station through the smoke, but could not. There was no sign of Will James.

Disorganized Vanir companies were climbing back toward the cannon. Clearly, there had been some kind of counterattack. With them were large groups of Glassey prisoners. Other men struggled to move the wounded toward the rear. The dead were so numerous that they appeared to be a carpet of pea-green, gray, and blue. Here and there lay a dead horse, lying on its back, its legs hanging limp and up in the air.

Jarl continued to watch for the remainder of the day, waiting for another Glassey onslaught, but none came. Toward dusk, news arrived that Hisson had held the steppe, this time decisively defeating the Glassey cavalry. And on the following morning, after four hard days of battle, Guslov Kivlor and his mighty Glassitron army began their long retreat west toward Cimarron.

CHAPTER SEVEN:

THE PEPPER FORD STATION

Jarl did not go with the Vanir army as it pursued the Glasseys west along the southern edge of the White Plains. His sickness became worse and, within hours of the final attack of the battle, he was far too weak to stand. At dusk, as he lay wrapped in blankets and propped against a tree, it was all he could do to attend the funeral for Teague Walker and the fourteen Rangers who were buried at the forest's edge. Then, his strength spent, he spent the night wrapped in several woolen blankets, shivering, and cowering close to a large fire.

Daylight found him no better. The Rangers carried him down the mountainside to the aid station, where a doctor said he was to have nothing to eat or drink. Jarl asked for both his blasters and pack, but then could not remember the answer. He vaguely recalled Mylea's concerned face as he was crammed into a straw-filled cart with seven other wounded soldiers. A light rain had begun to fall and someone covered the invalids with a heavy canvas tarp. Then, with a slow lurch, the cart began a bumpy journey down the valley to the Foord Road.

After what seemed an eternity, someone said they had reached the road. Here, the cart turned east and joined a long, slow procession toward Atrobee. Jarl's world became dull and thirsty, wet from the rain and dark from being under the tarp. He sweated and then froze, and hovered in a timeless void between consciousness and unconsciousness. He vaguely remembered large clusters of troops marching east along the highway, long lines of dejected, mud-covered Glassey prisoners moving in the same direction in the fields next to the road, and the jolting, jarring ride in the high-wheeled wagon.

A heavy rain came at dusk. Someone stopped the cart, and Jarl was unloaded and tied onto a horse's saddle. He was wrapped in a heavy coat and given a full canteen of water to drink. Jarl took great gulps of the cold liquid, spilling a small river down the front of his coat. Then the horse was led away from the road and into the nearby hill country.

The journey was slow and marred by the intermittent rain and Jarl's violent shivering spasms. Consciousness came and went. Once he recognized young Stefan Ker at the horse's head. It was well after full dark when they forded a river and halted in front of a huge stone house or tavern. The rain, for the moment, had increased and become heavy. Large swaths of yellow light fell onto a muddy courtyard.

Someone untied him from the horse, and despite his best efforts to hold onto the mane, Jarl fell into that person's waiting arms. Three men—two of which were Otis and Stefan—carried him across the threshold of the house into a large common room. Jarl had a vague impression of a large fireplace and of many people hurrying back and forth across the crowded room of wounded soldiers, then he was laboriously carried up a narrow, steep set of steps to an upstairs bedroom. He was tucked into a wide bed under the direction of a large woman, and he remembered—dimly—someone being ordered not to spit.

Jarl's days and nights slowly became a hazy memory of a feather tick, a tall bureau—at night sometimes lit by a smoky whale-oil lamp—a high, dirty ceiling, a walnut footboard, and a gentle young girl—who, no more than fifteen, tanned and wide-eyed, gave him an endless supply of water and, twice a day, large bowls of hot soup or broth. His joints ached, his chest hurt, and his nose ran all the time—in fact, it often bled copiously. Rarely was he strong enough to stand and, any time he left his warm blankets, he quickly began to violently shiver.

Gradually, he became well enough to sit up in bed for long periods of time and to move around the small room. The young girl's name was Marri Stephenson, and she was full of information. She said that the Glassey army had retreated west to the Province of Cimarron, and there had been one last battle for a fort there. The war—she said—was almost over.

Marri also said that the stone house Jarl was staying in was the oldest and largest of the structures that made up the Pepper Ford Station. Here, fresh horses replaced the tired teams that pulled the King's stages along the

Foord Road. To the west, about a one-day ride, was the site of the recent battlefield and the Burkes Ford Station, the next stop along the stage line.

The Pepper Ford Station had been built next to the Snowy River, which flowed north out of the heavily forested Blue Hills and onto the White Plains. When the river was low, the Snowy could be forded in many places—and many travelers preferred to do so out on the White Plains and avoid the roundabout trip to Pepper Ford. But in times of high water or wet weather, the Snowy could only be crossed at Pepper Ford, and so the Foord Road made a long loop behind Roundbottom Hill to the Station.

Here, and in all weather and seasons, Marri and her family changed out the stages' horses and fed the passengers. Usually, depending upon the status of the frontier and the nebulous relations with the Glasseys, there were two stages daily, one eastbound to Foord and one west to Atwa, the provincial capital of Kettlewand. When Marri's father had been a boy, the young girl said, before the Vanir had lost the Cimarron Province, the western stages had run all the way to Horst, on the Cimarron Sea. To the east, the Foord Road continued through the Atrobee and Nowell Provinces, where it joined the northern Greenlands Road, and turned south to Tyr, Smyrna, and Southern.

Marri's mother was the portly, but kind, woman. Her name was Iajore. Marri's father's name was Kevin, a jolly, robust, clean-shaven man, who Jarl met only once the entire time he was upstairs in bed. The young girl had one older brother, who was off fighting with the army, and no less than five younger siblings. Also staying at the Station was Marri's cousin, whose father was also off campaigning.

Marri told Jarl that, when he had arrived, she and her mother had spent the first two days at his side, afraid that, if had they left, the scar-faced stranger would die. She also said that Jarl had briefly shared his room with first a wounded pikeman and then an officer from Atrobee, but—the young girl became very sad-eyed and serious—both had died. Many wounded had also died in another bedroom, in the common room, and in the barn, all of which had been used as hospital wards. However, most of the casualties had recovered and had gone elsewhere, and only a few remained at the Station.

Because Jarl had no home that anyone knew of, Otis had made arrangements for him to stay at the Pepper Ford Station, which was the winter base for the 7ᵗʰ Kettlewand Rangers. It was also Otis who had cached Jarl's weapons and pack in one corner of the upstairs bedroom, and it had been Otis who—not trusting the first doctor's advice—had talked to a second surgeon, who had said to give Jarl all the water he wanted. At present, Marri said, the small Ranger company was off campaigning against the Empire's army, but soon they would have to come home—with the onset of autumn, the Ghost Raiders would soon be raiding the Kettlewand communities, and the Rangers would be needed for protection. Once, Marri had tried to speak of Teague Walker, but her voice broke and she began to cry. The man had been a close friend of her family.

Jarl assumed the guise of a native of Cimarron who had accidentally been caught up in the war. From Marri, he was able to discreetly learn that the Vanir planet had twelve months, all named after and having the same order as the Earth months. The Battle at Burkes Station had been fought at the end of August and it was now mid-September. The Vanir year contained 379 days, with every fifth year being a leap year of 380 days. The Vanir day was 24 hours long, and each hour contained sixty minutes, and each minute sixty seconds. But this information was deceptive. By Jarl's estimate, a Vanir minute was slightly longer than an Earth minute, so the Vanir day was somewhat longer still.

The Nation of Vanir was a monarchy, ruled by His Supreme Majesty King William Host Lostkoth, of the ancient lineage of Vanir, and his wife, Queen Gretchen Bergelmire Lostkoth. Marri spoke of the two monarchs with great emotion, obviously in awe of both. Jarl never exactly understood the greater good they had brought to Vanir, but Marri was utterly sure that, because of the present two rulers, the quality of her life was much better than that of her parents. One thing Jarl did comprehend was that the king had stopped the erosion of his nation that had begun during his father's reign. During those dark times, the Dominion of Roomia had taken the Province of Freyr, and the Royal and Most Holy Empire of Glassitron had conquered the entire Province of Cimarron, taking Horst, the Vanir's only western port on the inland Cimarron Sea.

Marri's eyes burned with a fierce admiration. "If the King's forces had not stopped the recent invasion by the Empire," she said, "the entire Province of Kettlewand would have been lost." Then she paused, and her face turned apprehensive. "But the King and Queen have only one son, and he is a bookworm. Surely the Empire will conquer the Kettle when he becomes king!"

"What's wrong with books?" Jarl asked.

Marri rolled her large brown eyes in wonder—did this strange, inquisitive man know nothing? Most books were evil. Many had been banned by the King or the Church; and within the Empire, which Jarl was surprised to learn was a theocracy, there were only a few books approved by the Church-State. The rest were illegal to own or read.

Marri counted not only the Empire as the enemy of the Vanir, but also the Ghost Raiders, of whom Kvasir had spoken. These were a fearsome people, who, each winter, preyed on the Kettlewand people, stealing food, cattle, and occasionally children. The fast-moving nomads would sweep down off the cold, northern plains, mounted on small, agile war ponies, attacking and raiding Kettle households, leaving good Kettle folk dead and their homes in smoking ruins. Once, when she had been a very young child playing beside the Snowy River, Marri had almost been captured by a surprise attack. The young girl trembled when she remembered the moment, and mumbled a sentence Jarl could barely hear, that the Ghost Raiders ate human flesh.

When Jarl asked about the captured children, Marri trembled and looked away. But she continued with her descriptions, "The barbarians are trained in combat since birth... the weak are cruelly killed as babies... those men and women who are unwilling or too old to be warriors are abandoned... in summer, when not raiding the Kettlewand people, the Ghost Raiders fight among each other and fish along the Western Ocean and the Coldspray Ocean."

"Where is that?" Jarl asked.

"North of the White Plains."

Jarl was astonished when Marri described the Raiders' appearance. The nomads were blond men and women identical to the samurai-sword carrying soldiers in the Vanir sword companies. "Those are Ghosts hired by the King for their endurance and war abilities," Marri explained. "They are called Tame Ghosts. Wild Ghosts paint their faces and bodies in wide stripes of wild, outlandish paints and decorate their hair, clothing, and weapons with feathers."

Jarl recovered slowly. By the time he was moved downstairs into a side room, only one other Vanir soldier remained—an old campaigner named

Orr, who was now missing the bottom of his left leg. Near the end of September, Jarl was able to join the Stephenson family for meals. There, he met Jorm, a very serious boy of thirteen and the oldest brother remaining at the Station. The remaining children were Molly, a brown-skinned girl who had large, deep-brown eyes, and a boy of six, and two girls of five and two.

The household terror was Marri's thirteen-year-old cousin, Chadwick Branson. The first time Jarl met Chad, the boy's manner was very quiet and respectful. But Jarl was in the know, as Marri had informed him that Chad's latest escapade had been to burn down the family chicken house during some kind of experiment with black powder, killing nearly two dozen of her mother's prized hens. Of course, it was an accident; Marri had rolled her own large brown eyes heavenward. This last straw had tested even her father's eternal good nature and now, under orders from Marri's mother, Chad was attempting to survive a period of probation at the Station. One more incident of mischief would result in his exile to live with a disliked great-aunt in Tyr.

Whatever misgivings her family had about Chad, Jarl quickly discovered that Molly had no such doubts. The young girl adored Chad and was his ever-faithful companion and champion. According to Marri, the two had spent a good deal of time on the Snowy River during the summer, fishing for trout and bass, and staying out of the sight and mind of the elder Stephensons.

The Station's hired hands, Tres and Hjad Glades, also attended the family meals. "The brothers," Marri said bluntly, "are not too bright. But father had no choice but to hire them. All the better help is off campaigning with the Vanir army."

The Stephenson meals were simple county affairs. Breakfast was bacon or sausage, bread, and a rare egg, usually eaten while serving Chad with dark looks. Lunch was sandwiches of cold meat, cheese and bread—Marri said they would serve soup in the winter. Dinner was called supper and was a good deal more diverse, although lately the Stephensons had been forced to eat a lot of chicken. Typically, there were greens and potatoes, and perhaps squirrel, pork, beef, or fish, depending on who had been afield and where. Evidently, both wild cattle and hogs roamed the nearby forest, but many of these animals were dangerous and were hunted only with extreme caution. For this reason and others, the Stephenson family was happily anticipating the arrival of the 7th Kettle Rangers.

By late September, Jarl was finally allowed on the extensive front porch of the Stephensons' home. There, he and Orr could sit and watch the stages arrive and the teams of horses changed. Jarl was still very weak, but he soon found that he could climb down the short series of steps into the courtyard. Only the pains in his chest, his occasional bloody nose, and his intolerance to cool weather remained.

From the front porch, Jarl watched the traffic of the Foord Road. The two daily stages were pulled by six-horse hitches, and the Station maintained a herd of fifty-some horses, making them choice pickings for Ghost Raiders. The coaches themselves were square-box affairs, with a canvas roof, built over iron leaf springs or having no suspension at all.

Pepper Ford was also a relief station for the stage drivers. One driver was old, worn like Otis and Orr, two were middle-aged, and the fourth was very young, in his late teens. Each wore a gray uniform with a short cloak and each carried a whip, which was never lent or borrowed. They were valuable people, exempt from military service and admired by most of the population. Even Chad managed respect.

But, what Jarl found especially fascinating during his lengthy time on the front porch, was the cross-section of the people that traveled literally beneath the Stephensons' doorstep. Mercenaries, E'landota, soldiers, salesmen, carpetbaggers, monks and clergy, tramps, messengers for the King, Kettle Rangers, High Ejliteta, bureaucrats, even a rare Tame Ghost: they all passed the Pepper Ford Station.

Some came on foot, in groups of two to twenty; many rode horses, often traveling in small numbers; some came in carriages, with large armed escorts; and of course, twice a day, the stage brought its complement of passengers. Most of the travelers wore pants and shirts, or dresses and skirts, if they were women, in what Marri called the New Style. Others wore the Old Style clothing, which were often heavy wool robes, identical to Kvasir's. There were different accents, unusual customs, strange habits, and hard-to-believe proclamations. For the casual or astute observer, everyone and everything traveled through the courtyard of the Pepper Ford Station.

All—that is—except one kind of person. If any sorcerers traveled the Foord Road, Jarl was unable to identify them.

CHAPTER EIGHT:

THE BULL

The first week of October had just begun when someone noticed smoke coming from the chimney of the Rangers' barracks, located about two hundred meters behind the main Pepper Ford house. Jarl could now walk at a reasonable pace, and he and Marri strolled over to see if the Rangers had returned.

They discovered three Rangers in their barracks, airing straw ticks and stoking an iron pot-bellied stove, taking the chill off their quarters. Two helpers, Chad and Molly—huge smiles on their young faces—were laughing and chattering aimlessly as they vigorously swept the floor of the building. The leader of the Rangers was Mylea Orlando, who, amid the billowing clouds of dust, grinned and shook Jarl's hand, happy to see him healthy again. Marri was soon bubbling over with joy, glad to see the first of the returning militia; then she began to scold the two youngsters with little success, trying to get them to stir up a little less dust.

Amidst the noise and confusion, Jarl asked about Kvasir. The thin woman had no news, but she said Aaron would be returning later in the day. He would have more information.

Mylea was good to her word; within hours a contingent of thirty-one Kettle Rangers, fifty horses, and four or five stray dogs rode into the Pepper Ford Station courtyard. Aaron was at their head, his expression grim and unsmiling. The men and women dismounted, stiff and saddle sore. Except for the old man who trailed at the rear, all appeared exhausted and disillusioned. Otis had been the last to ride into the courtyard; nevertheless, he quickly jumped off his horse and limped up onto the porch, grinning at the sight of Jarl and spitting tobacco at a passing dog. With excited children and canines underfoot, Iajore and Marri served everyone cold lemonade. The Rangers' mood quickly improved and only the needs of their horses prevented them from lingering on the porch, laughing and enjoying the many conversations.

Aaron alone remained. He looked older, perhaps from the weight of his new command, and he had little additional news. His report was not good. For the better part of a month, the Rangers had attempted, with little success, to harass the retreating greencoats, fighting only two small, indecisive battles. Aaron bluntly blamed the leadership, himself included. Most important to Jarl was the lack of news regarding any Vanir prisoners, particularly of Kvasir. The tall Ranger spoke with bitterness: "I don't think that anything more can be done. The old wizard has not been recaptured, and no one has heard of him. By now, he is probably dead or on board a Glassey ship, on his way to the Empire."

The lack of word concerning Kvasir was what Jarl had been expecting, and what he had been dreading. His hopes were nearly dashed—obviously the old wizard had been separated from his crystal or had been badly beaten or killed. There seemed to be nothing, short of going to the capital and pleading his case with the King or locating some private person or organization with power inside the Empire, that Jarl could do to find and free his friend. He was disheartened, and doubly despondent—not only had he lost the best friend he had on Vanir, he had also lost what little means he had of returning to the *Cassiopeia*.

October on Vanir was like October on Earth's Northern Hemisphere. The leaves changed to yellow and red and then fell to the ground. The nights were cold and the days, for the most part, remained hot. The horses and cattle grew long, shaggy winter coats. The nightly meals at the Station now included squash and pumpkin. The men and women—the Rangers included—chopped wood and hauled it on a horse-drawn sled to the Station. Buildings were prepared for the coming winter and the raids of the Ghost Raiders. Jarl and Orr braided ropes and mended the stage team harnesses. Before the month was out, Jarl was strong enough to hold the dancing, half-broken horses while Kevin or Hjad changed out the exhausted teams. The two or three of them would then hitch the largest two horses, the wheel team, in front of the stage. The swing team was harnessed next, followed by the relatively small lead team. There was little time to dawdle, as each stage spent only thirty minutes at the Station, while the passengers hurriedly ate and ran to the outhouses.

Otis had somehow procured the dapple gray that Jarl had ridden during the battle, and as his endurance increased, Jarl saddled the horse and rode with small groups of Rangers along the Foord Road. Often they cantered east along the highway, then turned north and forded the Snowy River on the edge of the White Plains. There, they would rejoin the Foord Road and return to the Station from the west, splashing across the river at gravel-bottomed Pepper Ford. On other occasions, they would patrol up the small creek behind the Station, Getout Run, into the Blue Hills. This was a dark and somber forest, for the most part full of ancient, giant trees with huge, crooked limbs hanging down and massive, knobby roots protruding from the black forest soil.

The fall days seemed lazy, yet sped by quickly. Under Mylea's and Otis' careful instruction, Jarl learned how to load, prime, and fire two flintlocks, a long rifle and a pistol. The Rangers mined saltpeter from under the outbuildings of the Station and, using sulfur brought by the stages and homemade charcoal, manufactured black powder. Flint was collected from a small outcrop at the base of Roundbottom Hill, and lead arrived via stage from the Province of Smyrna. Hogs were butchered and hung in meat sheds for the winter. The men squeezed cider and the women boiled apple butter. Except for his nagging concerns about Kvasir and his friends on other worlds, Jarl found himself relaxing and enjoying life at the stage station. Feeling safer than he had in a long, long time, he cached his weapons in the upper bedroom, behind his blue pack.

With November, word came that a treaty had been signed a fortnight earlier between the Vanir and the Empire. Kevin broached a keg of cider and that evening, everyone—the Stephensons, the Glades, the Rangers, Chad, Orr, and Jarl—celebrated their good fortune. Chad spoke enthusiastically of his father, who served with the Vanir cavalry, and who intended to retire from the army at the war's end, collect his son, and go into some unspecified occupation. Jarl honestly looked forward to meeting the man.

Jarl found himself doing all sorts of odd jobs at the Station. One warm day, near the middle of November, he was helping Marri carry food to the long table on the porch of the Station. The eastbound stage had just arrived and the Glade brothers were changing the six-horse team, producing the usual swirling dust clouds. Kevin was helping one of the King's couriers switch from one sleek, long-legged horse to another. On the opposite side of the dusty courtyard, two Tame Ghosts were eating a small meal at the crude table set up for their use in the shade of the barn.

Passengers were arriving at the long table, discussing the trip and complaining of the ride. A tall, young man with a serious expression returned from an outhouse and asked for Kevin, and Jarl directed him toward the rising dust in the courtyard. Another passenger was commenting on the freshly baked bread, and Otis and Orr were sitting on a side porch, discussing a dimly remembered campaign.

Abruptly Jorm was underfoot, talking excitedly in a high voice. Iajore appeared from the kitchen, dragging a stage driver in tow. The peaceful day rapidly deteriorated into mindless confusion as Jorm's words fell over each other. Jarl understood only a handful: "Bull, Molly, swing, Chad." The swing was an old rope somewhere well behind the Rangers' barracks, hanging over a high bank on Getout Run. It, and the entire forest surrounding the run, were strictly off-limits to any of the Stephenson children and their inquisitive nephew.

Iajore's face was suddenly white, and Marri's hands flew to her face, covering her mouth and highlighting her wide, brown eyes. Jarl put a hand on the porch rail and vaulted it, landing lightly on the ground. Then he sprinted for the Rangers' barracks, with the words "Molly" and "bull" stuck in his mind. The Rangers had a habit of keeping a few saddled horses tied to a rail near their quarters, and Jarl hoped to find one or two there now—he knew he did not have the endurance to run the entire distance to the swing.

As he rounded the final corner of the path and dodged the last tree, Jarl could see that Stefan was holding a white horse while Mylea cleaned one of the animal's hoofs. Behind them, other horses were tied at the hitching rail. Someone shouted behind him, and then that someone—Otis—went flying by, his long legs and arms seemingly pumping in all directions. The two Rangers looked up, startled, and Aaron's face suddenly appeared in the open doorway. He quickly ducked back into the building, chiefly to make room for Otis to fly through the opening. Jarl was only a step or two behind.

It was dark inside the barracks. Someone was sitting bolt upright on a top bunk, his blankets falling to the floor. This man shouted, "Raiders?"

Otis yelled back, "Wild bull!"

Two other Rangers fell from their bunks and landed on their feet. Otis grabbed a loaded rifle from the rack, and Jarl helped himself to one of the weapons with which he practiced. He noticed, as he did so, that the space where Teague's long rifle was habitually stored was empty.

Outside, the horses were milling, excited by the commotion. Otis ran out the back door and, with an ease that would have done a much younger man proud, jumped onto the back of a side-stepping spotted mare. Jarl grabbed the reins of a roan, caught a swinging stirrup, and landed in the saddle before the horse realized his intent. Aaron sprinted to a third animal.

Jarl was unfamiliar with his horse. The animal danced sideways and arched its back to throw him off, but he slapped the animal's rear with the end of the reins and the horse's waltzing exploded into an abrupt run, as it suddenly spied Otis' mare and chased it into the woods. For a few moments, the two men had a fast horse race through the forest, dodging trees and ducking low-hanging limbs.

Then the two running horses entered a fern-floored forest of tall poplar trees. Aaron suddenly appeared on Jarl's right, mounted on a black horse, the wide brim of his hat bent back against the crown. His horse jumped a dead log and, as it landed, the Ranger captain stood in his stirrups and pointed with his long rifle. He shouted for Otis and Jarl to follow.

Jarl gave chase, as did Otis. The three horses were running all out, racing through the forest. Aaron led them into the creek, and silvery water splashed high around them, bright in the dim forest light. Then, in a small fern-covered meadow, lit by a single sunbeam, Aaron drew up. Ahead was a large sycamore, with massive roots that twisted down a steep bank and into a pool of water. From one limb hung the brown line of a rope, barely discernable against the dark forest background. No one—person or animal—was visible.

The three men stopped, letting their horses mill among the ferns. The ground underfoot was quiet, but the animals' breathing was hard and ragged after the fast run. Then, from downstream and back toward the Station, came the dull boom of a black-powder weapon. Otis' mare was facing that direction, and the animal jumped forward, sprinting toward the sound. Jarl and Aaron pivoted their horses and were soon in pursuit.

Aaron slid his black down into Getout Run, and there it ran, water again flashing in the air, until the Ranger found a place to climb the opposite bank. Jarl followed Otis through the ferns, staying beside the watercourse. The old man and his horse were one fluid body, dodging the pillar-like trunks of the poplars and occasionally jumping a log. Then Jarl saw a spot of moving brown ahead, across the creek. Otis' spotted mare raced up to the deep gully cut by the run and slid on its haunches in a hurried stop. The old Ranger stepped from the horse even before it halted. He ran a few steps and dropped to one knee, bringing his rifle to his shoulder.

Jarl was much more expedient in dismounting. Otis' mare darted in front of Jarl's roan and his horse abruptly shied, throwing itself to the right. Jarl made a belated grab for the animal's mane, missed, and continued in a straight trajectory over the horse's head. He flew through the air, with the green ferns rushing up to meet him. He bounced twice across the ground and smacked head-first against a rotten stump. Just as he hit the stump, he heard the explosion of Otis firing his black-powder rifle.

There was a dull thump as Otis' ball struck its target. Jarl tried to stand, but only fell back onto his rear end. Thirty meters away, across Getout Run, a massive bull snorted, swung its head, and danced on its hind feet. Even at this distance, the animal's black eyes were bright. Slobber sprayed from the moving head, and the horns that sickled through the air were a full two meters wide. Fresh blood ran down its rear flank, and it was dragging its left hind leg. A few scant meters in front of the animal, a young teenager stood, straddling a log, and wielding a long rifle by its barrel, waiting to club the massive bull.

Aaron was nowhere to be seen. To Jarl's left, Otis calmly reached behind him and into his cartridge bag and began to reload his rifle.

The big animal moved closer, stalking the boy, who turned slightly sideways, allowing Jarl to see Chad's scared, white face. Under his feet, part of the log moved and a second teenager appeared—Molly. Jarl, still sitting down, snuggled his rifle into his shoulder and eared the hammer back. He took a moment to sight the weapon, aiming just to the front of the bull's massive left foreleg. He squeezed the trigger and the hammer fell, shoving the fizzen up and out of the way. There was only a dull click, and no explosion of light and powder. The flintlock had misfired.

Jarl pulled the hammer back a second time. Otis was ramming his charge home. Gray smoke drifted across the creek. With his long rifle, Chad swung at the bull's head. The massive animal moved in the other direction, leery of Chad, leaving Jarl no clear shot.

A black horse skidded to a stop behind the bull, throwing broken ferns into the air. Aaron dismounted at a run, yelling for Chad to clear out. The young boy turned, and still holding the long rifle, reached down to help Molly. The bull began to rush the two youngsters, and Aaron fired his long rifle from the hip. There was another dull thump and dirt flew from the bull's left shoulder. The animal flinched and then began to swing his massive horns toward Aaron, dragging its wounded hind leg.

Jarl aimed at the center of the bull's swinging head and again squeezed his rifle's trigger. This time there was an explosion and the weapon pushed against his shoulder. But, toward the Station, Jarl heard the long whine of a ricochet—the lead ball had bounced off the animal's thick skull.

For a moment, Jarl could not see. The smoke was thick and the paper wad drifted between him and the bull. Someone fired another flintlock. Jarl heard yet another person yell far off in the woods.

Then the smoke cleared, and he could see that the bull was still on its feet and moving haltingly toward Aaron, who was holding a smoking pistol and—having tripped over a small log—was lying on the ground. Chad had dropped the long rifle and was still struggling to extricate Molly from the log. Jarl could see the young girl's stained face, white but not panicked. Then both youngsters stopped their struggles and, almost slowly, began untangling Molly's feet from the log. Behind them, Aaron rolled to one side as the bull buried one of his long horns into the black soil of the forest, trying to gore the Ranger.

Jarl jumped to his feet and leaped over the stump. He ran to the creek bank and launched himself into the water. The opposite bank was undercut and came to his chin. He tossed the rifle up onto the bank and used a root to pull himself up and onto the level ground. The bull swept its head in the other direction and buried its other horn in the ground. Once more Aaron rolled to one side, but now he was trapped, with one arm under his body.

Jarl grabbed his rifle and scrambled to his feet, and sprinted past Chad and Molly. He swung his rifle by its barrel and smacked the bull across its rear end. The animal spun back toward him. Jarl tried to block the horns with his rifle, but the enraged bull easily knocked the weapon from his grasp. The tip of one horn grazed his thigh and slobber sprayed across his pants, and only sheer luck prevented the sharp horn from slicing into his leg. Jarl stumbled, trying to back up, but the bull was already spinning back toward Aaron. He caught a glimpse of the Ranger captain hanging onto the animal's tail, then there was a dull explosion from across the run and Jarl heard the clap of another rifle ball hitting the bull.

This time—finally—the huge animal fell, landing awkwardly on his hurt hind leg. Almost immediately, it was staggering back to its feet, but Aaron was up and running. Jarl turned, and finding both Molly and Chad on their feet, grabbed one in each arm and fell over the bank into the creek. They seemed to hit water and sand at the same time. Jarl staggered to his knees and shoved both youngsters under the high bank. Two shots, close together, and then a third sounded from above. Dirt rolled over the lip of the bank, falling into the water in front of Jarl.

Jarl could see Otis through the smoke; the old Ranger calmly bit the end off a paper cartridge and poured a little black powder in the flash pan of his flintlock. He lowered the fizzen, and then he placed the open cartridge over the rifle's barrel and forced it down with the ramrod. He rammed the charge home, tamped it down, removed the ramrod, and stuck it into the soft ground. He next brought the weapon up and eased the flintlock's hammer back, nesting the rifle to his shoulder. After a moment's hesitation, the old man squeezed the trigger. There was a flash of fire, a dull boom, and the belch of heavy black smoke.

Jarl peered at Otis; Otis peered at the bull. The forest was quiet. The old Ranger finally looked at Jarl and said, in his dry manner, "I think it's dead." Then he reached for yet another paper cartridge.

Jarl herded the two, wet youngsters up onto the dry sand bank. He risked a tentative glance at the bank above, but saw only the unmoving, expansive brown back of the bull.

On the opposite side of Getout Run, Aaron was priming his pistol. A half dozen Rangers were spread out through the open woods. Most were reloading weapons, and heavy smoke drifted in the dim forest light and the woods reeked of sulfur.

After the reloading ritual was finished, Aaron found a long stick and poked at the bull. The other Rangers moved in closer and stood at the ready, waiting for the huge animal to come back to life. There was no response. Otis jumped the creek, and Jarl followed with Chad and Molly.

The bull was dead. Aaron retrieved two rifles—Jarl's and his own. Chad's weapon was underneath the massive animal, pinned by the great weight. As the two men reloaded, the Rangers gathered around and listened as both youngsters spoke, talking at the same time, trying to tell their story.

The three of them—Jorm, Chad, and Molly—had been playing Rangers, sneaking up toward the swing in the sycamore, staying in the deep cut of Getout Run to avoid the eye of any passing adult. Chad had seen a boot track, a Ghost Raider he had thought. Molly added Jorm had almost stepped on it. After a hurried conference, they left the creek and started to return to the Station. It was then that they encountered the wild bull. Molly had scooted into a hollow log, Chad had tried to divert the bull to the creek, and Jorm had run for help. The aggressive animal had followed Molly, rooting the log out of the ground, and rolling it along the ground. Chad had raced to the Rangers' quarters. He had grabbed Teague Walker's long rifle, and had run back to the creek.

Once there, he discovered the log was breaking apart, and that only Molly's small size had so far prevented her from being hurt. Chad had gotten close and fired at the bull, and it had turned and chased him. He ran to the creek, scooted along the run, and popped out to race to Molly's side. There was no time to free her; the enraged animal once again approached, this time stalking the two youngsters. It was then that Otis and Jarl had arrived.

Jarl's nose had started bleeding, and he slowly managed to get it stopped. Chad and Molly started to shiver—either from the cold water or the excitement. Nevertheless, Chad insisted on showing the Rangers the track by the stream. He led them upstream along Getout Run, and then unerringly down to a soft mud bank. There, next to the water, was a half side of a faint boot track, pointing upstream. The Rangers crowded around; some looked at the track and others scanned the surrounding forest for danger. Otis stooped and looked at the track, then he glanced up and down the small creek. Only when he spit did Aaron ask his opinion.

The old man almost purred, "Track's about five days old. It was made underwater; but the creek has gone down a bit during the last few days and now the track is above water. I'd wager someone waded downstream and scouted the Station."

He added, his voice dry and final, "It's a Raider boot." The old Ranger turned to Chad, "You did good to see it." Jarl, standing behind Molly and Chad, could see the respect in Otis' eyes.

Afterwards, Aaron, Jarl, Chad, Molly, and Stefan walked back to the Station, leading some of the horses, with orders to send back a sled. Mylea, Otis, and two other Rangers began to field dress the large bull. Three more Rangers followed Getout Run upstream, searching for additional Raider sign. Chad carried Teague's rifle. The youngster was ashen, and Molly clutched his arm to provide moral support—the butt of the dead Ranger's rifle had been badly cracked when the bull had fallen on it. At the barracks, Aaron took his cousin's flintlock and silently entered the building, saying nothing. Jarl washed the blood from his face, and then he and Molly and Chad walked the remaining distance to the Station.

As they rounded the last corner, Jarl saw that the porch was crowded full of people, both men and women, Station employees, and passengers. At the sight of Chad and Molly, there were sighs, shouts, and utterances of relief, with Iajore's being the loudest. While Kevin stood to one side, his face long and serious, the round woman ran forward and fiercely hugged Molly. She released the squirming girl after several second and, still holding her daughter by her shoulders, began questioning Jarl. Molly spoke first, her voice small and weak, "It wasn't Chad's fault!"

Jarl spoke quietly and slowly. At his first word, Jorm let a low whine slip threw his lips. He was doomed. "Jorm, Molly, and Chad got caught up Getout Run by a wild bull."

Marri gasped. Iajore's eyes widened with fright. Then anger washed across her face, and she looked at Chad, "What were you doing at the creek?"

Chad said nothing. Still holding Molly with one hand, Iajore reached around behind her. With one strong movement, she pulled Jorm around and placed him next to Chad. She repeated her question, this time directing it toward both boys.

When Molly began to stutter, Chad popped the answer out, "We were pretending to be Rangers."

"All three of you?" There was no nonsense in Iajore's voice.

Jorm answered, "Not me, I only went to tell them to come back."

Molly was indignant, "Not true, Jorm was..." A sharp glance from her mother silenced her. Iajore looked up at Jarl.

As simply as possible, Jarl recounted the story, not mentioning the broken rifle. Iajore listened, her face impassive. At the end, she looked at Chad. The youngster was shaking, and his face white. Jarl was not prepared for the violence of her reaction, "Go pack your bags! You are leaving on this stage for Tyr!"

Molly was even more shocked. As strong as her mother's grasp was, the girl broke free and ran to Chad's side, shouting, "It wasn't Chad's fault! It wasn't Chad's fault!"

Her mother was not listening. "You," now she looked at Jorm. "No more riding." Jorm flinched; he had a favorite pet pony. Iajore now looked at her daughter, "You both are going to bed immediately after supper for the next month. And you both have a meeting with your father in the barn." That, in the Stephenson family, amounted to a severe spanking with a willow branch. Jorm paled, but Molly was quiet—she had been crushed by Chad's sentence and nothing more could hurt her. Iajore looked back at her nephew and roared, "Move!"

Chad ran silently into the house. Iajore caught and restrained her daughter. Jarl caught a glimpse of Kevin's ashen face; behind him was the passenger who had asked for Kevin, his face equally white.

Suddenly, something in Jarl's throat caught. The passenger had a military look to him and he was coming from the border forts, en route to the capital. Jarl reached out and caught Iajore on the arm. His voice was weak and dry, and somehow not his own, "Wait..." In the courtyard, the stage driver had rounded up most of his passengers. They were boarding the stage.

Jarl spoke again, his voice stronger, "Wait..., there is always tomorrow's stage."

Iajore looked at him sharply, "No! I want that boy on that stage today! He has been nothing but trouble ever since he got here. He can stay with his aunt until his father picks him up."

Jarl looked at Kevin. The man spoke for the first time, "The boy can take tomorrow's stage, Iajore." His voice too was weak.

The round woman exploded, astounded at her husband, "No! I want him on today's stage! Before he gets our daughter killed!" Molly suddenly broke free from her mother and, almost in the blink of an eye, was gone. The stage driver was trying to coerce the last person into the stage, the passenger who had spoken to Kevin. The young man was poised one step on the running board, his face still white and strained.

Kevin spun on one heel and bellowed at the driver, "Leave!" Then he turned to his wife, caught her by the arm and propelled her toward the barn. Jarl followed. Behind him, even before the stage door closed, the driver wheeled his teams out of the yard.

The inside of the barn was dark. Iajore's voice was high-strung, and she shouted at her husband. He allowed this, until she calmed enough to demand an explanation.

Kevin was at a loss for words. Jarl asked him, "What happened? What did the passenger say?"

Iajore was now quiet, her hands on her wide hips, still angry, and still waiting.

Kevin's expression was pained, a fact that was highlighted by a white swash of a single light beam across the dark interior of the barn. His response was long in coming and, when he finally spoke, his voice was slow and halting, "Jauush Branson was killed ten days ago on the frontier."

Iajore was confused. "That is impossible! The war ended three weeks ago!"

"They hadn't heard. Jauush's unit was ambushed. He could have gotten away, but he stayed behind, helping his men. The lieutenant said he was a good officer. Several of the greencoats rode him down."

It was Jarl who spoke, "The lieutenant was the passenger on the stage?"

"Yes. He is an aide to one of the cavalry generals. He had served with Jauush some." The man turned back to his wife and asked plaintively, "What are we going to do now?"

There was another long silence, and again it was Jarl who broke the silence. "Don't send Chad away, not now. With his father gone, he would get into impossible trouble in Tyr. The aunt would probably never be able to control him and... I think it could ruin him."

Iajore glared at Jarl, but his eyes were elsewhere and his voice was choked with emotion. "Let Chad stay," he softly said. "When we found them in the forest, he was standing over Molly with an unloaded rifle, trying to protect her. He would have died before he let the bull near her."

It required most of a minute, but Iajore softened. She looked up at Jarl, "Chad is a troublemaker. Sooner or later, he will get someone killed or seriously hurt."

"No... he gets into trouble a lot, but it is not the same thing. Would you really send him off now?"

The woman looked up at Jarl, long and hard. The answer came slowly, "No... he can stay... this time. You will be responsible for him?"

This was something Jarl had not expected, and a burden he did not want. His answer was just as slow, "I will try."

With that, the round woman turned and marched from the barn. For a long minute the two men stood there, and then Kevin asked quietly, "Jarl, would you do me a favor? Would you tell Chad about his father?"

Jarl looked at Kevin questioningly. The man seemed embarrassed, then he continued, "Ever since Chad cut off my mustache, I have not had that much to do with him... I feel that some of his mischief could have been my fault."

"Cut off your mustache...?"

Kevin hesitated, even less at ease. "Right after Jauush left Chad here, he was cutting something with Iajore's sewing scissors. I leaned over to see what it was and... he is rather impulsive... he reached up and cut off half my mustache. It was a handlebar mustache... a real beauty."

At another time and another place, Jarl might have laughed. "I can understand why you might be angry..."

Kevin smiled at the memory, but it was a sad smile. "I was pretty upset at the time. You're right about him. Chad is a good kid. He's not a troublemaker, but he would be in Tyr. I'm fairly certain his aunt is very old. She could never control him."

"How is Chad related to you?"

"Jauush's father and my father were first cousins. The boy has no other kin. Jauush courted a Lady of the High Ejliteta in Tyr. Her family was dead-set against the marriage, but Jauush spirited her away one night." The man stopped speaking, thinking of another time, another place. A smile momentarily touched his face, then vanished. "She died delivering Chad."

Jarl was quiet for a long time, then he spoke softly, "I will tell him."

"Thank you."

The two men left the barn, exiting into the shadows of the early fall twilight. Iajore had located Chad. He, Molly, and Marri were waiting on the front porch. Molly and Chad were scooted together, holding hands and sharing a dismal expression. For some reason—perhaps by Iajore's order—the busy Station courtyard was strangely quiet and empty.

It took only a few long, terrible minutes to break the awful news to Chad. At the first mention of his father, Chad brightened and became almost wildly enthusiastic. But when Jarl mentioned that there was bad news, his face became dreadful—it was almost as if he already knew what had happened, and he squeezed in even closer to Molly. Neither youngster cried when told about Jauush's death, at least not aloud, but tears streamed down both sets of tanned cheeks. Higher on the dark porch, Jarl could hear Marri softly sobbing. Then Kevin spoke for the first time, telling Chad that, for as long as he wanted it, there was a home for him at the Pepper Ford Station. Chad only stared straight ahead, and Jarl was unsure if he was seeing or hearing his uncle.

Then, from the deep shadows of the courtyard, a tall figure stepped forward. It was Aaron, who had arrived unseen on cat feet. As the tall Ranger moved into the light of the single lamp, Jarl could see that one arm held his cousin's long rifle, bandaged with a wet leather sheath.

The Ranger quietly extended the weapon to Chad. Although confused, the youngster slowly took the rifle. When the Ranger spoke, his voice was solemn and purposeful, and Jarl could feel the deep emotion. "I soaked the leather in water. It will become rock hard when it dries, and bind the cracked wood together." He paused, and then continued, "It is yours now. Take it, you deserve it. And, if you ever want it, lad, there will be a place for you among the Kettle Rangers. What you did today took nerve and grit."

Molly's brown eyes popped open in surprise. Chad's voice was weak and thin, "No, I can't... I don't deserve..."

"No, you deserve the rifle. And I meant what I said about being a Ranger. You got gumption, lad. I think Teague would be proud to know you have his rifle."

Chad tried one more time, "I can't..."

Another voice spoke out of the darkness—it was Otis. "Take the rifle, lad. You deserve it. Given time, your shot would have killed that bull." This statement, with its dry finality—and even without the punctuating spit—ended Chad's argument.

Sometime that night, in a late journey to the outhouse, Jarl—the hardened partisan from Jubal, inured to all kinds and forms of death—broke down and cried. Impressed by Aaron's magnanimous offer, Iajore had rescinded her own order and had agreed that Chad could stay at the Pepper Ford Station, to call it home, as long as he wished.

But, inside the great house, on the wide stone hearth of the massive fireplace, Molly and Chad sat, the giant rifle across their laps, staring unseeing from a tiny huddle of misery.

CHAPTER NINE

PATROLLING WITH THE RANGERS

The third week in November brought the first cold weather and the first snow flurries—late, according to Kevin. With the wintery weather, traffic on the Foord Road became less and less frequent, and the Kettle Rangers' patrols became longer, often venturing far out onto the White Plains in search of marauding parties of Ghost Raiders. The Stephensons' three dozen assorted animals—cows, bulls, sheep, horses, and the few remaining chickens—were herded into the one large barn. There, next to the stage horses, and theoretically safe from Ghost Raiders, the animals would spend the long, brutal Kettle winter. Every man, and many of the women, who lived at the Station began to carry a long rifle, musket, or shotgun, never to be left more than an arm's distance away. Orr sat on the porch, a bitter old man, a flintlock shotgun across his lap, waiting with a grim anticipation for his first sight of the Raiders.

Each stage now had two guards, who both rode on top of the coach with the driver and were bundled in heavy coats, protection from the chill air. One faced forward and the other rearward, and both carried double-barreled shotguns. Occasional units of cavalry also escorted the stage, and once a quiet officer stopped and spoke solemnly with the Stephenson family, leaving a long cavalry sword and a small number of Jauush Branson's personal possessions with Chad.

Jarl spent a great deal of his time in October and November teaching the Stephenson clan to read, write, and do simple arithmetic. Chad—anxious to redeem himself for the incidents with the chicken house and the bull and deeply afraid of permanent exile to Tyr—became Jarl's best student, intently poring over the single words and simple phrases that Jarl produced with chalk on a piece of large black slate. Molly, either from her own desire to learn or her customary imitation of Chad, was just as serious in her studies. Even Marri, despite her poor opinion of books, joined in, displaying a natural desire to learn. Iajore had never been happy with her own inability to read and write, and Jarl soon discovered he had earned her gratitude for teaching her children some of the basics. Indeed, Chad found himself in a totally unfamiliar position—instead of the round woman continually watching him for potential trouble, she was now persuading her own children to follow his example of industrious study.

In mid-December, Jarl became a member of the 7th Kettlewand Rangers, signing up for a salary of three dollars a week. The other Rangers laughed and told him that a rich man could well afford to give up his three dollars for his companions' beer and food. Jarl smiled and quietly pocketed the money, but—by Vanir's standards—he was indeed a rich man.

During the Thanksgiving celebration in November—evidence of the Vanir's dim memory from Earth—Jarl had cornered an agent of the stage line and offered a design of a better stage vehicle. His drawing had been nothing more than a Concord Stagecoach, used throughout the North American west in the late 19th Century. It had a high luggage rack on top, and a spacious baggage compartment in the rear, but what sold his idea to the stage line was the high wheels, rounded bottom, and leather suspension, which would rock the stage over each bump, helping the horses on a rough road, instead of jarring both the passengers and the animals in each pothole.

The stage line had agreed to pay Jarl one hundred dollars for the design and ten dollars for each coach constructed. With the initial payment, made in silver and stamped with the King's bust, Jarl became a wealthy man. But, with his new-found wealth came new responsibilities. After a long argument, where he discovered that many of Vanir's teachers worked for free, he had to start paying Kevin rent.

Rich or poor, Jarl was now a Kettle Ranger. His first patrol was an expanded version of one of his previous rides. Twelve Rangers, led by Mylea and Otis, left before dawn, crossed the wide Pepper Ford, and traveled west along the Foord Road. The battle site at Burkes Ford was in view when they turned north and rode far out onto the White Plains. The Rangers nooned along the Snowy, and then followed the river north to an obscure ford Otis knew of, where they waded their animals across sixty meters of cold, knee-deep water. They then cut across country and rejoined the Foord Road east of the Station. It was an hour after dusk when the tired Rangers returned to the Station. The only Ghost sign they had seen all day had been along the river, and it had been more than a month old.

Jarl found the White Plains fascinating. It was a treeless steppe, with grass close to knee high. The relief, other than along the wide, broad valley of the Snowy River, was seldom more than a few score meters. Along the river were clumps of willows and tall, old cottonwoods. Otis, as usual, was full of information. His knowledge was slowly dispensed, with long intervals, over the following days. In fact, once on the plains, all talk took the form of intermittent sentences strung out over the long hours. The conversation seemed to hang forever, and with no hurry to talk, the Rangers could better listen to the never-ending wind of the plains—and for any noise that might precede a Ghost Raider attack.

Otis said that kilometers and kilometers of the plains were rolling grassland, with valleys of stunted, wind-whipped willows, and that some sections were table flat, with abrupt arroyos that cut deep into the landscape. The White Plains were drained on the west—Otis said—by the small Cimarron River, to the south and east by the Snowy River, and to the north by the Cold River. Jarl was surprised to learn that the Sulfur Hills, located far to the north by the Coldspray Ocean, were tree covered, and evidently by tall trees at that. Otis had no explanation for this, but he did say that the Coldspray Ocean was open water, never freezing over, and only rarely dotted by drifting ice.

It was Otis who taught Jarl the night sky, showing him the two stationary stars, teaching him to tell time from the rotating constellations and how to locate the bright northern star, Ydalir. The old man was also knowledgeable in regard to the nomadic Ghost Raiders, who counted their wealth in the number of horses and cattle they owned. As far as Otis knew, each clan lived in a certain general geographic location on the Plains, but they could often travel incredible distances, occasionally in an astoundingly short period of time.

The majority of the Kettlewand Rangers felt that the Ghost Raiders were a savage, lean people, who often ate human flesh, and particularly enjoyed the meat of young children. And of course, the nomads took great pleasure in torturing and slowly killing their prisoners. Once, after one of the younger Rangers gave a lengthy oral dissertation on Raider atrocities, Jarl gave Otis a long questioning lock. The old man only glared back, obviously angry, and then had spit.

Later, when Otis and Jarl were scouting alone along the flood plain of the Snowy River, the old man had elaborated, "Ain't never seen no sign of Raiders eating people. Guess they might in a hard winter, but then so might some of the Kettle folks. Mostly, the Raiders chase down bison, antelope, deer, musk ox, and mastodons."

Jarl's simple theory that the planet had been colonized by modern space explorers was utterly destroyed, and he nearly fell from his saddle in astonishment. Otis momentarily stopped talking, his face breaking into amused surprise. Then the old Ranger continued, "As for them children, you ain't never seen nobody that likes young 'uns... anybody's young 'uns... the way the Raiders do. You wanta get a Raider mad, you harm a child."

Otis then snorted and spit. He was angry. "Ghost Raiders eating children is pure Kettle bunk! Why... a Kettle child would be just as safe with the Ghosts as they would be sittin' on their own front porch."

"Then what do they do with the Kettle children they kidnap?"

"They raise them as their own. They replace their battle and winter losses with Kettle and Atrobee children. Treat 'em as good as their own kit. The Raiders are a proud and arrogant people, but in many ways they are more knowin' than the Kettle people."

The old man paused, obviously considering what he had to say. "The trouble is... the Kettle folks hate the kidnaping even more than seeing their kin killed."

"Why?"

Otis gave Jarl a stern look. "Because the Kettle folks don't know what happens to their kids. They worry about it, they think the worst, and they imagine that it is their own kids who are coming back and raiding them."

Jarl nodded, and said, "They get closure for the people who are killed, but not for the children who are kidnaped."

"I've got no idea what this 'closure' is," Otis said, "but it sounds like you've got the right of it."

"Do Raiders torture their prisoners?" Jarl asked.

Otis spit and growled, "Yeah... but if you got somethin' against that, then you don't want to be around if we ever capture a Raider."

The old man was disapproving, but Jarl was unsure if it was toward his questions or toward the torture. He started to ask Otis how he had acquired his knowledge, then he reconsidered and changed the subject. "Have you ever seen a mastodon?"

Otis turned around, surprised at the question. His voice was dry and matter of fact, "Sure. Ain't you?" That ended the conversation.

At first, the Rangers spotted no wildlife on the White Plains, save the occasional buzzard, hawk, or borrowing owl, and a rare faraway eagle. Then, toward the end of December, they saw immense herds of bison and pronghorn antelope, and once a nearby group of wild horses, running from some unseen threat. The Rangers dismounted and jogged along beside their own animals, moving toward a spot well behind the spooked horses. Then they walked, rifles at the ready, to the crest of one of the long, low White Plains ridges. To the north, in the far distance, was a second herd of cantering horses. After setting his blaster's magnification on maximum, Jarl could make out blond-haired riders. It was his first glimpse of Wild Ghosts, but the Rangers did not pursue them.

It was also his last excursion that month onto the White Plains; Jarl switched from Otis' and Mylea's group to another unit and helped patrol the deep hollows and steep, knobby foothills of the nearby Blue Hills, now searching for Raiders who climbed the high ridges and descended Getout Run to sneak up on the Station from the south. As on the steppe, the Rangers spotted birds of scavenge and prey, but now there were also small herds of forest bison, elk, mule deer, and the smaller white-tailed deer. These patrols were led by Aaron, and they usually moved at a slower pace and stayed out for one night, often returning to the station with a deer or part of an elk draped across the withers of one or more horses.

Neither group spotted any Ghost Raiders, but Jarl learned the surrounding countryside and discovered that the dapple gray was a good horse in both the mountains and on the plains. The first Ghost blood was scored, not by a Ranger, but by Orr, who claimed he had spotted a Raider from the front porch of the Station. Kevin swore the old soldier had concocted a story, but Otis found fresh Ghost sign near the Station. He could not, however, find any sign that Orr's one shot had struck a target.

The Rangers and all the Station's people considered themselves lucky; there had been no serious skirmishes with the Ghost Raiders. Then, in early January, four close-together snowstorms swept the plains, closing the mountain trails for winter, making the Foord Road impassable, and stranding two stage loads of passengers at the Pepper Ford Station. All the Rangers had returned to the Station, with Otis' group staggering in during the wee hours of the morning, during the first and worst storm. For more than a week, everyone shoveled snow and mended gear. Jarl resumed his teaching, now instructing the children on multiplication and division, and more complicated reading. He was assisted by a stranded elderly woman passenger, who produced an ancient, hand-written book of the Vanir King's pedigree.

A warm wind melted most of the snow one night in mid-January. The next morning, Kevin harnessed a six-horse hitch to each stage and then both vehicles departed in their respective directions along the Foord Road. Otis and Stefan led the one stage's escort west; Aaron and Mylea—with Jarl—led the other east.

By two in the afternoon, the small group was well past the halfway point to the next station east, Judy Station. They had given up hope of encountering the westbound stage, resigning themselves to escorting the Pepper Ford stage all the way to Judy. Aaron was disgusted—and scared. More than once he muttered aloud that he hoped Otis' patrol would return to the Pepper Ford Station before dusk and protect it through the night.

Then, all thoughts were rudely jerked to the present as a series of shots sounded just ahead. Aaron refused to split his small force, fearing the noise was a diversion to separate the Rangers from the stage vehicle. Together, with the Rangers in front and the two stage guards nervously watching the rear, the tired squadron cantered east along the now quiet road.

As the small patrol rounded a final bend, Jarl caught his second glimpse of the Ghost Raiders. The westbound stage from Judy Station was stopped in the middle of the road. Both the near lead and swing horses were down in their traces, dead from a Raider volley. One man was inside the stage, and as the Rangers rode into view, there was a puff of blue smoke from the rear window and then the dull boom of a black-powder weapon. Three other figures, dark against the white snow, crouched in a ditch next to the stage. To the right, two Raiders were visible next to a clump of trees, caught out of position by the Rangers' sudden appearance.

One Raider turned and fired at Aaron's group. Three Rangers returned fire. Aaron shouted for his men to move to the right and into the woods—it was the high ground. A dozen horses turned from the road and ran toward the crest, but soon foundered in deep snow. Jarl, leaning low over the dapple gray's back, worried for his horse. His mouth tasted the spent black powder and his mind caught the edge of a short mindbeam. Then, from an unseen position, a rifle boomed and a Ranger toppled from the saddle. Two Rangers fired at the sound; then the Vanir were in the trees. Jarl jumped from the saddle and fell in the deep snow, letting the gray go. He quickly staggered to his feet, skirted one tree, and ducked, on hands and knees, under a low bush, knocking wet, heavy snow onto his camouflage jacket. Then he scooted to the protection of another tree and waited, listening.

The sound of another shot came from the westbound stage. Another bush shook and Jarl spun in that direction. Mylea appeared, and squatted next to a tree. Both of them listened and waited. When there was no sound, Jarl moved forward, encountering a single trail of Raider footprints in the snow. He and Mylea silently followed the trail. It was joined by two additional sets of prints and, from behind them, three more Rangers emerged from the bushes. Finally, after Aaron bellowed a loud "All clear!" they located a hidden stand of trees where a dozen horses had been held. Boot tracks converged on the stand of trees from several directions and hoof prints led northeast toward the Foord Road.

The Rangers returned to the Judy Station stage. A fat man stood nearby, holding two long-barreled pistols and shouting that the Raiders had crossed the road and escaped to the plains after the Rangers had entered the woods.

At the stage, Aaron, wanting to arrive at Judy Station before nightfall, had matters firmly in hand. Two horses were dead, and Grayson and the driver of the Judy stage had been wounded. Aaron replaced the downed animals with Grayson's horse and a spare mount the Rangers had brought. Grayson, his injured arm in a sling, was bundled into the Pepper Ford stage—it had one fewer passenger. Mylea climbed into the driver's box of the Judy Station stage and then, with a loud "Yaaa!" turned the coach in the road and started east, toward Judy. The snow in that direction was wetter and heavier, but the trail had been broken by the stagecoach.

The Rangers crested the last hill before Judy under the full moon of Kmir with its yellow ring, while the stars were appearing in the night sky. Although the bright moonlight provided ample light to spot any hidden Raiders, it aggravated Aaron, because this was a condition the northern marauders preferred for raiding and—with half the 7th Kettle Rangers at Judy Station—there was no telling what havoc the Raiders could cause at the Pepper Ford Station.

Jarl had expected Judy Station to be another few houses, clustered around a central stage station. He was surprised to find it was in fact a small village, built in front of a series of low hills less than a hundred meters high. Not counting the small sheds and outhouses, there was close to one hundred buildings, and judging from the trails of drifting wood smoke, almost all of them were occupied dwellings. The Foord Road became one street, with a parallel avenue behind it. There were a dozen or so cross streets, and in some places a low wall surrounded the town. Only two structures were higher than one story—one was the church and the other the Stage Station. The longest building in town was the military barracks.

After dispatching Jarl and several Rangers to help Mylea with the stages, Aaron turned his own horse toward the barracks. The town lay in an intense quiet, magnified by the night's cold. There had been no guards at the low wall and Jarl was fearful, watching for a trap—could the entire town have been captured by the Raiders? And why wasn't someone awake and waiting for the Pepper Ford stage? He carried his blaster carefully in the nook of his arm, a naked finger on the safety, and intently searched the village for danger.

The two stages and the many horses only made a few soft sounds on the half-frozen snow of the street. But it was enough noise that, with a harsh grating sound, one of the Station windows slid up, throwing a bright yellow rectangle of light across the street. A fat man, wearing a faded nightshirt and a tasseled cap, popped his head through the opening and yelled down, wanting to know what was going on. Mylea stood in the driver's box of the stage, and cursing—at a much louder volume—told the man that two stages had arrived and there were passengers and horses that required attending.

With that, the town of Judy Station came to life. Other windows flew open, dogs began barking, doors slammed, men ran into the street, and a score of people began shouting confused questions to each other.

The fat Station Master stood frozen in one place for a long moment, his face turning red, while his wife's high-pitched voice drifted down into the street below. Then, finally, he slammed the window down and—while his wife shouted more questions—stomped down the stairs, unbarred the door, and stalked out the street, wearing only his nightshirt and cap, his booted feet sounding ominous on the wooden boardwalk. He was angry, his face was still red, and he held a whale oil lamp high, looking for the person who occupied the driver's box. But the top of the stage was now empty, and before he could equate Mylea with the individual who had so recently debased his ancestry, the woman Ranger opened the stage door and started to slide the wounded driver out of the vehicle. The Station Master stomped toward the stage and shouted, "Here, what's going on?"

His answer was immediate. Mylea dropped the driver square into the fat man's arms. The oil lamp flew into the air and the round man bounced backward onto his backside in the street, providing the nearly unconscious driver with a soft landing.

The fat Station Master began squirming, and trying to get the wounded driver off of him. Another townsman stepped from around the stage and helped pull the driver up and onto his feet. This man then looked at the stage master and said, "Hey, Burt, why are you sitting down there in the snow on your naked bun?" The fat man popped to his feet, brushed off his backside and gave an indignant shout, and then stomped back into his station.

Together, Jarl and the local carried the driver into the station house. They met Burt's wife in the doorway. For a moment this confrontation seemed to be destined to be a repeat of the first—the woman was white-faced and wide-eyed, wearing a nightshirt that she clutched at the collar, and holding a second whale oil lamp in front of her. She attempted to use it to force her way into the open door, but Jarl and the local shoved through first, pushing the woman back, while she sputtered commands to stop. She fell over backward, landing in an over-stuffed chair with a loud "Oof!" She jumped right back up, her face full of anger. Then—abruptly—she held up a blood-covered hand and ran from the room with a high-pitched squeal, holding the lamp and her ruined nightgown in front of her.

Jarl caught a brief glimpse of two small children standing on a dark stairway, wide-eyed in their night clothes, before the room became pitch black. Another man shoved his way into the room and said something about a bench. Somehow, unseeing, they levered the wounded driver onto the wooden platform. Light entered the room from the street, as Mylea, holding the Station Master's lamp high above her head, slid into the room.

As the woman Ranger edged forward, providing more light, Jarl opened the driver's coat and his shirts. He discovered no wound, but he followed a thin trail of blood upward and across the driver's body to his upper chest. Slowly and carefully, Jarl eased the man's coat off, until he found the hole of a rifle ball below the driver's shoulder blade. It was an ugly wound, rubbed raw by the stage's rough journey to Judy Station. Jarl turned to the man who had helped and spoke quietly, "I will need water. Lots of it."

The man—who someone called the sheriff—ordered someone to fetch a bucket of warm water and another lamp. When both arrived, Jarl washed the now unconscious driver's wound and then let him rest, and then cleaned and bandaged Grayson's wounded arm.

Then, with the help of a bent and withered woman, whose brown, ancient skin was wrinkled into a thousand folds, Jarl used a thin knife to remove the rifle ball from the driver's shoulder. The driver did no more than softly groan as Jarl worked, while the old woman pressed her bent, arthritic hands against the hurt man's head. But, from the back of the crowded room, Jarl heard a hushed whisper, one spoken with both fear and hate, "Witch!"

Jarl then bandaged the driver's shoulder, and the two wounded men were moved upstairs. Someone had scooted the passengers off to other rooms. Footsteps sounded on the boardwalk outside, and Aaron stomped into the room, shouting that the local militia commander had not thought to send an escort with the Judy Station stage.

The Ranger captain was in an extremely foul mood. He wanted to leave immediately for Pepper Ford Station. The local commander had agreed to escort the next day's stages westward. They would also herd the Rangers' tired horses with them.

Saddles were switched from the Rangers' tired animals to fresh horses. Despite Aaron's objections, a hot supper was fed to the Rangers and, as Jarl swung into the saddle of a black gelding, the sheriff thanked Aaron for bringing the stage safely back to Judy and said that Grayson would be well looked after. Then, a gloved hand caught the black's reins, and the sheriff thanked Jarl for helping the stage driver.

With a wave of one hand, Aaron ordered the Rangers toward home. The small band, numbering only eleven, moved out of town at a trot, riding west along the Foord Road. They galloped for two kilometers, then walked the horses for half that distance. The one full moon and the reflective snow gave the night a surreal quality, making it possible to see kilometers along the road and across the White Plains. The night was icy cold, and the Rangers and their horses' breath came in steamy bursts.

The long night ride went quickly, as the trail was already broken and the men and woman moved at a speed more typical of the fast-moving Kettlewand stages. Judging by the stars, it was well after midnight when the Rangers reached the turn where the road left the endless edge of the White Plains. The Snowy River flowed west of Roundbottom Hill, so only silence greeted their ears as they rode into the hollow east of the hill, a bottom that was intensely dark after their moonlit ride beside the plains. Jarl brought his modern weapon to his shoulder and used the electronic night vision to see if there was any danger ahead.

The Rangers now moved slowly, feeling and hearing their way along the road. They were within a few hundred meters of the Station and were beginning to relax, thinking their hard ride had been for nothing, when Jarl—in the lead—caught a slight whiff of spent gunpowder. Without speaking, he slid from his horse and darted quietly to the edge of the road. Instantly, Mylea moved to his side. Together they squatted in the snow and attempted to peer along the road. Twice they eased slowly forward and between each movement, squatted and listened. Kmir had now set and the darkness had become even deeper. There was nothing to be heard or seen.

Aaron came forward, and moved the Rangers off the road and into the forest on the left. They immediately discovered a fresh Ghost trail, no more than a few hours old. Two men took the horses, and the remaining Rangers eased toward the Station in a slow stop-and-start hunting fashion. A bit more light played across the white snow as the forest became more open.

Jarl began to shiver. Finally, close to an hour after he had first smelled the spent gun powder, the dark outline of the Station's buildings could be seen through the trees. And then, although he could not comprehend the language or the thoughts behind the sender, he felt a brief, but powerful and well-directed mindbeam.

Slower still, the Rangers crept forward. As yet, no Ghost Raiders were in sight, and there was no indication that the Station personnel were still inside the buildings. Then, abruptly, the stillness of the night was broken by a short volley of gunfire, followed by a second ragged series of dull explosions. With the last, came the slap, slap, slap of rifle balls against the Station's walls. Jarl saw one white flash of a rifle, far into the woods, on the opposite side of the Station house. Then three of Aaron's Rangers fired. For a moment the mindbeam became strong, but then it departed, too quickly for Jarl to understand what was said. Two more quick shots came from the direction of the barn, and Jarl caught a glimpse of a shadow flitting around one corner of that building.

For a long time everyone waited, not moving. Jarl swept the area with his night vision and saw nothing. Finally, shivering intensely from the cold, he eased forward to a large tree next to the courtyard.

Immediately came the sound of rushing air and then an arrow smacked a bright patch on the old tree, a sycamore with flaking bark. Jarl dropped into the snow.

Someone nearby fired at a Raider. Jarl had a feeling a marauder near the barn had fired the arrow. He waited, peering through his scope until the edge of the nomad's head appeared over a snow-covered wood pile, next to the edge of the barn. He increased the magnification of the scope and concentrated on the edge of the head for a long moment. Then—just as he began to shiver again—he squeezed the trigger of the blaster. His shot was a clean miss; the red pulse of light flashed over the Ghost Raider and exploded in the woods behind. Jarl caught a momentary melody of mindbeaming, emitting from several different sources, and then a rifle banged on his left, followed by another, across the courtyard. There was a spatter of firing from behind the house, near the Rangers' barracks, and—after a short wait—horses could be heard on the ford, splashing across the Snowy River.

Aaron waited another half-hour, slowly moving about the area. He hello-ed the people in the house and the Rangers scooted inside. After a brief conference, Otis and a half-dozen warm men moved outside. They checked the people in the outbuildings and brought the horses and the two cold men with them into the barn. Jarl stood by the hot wood stove, shivering and drinking hot tea. Then he retired to his upstairs bedroom. Other than from the cold and fright, there had been no Vanir casualties.

CHAPTER TEN:

THE MURDER OF THE RAIDER

Jarl slept late the next day, finally joining the Stephensons for lunch. Seeing that he was still shivering, Iajore ordered him back to bed, but Molly discovered him awake in the early afternoon and coerced him downstairs to the front of the large fireplace to teach reading and arithmetic to her, Chad, Jorm, Marri, and the remaining Stephenson children, who were confined to the Station house until the Rangers were sure that the Ghost Raiders had left the area.

The Raiders had arrived at twilight the previous day, following Otis' squad and the eastbound stage. A sharp-eyed Jorm had spotted them crossing the Foord Road and, for the next seven hours, the two groups had fought a sporadic and intermittent battle, with the Raiders not able to penetrate the Station's defenses and the Vanir unable to drive off the nomads. There had been three main points in the Kettle defense—the barn, the barracks, and the house, each with about a dozen people trapped inside. The Raiders had stolen no stock—it was all crowded into the barn—and, for some reason, they had set no fires, although both brush and firewood were readily available.

The next day, while Jarl was bedridden, Otis tracked seventeen Raider ponies and thirteen sets of footprints, but found no indication that any of their enemy had been wounded. Toward evening, just as the crowded stage arrived from Judy Station along with Grayson and the Rangers' horses, the small band of Raiders was sighted at the edge of Roundbottom Hill. Twenty or so Rangers went in pursuit of the marauders. They returned, discouraged, well after dark; the nomads had given them the slip. The next day, Otis trailed the small group well out onto the White Plains.

Jarl spent a week in the Station house—Aaron docked him three dollars in pay—teaching more reading, writing, and arithmetic. Finally, well rested, he was Aaron's first choice to lead a small patrol to the lookout on Roundbottom Hill. There, in the cold afternoon and evening, they spotted no Raiders.

In summer and good weather, the stages could travel long distances each day, passing three or four stations, and often traveling after dark. Now, once again, the stages began running daily; however, their rate of travel was slower, limited by the short winter day and the condition of the road, and it was seldom that passengers did not spend the night at Pepper Ford Station. Moreover, small squadrons of cavalry began escorting the stages on a regular basis.

Raider sign, both close to the Station and far out onto the plains, became more prolific. One stage brought news that a house near Burkes Ford had been burned and all the inhabitants killed. Once, a squadron of Rangers under Aaron became involved in a long fight far out on the White Plains. The battle had lasted more than six hours and had ended when both sides withdrew into the coming night. Aaron's force had numbered nineteen Rangers, and Jarl was not surprised that, altogether, they had fired less than thirteen rounds—fights with the Raiders had the habit of quickly becoming battles where both sides hid well, moved little, and fired only well-aimed arrows or rifles.

On another occasion, Mylea and a mixed group of Rangers and cavalry were escorting a westbound stage from Judy Station. The Vanir had surprised a small group of Raiders, and a running fight had developed. Again, there were no casualties and, despite the fact that the stage had been left unprotected, it had safely arrived at the Pepper Ford Station. But the following day, the Vanir were not so lucky. A band of Rangers led by Otis, Jarl included, discovered five mutilated bodies littering the road ten kilometers east of the Station. The small group of mid-winter travelers had been surprised and killed by the nomads. They completed their journey to Judy in the back of a springless farm wagon.

By early February, Jarl was again going on the long patrols onto the White Plains, while more and more Vanir cavalry escorted the stages along the Foord Road. Twice, Jarl was with Otis when the old man attempted to ambush moving bands of Raiders. The first time, the marauders simply chose another trail, leaving the Rangers empty-handed. On the second occasion, a Raider saw or smelled something and quickly waved his group off. Three Rangers had fired shots at the retreating Ghosts, but, because their horses were hidden a short distance away, the Kettle militia did not pursue.

On the next day—and without Otis—more due to good fortune than planning, Jarl was able to organize a quick ambush along the Foord Road. As a small group of Raiders followed a frozen creek upstream under the short span of a tall, wooden highway bridge, Jarl quickly posted his men along one side of the steep gully. The quick firefight left three Raiders wounded, hanging to the sides of their running horses, and another dead, lying face down on the ice-covered stream.

Once again the nomads made good use of their slight head start, expediently racing out onto the White Plains, and the Rangers did not pursue. Afterwards, Jarl slid down the frozen bank and rolled the dead Ghost Raider over onto his back. It was a young man, with pale-blue eyes and wide swaths of red and black paint streaked across his wind-burnt face, and who had the carbon mark of a blaster in the center of his chest and the hole from a rifle ball in the middle of his forehead. His long hank of gray-blond hair was pulled back into a pony tail and decorated with the feathers of a red hawk, and his clothing was a drab gray color that blended in well on the winter plains. His weapons were a samurai sword and a short, powerful recurve bow, constructed of several types of laminated wood unknown to Jarl. He allowed his men to strip the corpse of its outer clothing and weapons, but he forbade them to mutilate the body. The next day the body was gone, and Jarl was never sure if it was stolen by the Rangers or reclaimed by the Raiders.

February was much the same as January. On some days they spent as little as four hours in the saddle; on others they would patrol from well before first light until well after dark, often taking a second and third horse for each rider. Meat at the Station ran low, but was supplemented when a group of Rangers—Jarl included—accidentally encountered a herd of wild pigs behind the Station. Kevin slaughtered an old cow, and once Otis returned with a brace of dead turkeys and news of another wild bull.

The following day—while Aaron led a mixed group of Rangers and cavalry on a patrol west along the Foord Road—Otis, Stefan, Grayson, and

Jarl took it upon themselves to locate the bull and dispatch it, not only for the meat, but also to eliminate the danger. Jarl had recently found a pair of old snowshoes hanging on the wall in one of the Station's outbuildings, and he led the way, stamping out a path through the deep snow up Getout Run. The four Rangers finally located the large animal in a dense patch of brush, but the bull saw them and charged, throwing a white spray of snow skyward. Stefan and Grayson's horses became tangled together, and Otis' shot ricocheted off the bull's massive skull. But Jarl, aware that he could not run wearing snowshoes, took his time and fired two lethal blaster shots into the animal at a range of less than fifteen meters. Stefan and Grayson were sent for Kevin's heavy wood sled, and by early afternoon the foursome was back at the Station, struggling to butcher the immense animal.

This job was almost finished when suppertime arrived. But, just as they sat down to eat, two men rode into the Station yard from the west, their horses lathered and trembling from a long, hard run. It was English and a Vanir cavalry trooper.

Everyone rushed outside, and found that English had a grim story to tell. Late in the afternoon, Aaron had been returning to the Station with his squadron when they had been ambushed by a party of Raiders. Two Rangers and the cavalry officer had been shot, and Aaron had ordered the survivors to charge directly into the ambush, but instead the cavalry had rushed to hide in a nearby—and very convenient—ravine.

The result had been a slaughter, as the main Raider force had been hidden on the opposite side of the deep gully. Eight cavalrymen had been killed and another six wounded. Aaron and his handful of Rangers had ridden directly into the original line of fire, but the few Ghosts there had slipped out on well-packed foot trails that wove through a dense thicket. The Rangers came out empty-handed. All they could do was turn and fire on the main force of the Raiders, who now, without as much as a single casualty, slipped out over previously made paths in the snow.

Of thirty-two Vanir, ten were dead and another seven were wounded. Fifteen still patrolled the road, and since Aaron had estimated the marauder force to be no more than twelve or thirteen, he figured there was no immediate danger. Nevertheless, English said, he wanted reinforcements and wagons for the wounded. Because Mylea was leading another mixed unit of Rangers and cavalry in the other direction, east toward Judy

Station, there were only eleven Rangers at the Pepper Ford Station. Otis had horses saddled and two wagons readied, but—fearing a Ghost attack on the Station—it was not until Mylea's group was in sight that the old Ranger gave the order to mount and proceed to Aaron's side.

Pepper Ford was, in reality, two fords separated by a long, narrow island. The horses and wagons quickly crossed the river, walking on top of the thick winter ice. The stage road was rutted and the Rangers made good time until a small squad of cavalry joined Otis' force from the rear.

It was more bad news: despite Mylea's and Kevin's orders and pleas, these men had left the Station and had come, on already exhausted horses, to help rescue their comrades. After a short, angry argument, the horsemen rode on ahead of the slow-moving wagons. It was more than six kilometers later, at the site of the ambush, that the Rangers caught up to the cavalrymen, who were standing next to their exhausted horses and well away from their injured comrades, not helping and not watching for Raiders.

While Aaron loaded the dead and wounded into the two wagons and killed two incapacitated horses, Otis, Jarl, and eleven Rangers followed the Raiders' trail a half kilometer onto the White Plains. Afterwards, the combined force returned to the Station, walking a large part of the way because of the cavalrymen's trembling mounts. They arrived at the turnoff from the plains at dusk and crossed the ice-covered Snowy River just before full dark. The Station courtyard was lit by torches and people were standing on the wide veranda, anxiously awaiting their return.

It was a long night at the Pepper Ford Station. Marri and Iajore had bandages and hot tea ready. While Iajore, Jarl, and Otis treated the wounded, Mylea led a large group of Rangers west along the Foord Road, then across the north side of Roundbottom Hill, and finally a short distance east along the Stage Road. She returned before midnight, reporting no additional Ghost sign.

Otis, Iajore, and Jarl had their hands full. Two cavalrymen had chest wounds, one of which made loud sucking sounds. That man had also been wounded by an arrow in his left leg. Two other cavalrymen were shot high in the left arm directly above the heart, both by arrows. One Ranger had died; the other had been shot through the fleshy portion of his neck by a rifle ball. Although bleeding badly, it was not a serious wound. Jarl cleaned it, using almost an entire bucket of warm water, and then applied a dressing and a bandage. One of the remaining two cavalrymen was shot in the leg, the other in both the leg and arm. Otis and Iajore cleaned these wounds, removing a rifle ball from one leg.

Wide-eyed and frightened, Marri, Chad, and Molly—despite her mother's protests—hauled water and ran countless errands. Kevin, the Glades brothers, and Jorm saddled and unsaddled horses. Many of the surviving cavalrymen gathered in one corner near the great fireplace; others returned to their makeshift barracks in one of the outbuildings. The Rangers guarded the outside of the Station, but no Ghost Raiders returned.

Just before dawn, as most people slept and despite the best efforts of Jarl and Iajore, the cavalryman with the punctured lung died. It was a grim squad of Rangers that Aaron led across the White Plains that day and the next, but there was no sign of any of the nomads. Within two days, two dozen more cavalry and a sour-faced lieutenant arrived at the Station, but despite the increased number of patrols and the renewed determination, no Raider parties were sighted. In fact, no fresh sign was even found.

Snowstorms followed. This time, with increased personnel, the stage line quickly and safely resumed its schedule. Rations arrived from the east so that the horse soldiers could stay on at the Station and continue their escorts. Jarl joined Otis and twelve Rangers for a long, fruitless patrol that followed the Snowy River downstream for forty kilometers to the point on the plains where it turned abruptly east toward Atrobee. They traveled north for a half day from the turn, which was called the La Sinuosite by the Rangers. Far to the north, with the Snowy far behind them and out of sight, the frozen grass was now only hoof deep and had been swept almost free of the snow by the wind. With no immediate assistance from the Station, the tiny Ranger force was very vulnerable, and more than one man breathed a sigh of relief when Otis finally turned his small squad south and rejoined the Snowy River some fifteen kilometers down river from the La Sinuosite.

The Rangers spent two nights on the Snowy, seeking refuge from a violent snowstorm in a narrow alluvial gully that led down to the river. Rations were low, but the men were able to fire their weapons in the air and scare a dozen large plains wolves from a freshly killed bison they discovered along the river. When the storm abated, the Rangers returned to the Foord Road, taking turns breaking the trail and traveling through a light, powdery snow that often touched the bottom of their stirrups. For half a day, the black plains wolves followed, hoping to kill a horse or man for food.

The small party of Rangers spent the night in the foothills of the Blue Hills, hidden in a small fold in the hillside and surrounded by a willow thicket. The next day, Otis—not one to do things normally—led them up a long, deep hollow. From here, the men climbed a steep headwall in deep snow. With Jarl breaking the trail on his snowshoes, they crossed over the tops of two more ridges and slid down the eastern slope of a mountain to what Otis hoped was Getout Run. The snow was deep and the energy of the small force were exhausted, but Jarl found a game trail that led to the Pepper Ford Station. Of the fourteen men on the patrol, only Jarl was still on speaking terms with Otis by the time they returned to the Station.

The first day of March was heralded by a snowstorm that dumped more than a meter of snow on the Station. It took almost two weeks before the stages were running with any degree of regularity. The wounded cavalryman recovered sufficiently for him to board an eastbound stage to Judy Station. With no sign of the Ghost Raiders, the remaining troopers were becoming more and more bitter. They made fit company for Orr, who Iajore was now openly lamenting would leave the Station in early spring.

In the second week in March, Jarl was one of a mixed group of Rangers and cavalry that Otis led as a stage escort west along the Foord Road. In an effort to break the trail and scout for Ghost sign, Otis allowed his unit to get more than a kilometer ahead of the westbound stage. Around noon, they encountered the eastbound stage and its escort from Burkes Ford Station. Otis turned his squadron and, at a canter, led that stage toward Pepper Ford. As they rounded a slight turn in the road, they spotted two Raiders on foot, squatting behind a snow-covered rock south of the road. One nomad let loose an arrow, hitting the near lead horse on the eastbound stage. Another half dozen nomads—all on horseback—charged from hiding, intending to complete the ambush, but when they saw the Rangers, they turned and fled into the brush. As the two Raiders on foot sprinted toward their horses, Mylea eared back the hammer on her long rifle, stood in her saddle, aimed, and fired.

One Ghost stumbled and fell, measuring his length on the cold packed snow of the Foord Road. Jarl was not so accurate; his red light burst dropped the other Raider's horse. That Ghost landed on his feet, turned, and neatly placed an arrow into the throat of one of the cavalrymen. Otis led the main group of Vanir off the road and into the brush on the right, beginning a sporadic firefight. Smoke erupted from the stage as passengers and guards fired black-powder flintlocks into the undergrowth, shooting at unseen targets. Mylea rode down the surviving Raider with her horse and knocked the small, gray-clothed marauder into the snow.

Jarl was first to dismount, but he floundered in the deep snow beside the road. Mylea was trying to turn her animal, but it slipped and then sat on its haunches. A fat cavalryman more fell than jumped onto the Raider. There was a momentary struggle and then both combatants popped back up, stumbling in the snow. The larger cavalryman had the clear advantage; his arms were locked behind the smaller Raider's neck, bending the Ghost's shoulders backwards. Jarl regained his feet, but the nomad suddenly threw both feet into the air and kicked him back into the snow.

Jarl caught a brief glimpse not of not a savage and determined warrior, but rather of a small and badly frightened young girl—her face white beneath her wind-burned tan, her forehead and cheeks smeared with wide stripes of red and yellow paint, her blond braids and feathers swinging in the air, and the brown skin of her belly showing through a gap in her clothing at midriff—struggling to free herself from the grasp of the big man. As Jarl stumbled back to his feet, something hit him hard from behind and he plowed face first into the snow. At the same time, he heard Mylea scream a loud, desperate, "No!"

Then there was a sound he could not identify. For the third time, Jarl struggled up and out of the snow. He had a vague feeling of Mylea's strained face, her wheeling horse, and her pointing rifle. Less than two meters away, the large cavalryman still held the young Raider, but now the girl was no longer struggling. A trickle of blood ran from her mouth. Jarl's stomach became queasy, and for a moment he thought he was going to be sick. A second large trooper was withdrawing a long, bloody cavalry sword from the young girl's chest. The sound he had heard had been steel grating on bone. The second man was grinning wildly, and—as he looked up at Mylea, who was cocking her flintlock—he began to laugh, plainly enjoying his words, "Go ahead, lass, that rifle ain't loaded."

Jarl brought up his own blaster. "But mine is," he said.

Even through Jarl's concentration was on the second horse trooper, he saw Mylea's face become paler, and her eyes were shouting, 'No!' He glanced over his shoulder, and then half turned, looking behind him. A third trooper stood about two meters away, pointing a long, single-barreled, black-powder pistol at his head. The hammer was eared back, and Jarl could see a heavy stain of blood—his blood—under the butt. The man had a malicious smile, and it was clear he wanted Jarl to give him an excuse to shoot. Then Mylea gasped, and Jarl turned back toward the dead Raider. The first horseman dropped the girl into the snow and the second man ran her through with his saber a second time. Again, the sound of steel on bone was sickening. The man with the pistol called Mylea a 'damn Ghost lover' and he called Jarl a wizard. His voice was cruel and full of hate.

The three horse soldiers forced Mylea to dismount. Then, they herded the two Rangers up onto the highway. Mylea made a small effort to reach for a pistol, but the grinning men were attentive, and in the end, both she and Jarl had to stand quietly by and watch the cavalrymen mutilate, scalp, and rob the two dead Raiders.

There was a renewed spatter of firing from the eastbound stagecoach. All this time, it had been standing less than fifty meters away, while its occupants searched the brush for more Raiders. Now a small group of mounted Ghosts broke from the undergrowth and raced west along its packed road. Rangers and cavalrymen rushed toward their horses. The three troopers with Mylea and Jarl quickly completed their work and caught their horses, then—whooping and hollering—ran their animals after pursuing Vanir.

To the east was the sound of horses and, several seconds later, the westbound stage arrived. Then, for the first time, the passengers on the eastbound stage noticed the two Raider corpses lying in the snow next to the highway. Without hesitation, they began to cheer. Mylea, her faced pinched with anger, was reloading her long weapon, forcing the ramrod up and down in hard, sharp jerks. Jarl walked over, and using his feet, pushed the two corpses together. Then, while the twenty people quieted and watched—now knowing that something had happened that they were unable to fathom—Jarl and Mylea chased down their horses, mounted, and chased after Otis.

They found the old man returning with a half-dozen Rangers. Two other Raiders had been killed, but no other Ranger and cavalryman had been hurt. Otis had called off the horse race, seeing little sense in wearing down their animals in a futile chase. But then the three cavalrymen had joined Otis' squadron combined squadron of Rangers and cavalry, wielding their bloody trophies, and all of the Vanir horse soldiers again chased after the Raiders, leaving the Rangers behind, and calling them cowards and Ghost lovers.

As Mylea and Jarl told their story, Otis' face became grim and unreadable. When he asked Jarl about his head wound, Mylea jumped, shocked that she had forgotten the injury. Her long, strong fingers quickly probed the small cut—it proved to be little more than a bruise, and the bleeding had already stopped.

It was a long, quiet ride back to the Pepper Ford Station. The Rangers were not happy. A horse trooper had been killed and was now tied face down over the back of his mount, one of their own had been assaulted from behind by a cavalryman, and a good portion of the unit was chasing an enemy through deep snow who could turn on them at any time and wreak havoc. Their feelings were amplified by the cold and the approaching dusk, and the fact that they were short-handed. But there were no ambushes and, a full hour before the early winter dusk, the Rangers and their stagecoach crossed the ice of the Snowy River and walked their tired horses into the courtyard of the Station.

It was another two hours later when the nine cavalrymen arrived, still jubilant at their earlier success, but returning empty-handed from their chase. Orr took great pride in their trophies and produced a bottle of whiskey. The men celebrated late into the night, joined by Orr and their lieutenant, who did not care that his men had abandoned the two stages.

Two days later, Jarl resigned from the Kettlewand Rangers. Six days after that, tired of hearing Orr's jeers and snide remarks, he saddled the dapple gray and—alone—began a long trip to the Vanir capital of Tyr.

CHAPTER ELEVEN:

THE ROAD TO TYR

Jarl found it difficult to tell Otis that he had quit the 7th Kettlewand Rangers. When he did so, the old man had spit, his face sour and uncompromising. Then he looked long and hard at Jarl and spit again. Jarl knew Otis was angry at him because he lacked the gumption to stay after their one prisoner had been killed.

But he had totally misread the old Ranger—somehow and somewhere, Jarl had made one good, solid friend. Otis abruptly grinned, grabbed Jarl's hand and flat-out said that he would miss him. Jarl was taken aback, both from the statement and because he could rarely remember Otis smiling so broadly. The old Ranger had not thought much of the cavalrymen's treatment of the young Raider; but then—he had to admit—he had never seen the capture of a Ghost Raider that had not ended in disaster, often with the prisoner's suicide.

It had been Otis who—despite the nervousness and downright fear of the Rangers and Vanir cavalry—had originally convinced Jarl of the common sense of taking his modern blaster on patrol, and, ultimately, it was the old Ranger with whom Jarl discussed his decision to leave the Pepper Ford Station. The old man was full of useful information concerning the highway, the towns, the rivers, and the capital city. It was a sad day in mid-March when Jarl mounted the dapple gray and rode out of the muddy courtyard of the Station, leading a mouse-colored packhorse, but—on that day—he had a fair-to-good appreciation of the hazards that lay before him, thanks to Otis' lengthy advice.

Jarl had two good reasons for traveling to Tyr. First, Alfheim Vail, the agent for the stage line, had written him a letter asking that he come to the capital and inspect the construction of the new Concord Stagecoaches. Second, because he had not met any sorcerers while living at the Pepper Ford Station, Jarl wanted to discover, either through official or private channels, if there had been any word of Kvasir at the Vanir capital.

The evening before he left, Jarl and Otis talked long into the night, sitting on the dark porch of the stage station. When Jarl had inquired if Otis had ever witnessed any witchcraft, the old man was silent for a long time. Finally he said, in his dry, matter-of-fact voice, "'Cept once, I ain't sure I've ever seen anybody do anything I'd call magic..."

"Including Kvasir?"

"Yep. Including Kvasir."

"And that one time?" Jarl asked.

"I didn't see anything that one time either, but I was only a step or two from someone and he didn't see me. And he should have, 'cause I was in plain view and standin' full in front of him."

Otis paused for a moment, remembering, then he continued, "The woman I was with claimed she was a witch, but—other than that one time—I never saw her do nothin' that could have been considered witchcraft."

It was too dark to read Otis' expression. Jarl was silent, thinking, enjoying the quiet of the night, and nervous about leaving in the morning. Finally he asked, "Well, what is sorcery supposed to be then?"

"Things like shape changing and..."

"Shape changing? You mean wizards and witches can change themselves into other things?"

"Yea..." the old man was hesitant. "Least that's what I hear. They can change themselves into other people, or into animals, like black cats and dragons." He paused, thoughtful. "They can change the weather and see in total darkness, such as in caves and such. And they can heal people who are dying. They can put a spell on you and make you sick, or make you fall in love, or keep a woman from becoming pregnant. And they can make your horses founder or make your cows dry up. That's a common thing witches do—make cows dry up."

"Why?"

"I don't know. It is just somethin' they do..."

"But you've never seen any of this. Has anyone you know... anyone that you trust... seen witchcraft?"

Again Otis was thoughtful. He answered slowly, "No."

"Have you ever seen a dragon?"

"No."

"Have you ever met anyone who has seen a dragon?"

"Not nobody I trust..."

Jarl considered that for a while. "What's the punishment for sorcery?" he asked.

"If you're a Ghost Raider, they banish you." Otis did not say how he knew this. "If you're Vanir they imprison you or put you to death."

"Death?"

"Yea. And it ain't a good death either. The Church likes to burn sorcerers at the stake. They say it frees their souls. In Tyr, they used to burn dozens of wizards and witches a year."

Jarl was shocked. "Do they still do that?" he asked.

"Yea, but not so many. It might be there are fewer wizards and witches about."

"Or they are in hiding. Is sorcery a crime?"

"It's a crime against the Church."

"Is there a trial?"

"Sometimes, but it is often just for show..." Otis' voice was very dry.

Jarl thought for several moments, then he asked, "If you never saw Kvasir do sorcery, then why do they call him a wizard?"

"I don't know. That was just his reputation. Besides he lived in Vor, and they're all witches and wizards there."

Jarl wondered if he should travel to Vor, instead of Tyr. "What do you know about Vor?" he asked.

"Not much. I ain't never been there. It's somewhere out west across the White Plains, near Raider country, so it's damn dangerous to get to. Plus, with all the wizards and witches living there, there's supposed to be bunches of spells protecting it, so even if you were in sight of the city, you can't see it. It's supposed to be a shiny city, with high towers, and the streets paved with gold."

"Gold?"

"Sure. All them wizards and witches can change rocks into gold. At least that's what people say."

"Kvasir didn't look like someone who could turn rocks into gold. In fact, he looked downright poor."

"True," Otis allowed, "but looks can be deceiving. And he was supposed to have run the high council of Vor for a bunch of years."

"That's what I heard..." Jarl said, thoughtful. "Have you even met another wizard or witch, other than Kvasir and that one woman?"

Otis' answer was slow, but then that was his manner. "No."

"Do you know where she is now?"

There was something in Otis' voice that Jarl could not fathom. "No. It was a long, long time ago. And out on the Plains. God only knows where she is now, if she's still alive."

Jarl did not pursue the subject. Instead, he thought for a minute or so, then asked, "A city of sorcerers... has it always been that way?"

Otis brightened. He seemed happy to change the subject. "No. At one time it was the provincial capital of Olympic. There used to be a highway out there. Back then, it was a part of Vanir. The Ghost Raiders were a part of Vanir too. It used to be the roads were better and there were a lot more bridges. You could send a letter from one end of the nation to the other. And there were more books. I remember that from when I was real young. And my father used to say that long ago they had metal cartridges for their rifles. They didn't have to ram the charges down their rifle barrels like we do, and some rifles could be shot more than once, without reloading, like your gun..."

The old man stopped for a long moment, then he continued, "But each year, the roads get a little worse, the nation gets a little smaller, and it seems to get harder and harder to make do or get around."

Jarl said nothing more. The next day, his departure from the Station was painful. Iajore and Marri cried and asked him not to go. Kevin offered him a home if ever he needed it. Jorm and the Glades brothers stood to one side and said nothing. Aaron was hard-faced, saying the skirmish had been the fortunes of war, and what had happened was nothing compared to what the Raiders would have done to a captured Ranger. Mylea, now that she had talked things over with Aaron, agreed with him. Orr sneered and, like the arrogant cavalrymen, was glad to see Jarl go. Molly cried and cried, and Chad held her hand and appeared close to tears. That—for Jarl—was the worst moment, as he had become quite fond of the two teenagers. They—and Marri—promised to continue with their studies.

Jarl arrived at Judy Station well before dark, after a long, cold day in the saddle. He was surprised to see that the village was pleasant-looking during the day, and he spent the night with the sheriff and his family. The next day he was again in the saddle, following the Foord Road east. The days passed quickly. One day he would travel with a group, the next day alone.

Eastern Kettle was more settled than the western portion of the province. Here, the danger from Ghosts decreased, but the danger from bandits increased. The villages were larger and the easternmost town in Kettlewand, Desjhan, was large enough to be considered a small city.

Still, even a day's ride from Desjhan, there were long, lonely, uninhabited stretches of the highway. Low hills remained on the right, stretching southward toward the still unseen Sabre Mountains. At one place the road became a rutted series of red tracks and climbed onto a flat plateau that stretched northward for ten kilometers. This was called the Rhombus, an ancient name for a place that—according to the people at the tavern where Jarl had spent the previous night—was drained mostly by caves, all reputed to be haunted. Now, as the gray ascended the short grade onto the Rhombus, Jarl searched for sinkholes and limestone outcrops.

He saw none, and the scenery became dull. He daydreamed and lost touch with his surroundings. Then, suddenly, a small group of running horses jumped from a hidden gully, and he was abruptly jerked back to reality. Jarl hooted and the gray lunged forward and broke into a fast run. After a sharp tug on the lead rope, the packhorse followed. There was the dull boom of a gunshot and everything became a kaleidoscope of bright colors and running horses. The leader—a fat, dark-haired man on a roan—fired the second barrel of a long, double-barreled shotgun into the air. The cloud of blue smoke was quickly left behind. A second rider let loose an arrow. It flashed by, far in front of the running gray.

Then there was a third gunshot. Jarl glanced over his shoulder at the tightly bunched group of riders. All the horses were now running at full speed, throwing clumps of wet, red clay into the air. For a few moments the race continued east along the rutted road, with Jarl's two horses gradually pulling ahead. Then, suddenly, from a cluster of snow-covered sandstone boulders on the right, another group of highwaymen appeared. The first band of attackers had clearly intended to scare Jarl and tire his horses; the second bunch planned to cut him off. But the second group of bandits had made a mistake—likely they had set their trap while the ground was still frozen. Now the surface had thawed into a thin, slick mud covering, and their horses made work of the slight uphill grade onto the road.

Jarl crouched low behind the gray's neck and sped by within a few meters of the second group of men, and they had a fast horse race for more than a kilometer. At one place the road dropped a few meters down onto another flat. The gray slid down the slick grade on its rear hoofs, while Jarl held his breath and tried not to pull on the reins. His pursuers descended the short mud slope with a similar wild abandonment. To their credit, most of them arrived at the bottom intact, but two animals fell, one in the middle of the group. Other horses attempted to jump the fallen animals, and the result was a confused tangle of falling horses and riders. When the bandits reached the flat bottom, their numbers had been halved.

Although the gray was now breathing in hard grunts, the animal was leaving the bandits' horses far behind. Then there was another gully on the right—it seemed almost man-made—and a third group of horsemen appeared from it, their horses already racing full out. Even with the gray's tremendous speed, these men would cross the road many meters in front of Jarl, cutting him off.

The lead highwayman was a large, red-haired man, mounted on a big red horse that was running a step ahead of the tight cluster of bandits. He raised a long-barreled pistol high into the air and began to slowly bring the business end down, pointing it toward Jarl. The distance between the racing horses was rapidly decreasing. In one smooth motion, Jarl brought his blaster up off the nook of his left arm, flicked off the safety, and fired the moment the weapon touched his shoulder. His first shot struck the red man just below his throat. The pistol exploded, still pointed skyward.

As the leader toppled backward off his running horse, one of the other riders reached sideways to catch the body. Jarl's second shot took this man in the center of his chest, and then he, his horse, and the red-haired bandit went down in a huge collapse of moving men and animals. Two other horses tripped and fell, one somersaulting onto its rider. A horseman on the near side of the tangled group attempted to rein up, but his animal slipped on the thawing clay and also fell to the ground, sending its rider tumbling through the air.

Only one man was able to stop, narrowly avoiding the collision, but then his horse was kicked by one of the fallen animals. As the gray raced by, Jarl caught a glimpse of a startled, dirty face before the bandit's horse arched its back and jumped clear of the thrashing men and animals on the ground. The rider made a hurried grab for his saddle horn and stayed with his horse, bouncing off the highway and leaving his hat hanging in the air behind him. Over his shoulder, Jarl could see the other two groups of bandits, now one mob, beginning to pull to a slow stop on the slippery highway.

Jarl let the gray run for another half kilometer. The bandit leader's horse ran easily alongside. Then, as the packhorse began to pull against the lead rope, Jarl slowed the gray to a canter and then to a walk. Behind him, through the blaster's scope, he could see the cluster of would-be robbers, some sitting on their horses, some huddled in a group on the ground, but none pursuing him. The red horse continued running ahead of Jarl and his animals. Now as he watched, it kicked its hind feet into the air two or three times and then angled north, cantering out and onto the Rhombus. The last he saw of the animal, it had turned and was trotting back toward the would-be highwaymen.

That evening, about an hour before dusk, Jarl rode through the western gate of Desjhan. According to Otis, the community had close to five thousand inhabitants, a thriving iron industry, and was a prominent fort and crossing of the mud-colored October River, which flowed north to join the Snowy. The homes were for the most part well built, made of wood or stone, and occasionally constructed over a barn or pig sty.

There were a good half-dozen east-west streets, bisected by twenty or so cross-streets, each a different length, that ran back toward a high hill on which was constructed a tall stone citadel, one that overlooked all of Desjhan. Directly under the fort was the second-largest building in the city, a stone church, with a high tower and sharply pointed roof. Most of the streets were cobblestone; the remainder were red dirt, or more accurately—at this time of the year—liquid mud.

Jarl spent the night in a boarding house with a large yellow sign, and he made no mention of his brief fight on the Foord Road earlier in the day. The next morning he met Alfheim Vail at the stage station. After a loud hello and hearty handshake, the agent said that five new coaches had been completed and there was an additional fifty dollars waiting for Jarl in Tyr.

Together Jarl and Alfheim crossed a stout, well-made wooden toll bridge—free because they were on stage business—leaving both Desjhan and the Province of Kettlewand. Now, they traveled through Atrobee. This was a much more populous land, with small communities every few kilometers along the main highway. There were also many forks in the stage road. Some of these led south into the famed Forests of Atrobee, while others led north onto the settled fringes of the White Plains. The two men spent each night in the stage line's Stations, sharing Spartan, but adequate lodging with the stage drivers and other agents.

With each day's travel to the east the roads became better and, despite the heavier traffic, Jarl and Alfheim were able to make better time. Nevertheless, it took Jarl ten days to cross Atrobee, passing forty kilometers north of the congested provincial capital, Sweetroll. Alfheim was not so fortunate—his business required him to turn south, and at one prominent junction, he and Jarl parted, each traveling their separate ways.

Next were the Province of Nowell and its capital city of Foord. Now the residents called the stage road not as the Foord Road, but the Atwa Road, as it led to the provincial capital of Kettlewand. Despite the congested traffic and Jarl's frequent conversations with other travelers, he was lonely, missing Alfheim's easy company, and it took him another week to reach Foord. Twice he passed blackened, charred posts set a short distance from the highway, where other travelers said sorcerers had been burned to death, freeing their souls for their afterlife. And it was in Foord that he intersected the road from Greenlands and, after two sets of conflicting directions, found the highway to Tyr.

The elevation in Nowell was less than the Kettlewand Plateau and, as the weather warmed, it suddenly seemed as if every hardwood tree was budding and everywhere, flowers and green grass sprouted from the ground. Toward the east were the flat coastal plains of Ringhorn, and the high, precipitous massif of the Sabre Mountains now dominated the skyline to the south. Somewhere in that direction, at the base of the mountains, was the city of Tyr.

Jarl traveled the next few days with a group of merchants who were hurrying south to some appointment; however, at a high, arched stone toll bridge that crossed the cold, white-crested Nanoo River and marked the guarded border between Nowell and Kamiar, the province in which Tyr was located, there was some confusion and delay over a product the traders were carrying. Jarl rode on ahead and spent the night at a small inn that had been constructed around the intricate root systems of two huge living walnut trees. The next day, he lingered, waiting on his merchant acquaintances, but by mid-morning—when they had not arrived—he mounted the gray and followed the highway south toward the tall line of mountains.

He nooned on a high knoll, west of the road. He could look east, out across a lowland of deep, blue-green grasses and trees. This was the Province of Ringhorn, which lay between the young mountains and the Aegonian Ocean, located some two hundred kilometers to the east. Directly below his feet flowed the Nanoo River, now a sluggish liquid highway winding through the agricultural heartland of Vanir, blocking all travel in that direction.

Finally, after a short nap, Jarl tightened the cinch on the gray, mounted, rejoined the road, and turned south. Five days later, in a cold April drizzle, he passed through the northern gate of Tyr, capital city of the Nation of Vanir and home to both the Vanir Church and his Supreme and Royal Majesty, King William Host Lostkoth, of the ancient lineage of Vanir.

CHAPTER TWELVE:

TYR

Jarl had been born and raised in a rural and sparsely populated area of Earth. Nevertheless, he had been to many of the great, congested terrestrial metropolises, such as New York, Denver, Calgary, San Francisco, Honolulu, and Jakarta; to Lunar, Dejah Thoris, Ganymende, and Jasper, huge urban areas on other planets and moons within Sol's solar system; and to the two great three-dimensional cities that hung in deep space, Echo Blue and Discount. Compared to these, Tyr was a small town, a tiny village. But, nevertheless, the Vanir's capital bustled with a relatively frantic activity, and the residents carried themselves with a certain pride, sure in their knowledge that they were just a little bit better than their countrymen, simply because they lived in Tyr, not only the capital city of the nation, but also the provincial capital of Kamjar.

Tyr was located at the confluence of the Nanoo and Vilyur Rivers, which formed the brackish Greymist River, a sluggish, wide tidal estuary that flowed slowly across the wide agricultural plains of Vanir to the Aegonian Ocean. Behind the city rose the inevitable highland; but, instead of a low, rounded series of hills, Tyr was back-dropped by the steep, outright precipitous Sabre Mountains, whose lesser peaks dominated the western skyline. South, along the edge of this massif, were the provinces of Smyrna and Southern, the latter guarding Bell's Pass, the gateway to the Royal and Most Holy Empire of Glassitron.

Four tall columns of jet-black volcanic stone, two on each side of the highway, marked the northern entrance to Tyr. Behind each set of columns, a low stone wall led off into the distance. On the right were the inevitable military barracks and, on the left, was the acient, tall, volcanic statue of a virile, one-armed warrior, who Jarl assumed was the old Norse war god for whom the city was named. A score of foot soldiers, armed with short pikes, stood in relaxed poses on both sides of the road, but no one made any attempt to stop or question Jarl or any of the other many travelers. There were no gates, nor was there an arch over the columns.

To Jarl's right, about two kilometers away, was the square bulk of the capitol, constructed of a massive red stone, and despite the cold drizzle, pink in the early morning light. Clustered around it were other large, but relatively smaller structures, built of the same stone, which Jarl assumed served some purpose in the business of the State. Across a square dominated by an immense, black obelisk was a tall, dark, steep-roofed building, easily the second-largest structure within the city. This, Jarl knew, was the city's cathedral. Built into the steep mountainside behind the capitol building was the wide, stately home of the King and Queen, a many leveled palace with an appearance of great bulk. Behind the city was a high, craggy peak, small compared to the broken massif in the background, and a grassy mountain valley, from which a long, silver thread of water fell, becoming the Vilyur River. Tyr, with its red buildings and backdrop of steep, snow-covered mountains, was an incredibly beautiful city.

In the other direction, below the highland and next to a wooden bridge across the Nanoo River, Jarl could see many small sailing vessels tied to a long series of wharfs. Each ship had between one and three masts. Some were lateen-rigged, others had furled square sails. To the southeast, the Greymist River widened and became bay-like, with dark shores of conifer forests. Far along its northern shore, Jarl could see the smoke and buildings of another town.

Otis' directions for Tyr were very straightforward; also the tavern the old man had told him to seek out was located on the main highway, which was again called the Foord Road, and close to the northern gate. Soon Jarl sighted a large wooden sign marking the Soo-Hoo, a large, two-story inn built of stone and heavy oak. A thread of smoke flowed from one of the two brick chimneys. Behind the tavern was an equally large stable and in front of the building were two long benches, a hand pump, a water trough with a metal cup, and two hitching rails, empty of horses. Jarl dismounted and tied both horses to the rail, and slowly climbed the steps to the tavern.

It was dim inside. Half the first floor was a large common room, lit and heated by a huge fireplace. There was a wooden floor, tables and chairs of heavy oak, and a long plank bar across the back wall. A teenaged, white-aproned girl stood behind the bar, drying heavy ceramic mugs. As Jarl entered, she looked up questioningly. When he mentioned Otis' name, the girl turned and shouted through an open doorway for her mother. A moment later, a stout woman bustled into the room, and Jarl introduced himself, repeating Otis' name.

The matron immediately hugged him in a bone-crushing embrace. She introduced herself, Thir Ahlum; her daughter, Sunny; her husband, Fjlar; and her son, Lif. The two men were visible through the open top half of a rear door, where they labored next to a small forge, shoeing a gigantic work horse. Despite Jarl's objections, Fjlar stopped his work and disappeared around the side of the house to bring Jarl's two horses to the barn. Thir explained the rent—it was twice that of the Pepper Ford Station, but included shelter, grain, and water for the horses. Meals were extra.

The woman seemed to be in a perpetual hurry. She led Jarl toward his room, winking and saying only the best was good enough for a friend of Otis', then she asked about the health of the old man and Teague and Aaron. She talked on, bubbling over with an internal joy, but Jarl managed to bring her to a stop long enough to tell of Teague's death. Thir flung her hands to the sides of her face and stood silent for most of a minute, then she led him up a narrow and dark stairway to an equally narrow hall. At the end of the hall—the house was L-shaped, and there was more of it than first met the eye—was a small bedroom with one shuttered window, which the woman threw open for a view of Fjlar leading Jarl's two horses into a stable.

Jarl rushed downstairs and helped the man unsaddle his horses. Then, with the same speed, he carried his two packs upstairs and put them in his room. He hid his modern weapons, keeping only his small projectile pistol, which he secreted in a pocket of his camouflage jacket. Afterwards, he helped Fjlar brush and feed the packhorse and the gray, and he paid one month's rent, giving Thir a little extra money as credit toward his meals. Then, after eating a small lunch with the Ahlums—where they lingered long at the table, discussing mutual friends and the long road between

Tyr and Kettlewand—Jarl wandered out into the great city, to explore it for himself.

Most of the avenues and alleys of Tyr were cobblestone or brick, with ample drains for water and sewage. Because the High Mayor of Tyr paid men to collect the garbage and haul it somewhere outside the city, the place was much cleaner than any of the other Vanir cities Jarl had visited. He spent the next few days walking the byways, seeing what was open to him and what was not, sampling the many foods and wines, having meals in different taverns, and listening to the conversations of the city's residents and its many travelers. He attempted to meet with a representative of the King; he asked about Enrick von Rhinehart and Liebs Hisson, and was told they were off campaigning; and once—from a distance—he caught a glimpse of the Glassitron ambassador.

Most of the people of Tyr wore clothing of the New Style: practical trousers and dresses, with many buttons and long sleeves. Along the long road from Kettlewand, Jarl had seen many of the Church's men and women, and—with few exceptions—they had all worn drab gray robes of coarse, inexpensive wool. In Tyr, however, both the Glasseys and the Vanir clergy worn Old Style clothing—expensive, long-flowing, brightly colored robes and wide-brimmed hats, from which multicolored tassels often hung. Another indication of the Church's power was the three-meter-high brick wall that encircled the tall, black cathedral—which was the only place of worship in Tyr and which had been constructed with many wide doors. This was a surprise, and Jarl found that—except on Sundays—the church was not open to the public.

One morning, Jarl mounted the dapple gray and rode south. He crossed the Vilyur River on a long, well-built wooden bridge constructed directly above the flashing white water where the river dropped to become the Greymist River. He rode through the outskirts of the city and encountered a small group of dirty women with tear-streaked faces, wailing, and coming from a path to the right. Jarl turned his horse and followed that crude road for a half of kilometer. He passed two small carts, each pulled by a single ox, a dozen sword-carrying guards—all wearing green armor—and two clergy, who wore the red robes of the Church's ruling class. From behind them, up the way they had come, he could hear screaming, a terrible pain-filled sound.

No one barred his way and he continued up the trail. The screaming had stopped by the time he arrived in a small hollow next to the steep side of the mountain. There, Jarl discovered a repulsive sight—the hollow was a place of pain and death, where the Church executed sorcerers, burning them alive. Piles of deep, white ash surrounded three fire-blistered iron posts, and bent and grief-stricken family members rooted among the still hot coals, attempting to recover the black and twisted remains of their loved ones. Other clusters of mourners walked this way and that, crying, wailing to the sky, searching for someone they could not find. Two dried corpses hung, unclaimed and unwanted, waiting to be cut down.

Two fires still burned. One was at the feet of an ancient man, who was a naked, shriveled ball of half-burned flesh. While Jarl watched, the cord that bound him broke and he fell, throwing ash into the air. The other prisoner was the black skeleton of a young girl, who still wore part of a filthy dress. Dirty, armored guards piled more wood around the feet of both corpses. To one side stood three more of the Church's priests, suspiciously watching Jarl. There was nothing Jarl could do, and he turned the dapple gray to the northwest and rode up a long hill, leaving the awful bowl-like depression. He rejoined the river, and walked his horse upstream, attempting without success to forget what he had just seen, until he was under the cold spray of the towering waterfall at the head of the narrow mountain valley.

On another day Jarl crossed the Nanoo River on a second wooden bridge and rode south of the city to Ispwich, the town by the Greymist River. On yet a third occasion he skirted the portion of the city south of the Vilyur River and rode into the steep foothills of the Sabre Mountains. Once he spent a full day walking along the docks and wharfs, and—after being invited—climbing through and inspecting several of the coastal and ocean-going sailing ships.

Jarl spent three days in a large open warehouse that belonged to the King's stage company, making suggestions and helping to build the new Concord stagecoaches. Eight were now completed, and the manager there paid him 80 dollars in newly minted silver money. This—and his traveling money—he secreted in a sack he hid behind the head of his bed. He also dismantled his modern blaster rifle and hid that and his blaster pistol in his packs in his upstairs bedroom.

Despite his numerous trips to the capitol and the palace, Jarl never received an appointment with the King or any of the King's representatives. Finally—close to two weeks after he had arrived in Tyr, and following an all-morning wait—he was able to meet with an agent for an importing company that regularly traded within the Royal Empire of Glassitron. The man was haughty and overweight, but was willing to accept a bribe and allow Jarl to pay for an over-priced lunch at Tyr's most-exclusive restaurant. Afterwards, the agent promised to see what could be discovered within the Empire about Kvasir's whereabouts. Jarl left the meeting feeling depressed and knowing it had been an expensive waste of time. With few options left, he decided to prowl the riverside bars, searching for sailors with a knowledge of the Empire, but he knew—somewhere deep inside himself— that the only way to find Kvasir was to travel to Glassitron himself.

Jarl spent most of the remaining afternoon at the stage building inspecting the new Concord coaches. Then, a full hour before supper, he returned to the Soo-Hoo and allowed Thir to shuck him out of the camouflage jacket, which she said needed cleaning. He then climbed the steep, narrow steps to his room, and collapsed on the bed. Although it was not his intent so close to meal time, he fell fast asleep.

The loud crash of the bedroom door against the back wall woke him. Jarl rolled, trying to be quick, and he reached for the one blaster pistol not in his packs. But the bed was soft and the weapon had slid down next to his body. His one mis-grab was the only chance he had. Two strong, heavyset men, who smelled of sweat and grease, jumped on top of him. One man tore at the pistol, which Jarl released when the man started to break his fingers. The men—and the three who followed—carried long broadswords and were dressed in heavy green leathers, polished to a bright sheen. Jarl had a brief glimpse of a thin, spiteful-looking man with a clean-shaven head, wearing heavy blood-red robes, and then a dirty burlap sack was thrown over his head.

Fists pounded into his side, and something hard was knocked against his head. His hands were jerked behind his back and tightly bound, and the sack was tied in place around his neck. He was hit a half-dozen more times, then his feet were bound together. One of his assailants picked him up and threw him over one shoulder, as if he was a heavy sack of feed. The man carried him down the hallway and narrow stairs. His head smashed against a door lintel, causing a loud thump, and something fell from one of his pockets and clattered down the stairs. On the first floor, he heard Thir's sharp and high-pitched protests, then the woman became abruptly silent.

Jarl felt the warmth of the sun on his back, then someone—he assumed it was the thin man in the blood-colored robes—gave an order, and he was thrown, face-down, into some kind of cart. He began to feel sick, and he could feel blood running down the side of his face. He started to tremble from fear and apprehension. Then, slowly, the cart bumped and creaked away from the tavern, its wheels sounding hollow and ominous on the cobblestone street. Then Jarl was clubbed once more over the head. This time, he passed out.

The next week was a nightmare. Jarl woke up in a small cell, less than three meters square, and constructed of massive, black sandstone blocks. The door was heavy oak, with no handle or window. The ceiling was also oak, black from age. In one corner of the cell was a small square hole that looked and smelled like a latrine. Two meters above this hole was a narrow slit, only a few centimeters wide, through which—during the day—a bit of reflected light entered the cell.

He had been beaten badly. The left side of his face was bloody and that eye was partially swollen shut. Two teeth were loose. He could hardly move his right arm and his little finger ached from where his pistol had been wrenched from his grasp. The outside of his left thigh was bruised, from where he had been kicked, and Jarl was in such intense pain that it was all he could do to crawl across the tiny cell. His wrists and ankles had been cut by the narrow cord that had bound him, and his belt and good Kettle boots had been stolen.

Each afternoon Jarl was ordered against the back wall while the massive bolts behind the door were withdrawn. The oak door was opened and an unseen person would set a small loaf of hardtack and a wooden bucket of water inside the cell. The water had a faint smell and occasionally had a slightly greasy feel, but Jarl drank it and suffered no ill effects. Once the bread was moldy and he could not eat it, but usually—after he removed the crawling bugs—it was edible.

Jarl shouted at the guards, demanding someone in authority and questioning where he was. Once a chain was slammed against the outside of the door and someone yelled at him to quit his yapping, but the only answers he usually received were taunts and threats. The hard, stone floor was chilled from the long winter, and Jarl found it impossible to sleep on. He often trembled, terribly frightened and anxious because of his imprisonment, and he learned to rest, after a fashion, by squatting against one of the damp, cold walls. At least—he thought—there were no rats, but with nothing to occupy his time, the boredom was mind-numbing.

On the fifth morning in his cell, with no warning, there was the sound of the bolts sliding behind the door, and then the heavy oak door was slammed open. Two guards, wearing highly polished green leather, paced into the room. They grabbed Jarl and violently shoved him face first into one of the hard, stone walls, then they tied his hands together with thin strips of rawhide and pushed him out of his cell and into a stone-lined corridor. The passageway was lit only by one torch, set in an iron bracket near the end of the corridor.

On each side, every few meters, were oak doors, leading to other cells. At the end of the hallway was yet another heavy oak door, strengthened with black iron reinforcements. One of the guards—he was a big man with badly yellowed teeth—bellowed an order and then, after the bolts were pulled back, this door was opened, causing the single torch to flicker. Jarl was shoved through the opening and into a corridor lit by an unseen skylight. The guard there kicked him in the seat of the pants.

Jarl collapsed and rolled into a ball. The man kicked him in the ribs. The guard with the bad teeth shoved the first man away and hauled Jarl to his feet. He growled, "Upstairs," and pushed Jarl toward a short set of stone steps. Once more Jarl fell, but the guards pulled him back onto his feet and hauled him up the stairs. A second set of steps followed the first, and then there was a third oak door. One guard shouted, and the heavy iron bolts were slid back and the door was opened by someone on the outside.

Jarl was shoved through the opening. Now the walls were lined not with coarse rock, but with a brown sandstone, cut into smaller blocks and evenly finished. Sunlight entered through a series of high, vertical slits, placed every few meters along the corridor. The floor was a dark marble, with white calcite intrusions, polished to a bright hue. Jarl was pushed through a series of hallways by his guards, and was brought to a high double door, made of some wood other than oak. There they waited, with Jarl shaking so badly from fear that he could hardly stand.

After more than an hour, one of the doors opened and a figure stepped out of the room beyond. It was the thin, red-robed man from the Soo-Hoo. He glared at Jarl and motioned to the big guard with the bad teeth, who opened the other door. Jarl was shoved through the wide portal. Two of his guards followed, and—with a loud, ominous sound—the two doors were slammed closed.

Even as an outsider, Jarl quickly recognized the spacious, high-ceiling room as a courtroom. Bright sunlight poured in through a series of wide, tall windows. Expensive benches were set along each wall. On these a half-dozen nervous people waited. Jarl recognized no one. A line of guards, wearing green leathers lacquered to a high sheen, stood at rigid attention along the walls. Across the front of the room was a low wooden railing, polished with dark stain. Beyond that was a massive podium, where a thin figure sat, his head shaven clean, wearing the lemon-yellow robes of the Church.

Jarl was shoved forward through an opening in the wooden railing. To the right, a red-robed scribe sat behind a long, broad table with a heavy, black book in front of him. The man wore a distasteful expression. On Jarl's left was another long table. As near as he could tell, it was covered by his personal possessions, including the dismantled blaster, his samurai sword, his pistols, and his blue pack. The big guard shoved Jarl to his knees, then grabbed his hair and pulled his head back, forcing him to stare at the thin figure sitting high above him behind the podium.

This person—Jarl could not decide if it was a man or a woman—had a narrow, spiteful face. One bony hand rose in the air, and Jarl glimpsed the brown flash as a gavel slammed against the top of the podium. The hollow, loud sound echoed around the room. Jarl had ceased to shake when he had entered the room, but now his right leg began to uncontrollably quiver—he was that terrified. Then the person—judge, bishop, or priest—spoke, in an ominous, high-strung voice, empty of all emotion.

"You stand accused of sorcery against the High Church of Vanir, Protector of the Old Religion. How do you plead?"

Jarl was never more aware of his unwashed and unshaven condition. He had seen the terrible fate that awaited sorcerers in the valley south of the city, and his entire body was now trembling. But he made his voice as strong as possible and answered, "Not guilty!" The two words warranted a hard rap to the side of the head.

The voice boomed out once more, repeating the words, "You stand accused by the High Church of sorcery! How do you plead?"

"Not guilty!" Again his head was hit, this time with such force he fell to his side. The guard pulled him back to his knees and his head was again bent back, so that he had an uninterrupted view of the judge-priest. The face seemed even more spiteful, more hateful, more full of distaste. A tap-tap-tap sound filled the courtroom—it was one of Jarl's knees rapping against the cold, hard floor.

"Do you deny that you are a wizard?"

"Yes."

Jarl was again knocked to the floor, and he noticed—for the first time—that someone was marring the polished marble and calcite with fresh blood. Then, by his hair, he was hauled back to his knees, facing the judge-priest again. Warm, salty blood flowed from his nose, forcing him to gasp for air through his mouth.

The judge-priest continued, "Do you deny that seven weeks past, on the road between Foord and Atwa in the Province of Kettlewand, you, for no reason and with no provocation, shot and killed the High Sheriff of Glad, a man who was doing no more than his sworn duty to his Church, his god, and his nation by requesting a just and reasonable toll from you as you crossed the Church lands known as the Rhombus?"

Jarl said nothing. He was tired of examining the floor with his face.

"Do you deny this?"

Jarl remained silent, but he was even more terrified, again remembering the burned corpses south of Tyr.

"Do you deny that you used a witch-weapon to kill the High Sheriff, who was a duly appointed representative of the Church and King?" The bald judge-priest's face was pale white, and the mouth—when closed—was a thin red line. He-she waved a bony, white hand toward the table on Jarl's left. It suddenly occured to Jarl that the Sheriff of Glad was the red-haired bandit he had killed in eastern Kettlewand.

He was again clubbed on the side of his head. This time, he managed to stay on his knees.

The disembodied voice above him continued, "Do you deny that you used this same witch-weapon against the soldiers of the Church of the Royal and Most Holy Empire of Glassitron?" A pause. "We have reliable reports of your sorcery at the Battle near Burkes Ford."

Jarl felt dizzy and his mouth was dry. '*Was this person siding with the Glasseys?*' he wondered. He spoke, making his voice as strong as he could, "I deny it!" This warranted another hard rap to his head.

The judge-priest leaned over the podium and glared at him. The loud voice engulfed him. "Are not these your immoral tools of your witchcraft?"

Jarl did not answer. He was again knocked onto his face. More blood marred the marble floor. He was pulled back to his knees, and the judge-priest spoke again, this time in a voice that was a low, purring growl, "Where did you obtain these tools of sorcery?"

The judge-priest then leaned forward even more, so that he-she was towering over Jarl. The question was repeated, even more softly, "Where did you get these tools of sorcery? These weapons? Tell me where you obtained them!"

Jarl knew he could not answer this question. He said nothing, and he was again knocked forward onto the floor. A guard pulled him back to his knees. The bald judge-priest leaned back, almost out of Jarl's sight. There was a long, loud sigh and the person bent forward and, once again, glared down at Jarl. The thin line of the mouth disappeared with disapproval. Jarl decided, clean-shaven head or not, this person was a woman.

The voice rang out again, "Do you deny that you are a wizard, a sworn enemy of the High Church of the Old Religion and of the people of the exalted Nation of Vanir, and a traitor to the High King?"

Jarl managed to squeak out a weak, "Yes, I deny that," before he was slapped sideways by the big guard. His head was then pulled back once more, so that he was again facing the judge-priest. The blood continued to flow down off his chin, and—for a moment—the room spun and he felt as if he would throw up.

The woman leaned back slightly and turned to her scribe. Her voice was arrogant and full of authority, "Let the record show that this wizard should be burned at the stake at dawn."

Jarl felt his heart catch in his throat, but the woman continued, "However, I am in a lenient mood today. He will instead be sentenced to five years hard labor at a Church prison and all his worldly possessions duly confiscated by the Church. May God have mercy on his soul! Court dismissed!" Once more the pale hand rose into the air, and once again there was a streak of brown and the hard slam of the gavel.

Jarl shouted, "Don't I get a chance..." He was interrupted by a violent slap to his head. The big guard then shook him, so that blood sprayed everywhere, then the man grabbed his hair and bent his head backward yet again. This time the judge-priest appeared to be reeling in a hazy fog.

The woman was incensed. She leaned over the podium and bellowed down at Jarl at the top of her voice. "Are you so insolent that you have no respect for your Church, your God, and your state? Are you so arrogant that you cannot even be silent for a few holy moments, while..." The woman was sputtering and spitting, and excitedly waving one of her hands, "While... while... the Holy Church takes some of its precious time to show mercy on your most unholy soul and allow you the one chance for the holy redemption that you are so unworthy of?"

The woman sat down, slowly and with purpose, then she continued, her manner and voice more reasonable. "You should be most thankful I have not ordered you burned at the stake, wizard, to free your soul from the Devil you so gladly gave it to, to obtain your craft of sorcery." She paused, then spoke again, in almost a whisper, "I will make you a deal. I will not burn your worthless person at the stake, if you only tell me where you obtained your witch-weapons."

Jarl's trembling began again. He said nothing.

The woman waited for most of a minute, then she leaned forward again and spoke again, this time in a loud voice, "You may count yourself very lucky today, wizard. I will not have you burned, and I will only add two more years hard labor to your already lenient sentence. Next time, show more respect to your Church, wizard!" With that, the woman slammed down her gavel one last time and again bellowed, "Court dismissed!"

Jarl was hauled to his feet and led from the courtroom. The red-robed priest, now wearing a very satisfied smile, waved with one hand and two guards dragged Jarl through a series of stone corridors and an outside door to a large iron cage with high, iron-rimmed wheels. Seven despondent and dirty prisoners were already inside, many dressed only in a few tattered and pungent rags. A few were fettered with iron chains around their legs and arms. A guard opened an iron door, and, after his thongs were cut, Jarl was unceremoniously heaved inside.

There he lay for a few moments, brushing the dirty, foul-smelling straw from his eyes. Then he crawled over to the wide iron bars, and the red-robed bald priest secured the door with a long spike of iron and gave him a last, long look of satisfaction. Then the vehicle lurched forward, rolling down the street, pulled by a single ox.

The journey was slow. They proceeded south, bouncing over the rough cobblestone streets. Green-armored guards led and followed the wagon. People stared or quietly watched. Others threw bits of garbage or spoiled food, shouted profanities, and called them demons and wizards. Jarl saw no one he knew. He cursed himself for not noticing the Church's spies who must have been watching him, and for allowing himself to be taken prisoner.

By early afternoon they had left the city, rumbling across the wooden Nanoo River bridge and descending onto the flat coastal plain. There, the cart and the seven guards followed the main road east, finally turning off on a sandy sidetrack that led southeast.

The night was spent under the bloody eye of Mytos, next to a small stream and a dark grove of tall conifers. From somewhere in the forest, a screech owl voiced its lonely lament. The guards gathered around a campfire and drank whiskey until they passed out. Jarl knew this was his one chance to escape, and he crawled around the interior of his cage, moving the other seven dispirited prisoners back and forth. It was a desperate situation—all the bars along the sides were tight and strong, as was the iron lid across the top. The wooden floor, discolored from the excretions of many men, was oak solid. The hinges of the door were strong and well-made and it did not matter how easily he could remove the iron pin, as the guards had taken the precaution of backing the cart up against one of the massive conifer trees. The door would not open, and with the cart's tongue buried in the soft sand and weighted with a large rock, Jarl could not rock the vehicle forward more than a few millimeters. Daylight found him tired, and still trapped inside his cage.

The next morning, the guards ate a slow breakfast and then, once more, the ox was hitched to the front of the cart and they began their snail-like journey, now to the east. Jarl hung on the bars, as despondent as the other prisoners. Twice they passed small groups of priests heading toward Tyr, heads bent under gray cowls. It was late afternoon when the cart and its escort arrived at a fenced camp. There, wooden gates swung open and the high-wheeled vehicle rolled into a wide, sandy compound.

The green-armored guards of the Church were everywhere. Many carried whips or leather bludgeons. There were nearly a dozen wooden buildings, several of which were half buried in the yellow sand. To one side was a forge and anvil, set over a slab of gray crystalline rock. Beside that, four groups of two inmates waited, each of who was chained to a dead man lying on the sand.

Of the new arrivals, Jarl was freshest. He now wondered how long his fellow prisoners had been locked in those hard stone cells, waiting for their trial, and he worried that this was how Kvasir had met his fate. Had the old wizard been one of those who died, condemned as a sorcerer, locked up in some small, dark cell somewhere in the Empire?

Jarl was pulled from the cage and shoved to the forge. Two chained prisoners, dragging their near-naked corpse with them, moved of their own accord toward the rock. While Jarl waited, forced to his knees, a barrel-chested smithy raised his heavy hammer high in the blue sky. Then, in a blur, he struck at the leg iron on the corpse. With that one blow, the rivet sheared. Jarl was hauled to his feet and shoved forward, over the dead man. He was brutally twisted around, so that the back of the leg iron could be pressed against a small indentation in the anvil. Using tongs, a guard placed a small, red-hot rivet into the square slot in the cuff. The back of the cuff was pressed against the anvil, and the smith's hammer rang down— terrifying in its violence—no more than twice. The rivet was set in place.

A guard stepped forward, and—pushing—ordered Jarl away from the forge. Somehow, in spite of the short iron chain, Jarl was able to move backwards. A whip slapped across his back, bringing a sharp pain. The prisoner on the opposite end of the chained trio, a man about his own age, grabbed the corpse by one leg, and Jarl did the same with the other leg. The third and middle prisoner—an elderly, stooped man with a long, filthy beard—stood unmoving in one place, muttering to himself, and getting in the way. Jarl imitated the younger man and guided the old, fumbling man with his free hand. A guard motioned them toward a deep ditch.

Somehow—and in spite of the old prisoner—the two younger men pulled the corpse to the trench, which was a latrine, and heaved the dead man in.

They then waited by the trench until three prisoners had replaced the three corpses lying on the ground. The remaining three inmates were then chained together into one group, and they all shuffled off to a large, open pavilion. Here, they sat on the ground, waiting, and watching a dozen unchained inmates stir large, black iron caldrons of some unknown liquid.

Finally, near dusk, Jarl heard the sounds of shuffling feet and the shot-like sounds of whips. Then, from the south, together with a low cloud of yellow dust, there appeared a long line of dirty and exhausted prisoners. The inmates with Jarl were ordered to their feet. One man took too long to stand and Jarl saw the flash of a whip and heard it crack on the man's back. The inmate fell, but his two chain mates, fearful of the same whip, quickly pulled him back to his feet. Jarl and his two companions stumbled forward and, with the long line of dispirited prisoners behind them, each took a wooden bowl of some vile-smelling green goulash. Then, using their fingers, they began to eat.

CHAPTER THIRTEEN:
THE CHURCH'S PRISON CAMP

The Church's prison camp consisted of eleven buildings surrounded by a tall lattice fence and a dark, uninhabited conifer forest. There were two sets of gates, one in the front and a second, behind the stables, facing the morning's sunrise. Four of the buildings were half-buried log structures, and each held between 200 and 300 prisoners. The remaining structures were all built above ground and, other than a small stone spring house, were either stables or bunkhouses for the guards. Meals were served from an open shed that was nothing more than a roof supported by four posts.

The days in the camp slowly became weeks, and the weeks settled into a long, hard, brutal routine. The nights were spent in the rough-hewn log structures. Entry was through a massive trap door that, each morning, the guards lowered to form a ladder. After climbing out over the trap door and shuffling off the flat roof onto the adjacent sand dunes, the chained trios of prisoners were divided into rough phalanxes and counted. Thirty minutes was allowed for visits to the slit latrines and breakfast, which consisted of a cold bowl of rice or stew and an occasional bit of hard, salty bread. The cooks were unchained prisoners—many of whom were missing arms or the lower part of their legs—who also filled in and dug the long slit latrines, and removed those prisoners who had died during the night from the log prisons.

After their short breakfast, the inmates were marched—if the slow discouraged stumble of many chained feet could be called a march— through the rear gate and east for two kilometers. There, protruding from the flat coastal plain, were two large, rounded hummocks of granite. Tools were produced from an open shed and, each day, the prisoners drilled and cut the hard, fine-grained igneous rock into large blocks of gray stone. Then, using ropes, pry bars, pulley systems, and oak rollers, these blocks were wrested first from the quarry and along a flat, sandy road. A long half kilometer north was a wide, shallow estuary. Here, the granite was carefully loaded onto sailing ships owned by free merchants or onto foul-smelling, oared slave ships belonging to the Church.

On Jarl's first day at the quarry, a thick manila rope broke and, as the long line rattled and whisked through the wooden pulleys, one of the massive rocks slid downhill and over three teams of chained prisoners, instantaneously crushing eight of the men. The guards were in a grim mood, and they axed the last man, who was uninjured by the accident. Then, after the chains had been removed by severing the legs of the dead inmates, all nine corpses were thrown into the water of an abandoned section of the quarry and, for the next week, the bloated, sun-blackened remains floated in one corner of the deep, green pool.

The prisoners were allowed only one thirty-minute break each day, which was the only time they could relieve themselves, while the guards ate a noon meal. Starvation, dehydration, and disease were rampant. Each day, one hour before dusk, the prisoners returned their tools to the shed and then shuffled, bone-tired and dispirited, in a huge cloud of yellow dust, back to the prison camp. There they stood, half asleep on their feet—rain or shine—and listened to a long sermon to the greater glory of god and an afterlife that most of the prisoners—including Jarl, convicted of sorcery—would not be permitted to enjoy. Finally, after they were served more rice or soup and counted one last time, they were herded off to the slit trenches and the log dungeons. Often, because of the chilly nights, they had to spend the nights huddled together for warmth.

The middle prisoner of Jarl's trio was an old, white-haired man, thin from untold years in the Church's care, who had a filthy beard that reached his waist and who provided his two companions with a continual source of lice and other small bugs. The old man raved, drooled, talked to himself, and swung his hands this way and that, often slapping his two chain mates in the face. He could be counted on to tangle the shackles, to fall off the ladder while climbing in and out of the log structures, to almost slip into the slit trenches, or to knock over the stacks of wooden bowls in the so-called kitchen. Each offense brought a guard with a whip or a club, and each time the punishment was doled out, not just to the old man, but to all three men in the chain gang.

Sleeping, the old man was no better as a companion; he snored, scratched, kicked, and would jerk the short chains toward him. At the quarry, he was downright dangerous, often stopping in front of the moving granite blocks, tangling the ropes, and once, falling into the green pool beside the quarry, dragging the two men chained to him into the dark, dirty water.

But, as bad as his situation was, Jarl counted himself lucky—immensely lucky in fact. The third man of his chain gang was an intelligent, sharp-eyed, dark-haired man about his own age who hailed from the Province of Nowell. The man was small and agile, and surprisingly—despite years in the prison—had no more than a shadow of facial hair, less than Jarl's beard when he arrived at the work camp. The first night, after they were herded into the log dungeons, the man introduced himself as Navee Odror, imprisoned for—of all things—punching a high priest in the nose. Navee was, in spite of the prison camp, almost always in a good humor, and telling his story was no exception.

However, when Jarl asked the little man how long he had been in the prison, Navee had become silent. The answer was a sobering six years. Twice, when the elderly prisoner was otherwise occupied, Jarl attempted to mindbeam Navee, keeping his thoughts concentrated and narrow. But both times, the little man did not answer.

Navee told Jarl that the old man he was chained to was a very famous prisoner: Jonson Baeldaeg, a rogue priest who—twenty years before—had, together with several companions, translated the Church's Bible into English. At the time, there had been a large, well-publicized trial in Tyr. All of Jonson's friends had been executed, and he alone had been kept alive, mostly to locate the surviving translated Bibles. Navee shook his head, perplexed when Jarl said he had never heard this story—the trial had been widely publicized, even on the remote Kettlewand frontier.

Jarl quickly discovered he had a valuable trade item. Even though his torn Kettle shirt quickly turned to rags and fell from his body, his long trousers, although worn, were very much in demand. The prisoners all wore short pants in various degrees of disrepair. Someone had had the forethought to smuggle several iron needles and thread—an invaluable commodity—into the camp, and a few of the prisoners used scraps from Jarl's trousers to repair their own thin pants. As the weeks grew into months, and spring became the muggy heat of summer, Jarl traded lengths of his ever-shortening trousers for an extra drink of water or bowl of food, a crushed fern that relieved the pain of his broken blisters, a cleaner spot for the three of them to spend the night, and even—once—a small bar of soap.

One night, about a week after his internment, Jarl, Jonson, and Navee were approached by another trio of prisoners. Two of these men were huge, and the third was an ancient, stooped man with a long, dirty beard and a face full of open sores, who the other two pulled across the crowded dungeon floor. These three inmates commonly beat and took food from other prisoners, and now, as they shuffled across the dark, moon-lit interior of the dungeon, the larger two men kicked and shoved sleeping prisoners out of the way. No one fought or pushed back.

The two larger men concentrated on Jarl. One of them pointed at Navee and snarled, "Stay out of this, little man!"

Jonson cowed against the wall, huddled into a small, whimpering ball of trembling hair and flesh. He hampered Jarl by pulling tightly on the short chain.

Jarl was terrified, as he was almost powerless, and he knew these men were bullies and victim makers of the worst kind. He spoke, fighting to keep his words strong: "We want no trouble."

Navee tried to stand, at the same time calling the largest man Jessup. With one hand, that man shoved Navee back to the floor. The thump of the smaller man against the rough timbers of the wall and the rattle of his chains resounded across the dark interior of the log building. Jarl glanced skyward, through the lattice work of prison roof, but no guard was silhouetted there—not that they would have helped.

Jonson had been pulled off balance when Jessup had knocked Navee against the wall. Jarl took the opportunity to pull the chain toward him, and he rose to his feet as he did so. He waited in a half crouch, his weight on his chained left foot, his right foot well behind him, for the big man to move closer. Jessup was very sure of himself. The big man grinned, a slow greasy sort of smile, evil in its implications. He wove his hands in a confident manner and moved closer. The other two men shuffled along behind him, attempting to keep up.

Then Jonson, who had resumed his curled fetal position, yanked hard on the chain and pulled Jarl's left foot out from under him. As he fell, Jarl had a glimpse of the old man, his eyes wide, his hands against his mouth, shivering against the wall. Jessup lurched forward, reaching down for Jarl.

Jarl pivoted on his back, trying to get his one free foot into the air, between his body and Jessup. To his left, he heard a hard slap, slap, slap—the impact of a solid object against flesh. One of Jessup's chain mates fell on the floor, followed by the second. Jessup spun on the balls of his feet toward the unseen threat, and Jarl saw a quick flash of something white hitting Jessup's knee. The white object flashed again—it was one of Navee's feet. This time it hooked behind the knee and pulled the bigger man off balance. Navee was lying on the small of his back, kicking, and—even as Jessup fell—his free foot flashed out, three more times in quick succession, twice striking Jessup on the side of his thigh, and the third time, full in the big man's face.

Jessup rolled on the floor, withering in pain, blood pouring from his mouth, holding the outside of his thigh. He started to stand again, but Navee's foot again smashed into his mouth. Then, slowly and full of pain, the big man and his two friends crawled moaning back across the confines of their dark prison. Jarl was finally able to pull himself into a sitting position, a little away from Jonson. He looked at Navee in wonder and said a quiet thanks.

As the days passed, the blisters on Jarl's hands became calloused. His back became sunburned and then tan, crossed by the many marks of the guards' whips. Navee smeared it with mud his first few days at the quarry, to keep it from burning too severely. The little man said that, in summer, many of the newly arrived prisoners became so burned that they chilled and died in the cool nights. Jarl's feet became hard and his digestive system managed to withstand the poor quality of the food. He lost weight, but he did not become as rail thin as many of the inmates. And he discovered that all the inmates—himself included—suffered terrible bouts of diarrhea, even after their systems had become conditioned to the food and water.

The wounds and bruises Jarl had received at the hands of the Tyr guards gradually healed—they had been for the most part superficial—but he acquired new injuries daily, usually from the guards' whips and clubs, but sometimes rope burns, or bruised fingers from the hammers and drills, and once a smashed thumb, received while pulling Jonson out of the way of a large granite block.

Navee was the most important person in the work force. Not only did he understand the quarrying methods, but it was he who taught Jarl how to swing the heavy hammers while hitting the long iron bit that Jonson held, supposedly turning it a little between each blow.

All morning long, while unshackled inmates brought sharpened bits from a forge at the base of the quarry, the three men would drill holes in the hard granite. To achieve the required depth, an iron extension was attached to the bit. Often, the bit would wedge in the hole, particularly when Jonson was slow to rotate it. This warranted a beating from the guards, one that was brutal and often migrated to Jarl and Navee, but nevertheless, the long iron rods were occasionally stuck so badly that they had to be left in the hole. Finally, teams of prisoners, using iron pry bars, would attempt to crack the rock away from the face. Sometimes they ruined the granite block, but most of the time the massive rock popped free.

Jarl was immensely thankful the jobs were rotated at midday. Even after working half a day, his hands were so strained that he could hardly lift the heavy hammer, much less swing it. The afternoons were spent using long hemp ropes to pull the heavy granite blocks along wooden rollers from the quarry to the estuary. There was a wharf at the water's edge, and another group of prisoners worked a monstrous oak crane, lifting each stone and carefully setting it inside the vessel.

Jarl had no intention of spending his entire sentence in the Church's prison. Since Navee was to have been released the previous year and had not been, he too was eager to leave. The two men talked of escape constantly, but with close to a hundred guards, they knew their chances were slim. Over the weeks they managed to wander the length of their log stockade, dragging an unwilling Jonson with them. No timbers were rotten or broken and, although the floor was sand, there was no way, without timbering materials, that they could dig under the log sides of the prison. There were too many guards in the camp to escape over the high wooden camp fence, especially dragging an unwilling Jonson, and Jarl was unsure if he wanted to leave the old man behind to be noticed.

With the camp eliminated as a place from which to escape, all that was left was the quarry and the estuary. The best plan the two men could think of was to wait for a convenient diversion, break their chains open with the hammers, and then make a run for it. Since none of the guards carried firearms, it would be a simple matter of dodging their wardens and sprinting to the conifer forest, three hundred meters away. The problem was there was always a mounted patrol somewhere in the vicinity of the quarry, and the one time Jarl and Navee saw three prisoners break and run for the woods, these horsemen had easily ridden the stumbling men down and killed them with the long pikes they carried.

Navee's eyes often narrowed and glowed with an animal-like cunning, and he advised caution. One night he confessed that he was an E'landota, trained since childhood in the arts of stealth and close combat. "Perhaps," he said, "if we are ever left with just one or two guards, we might be able to kill them and escape."

Jarl was not enthused about that plan, and he suggested that it might be possible to hide in the quarry or the estuary one evening and then sneak away after everyone had left. But, whatever their differences on how to escape, they were both in agreement on one thing, and that was that they would only have one chance—all prisoners who attempted to get away and who were caught were killed on the spot. And with an ancient, rogue priest, who would probably do everything he could to hinder their escape, Navee and Jarl would be doubly handicapped.

And if they escaped, Jarl was in favor of fleeing toward the mountains, whose snow fields were easily visible on a clear day, hanging cloud-like above the flat coastal plain, about a full day's hard march to the west. But Navee was insistent; not only were the mountains too far away, especially while dodging the Church's patrols, but their clothing was too light to withstand the cold mountain temperatures. "If would be better," Navee said, "if we hide in the swamps to the east."

As the summer wore on, Jarl's muscles became stronger, his tan darker, and his pants shorter. Once more, Jessup and his two friends tried to manhandle Jarl, Jonson, and Navee, this time trapping the small E'landota in a corner on the quarry. But Jarl pushed the stooped man off a ledge, which in turn pulled the second prisoner to the edge. As the guards moved in with their whips, Jarl, Jonson, and Navee quickly darted away, going back to work. The three bullies spent the next two days without food and water, imprisoned in a tiny log box buried in the hot sand inside the prison camp. They were in a foul mood when they were released, and Jessup glared insolently at Jarl, but they stayed well away from Jarl and Navee.

No diversion for escape at the quarry ever presented itself. One day, when the guards were distracted by a prisoner who had been crushed by one of the huge granite blocks, Navee quickly grabbed the chain at his feet and held a worn link against the head of his hammer. Jarl hit the link with his hammer. The sharp sound was obviously different than the dull noise made by a hammer striking a drill bit, but no guard paid any attention. But, with the second hammer blow, Jonson dropped the drill. It clanged against the rock and a guard turned, and Jarl and Navee had to quickly pretend to be working. The guard then looked away, disinterested, and watched as the huge granite rock was moved off the crushed prisoner. Later, during the midday break, Navee and Jarl inspected the link for any damage caused by the two blows. They found none; the heavy iron chain was stronger than it appeared.

The two men could find no place to hide along the estuary—the water was frustratingly clear and there were no high grasses next to the wharf. The quarry was always searched in the evenings, and there were no places big enough to hide in. Jarl, Jonson, and Navee were never picked for errands and there always seemed to be a multitude of guards nearby. Desperate, Jarl even tried digging out of the log structures. With no materials for timbering, his tunnel caved in before he had dug half his body length. Navee and Jarl contrived to be thrown into the tiny log prison for a day and a night to see if they could dig out of it after all the guards had left for the quarry. Here too, they were frustrated. The roof, ceiling, and walls were all thick pine logs, impossible to scratch through. The heat was so intense in the tiny building that, afterwards, it was all Jarl could do to stagger to the larger, square dungeon. The next morning, when he finally got his first drink of water, he was dizzy and sick from dehydration.

For three days, Jarl and Navee carried silt in their hands back to their prison-camp dungeon. Then, one night, as rain poured in through the open lattice roof, they mixed up a liquid mud and applied it to the inside of the shackle holding Jarl's ankle. While Navee pulled the chain in one direction, Jarl tried to pull his foot free of the chain. The iron cuff did not even come close to slipping off. They tried the same technique with Navee, with the exact same result. Finally, for lack of any plan at all, Jarl spent several hours each night rubbing one link in the chain with wet sand, hoping to wear it in two. During the day, he covered the shiny place with dirt, hiding it from the guards' eyes. Navee dryly observed that at the rate Jarl was wearing the link away, he would be lucky if he escaped before the next decade.

The summer wore on. Every five or six days, the ox-drawn, high-wheeled cart arrived, bringing more prisoners to replace those who had died or had been injured too badly to work. Every two weeks or so, a ship brought food supplies and another ox-drawn cart hauled this freight to the prison camp. Once, in mid-summer, several dignitaries of the Church inspected the quarry, traveling in brightly colored carriages draped with heavy cloth and pulled by matching teams of brown horses. The coaches were protected by a dozen of the Church's E'landota. Unlike the guards, these men wore not the dark-green polished leather, but rather a rose-colored leather, covered by flashy steel breastplates.

Jarl noticed Navee watching the Church's E'landota, nose flared and breathing quick, like a bird of prey, waiting for a meadow mouse to move. The clergy themselves were richly dressed in long, blood-red robes and wide, floppy hats trimmed with tasseled red balls. Jarl stared long and hard at the horses, and asked if it would be possible to steal one. Navee snorted, "No, pulling an armed E'landota from the saddle, even one of the Church's poorly trained E'landota, would result only in a quick death... Yours, not his."

By the end of August, Jarl had all but given up on escaping. He was waiting for cooler weather and some change in the routine. One night, the two friends had talked long after Jonson had fallen asleep, whispering around the old man's snoring. Navee spoke quietly, "We should be issued new pants about the end of October."

Jarl sighed. It was a long, desperate sigh. "Does it get that cold here in the winter?" he asked.

"It doesn't snow that much this far out on the coastal plain. One time, when it did, we were forced to tramp out a path to the quarry in our bare feet. Then we spent the day shoveling the snow off the rocks. But the next day, when we returned to the quarry, a warm wind had melted most of the snow."

For a long time Jarl was silent, envying his friend's clean, beardless face. Then he asked, "Tell me about your E'landota training."

At first Navee said nothing, then he spoke slowly, "I trained for ten years at the Great Southern Citadel... That's a tall castle in the southern Sabre Mountains constructed especially for that purpose..."

"How old where you when you started?"

"Thirteen..."

"How did they pick you?" Jarl asked.

"I was good at games. My family was poor and couldn't feed me. So I signed up."

"And the training?"

Navee shrugged, "It was hard, but nothing mysterious... Mostly they taught us unarmed combat, called the Open Hand. But they also taught us to use many weapons."

"Such as?"

"Flintlocks, crossbows, throwing knives, swords, long ash poles, garrotes, and shirvken..."

Jarl interrupted, "Shirvken?"

"Throwing stars with sharp points."

When Navee said nothing else, Jarl said, "Tell me more."

The little man paused for a long, long time, "Some E'landota are employed by the King, others work for the Church, the Vanir government, the Empire, the Roomians, and even the Ghost Raiders. There are also many Free E'landota, who owe their allegiance to no government or Church, and who work for merchants. All the E'landota, no matter what school, are trained along guidelines set down long ago, and each school's style is somewhat different and each says much about the individual E'landota."

"How many schools are there?"

Navee squinted, thinking, "All told, there are eight E'landota schools... one just outside New Hope, run by the Church... one in Southern... one in Greenlands, two in the Empire, one in Roomia, and a mysterious academy on one of the islands in the Cimarron Sea."

"And the Ghost Raiders?"

"I know nothing about their school, only that their E'landota are very good. And that they train women."

Jarl thought for a second, "The Roomians, Vanir, and Glasseys all have one religion, and the Ghost Raiders supposedly another. What do you know about that?"

Navee shook his head in exasperation., "Next to nothing... All I know is that, like the E'landota, the religions of all three countries are tied together, dating back to the beginning of time. And I know that the Church's E'landota are not very good. They spend too much time studying their scriptures and not enough time practicing the way of the E'landota."

About the middle of September, Jarl noticed the first advance in the snow fields high in the Sabre Mountains. One morning they tripled in size, and as the day warmed, they slowly became smaller and smaller. At noon, as the prisoners took their midday break, a carriage and an E'landota escort arrived. Again Navee watched excitedly. "These," he whispered, "are not from the Church. They are the King's men."

Three men disembarked from the coach. Only one wore the red robes of the Church; the other two wore dark, fashionable suits of the New Style. The captain of the Church guards joined the three men, then so did the captain of the King's E'landota. Three more of the King's E'landota walked behind the small group, their hands on the hilts of their curved samurai swords.

Some of the Church guards began to move toward the small group, but when the King's E'landota's nervousness increased, the red-robed priest waved off these men. Even from the distance, Jarl could see that the bald priest was upset and aggravated.

The priest gave an order and the captain of the Church's Guards repeated it. Other guards ran into the quarry, shouting at the prisoners, herding them down onto the flat in front of the quarry. Jarl and Navee moved slowly, hoping to find a chance to escape. But there was no opportunity. Together with the other inmates, they were forced down onto the flat. There they were grouped into their rough formations, similar to those in which the morning and evening head counts were taken. Navee's eyes were strangely excited and Jarl was intrigued, wondering what was afoot.

The Church guards were not happy. The King's E'landota were watchful and filled with a calm energy. Jarl suddenly realized that their numbers had somehow doubled—something important indeed seemed about to happen. The taller of the two King's representatives stepped forward, facing the prisoners. In one hand he held a yellow parchment. The man spoke, the paper still at his side, and his voice was loud and authoritative, easily carrying across the ragged lines of inmates.

"By order of his Supreme and Royal Majesty, King William the Third, the fifteenth ruler of the Nation of Vanir, on this, the last day of August, in the 712th year of our colony, it is hereby decreed that one fifth of all prisoners and slaves within the realm of Vanir shall be set free, on this, the first anniversary of the Great Battle at Burkes Ford, which took place in the Province of Kettlewand, on the body of water known as Bryan Creek, where General Enrick von Rhinehart and General Liebs Hisson defeated Guslov Kivlor, commander of the combined armies of the Royal and Most Holy Empire of Glassitron."

Jarl was startled. One part of his brain was frozen, not daring to hope that he would be set free. The other portion was racing, fleetingly noticing many facts. He memorized the year, and he wondered how the Vanir had lost their great technical skills in a mere 700 years. And mastodons—he had never seen a mastodon. Did they really exist? And, if they did exist, how did they come to be on this planet? In the short time he had known Otis, the old man had seemed to be neither a liar nor one to exaggerate.

And—Jarl's mind was still racing—space travel faster than the speed of light had only been achieved some 100 years ago, so how could these people have been on their planet for more than 700 years? And von Rhinehart was now a general—that was good, the man certainly deserved it. And, if this proclamation had been issued three weeks ago, why had it taken so long to travel a single day's ride from Tyr, the capital city?

Three of the Church's guards, the red-robed priest, the King's representatives, and two of the King's E'landota began walking the long lines of prisoners, indicating that each fifth chain gang should drop out and move to a point behind the coach. Occasionally, the tall representative would point to another chained trio and the fifth chain gang would be left standing with the remaining prisoners. Jarl, Jonson, and Navee were in the second line, and Jarl could not see the expressions on the rejected men's faces. Once an inmate jumped forward, grabbing the tall King's representative's feet, pleading to be taken. There was the sharp crack of a whip, but—in the end—two of the green-coated guards had to step forward and drag the resisting man back into his place in the line.

Jarl was finding it hard to breathe. He closed his eyes and listened to the prisoner crying and the two guards brutally beating him.

He opened his eyes. The small group of Church, E'landota, and the two King's representatives had turned the end of the first line and had started down the second line. Jarl leaned forward and tried to count ahead, to see what his number would be. He glanced at Navee. The little E'landota was standing quietly, his face expressionless, gazing unconcernedly off toward the conifer forest. More chained groups of three prisoners shuffled to the point behind the carriage. A wagon from the prison camp arrived, hauling the anvil and the smithy.

Finally, the oncoming group was close enough that Jarl could make his count. He, Navee, and Jonson were group number four. The three men immediately to his right were group number five. Jarl rocked back on his feet, feeling the count like a physical blow. He wondered if he should plead his case to the King's representative. He had fought at the Battle of Burkes Ford. Did he deserve his freedom any more than the other inmates? Perhaps Navee, imprisoned for a year longer than his sentence, would be a better person to argue.

Nearby, on his left, there was a harsh crack of a whip and Jarl was startled out of his self-pity with a jump. Now he could hear the voices, as the captain of the Church's guards counted off the chain gangs. Jarl closed his eyes, praying that he had counted incorrectly, or that the captain would count wrong.

This time, when he opened his eyes, the small group was directly in front of him. Jarl had counted correctly—he, Navee, and Jonson were number four. The captain of the guard waved the trio on their right toward the back of the coach. There, Jarl could hear the first rings of the iron hammer against an iron bracelet.

But then, the King's representative held up a gloved hand. He pointed at Jonson, and said, "We will take this group." His voice was a whisper.

The red-robed priest became even more nervous. His voice was high and strained, and his face suddenly white, "No, this group!" He pointed to the fifth trio, inmates so dispirited that they did not seem to realize they were on the verge of being set free. Jarl fought to control his frustration and fear. Never before had the priest argued when the King's representative had suggested changes.

The representative of the King merely arched an eyebrow skyward. He was a tall man, with craggy features, wavy brown hair, and incredibly shaggy eyebrows. He was dressed as a rich High Ejliteta, with expensive clothing and high felt boots that came to his knees. Jarl could see that his eyes were hazel, calm, and slightly amused.

The red-robed man repeated himself, his voice impossibly high, "This group! This group!" He pointed to the three men on Jarl's right.

For a long moment, the tall man simply stared down at the priest, then he again pointed at Jonson and said, in a voice almost too quiet to hear, "This group."

The clergy tried to speak one more time, but the captain of the King's E'landota stepped forward and placed one hand on the red-robed chest. The priest stopped sputtering, frozen at the action, as this was obviously an unthinkable atrocity against a clergyman. The air was suddenly very tense. The captain of the Church's guard moved forward, as did the guard behind him. But there was something in the calm expressions of the E'landota captain and the High Ejliteta that made the Church's captain pause. Then the tall man representing the King motioned, not at Jonson, but at Navee, and Navee stepped forward, dragging Jonson with him. Jarl risked a glance over his back. His shoulder blades had been crawling with the sensation of impending pain, either from a whip or sword blade. One of the Church's guards was directly behind him. This man smiled confidently at Jarl, his malicious eyes conveying some kind of unspoken message.

Afraid that the Church would somehow make their power felt, Jarl hurried Navee and Jonson toward the wagon with the anvil. There, instead of joining the lengthening line of prisoners, he moved to the front of the line. No one noticed. The smithy had hit his stride, and with each swing of the hammer, there was a loud clank and another rivet was sheared, another leg iron fell off, and another man was free.

Soon it was Jarl's turn. His leg was jolted by the blow, the iron cuff fell to the side, and—for the first time in five months—he stepped forward unencumbered by the heavy weight of the leg iron. Another two swings of the hammer and Jonson was free. A fourth swing and Navee was free.

One or two prisoners had begun hurrying west, looking over their shoulder, as if they were unable to believe their good fortune. Larger groups began to follow. Some freed inmates stood behind the wagon, staring off into space, unsure what to do next. One old man, his long beard brushing against his bony knees, was wandering back to the quarry, as if he was going back to work. In front of the wagon and coach, the red-robed priest and the representative of the King were still counting off the chain gangs of prisoners. Navee motioned at Jarl, and pointed west along the road. Jarl grabbed Jonson's arm and began propelling the old man in that direction.

Navee was perplexed, but when he saw that Jarl had no intention of leaving the rogue priest behind, he came back, grabbed Jonson's other arm, and together the two men began to push Jonson west toward the prison camp. Jarl risked one last look at the long line of inmates. The guard who had stood behind him was now relaxing against the wagon that had brought the smithy, his arms folded across his chest, looking directly at Jarl. That man caught Jarl's glance and, once again, he slowly smiled.

It was an ugly smile, and Jarl knew, somehow, this guard had special plans for him.

CHAPTER FOURTEEN:

THE ESCAPE

Jarl and Navee pushed and pulled Jonson down the sandy road, toward the prison camp. Jonson babbled and swung his hands this way and that, and twice he slapped Jarl in the face. Jarl was worried, mindful of the one guard's long stare, and afraid the Church would somehow renege on the pardon. The tension in the argument between the King's representative and the red-robed priest left him with the feeling that the Church had some particular interest in him, and him alone. Of course, he had to admit, they may have been concerned over Jonson, as the rogue priest had been an important prisoner.

Of the pardoned inmates, Jarl and Navee were by far the most determined to leave the quarry, passing and then leaving the other westbound refugees behind on the sandy road. The prison camp was just beginning to edge into view when Jarl stopped, still holding one of Jonson's arms. It took a few seconds for the old man's momentum to slow. Navee looked questioningly at Jarl.

"Do you really think the Church is going to let us go free?" Jarl asked.

"They have no choice," Navee said. "It was a King's pardon."

"I'm not sure. That one guard... he looked like he knew something we don't."

"Do you think they'll arrest us as we pass the camp?"

"I don't know."

Navee was still certain. "Even the Church cannot revoke a King's pardon. Do you want to wait for the representatives of the King?"

"Would they help us now?"

Navee thought for a long moment, hanging on to Jonson's arm as the old man wandered in a wide circle. "No," he answered. "We have been pardoned, but if something else were to happen... arranged by the Church..." He paused, thinking, then he asked quickly, "What do you want to do?"

"Go with our original plan. Head east."

"But we'll have to go back past the quarry."

"No. We'll take to the woods here and cross the road that leads to the wharfs. No one should be using them today. Then we'll keep going east, swing wide to the south, and keep off the main roads."

"Why not go east here?"

"There's too much of a chance we'd be caught."

"Are you sure about this? The Church can't revoke the King's pardon." Jonson had now completed a full circle and was facing west, toward the prison camp.

"But something can always be arranged. We could always be arrested for some minor offense. That guard seemed to have a special interest in us. And we were the only group the priest argued over."

Navee's eyes were wide. "That could have been a coincidence."

"Do you want to bet your freedom on a coincidence?"

The little man's eyes suddenly became narrow slits and his expression hardened, "No." He looked toward Jonson, silently asking an obvious question.

The ancient man was unneeded baggage and could call attention to them, but Jarl said, "For now, let's keep him with us. It would look suspicious if he was wandering by himself."

Navee shook his head, "I disagree. One old man alone won't bring attention to us... especially with so many newly freed prisoners wandering about, but if you want to take him, we will take him." He started to push the ancient priest toward the south side of the road, into the dark conifer forest.

Jarl caught Jonson's other arm. "Wait, they might have seen us from the camp." Navee stopped, and together they waited until the first group of pardoned prisoners reached their location on the road. Then, hoping the guards at the prison would be confused by the increasing numbers of men,

Jarl, Navee, and Jonson moved back toward the quarry and—as quickly as they could—darted for the forest.

Under the tall trees and out of the hot sun, the air was cooler, but with less breeze, it was muggy. Sweat was soon dripping from Jarl's face. There was little undergrowth—only a slightly rolling forest floor, covered with a carpet of pine needles—and, in spite of Jonson's relatively slow pace, they made good time, stumbling and running through the woods.

Then the forest became more open, with tangles of greenbriers. They fought through these for a few minutes, becoming scratched and scarred by the thorns. There was a small clearing, and for one brief moment they could see the bright reflection of the estuary, only a short distance in front of them.

The three men retreated, backing out of the briers. They turned east, keeping in the deeper forest on their left, and continued with a faster rate of speed. Within another kilometer, they encountered another wide band of greenbriers. This time, they crawled under the undergrowth. Ahead was a narrow field that, on closer inspection, proved to be the road between the quarry and the wharf.

Navee crawled out onto the grass a short distance and slowly stood. No one was in sight. Again pulling Jonson, Jarl and Navee sprinted across the open area, leaving as few tracks as possible. There was no forest on the opposite side, only high reeds and another shallow, brackish bay. Jarl turned back to the north, toward the high rise of granite. Navee was surprised—they would be arrested for sure—but they had to get to higher ground. Travel through the inundated salt flats was too time consuming and energy draining.

The narrow peninsula led right to the base of one of the granite promontories. From this, the backside, there was no sign of the quarry. They managed to skirt the head of the brackish bay by staying on the sloping granite, at one point hanging onto a young maple tree to keep from falling into the water, then they climbed east among the small trees that grew on that side of the hill.

The high slopes gave them a view of the surrounding terrain. To the south and southeast, where the woods and water all blended together, were a series of low peninsulas, inter-fingered with wide, long brackish bays. The vegetation was dense, and there were many high reeds. Travel would be difficult there, if not next to impossible. To the east was a wide plain, where dark conifer woods mixed with open fields of short grass. Far to the northeast, next to another granite hill, Jarl could see the many smoke plumes of a tiny village. To their immediate east, about a kilometer away, was another pine forest, which came to a point near their granite promontory. But between the forest and the hill was a field of grass. Behind them, to the north and west, the high granite hill robbed them of a view.

Navee looked at Jarl questioningly and then asked, "Do you want to wait until nightfall before crossing that grassy plain?"

"No, I want as much distance between us and the Church as possible. Besides, as visible as we are going to be on that plain, we're a lot more visible standing on this hill."

Navee agreed. The three men carefully descended the eastern side of the promontory. They rested for a short minute at the bottom, gathering their breath and searching the plain for danger. Then they ran—even Jonson sensed the danger—toward the safety of the woods. Soon they were in the conifer forest, entering it in the narrow point closest to the granite hill. They looked behind them and, seeing no one, hurried deeper into the woods.

This forest too, was open, with another soft pine needle floor and tall, straight conifer trees. Jarl, Jonson, and Navee walked at a fast pace. Jarl's throat was already dry, and he was scared, worried that they might not be able to find any fresh water. Once they waded a narrow arm of the estuary and—in the middle—Jonson slipped and slid into the warm brackish water up to his neck. All afternoon they traveled east, wading three or more other narrow brackish creeks. Jarl became dizzy from dehydration. Dusk came and then dark, and still they traveled east. Finally, they crossed one more stretch of reeds and waded into one more body of water. This time, the water was cold and deep and they had to swim in the middle, where there was a slight current. Jonson dog-paddled, making noisy splashes. Jarl dipped his mouth into the water, and then he submerged up his nose, easing the cool liquid down his parched throat. When he surfaced, he whispered two soft words, "Fresh water."

The three man floated and waded downstream for many more minutes, drinking their fill. Then they climbed up onto the bank where there was no undergrowth, making sure they had left no tracks. They moved back away from the river, lay down behind a log, and slept, huddling together for warmth. For the moment, they were free men.

Jarl woke early the next morning. All was quiet. Under him was a scattering of dried leaves; that surprised him, for nowhere had he seen a hardwood tree. Above his head, next to the log he had slept beside, was a single sycamore tree. He rolled over and suddenly sat upright, causing Navee to wake. Jonson was gone.

Navee quickly rolled onto his feet. They looked along the shore of the river and then into the dark conifer forest. There was no one in sight.

Both men were silent, listening and looking for the old man, who—in his mental state—could have gone anywhere. It was Jarl who spotted the first smudge of dirty pine needles, and then the two men began moving away from the river, following the faint trail deeper into the forest. First there was another smudge in the pine needles, then an overturned stick. The minutes dragged on, and Navee walked ahead, searching for the old priest. Jarl stayed behind, slowly working out the faint trail of naked footprints.

Almost an hour had passed when Jarl heard a low whistle. Ahead, Navee waved, and Jarl moved forward. Navee led him to an inlet on a wide creek. There, sitting on a log and feasting on some kind of red berries, was Jonson.

Jarl and Navee also helped themselves to the berries, then they drank from the creek. The remainder of the day was spent exploring the forest, gradually working their way downstream. By mid-afternoon, they had arrived at the wide expanse of Greymist River.

They had eaten nothing but berries since the previous morning and now they spread out, searching for some kind of food. Jarl waded along the river shore and looked along the edge of the mud. Navee and Jonson began investigating a low rock bar, stopping and overturning some of the rounded stones, below a high alluvial bank. Jonson soon found a few tiny, sand-covered crustaceans, which he scooped up and stuffed into his mouth.

Finally, toward dusk, Navee discovered a bed of clams in one of the brackish inlets of the river. All three men carried great handfuls of the mussels to a rock bar and, there, for lack of a knife, they cracked the hard shells with the rounded granite rocks and ate their small and gritty catch. Then, still hungry, they attempted to fill their stomachs with the water from a small stream. They spent their second free night on the narrow peninsula between the brackish estuary and the freshwater stream.

The next day was also spent searching for food. Navee and Jarl each wove two fish traps from long reeds, and they floated these out into the river, weighting them with small rocks. Jonson continued to eagerly devour the small crustaceans he located under the stones on the rock bar. Afterwards, they walked back to the clam bed and ate their fill.

Thus the days continued. On some days they wove more fish traps, setting many in the brackish estuary. They found more clam and oyster beds, and occasionally caught a fish with a long pole Navee had sharpened on one of the rounded granite rocks. The traps yielded several kinds of fish, and after some experimentation with raw fish for bait, dozens of hard-shelled crabs.

Jonson seemed content to remain in close proximity to the narrow, forested point of land. That suited Navee and Jarl. Each day the two younger men ventured further afield, locating easy paths to and from their peninsular, and discovering noisy flocks of small green parakeets that fluttered this way and that in front of them. And, except for the very top of a lateen sail far off on the river, they saw no sign of any other human.

One week turned to two. The weather was warm during the day, but colder weather was certainly on the way. From a few places on their peninsula, they could see the high, faraway Sabre Mountains. Each day, it seemed that more snow was visible on their high peaks. Once, Navee found a thin piece of rusty iron in an old wreck of a boat. For part of two days, Jarl polished the shard of metal on a flat granite boulder. Finally, it was sharp enough for Jarl and Navee to trim the each other's shoulder-length hair, and for Jarl to trim his beard. Then, while Jarl held down Jonson, Navee cut the old man's hair and beard.

Then, one day, Navee did not return from a trip to the east. Jarl was worried and tried to erase the signs of their small camp, hiding Jonson several hundred meters back into the forest. That night there was a partial cloud cover, through which a half-face of ringed Kmir occasionally peeked.

Jarl paced between Jonson and the end of the peninsula, looking and listening for his friend. Because of the clouds, he could not see enough stars to tell the time, but sometime well past midnight, he was suddenly aware of the black silhouette of a log canoe on the Greymist River. There was one man in the small, narrow craft, which was hugging close to the shore and moving so silently that Jarl did not notice it until it was within an easy stone's throw of his location. The canoe turned into the estuary east of the freshwater river, and quietly moved upstream before the single occupant ran it ashore next to a partially submerged log.

Jarl moved silently toward the shore. The man in the boat climbed out and into the water. Then—just then—the moon peeked through the clouds. The man was Navee.

Jarl moved to his friend's side. Navee saw him and grinned. Together they took the canoe, which was nothing more than a hollowed-out log, out into the freshwater creek and carefully sank it, using rocks to weight it down. Then they waded back to shore, and climbed up and into the dark forest.

There, squatting, Navee told his story, whispering in a hushed tone. "I followed the Greymist River east, crossing..." The little E'landota stopped, counting on his fingers, "four brackish creeks. Finally, I came to a long point of land. Downstream was a small village. I crossed another small bay and waded across a tidal flat covered with high weeds and deep, greasy, black mud..." Navee paused and made an ugly face.

"I was about to give up, but I discovered a small freshwater stream. I followed that downstream until I found an old dead tree. Since I couldn't see or hear the village, I climbed the tree, until just my head was sticking up above the reeds." Navee stopped again, his eyes alight with excitement.

"The settlement was less than a half kilometer away; but, more importantly, there were several ships and small sailing craft, all beached on the low mud flat on the near side of the village. I waited until dusk, then moved closer. Most of the ships were small fishing boats, but one was an old canoe that had been hollowed out of a tree. I searched among the remaining vessels and found three paddles in the bottom of a small skiff. The canoe was heavy, but I pulled into the water, paddled out into the river, and came upstream. And here I am."

Jarl was for setting off at once, but Navee wanted to wait. His words were confident, "I am sure the canoe won't be missed and, by leaving now, we will be in the middle of the quarry's shipping lane just past daybreak."

Jarl wasn't happy with staying, but he wasn't happy with leaving either. In the end, they waited nervously all the next day, hoping that the rightful owner of the canoe didn't show up. Then, the three men stuffed themselves with clams and fish and drank large quantities of freshwater. Two hours before dark it began to rain, a cold, heavy downpour that became worse and worse until they finally called off their canoe trip. It was a wet and miserable night, but Jarl was glad they were not out on the open river.

It rained all night and then all morning, turning colder around noon. Jarl found the brackish water warmer than the rain and spent part of the afternoon fishing and collecting shellfish and crabs, eating them in the river. Then, just before dusk, under a cloudy sky, after one last feast and a final long drink, Navee and Jarl refloated the log canoe, and the three men gingerly climbed into the narrow craft and pushed off.

Navee took the bow. Jonson, with the oldest paddle, sat in the middle. Jarl, claiming some expertise in a canoe, sat in the stern. The boat was narrow and wobbly, and they had nothing to bail with, but even Jonson seemed to appreciate the situation and sat still. Because they were dressed only in their prison shorts, Jarl hoped they met no one on the wide river, as such an encounter could end in their arrest. Neither Navee nor Jarl tried to paddle quickly; each took long, strong strokes, careful not to splash water or reach out so far that they would tip the canoe. Jonson seemed to be capable of making only loud splashes, and Jarl was thankful when he finally placed his paddle inside the small craft and ceased helping.

At first, they paddled along the right shore. Then they arrived at the wide arm of the estuary leading to the Church's wharfs. Without hesitation, they set out across it. The trip became tiring. Occasionally Navee would whisper back a hushed, short command, telling Jarl to angle right or left. For a long time Jarl could not see what the E'landota was sighting on, then he realized that, high in the distance, two of the snowfields on the faraway mountains were visible. Jarl's legs, bent into a tight kneeling position, began to ache. He rocked gently back and forth, attempting to ease the hurt, but that did not help. Once, after midnight, they endured a sudden rainstorm, mouths open to the sky, trying to drink a few drops of the cold liquid.

Finally, far to the right, a low, dark land mass appeared. They angled the canoe toward that shore and were soon paralleling it. After a short distance, Navee found a place where the water appeared to be shallow. While Jarl leaned in the opposite direction, the little E'landota attempted to ease out into the warm water. There was a moment of awkwardness, then the canoe overturned, throwing all three men into the dark water. Jarl easily rolled clear of the heavy boat, but Jonson created bright splashes, struggling to keep his head above water. Then, abruptly, the old man quieted, realizing that the water was shallow enough for him to stand. Jarl swam back to the canoe, and he and Navee hung their arms over the bottom of their overturned craft, flexing the pain out of their legs, and wallowing in the luxury of no longer being confined to the cramped boat.

After an all-too-short rest, Jarl and Navee rolled the canoe over and bailed it out. Then came the ordeal of getting Jonson back into the narrow boat. Three times he upset the craft; each time the two younger men would right it and Navee would climb in and use his hands to bail the water out. Only after they moved closer to shore, where the water was only ankle deep, was the old priest finally able to climb into the canoe without upsetting it.

This was when Jarl and Navee discovered that Jonson had lost his paddle. They searched the water for it, without luck. At last, Jarl waded into the shallow water and carefully climbed into the rocking canoe. Then, after Navee handed him a paddle, the two men once again began paddling upstream.

They followed the shore westward for the remainder of the night. At no time did they sight a light or any sign of another human, either on land or in another boat. Occasionally, there were high reeds to the right, but most often, there was only the dark—and somehow comforting—conifer forest. At first, Jonson was a creature of nervous energy, rocking the boat and threatening to overturn it; but then—finally—the old man settled down and went to sleep, his head bowed and almost touching his chest. The night became silent. The only sounds were the quiet noise of Jonson's soft snoring and the hollow knock of their paddles against the side of the boat. Once, as the sky to the east began to brighten, they heard the long, lonely call of a loon, far off and up the river. Then they watched as a meter-tall red-headed woodpecker flew from an ancient skeleton of a tree and toward the dark smudge of a far away forest.

First light came and then dawn. The coast remained almost straight, curving slightly to landward, with high banks of sand, impossible to climb without leaving obvious tracks. Jarl suggested stopping several times, but

Navee always wanted to go a little further. Jarl's arms hurt, his back had become one wide sea of searing pain, and his legs had long since gone to sleep. The next long, wide turn came and went, and then the next.

Then Jonson woke and began his random twitchings anew, now almost violent in nature. Finally they found a small mud bar, half covered by a fallen cypress log. They beached the boat there, driving the bow into the soft ooze.

Navee fell sideways out of the boat. He slid in up to his elbow in the soft mud and uttered a soft curse. Jonson followed and then Jarl. For many long minutes they lay there, wiggling and moaning, trying to get the feeling back into their legs. Navee stood, as best he could, and clambered up over the log, leaving a muddy trail. With Jonson's help, Jarl passed him the bow of the log canoe and, together, the three men levered the heavy boat up and onto the bank above.

Then, Navee, facing backwards and with both hands on the bow of the boat, pulled it further away from the shore. Jarl boosted Jonson onto the log, and after much sliding and clawing—and after the priest placed a muddy, bare foot square full onto Jarl's face—the old man was finally able to crawl up and onto the bank. Jarl tossed the two paddles up and, using his hands, packed down the mud and threw water onto the bank, trying to make it look less as though someone had crawled out of the river. Then he clawed his way out of the water and onto the bank.

There was no sign of Navee or Jonson. Jarl followed the skid mark of the canoe for two dozen steps. There he found the small craft, two paddles, and Jonson, already lying beside the canoe, fast asleep. Navee was nearby, crouching next to the edge of a woods. Once again, the forest floor was covered in one wide bed of pine needles, easy on their naked feet and quiet to walk on. Jarl moved quickly over to his friend, and Navee placed a finger to his lips. Jarl groaned inwardly—something was not right.

The forest abruptly ended. Fifty meters away, across a grassy field, was a white, sandy streak of a highway. Despite the early hour, a tiny group of monks was traveling the road, heads bent under their hooded cowls. Jarl and Navee watched them as they slowly moved off into the distance, each step kicking up a small clump of dust. The two men waited a while longer, and then—without speaking—moved off in opposite directions.

Jarl soon discovered a low depression. After looking carefully in all directions, he ran down into it, hunched over and keeping low to the ground. In the bottom, despite the dry summer, was a bit of water, colored brown by tannic acid. Jarl dipped his hand into the liquid and tasted it. It was bitter, but fresh. He drank, then stood, searching for danger. He then continued to move along the edge of the forest, until he came to a point where he was surrounded on all sides by open fields. To his left was a small clump of trees and the Greymist River. To his right, a full kilometer away across a brush-covered swamp, was another large forest. Ahead and to the west, he could see the sand-colored highway stretching into the distance. Far along the road were other green forests and several dark dots that Jarl assumed were the monks. And above it all hung the white and blue precipices of the Sabre Mountains.

Jarl returned to the canoe, and Navee soon arrived, wearing his usual smile. The little man said that he had seen no danger and that he had found a ditch of stagnant water, from which he had drank.

They both wanted to set a guard on Jonson, but were too exhausted. In the end, they compromised. Both men slept, Jarl with his legs draped over Jonson's back, and Navee resting his head on the old man's legs.

It was Jonson who woke them, knocking them both aside as he staggered to his feet. The day was still warm, but sunset was approaching. They could hear nothing from the road. The three of them crawled over to the edge of the river. There, a brigantine, with large, dirty square sails on its foremast and yellow spankers set at the mizzenmast, was tacking upstream toward Tyr. They watched the ship for what seemed a long time, then—quietly—Jarl led the them back toward the depression where he had found the water.

At the first sight of the brown water, Jonson scurried into the depression. Jarl and Navee followed. The three men drank their fill, but—as they were leaving the depression—they spotted, far away, some kind of vehicle on the highway. They kept low, and moved back toward the forest. Then, while Navee took Jonson back to the canoe, Jarl lingered behind, finding a spot from which to watch the oncoming vehicle. Soon, he could see that it was one of the high-wheeled carts that the Church used to haul prisoners to their camp. Behind the cart walked six green-coated guards of the Church, and another walked beside the slow-moving ox, guiding it along the road with a long, thin switch. He could not tell if there were any prisoners in the cage.

Jarl slithered backwards into the forest and ran to the canoe. Once there, he found that Navee had the boat down to the mud bar. Together, they quietly slid it into the water, and then Jarl grabbed Navee's arm and lowered him into the boat. Bracing his feet and arms against the cypress log, he allowed Jonson to climb down him, as if he were a human ladder. The old priest, once on the mud bar, refused to climb into the small, cramped boat. But Jarl mentioned the Church guards on the road, and Jonson suddenly became impatient to leave. Soon they were on their way, quietly paddling toward the setting sun.

They quickly left the forest behind. Dusk came, and then night. Jarl had estimated they had paddled for five hours when Navee spotted a sandbar a hundred meters from shore. Far in the western distance they could see one bright light near the water. Above it, a half-dozen lights sparkled higher on a mountain or hillside. The three men stopped on the sandbar and rested for most of an hour.

They were just about to resume their journey when a lateen-rigged sailing vessel swept downstream, carried by the current and hurrying toward some unseen destination. One yellow lamp hung high on the stern, but evidently the ship's pilot knew the sandbar and stayed well in the middle of the river, and there was no danger of the three pardoned prisoners being spotted. Afterwards, shivering from the cold, Jarl and Navee loaded an uncooperative Jonson into the canoe and once again began paddling upstream.

The Greymist River was narrowing, reaching the confluence of the Nanoo and the Vilyur. Two hours later, Navee whispered that he could see a tall tree on the opposite bank, and Jarl turned the canoe into deeper water, leaving the eastern shore. After a long hour of battling the current they reached the opposite side of the river. They paddled on through the cold night, turning down a chance to rest on a grassy bank. Gradually, the sun began to rise, turning the tops of the snow-covered peaks pink and illuminating the small city at the base of the mountains. It was Tyr. Somehow, unseen and unknowing, they had passed Ispwich during the night.

With the sunrise, the numerous warehouses, houses, stores, and taverns unfolded before them. Higher on the mountain, Jarl could see the King's palace. To their right was the harbor, with its many ships outlined against the dark wharf, naked masts reaching skyward. To the left, they could see the falls of the wide Vilyur River, where white water flashed under the long, wooden bridge as it dropped over dark, wet rocks. Between them and the river, a light mist rose from the water, where the cold mountain Vilyur met the warm coastal Nanoo.

As they entered the harbor, they passed a fishing vessel heading downstream. It, like their night encounter, was a lateen-rigged ship, designed for maneuvering in shallow, narrow inlets and bays. The crew took no notice of the three near-naked men in the heavy log canoe. Silently, they paddled their narrow craft past the long lines of ships. Only a tiny number of people were up at this early hour, and they continued about their business, taking no interest in the three men or their small dug-out canoe.

They soon reached the end of the harbor, which was marked by the wooden, humpbacked bridge across the Nanoo River. The three men climbed out of their tiny craft and, ignoring the pain in their legs, dragged their canoe up a planked boat ramp and into a cobblestoned courtyard beyond. Then, as they had agreed upon before they had entered the harbor, Navee and Jonson found a discreet spot to sit and wait, huddled under an old canvas sail. Jarl handed Navee his paddle and turned his bare feet toward the Soo-Hoo tavern, desperately hoping he would still be welcomed there.

CHAPTER FIFTEEN:

THE ELDER OAK PRINTING COMPANY

Jarl quickly walked up the hill toward northern Tyr. Twice he stopped, and with his back to a stone wall, waited a few seconds, watching behind and in front of him. He saw no danger. Then, without warning, a man followed him around a corner.

Jarl quickly ducked down a narrow alley and ran to the end. There he waited, hidden in a recess formed where a high wooden fence was set against a brick house. The man turned into the alley. Jarl, one knee shaking, tensed for a moment; then he eased through a narrow opening in the fence. He drew up abruptly. The alley had ended and there was no way on. Behind him, he heard a knock on wood. Cautiously, he peeked around the corner.

The man was standing in front of a door that was just being opened. A young girl, wearing a long-sleeved white blouse and an ankle-length skirt, jumped out, shouting, "Daddy!" She threw her arms around the man's neck. The man laughed and twirled her in his arms. Then, chattering and laughing, the two entered the house. The door slammed shut, and Jarl quickly and soundlessly scooted back to the street. Once more he started toward the Soo-Hoo.

He approached the inn with caution. A well-dressed man, clothed in the latest fashion, stared at his scanty attire. On a bench, across the highway from the tavern, a robed man sat, apparently warming himself in the morning sun. From down the road, two groups of travelers approached. Jarl opted to make his way to the tavern from the back. He quickly walked up a side street, which was fortuitously empty of people, and climbed over a high wooden fence and into the Soo-Hoo's stables. He then ran silently across the worn cobblestones of the courtyard to the back door of the inn. As usual, the top half of the portal was open, and Jarl peeked inside. There was only one person in the common room—Thir, washing dishes.

As quietly as possible, Jarl reached over the lower panel and unlatched the door. He swung it open and stepped into the tavern, whispering "Thir," so as not to frighten the large woman.

She spun around. Her jaw dropped, her mouth formed a wide oval, and her hands flew to her face. A large ceramic mug clattered across the plank bar, but did not fall to the hardwood floor. For several seconds, the two of them stared at each other, Thir unable to believe her eyes, and Jarl fearful that the woman would scream, bringing help on the run.

But she did not. Instead, she ran around the bar, and fiercely hugged Jarl, crushing the breath out of him. Relief flooded through him, he felt as if his battle was won. Thir pushed him back and stared at him with large, damp eyes. She asked, in a hushed whisper, "Did you escape?"

Jarl found his voice dry, "No, I was pardoned by the King."

She held him at arm's length, "You wouldn't lie to me, would you? The King pardoned you?"

"Not him personally, but one of his representatives. I didn't escape."

The woman was still unconvinced, "Then why are you sneaking in here the back way?"

Jarl's voice was low and serious, "Thir, the Church arrested me once on trumped-up charges, what's to stop them from doing it again?"

The big woman considered his words, then she nodded. "It is wise you didn't come to the front. Someone has been watching us..." She stopped, thinking, "for just over two weeks."

"Who?"

"We don't know." The brown eyes were still thoughtful and serious. "Why were you pardoned?"

"The King set one fifth of all the prisoners free. It was the first anniversary of the Battle of Burkes Ford."

Thir nodded again, "They did that here too. The Church didn't like it, but the King released every fifth man of his prisoners and then forced the Church to do the same."

Jarl spoke, "The Church didn't like the idea any better where I was, but the King's representative gave them no choice."

"You deserved it. You were at the Battle of Burkes Station. Otis wrote and told us what you did."

"Thir, I have two friends. We all need help and clothes. If the Church is watching, it could be dangerous. We need a place to hide out."

Thir did not hesitate, "You cannot stay here. It would be too dangerous. But there might be a place... Are your friends inconspicuous?"

"Do you mean where they're hiding? Or what they're wearing?" Jarl paused for a moment, thinking, then said, "They should be all right where they are now, but one of them will stand out, either here or there. He's somewhat crazy." He did not tell Thir that the man had been one of the most famous prisoners in all of Vanir.

When Thir remained quiet, Jarl spoke again, pleading, "You're the only friend I have."

The big woman became angry, and it was clear she was upset that he would use that argument. "We will help you, but first we will have to find you some clothes. Come!" She pulled him into the dark interior of the other room.

"I have no money to pay you."

Thir gave him a strange look, and then disappeared up the front stairs. Jarl waited, hoping she wasn't sending a messenger down the back steps, running for the authorities. But once again, his suspicions were unfounded. The woman returned, carrying a large burlap sack. She motioned Jarl to a table and reached down into the bag, withdrawing his camouflage jacket. Jarl exhaled a long breath and quickly slid into his old familiar coat, checking the pockets. One had his black-handled sheath knife, another had the unmistakable outline of his small projectile pistol and its spare magazine. He looked at Thir and stammered a thanks.

The round woman was not listening; rather, she was upending the contents of a small leather bag onto the table. Silver coins chattered across the flat surface. Jarl's hand flashed out, quickly grabbing the red object that stopped on the first bounce: his multi-blade, utility penknife.

Once again he looked at the woman, beginning his thanks, but she spoke first, with a deep sadness, "Jarl, they took everything else of yours...

your other jacket, your weapons, your pack, what money they found, and your horses... Jarl, they even took your horses."

The brown eyes were large and tear-filled. "I know," Jarl said. "I saw some of my stuff at the trial. I never expected to see any of my things again, much less this much." There were tears in his eyes. "Thank you, thank you," he said. "You did good. I really appreciate your saving these things."

The woman looked down, silent and thoughtful. Then, as if she was seeing the money for the first time, she spoke, "There's close to 200 dollars here. The stage agent keeps bringing more around every time they finish a new coach. They're very worried about you."

Jarl wondered how much money the inn brought in a year—the sum had to be a small fortune to the woman and her family, and yet she had taken none of it for her own. He spoke again, quietly, "Thir, I am not a wizard, a witch, or a sorcerer. I want you to know that. The charges were made up. The trial was a farce."

"It was hard to watch them beat you. You didn't deserve their... wrath... There was so little we could do."

"You did what was right. Had you interfered, they would have just trumped up another charge and arrested you too." Jarl looked down at his few belongings and then back at the woman, "Actually, you did damn good!"

From behind him there was a quiet cough. Jarl whirled, expecting danger. But there stood FjIar, beaming. The man crossed the room, wrapped his arms around Jarl and hugged him, swinging his feet off the floor. Behind the father, in the open doorway, stood daughter and son. There was much talking. Despite Jarl's protests, Sunny forced him to eat a small sandwich, while Thir trimmed his hair and beard, and found him a pair of pants, socks and boots, a shirt, and an old tan sheepskin coat. Jarl dressed, and he sat quiet for almost a minute, tears again in his eyes, enjoying the feel of the wool socks and the old leather boots. Then he, Lif, and Fjlar exited a side door and, mostly using alleys and back streets, quickly walked to the northern end of the harbor.

Jarl approached the small cobblestoned courtyard cautiously, sliding into it through an open shop. His prudence was for nothing: there was no one lurking in the area. But as his eyes searched the empty courtyard, he realized—with a dismal start—that Navee and Jonson were missing.

He ran to where he had left them. The old sail lay in a small pile on the ground. Even the paddles were gone. Along the edge of the courtyard, the log canoe had likewise vanished. Jarl's eyes roamed the nearby ships, up and down the wharf, and then up the street. He could find no sign of his two companions. Lif and Fjlar stood nearby, their expressions apologetic.

Jarl walked a short way down the wharf. A white-haired, old man sat on the deck of a small sloop, mending an ancient fishing net. Jarl asked the sailor if he had seen two men—one old, the other young—waiting in the cobblestoned courtyard. The man shook his head no. Then Jarl asked the same question of the shopkeeper whose store he had slid through to enter the courtyard. The answer was the same.

He walked halfway across the bridge over the Nanoo River. To the east, along the road to Ispwich, he saw no one. There was no log canoe in the water or along the mud banks, north of the bridge. South of the bridge, downstream in the harbor, it was more difficult to tell—there were hundreds of hiding places between the wharfs and the many ships.

Finally, dejected, with his hands shoved into his pockets, Jarl walked slowly back to the old canvas sail. He carefully inspected it, lifting it and peering at both sides. He then searched the ground, the nearby stone wall, and the nearest buildings, looking in vain for a sign or message from Navee.

Fjlar and Lif were becoming nervous, worried that whatever had befallen Jarl's two friends might also strike them. The three of them walked several blocks south along the wharf and then returned, by way of several high streets, to the Soo-Hoo. Once back at the tavern, they told their story to Thir and Sunny. Jarl had been hoping that his two friends had been scared by something in the harbor and had made their own way to the inn, but there was no sign of them at the tavern.

Thir fed Jarl another meal and then sent him off to stay with Fjlar's brother in upper Tyr. Jarl stayed there for two nights until he discovered the man had an acquaintance who was some kind of metal artisan, on the outs with the Church and who lived in the southern part of the city, on the other side of the Vilyur River.

His third morning in Tyr, Jarl took his sheepskin coat, a few dollars, his pistol, and a carefully made set of directions and started out for the metalworker's home. The walk was about three kilometers, pleasant on the warm fall day and hot in the heavy coat. He crossed the Vilyur River and turned right at a prominent fork, then climbed a steep cobblestone side street. He found the house with little trouble. It was a two-story, white plank building set somewhat away from the nearest neighbors, abutting against a steep, treeless mountainside. In the opposite direction, fifty meters east and twenty meters below the house, was the main Tyr-Smyrna Road. Beyond that, as far as he could see, was the flat coastal plain, bisected by the Greymist River.

Jarl's knocks brought no answer at the front door, so he wandered around the back of the house, past a massive pile of split firewood. There, under a gigantic red oak and in front of two small outbuildings, sat two men, replacing the broken handle in a large, double-bladed axe.

One of the men was small with a shaggy red beard; the other was huge and seemed as broad as he was tall. The little man saw Jarl first and spoke quietly to his companion. The big man turned and gave Jarl a suspicious look. He then bellowed across the cluttered backyard, demanding to know what Jarl wanted.

Jarl was polite, and he quickly mentioned Fjlar's brother's name. The large man hopped up, walked across the yard—staring at Jarl while he did so—and then opened a rear gate with a massive hand and allowed Jarl to enter.

Introductions followed. The big man was Karl MacCulloch, who shook Jarl's hand with an impressive strength, causing Jarl to grimace in pain. The smaller man was Levi Balsdon, who stood and walked with a slight stoop over to shake Jarl's hand. Levi's handshake too was strong, and his eyes glittered with an internal energy. His beard, his bright eyes, and his stooped walk gave him a decidedly dwarf-like appearance.

For a short time, the three men talked, sitting on upended, unsplit logs. Karl produced a loaf of bread, a hunk of cheese, several filthy mugs, and an equally dirty pitcher of warm beer. Jarl asked the two men's occupation.

Levi answered, "I used to help haul the garbage to the dump across the Vilyur River. Karl was a silversmith at one of the shops near the wharfs, but now... we have lost our jobs..."

"Why?"

Neither man replied. Karl got up and walked into the unkempt house. Jarl thought he might be asked to leave.

But after many minutes, the massive man returned to the shade under the immense oak tree. In his huge hand was an object—incredibly tiny by comparison—that he handed to Jarl. It was a man's ring, made of silver, engraved with serpents, and set with a bright, red stone.

Levi explained, "One of the town's elders... a High Ejliteta... ordered the ring. He especially wanted the serpents and the garnet. The Church found out and had Karl tried..."

Jarl interrupted, "For what? What is wrong with the ring?"

"The serpents are some kind of evil. Karl was found guilty and the Church forced his boss to fire him. Karl didn't realize how bad his crime was until he tried to find work with the other silversmiths in town. Every one of them turned him down. One barred his door when he saw him coming toward his shop, and another had his E'landota throw him out of his shop..." Karl sat quietly on his up-ended log of wood, while Levi told his story, slowly clenching and unclenching his huge fists.

Levi continued, "After Karl couldn't find other work, he and I began to split wood in the evening after I was finished with my city job... But then I was fired, just for helping Karl..." Anger flashed in Levi's eyes. "The man who fired me was the same man who ordered the ring in the first place, and who I had sent to Karl."

For several long moments, the three men sat quietly, drinking their warm beer and not speaking. Then, quietly, Jarl told of his own encounter with the Church, of his recent pardon, and of his own fear of the Church. At the end of the story, he looked first at Karl, and then at Levi, meeting their eyes with his own. Then he slowly said, "I want you to know. I am not a sorcerer or a wizard."

Karl nodded. He picked up the dirty pitcher and refilled Jarl's mug with beer. While Jarl drank, the two men reached some unspoken, secret understanding. After Jarl had finished his beer, Karl cleared his throat and offered Jarl a job, cutting and splitting firewood in the foothills of the Sabres, hauling it on a rickety wagon—that at the moment stood behind one of the outbuildings—down into Tyr, and there selling it for winter firewood.

Jarl felt very old. "What kind of business would you have associating with a convicted sorcerer?" he asked.

That quieted Karl, but his solution was simple and quick, "You can work in the forest. Levi and I will take the wood into Tyr."

Jarl had to smile. "That should appease the good and righteous citizens of Tyr." He waited, while Karl refilled the three mugs, then he asked, "Where do people buy raw silver and copper in Tyr?"

The big man was suddenly suspicious. He answered the question and then asked Jarl what he had in mind.

Jarl was thinking; he had intended to search all of Tyr until he had found the right person or persons to meet his requirements, but it seemed as if he would do no better than these two men. Although Karl's home was cluttered and unkept, the large stack of split firewood to one side spoke highly of the two men's industry and motivation. And, most importantly, they had no love for the Church. He answered Karl's question, perhaps too simply, "I want to make books."

Both men rocked back on their seats. Their eyes popped open and Karl spilled some of his beer. The big man looked down at Jarl and said, "We are not scribes."

Jarl was intense. "That's not the way I want to make them. Not one by one. I want to make many books at the same time."

Karl and Levi said nothing and Jarl continued talking. He described a machine, constructed of wood, that would press small blocks of silver or copper against sheets of paper. Both men listened thoughtfully. Finally, Levi looked to Karl for the final word. After a long minute, the big man nodded his head in a slow up-and-down motion.

They talked for a few more minutes, but then Levi got up, walked back to the shed, and began to construct some type of contraption. It was not until Karl stood and walked over to where the smaller man was working, that Jarl realized that Levi was beginning to build a printing machine. He and Karl joined in, helping to build a crude apparatus, one that used a long hand lever to press a flat board into a second panel. Levi was unhappy— surely the machine could be improved upon. When Jarl suggested a foot pedal, the little man brightened; but it was dusk, and Karl and Levi had firewood contracts to fill.

The three of them loaded and delivered a large stack of wood to a well-do-to home on the outskirts of the city, and afterwards Jarl walked home to his temporary lodging. He spent a hungry night, having arrived too late at Fjlar's brother's for supper.

The next day, Jarl once again was at Karl's home, discovering that the two men had already reloaded their wagon with firewood. Together they delivered it to a small home in central Tyr and then, as Karl and Levi returned for yet another load, Jarl—using Karl's carefully written instructions—set off to talk to the few dealers of metals in Tyr, not about silver or copper, but—according to the big man's expertise—lead, which many people bought to mold bullets and would be easier to procure.

Jarl visited many shops, pricing copper, iron, lead, ink, parchment, and paper. The next day he returned to Karl's home in southern Tyr, and while the large man delivered another load of firewood into the city, Levi and Jarl constructed a second printing machine, utilizing a wooden screw similar to the kind the papermakers used to press their product. It worked adequately, but Jarl wanted to attempt a third press, one that would use the foot pedal, before committing to one design.

The next day, the three men delivered three more loads of firewood and took an order for a fourth; then in the afternoon, they constructed a foot-operated press. It too was only adequate, but Levi had several good suggestions. The following day, a Saturday, was spent delivering more firewood and discussing the different presses.

Jarl spent Sunday at the Ahlums, enjoying their company and their large noon meal. A nondescript man sat on the bench across the Foord Road from the tavern, forcing Jarl to again climb the fence and enter through the back door. Although there was no news of Navee or Jonson, Jarl was in for a surprise. The stage company had completed three more coaches and their agent—none other than Alfheim Vail—was visiting the tavern to deliver another payment. Alfheim and Jarl talked long into the night, discussing the new stagecoaches and the friends he had left behind in Kettleland.

Before he left for the night, Jarl casually mentioned he intended to purchase some lead the following day.

"Now that is something I can assist you with," Alfheim said, happy to help. "The stage company has the best lead available. We usually sell it only to the militias, but seeing how you have designed our new coach, I think we can manage to sell you a few ingots... and at a substantial discount too."

Jarl took a long way home that night, stopping twice to watch if anyone was following him. The next day, he moved his few belongings to Karl's home and made a bedroom in one of the outbuildings, where he could better hear during the night—and perhaps have a few moments to escape while the Church searched the main house.

Karl was suspicious when he discovered that Jarl could buy lead from the stage line. "They," he said, "have a better quality of lead, but they will not sell it to just anyone."

Jarl chuckled and explained his association with the new coaches, which had become the talk of all Kamjar. Karl and Levi were astounded, unable to believe that Jarl was the inventor of the stagecoaches and that he had been helping them with the poor business of cutting firewood.

The following week was spent delivering firewood, and, under the gigantic limbs of the red oak, constructing a foot-pedal-operated printing press. It was a dismal failure that was consigned to the wood stove. Jarl was depressed but the next morning, when he woke, he discovered Levi had already begun work on yet another press, one which used a hand lever and a wooden screw to press a block of wood against a horizontal platform. Before the day was over, while Karl delivered more firewood, the two men added a thin wooden plate that hinged over the press and slid under the heavy block of wood attached to the screw. The next day they took the entire machine apart and reconstructed it, using stronger materials and a better screw.

It took Jarl and Karl more than a week to carve close to seventy characters onto the narrow ends of small iron wedges. Next, using a hammer, Karl stamped a soft, small copper bar with each of the iron characters. The big man then placed each copper bar into a homemade form and poured liquid lead into the upper end, producing hundreds of letters, all backwards and all the same size.

Jarl bought small samples of ink, parchment, and paper from several different suppliers. One night, working late into the morning hours, the three men lined the lead characters into rows and tried different combinations of ink, paper, and parchment. The paper absorbed the ink correctly, which was fortunate—because the parchment did not work at all.

Then they placed a sheet of paper on the thin wooden plate and swung it down onto the inked lead characters. After shoving the plate up under the heavy block at the end of the screw, they pulled on the long wooden handle, turning the screw downward and pressing the heavy block of wood against the back of the thin plate. The result was black ink everywhere, on their arms, their clothes, in their hair, and worst—along the edges of their few sheets of paper.

Finally, as the first rays of light were creeping over the flat coastal plain and after Levi made a second thin wooden plate—which contained a rectangular hole and fit over each page, protecting the margins from unwanted ink—they successfully printed a near-perfect page of meaninglessly grouped letters.

Jarl had long been considering what should be their first book. During their nightly discussions and while hauling firewood, Karl had shown a flair for telling fairy tales, and for the next two days, while Levi and Karl cut more wood, Jarl sat at the kitchen table, using a quill pen, and wrote a series of children's stories and fairy tales. On the third day, a Sunday, the three men put together panels of lead letters, inked the characters and printed their first page. Levi could barely read his own name and Karl, while he was literate, was not proficient enough to proofread, and so Jarl ended up attempting to check his own writing—anxiously hoping his work did not end as the laughing-stock of all of Tyr. That afternoon, the three men began printing in earnest, or at least they tried to, until their limited stocks of paper and ink were exhausted. The next day Jarl bought the first of their extensive orders of paper and ink, raising more than one set of eyebrows in the various shops.

Progress was slow the next few days, because each page had to dry before the reverse side could be printed. During the next two weeks they printed four stories, two hundred copies each, and then a longer children's reader that, on the first page, gave Jarl a chance to promote a standard alphabet.

When Jarl suggested they hire a seamstress to sew the children's readers together, Levi surprised him. The dwarf-like man produced an equally short and bent woman—his wife, Sirota—who with a determination only equaled by her husband's, stitched first the children's reader and then books of fairy tales. Before she began, Jarl had to make a fast trip into Tyr to purchase the required needles and thread. While he was gone, Karl and Levi, on their own initiative, carved a special wooden block and printed front pieces for each book, establishing their enterprise as the Elder Oak Printing Company.

Jarl spent one evening conferring with Fjlar and Thir. At their suggestion, he borrowed a small booth, which he and Lif set up one warm October morning near the Nanoo River Bridge, next to where he had last seen Navee and Jonson. There, they attempted to sell the two books, as well as individual pages of the children's stories. In addition, they passed out printed advertisements for the new printing process. The first day, although many people stopped, took pamphlets, and examined the books, they sold not so much as one page of paper. Jarl was disappointed, but the next day, under a sky that threatened rain, the two set up their booth once again. The morning was a repeat of the previous day—if anything there were fewer potential customers and they only gave away two fliers. Jarl bought Lif lunch, then the two sat next to the booth for half the afternoon. Not so much as one person approached.

Finally, they had one interested person, but not one Jarl would have chosen. It was a haughty, red-robed, clean-shaven priest of the Church, but fortunately, not one of Jarl's previous acquaintances. The man disdainfully examined both books, then snorted to his two guards and strolled off down the wharf, to all appearances interested in the ships. Jarl watched him walk away. This was the first priest he had seen in two days and he could not help thinking the man had come down—or been sent—specifically to spy out his new publications.

Jarl's musings were interrupted by Lif's pulling on his shirt. They had their first customer, an elderly, silver-haired lady, High Ejliteta by her dress. The woman bought a copy of each book, entrusting the process to a young servant girl. Not once, as the money and books traded hands, did Jarl's and the elderly lady's hands touch. But their one customer was the start of something good. Before they closed their small booth at dusk, Jarl and Lif had sold twelve children's readers, eight copies of the fairy tales, and several of the individual stories.

That night, after Jarl returned to Karl's home, the mood was quiet and subdued. Karl was glum. "At this rate," he muttered, "we'll be broke before winter, especially selling each book for the mere pennies Jarl is asking." Jarl said little, but he was determined to sit in the booth for another day or two.

Jarl and Lif set up their shop once more the next day. The morning was again quiet, with no customers. But then just as the boy was scooting off to buy a small meal, no less than six High Ejliteta descended upon the booth, each purchasing one copy of both books. Some, even after Jarl explained that all the children's stories and fairly tales were combined into the bound books, bought both the books and the individual stories. Then a dirty, round woman pushed her way through the crowd and in a loud voice proclaimed her husband had bought one of the individual stories the previous day. She now purchased the children's reader. She was followed by several of her neighbors, each of whom purchased a reader and several of the individual stories. One bought a bound book of the children's stories.

The hectic pace continued. Once in the distance, although he was dealing with two customers at once, Jarl watched as a tall, handsome High Ejliteta hired a small boy to run to the booth and purchase one copy of everything they had to sell. Another time, he saw the red-robed priest standing on one of the high streets, suspiciously watching the small crowd that clustered around the booth of children books.

By three in the afternoon, with Lif paid and sent home, and after stopping and ordering more ink and paper, Jarl slowly made his way across the Vilyur River and up the hill to southern Tyr. He walked in the door of Karl's home, glum and dejected, his hands shoved deep into the pockets of the old sheepskin coat.

Sirota, stitching books in the kitchen, called her husband and Karl from the backyard, where they were printing more children's stories under the massive red oak tree. Levi's, Sirota's, and Karl's expressions soon mirrored Jarl's sour look. "What happened?" Karl asked. "Did the Church throw all the books in the harbor?"

Jarl kept his face sad. He slowly pulled one hand from a pocket and tossed a leather bag onto the kitchen table. It landed with a heavy thump, and a broad grin swept across his face. "Sold out!" he shouted.

For a few seconds the two men and the woman stared at him and at the heavy bag on the table. Then Sirota opened it and dumped it onto the table. Copper and silver coins rolled everywhere and onto the floor. For a few more moments the three stood there, their faces incredulous. Then, slowly, they too began to smile. Soon, the four of them were hugging each other, shouting, and jumping up and down.

The Elder Oak Printing Company was in business.

CHAPTER SIXTEEN:

NAVEE!

Fall rapidly became winter. Sometime, during the shortening days, Jarl decided Karl was one of the hardest-working individuals he had ever met, and certainly the strongest. Once, when they needed to move their heavy press, the big man simply wrapped his arms around it and picked it up; then grunting and swaying, he carried it the short distance to its new location. Still, as hard-working as Karl MacCulloch was, Levi and Sirota surpassed him. The two Balsdons, both stooped and short, simply never ceased working. Jarl could often get Karl to pause and rest by stopping and relaxing himself, but that trick did not work with Levi and Sirota. While he and Karl took a short break, the two Balsdons would simply move inside the dirty, white plank house, sweeping and cleaning the rooms and furniture.

No longer did Jarl have to sell his wares at a booth next to the wharf. Now people, common folk and High Ejliteta alike, came to a store they had set up in the small front room of Karl's home. There, Jarl would interrupt his own work and sell them a book or two. While Karl, Levi, and Sirota could print, trim, and stitch the books, they could not do the simple mathematics required to sell the books, nor were they literate enough to proof the characters lined in laminated maple trays, waiting to be printed. Thus, Jarl found himself trying to do all of the company's paperwork, ordering supplies, selling the books, proofing his own copy, and writing the short articles and more children's stories, of which Karl seemed to have an endless supply. And after their Thanksgiving holiday, when Levi mentioned he had finished the first children's reader—the busy man read late at night in one of the small outbuildings by the light of a single candle—Jarl began to write a second reader.

Levi constructed a second press. Karl poured more letters and numbers, now several different sizes, although still the same basic block letter. Jarl finished his second reader and then began writing an account of the Battle of Burkes Station. To his surprise, he learned that Levi had also fought in the battle, serving with a company of pikemen from Kamjar. Together, he and Jarl composed a twenty-page description of the battle. When Levi finished the second press, they used it for a full month to print nothing but the account of the battle, which quickly became their best seller.

Karl found himself cramped for space, and the big man sold his home to Jarl and moved into the house next door. Sirota and Levi were quick to move into the upper story of that building, and Jarl often saw the two of them, late at night, doing various tasks for the printer. He was sure that, in addition to their never-ending help, the big man was charging them rent.

As their work load increased, Jarl was forced to hire three more people. Karl began to teach two of the new employees, Graff and Gary, to be printers. The third person was an elderly lady, Ruth, a friend of Sirota's, who helped trim the pages and sew the bindings. Jarl had little money left, between the payments on Karl's house and his seven employees' salaries, but he still attempted to pay them each good money and give them half a Saturday and all of Sunday off, something unheard of in Vanir.

Jarl met with Tyr's only manufacturer of sewing machines, which were made exclusively for the three clothing factories that overlooked the Nanoo River. The company arranged for him to tour one plant, where women and children worked from dawn to dusk, cramped for space, their pay mere pennies. Even worse was the happy bald man who guided Jarl around the factory, explaining the dependability and quality of the sewing machines, his profit margins, and not once seeing the people slaving away for him in the dark building. After the sewing machine manufacturer promised to make some modifications to his specifications, Jarl ordered one of the massive machines.

Business became so good that Jarl had to work in the small store all day, with no time to write. Often, in the morning, there would be a short line of customers at the door when they opened. Finally, among his customers, Jarl met a thin young woman, Ali Vinyard, from a well-to-do merchant family. Ali was both literate and able to do adequate arithmetic, and Jarl hired her on the spot.

Using another name, Jarl began writing tales of a county bumpkin who always managed to get himself into some sort of unusual and humorous trouble. He sold these stories on separate sheets of paper and as part of a regular publication, which, together with the weekly news of Tyr, was printed each Tuesday. He also canvassed the city for letters, suggestions, and advertising, with little to no results. Finally, he allowed several merchants three weeks' worth of free advertising. Within a month most of the better shops, stores, and restaurants in Tyr were placing small advertisements in his newspaper, which quickly became his best seller, surpassing even the description of the Battle of Burkes Station. And, at no additional cost to themselves—Jarl thought that was a shrewd move, otherwise they would have charged him money to sell it—he allowed a dozen of the stores in Tyr to purchase his newspaper and then sell it at cost to their customers.

In addition, Jarl printed a simple form that allowed the stage company to keep better track of its rolling stock, horses, drivers, and passengers. Within three weeks, he found himself printing a half dozen forms for several of the companies in Tyr. And except for one or two spies who sat under a lone tree south of the house, watching the printing company, the Church left him alone, seeing little danger in his newfound power.

Now—in this corner of Vanir—all the stages were Concord coaches. The stage line continued to pay Jarl ten dollars for each vehicle constructed. One day, when Alfheim Vail offered to send some messages by way of the stage to Pepper Ford Station, Jarl quickly suggested that the stage line begin a daily mail service, charging a half-penny for each letter mailed. Alfheim thought that was a good idea, and promised to talk to his bosses about it.

Jarl's first letter to Kettlewand brought a speedy reply—not from Kevin, Otis, Marri, or Iajore—but from Molly, who said that everyone was healthy, Aaron and Mylea were now a much talked-about couple, there had been no sign of the Raiders, and that Chad was staying out of trouble. Jarl smiled at the child's crude letters, remembering that her idea of Chad's mischief was slightly different than the view shared by her family. The next day, the northbound stage contained a large package bound for the Pepper Ford Station; three sets of every book the Elder Oak Company had printed, including a new innovation, six books with blank pages, so that people could write their own stories.

One night in mid-December, during their first real snowstorm, there was a sudden rapping on the front door. Karl, who was working late, went to answer it. Jarl continued writing, completing another tale of the confused and always-in-trouble country bumpkin. Karl returned, obviously upset, saying that the man at the door would speak only with Jarl. The printer had left the man standing outside, freezing in the falling snow.

Fingering his projectile pistol, Jarl quietly walked into the front room, passing the two long benches that displayed their books. He peeked through a crack in the shutter.

There was only one person there, and he was holding a large package and swinging one arm to ward off the cold. The night was dark and there was no outside light, but after watching for several seconds, Jarl decided that the shivering man probably presented no danger. Holding his pistol near his side, he slowly unlocked the latches and eased the door open. The man turned and faced him, flashing a wide grin of recognition. It was Navee Odror!

Never sure where the Church's spies were, Jarl quickly pulled the little E'landota into the house. Jarl's smile was immense. He had given up hope of ever seeing the little man again, figuring the Church had somehow recaptured or killed him. He hugged Navee and then hurried him into the larger, back room, next to the hot stove. Navee shed his heavy overcoat and stood there, rubbing his hands, and grinning as if he was meeting the King himself.

After the introductions, Karl—now calmed down—went for food. Navee quickly admitted he had not eaten in a full day, being on the road from Southern. Jarl looked at his friend. His clothing was old and ragged. He had no gloves. Two toes protruded from one boot. His hair was again ragged and uncut. And he appeared thinner, although with the heavier clothing he now wore, it was hard to tell.

It had been almost three months since they had parted on the wharf next to the Nanoo River. Jarl tried to explain his business and what they were doing. Navee grinned, and Jarl was unsure that he understood. Then he showed him one of their books, titled *The Battle of Burkes Station*. Navee opened it and suddenly whistled, the smile gone from his face. Slowly he turned the pages, running a finger down each one, his eyes searching out the words. He looked up, eyes wide, and asked Jarl how many copies he had made. The answer—slightly more than three hundred—brought another low whistle and the little man's eyes became even wider. For a long moment, Navee stared straight ahead. Then he grinned again, his eyes narrowed to their customary squint, and he began filling himself with the food and beer Karl had brought.

Navee—while he ate—pointed to his oilskin-wrapped package, now steaming from the heat of the hot stove. Slowly, sensing that it was somehow important, Jarl undid the string binding it and then unwrapped the oilskins. Inside was an immense book, more than eight centimeters thick and forty centimeters square, bound in hard leather, but beginning to fall apart. At one time in the past, there had been some gold markings on the cover, but now they were too faded to read.

Jarl carefully opened the old volume. It was written in English, but the words were hard to decipher. He turned several pages, slowly, carefully running a finger down the words, imitating Navee's actions a few moments before.

Then, suddenly, as if someone had turned on a bright light in a dark room, Jarl realized this was one of Jonson's translated Bibles, more valuable than gold itself and worth the life of everyone in his small company if the Church found it on the premises. Jarl turned to the last page and then back to the first page. Never having seen a Vanir Bible before, it was hard to tell if the book was complete, but all appearances indicated that it was.

Jarl scooted Navee upstairs to change clothes and bathe in a bucket of ice-cold water that he forced the little man to fetch himself. After rewrapping the Bible, Jarl and Karl went out into the snow-covered backyard. After Karl moved the more massive of the two presses, the two men dug a four-foot-deep hole. Jarl put the Bible in a wooden box—paper had originally come in it—then the two men, together with a newly arrived and clean Navee, placed the box in the hole and covered it with two feet of dirt.

Jarl had recently brought all of his earnings from the stage company up to the printing company. Now he counted out two hundred dollars—Navee's eyes again widened in surprise—and placed the coins in a leather bag and then in a second, smaller wooden box. That container was placed in the hole, and Karl shoveled dirt onto the box, filling the hole. They scattered the remaining dirt around the back yard and Karl moved the press back to its original spot. Jarl cautioned both men to say nothing about the translated Bible to anyone, not even to the Balsdons, as it could well be the death of them all. Then, before they returned to the house, Jarl counted out another twenty dollars for Navee and told the little man he now worked for the Elder Oak Printing Company and—first thing in the morning—they would go shopping for new clothes and a good pair of Kettlewand boots.

But first there was a story to be told. Karl poured more beer and, seated around the wood stove, while the falling snow hid the evidence of their late-night work, Navee began his tale.

"After you left us at the dock... in fact, right after you left us, Jonson got up and started walking away. I grabbed him by the arm, but he shook me off. I thought he would only go a short ways, so I threw the paddles into the canoe and shoved it back into the water, and ran up the hill after him. I figured I could come back later and meet you."

"Where did he go?" Jarl asked.

"To the black church. He hid in the shadows and looked at the church for a long time, then he started walking south. I followed him. He followed the main highway for a long time. He walked right in front of this house. Never once did he look back. There were soldiers at the south gate, but they took no notice of Jonson..."

"Even though he was only wearing those short prison pants?"

"Yep. But, there were a dozen of the Church's guards south of the gate. They caught Jonson and held his arms. I ran up to stop them. There was a fight. I doubt if I could have won, but the soldiers got involved..."

Jarl interrupted again: "What happened then?"

The Church's guards began to argue with the soldiers. It became a shouting match, and Jonson and I escaped. Then we started arguing. Jonson didn't want my company, but I wasn't willing to be left behind. However, when the Church's guards began to chase us, Jonson relented and graciously allowed me to accompany him." Navee ended that sentence with a soft chuckle.

He then continued his story. "I remained awake that night. Just as I expected, Jonson sneaked off. I followed him all night. Truth was, night was cold and it was the easiest way to keep warm. Come morning, Jonson tried to steal a chicken from a farm. He got caught, and I again intervened. The old couple who owned the farm were very suspicious of us, but I managed to talk them into letting us work for a meal. Let me tell you, that took one hell of a lot of talking..."

Navee paused again, and the three of them listened to the storm outside for a while. Karl again filled their mugs, and Navee continued his story: "In the end, we cut down two trees and split so much wood that the couple fed us three meals, which was damn good, because we hadn't eaten much in three days. They also gave us two old shirts and two nearly worn-out pairs of trousers, and allowed us to sleep in their barn. Jonson had already tried to slip away once and now... I was exhausted... I waited until the family had gone to sleep and wrestled the old man to the ground and tied him to a wooden post with a rope."

The little man leaned back and stared at the ceiling, a smile on his face. "I slept damn good that night," he said.

"What happened then?"

"Jonson and I traveled south for close to four weeks, all the way to Southern Province. He tried to escape three more times. Once he actually succeeded, but I counted on his single-mindedness, followed the road south, and caught up to him just after he had stolen a chicken from another farmer."

Navee chuckled. "That was one good chicken, despite Jonson's foul mood. Often, we worked for a farmer for a small meal or so that we could spend the night in his barn. Once, I managed to steal an old pair of boots. More times than I can remember, I tied Jonson to a tree so that I could get a good night's sleep. Several times, we had to take to the brush to avoid roving patrols of priests or the King's soldiers.

"We had made it well into Southern by the middle of November, and Jonson began to wander aimlessly. After a day or so of this, I resorted to the one unbearable torture I knew the old man could not withstand..."

"What did you do?" Jarl was apprehensive.

Navee paused for effect, then said, "I gave him a bath!"

Karl snorted in laughter, and Jarl had to suppress a smile. Navee continued his story: "Jonson was now newly motivated. He led me into the forests west of the main road. I was considering repeating the torture when we came upon an ancient and overgrown castle, which I thought had been a part of some old fortification that had protected the Southern from an invasion by the Empire."

Navee stopped and leaned forward in his chair. When he continued, he spoke much softer. "But I was wrong. It was an ancient monastery. Either because of my threats of another bath, or because the nights were becoming cold, Jonson led me straight to a lower chamber. There, among the fallen blocks and timbers, was a narrow portal that led into some kind of back room. Hell, it might have been a secret room at one time. Inside the room, Jonson moved several large rocks and uncovered a large wooden chest set high into one side of the room.

"Inside the chest were two huge, leather-bound books. Jonson grabbed one and began to kick at me and shout old chants and curses. I had no intention of allowing him to escape until I had examined the other book, so I grabbed the other book and got between him and the only door."

"And the books were translated Bibles?" Jarl asked, his voice also a whisper.

"Yes. I let Jonson go when I figured that out. He took one copy with him. I took the other copy and wrapped it in my shirt. Then I went to see some friends." Jarl guessed that this was the E'landota School in Southern, but with Karl present, Navee did not elaborate.

"My friends fed me and gave me better clothes, some better boots, and the oilskin wrapping. I wrapped the Bible up and headed back to Tyr, hiding from soldiers and priests on the way. I often spent the nights in the same farmhouses we used on the trip south."

Jarl asked, "What did you do with the Bible at night?"

"Usually I hid it nearby..."

"Where?"

"In a hollow tree or under a rock... Believe me, I kept it close at hand. I waited for night to sneak through Tyr and I used the back streets to reach the Soo-Hoo. When I identified himself to the Stephensons, they told me how to find this place."

Jarl filled Navee's mug. When he began to fill the Karl's mug, the big printer waved him away; then put on his coat and stepped outside, heading toward home and bed. In the dark, silent backyard around the snow-covered press, the ground appeared undisturbed, as if nothing was buried there.

Navee spoke again, quietly, "Why did you hide those coins in the hole above the Bible?"

Jarl allowed himself a tired smile, "I hope that if anyone is lucky enough to dig open the hole, they will end their search when they discover the coins, thinking they have found the only treasure in the hole..."

"Can you trust Karl?"

Jarl hesitated, then answered, "The translated Bible is big secret, but I believe so. He has had his own troubles with the Church. And his troubles were as unwarranted as yours and mine." He paused for a moment, reconsidering, then added, "Well, as unwarranted as mine..."

Navee had one last story to tell. "Do you remember the other prisoners who were pardoned that day at the granite quarry?"

"Of course..."

"I heard that most of them were arrested on the road just west of the work camp."

"By the Church?"

"Yes."

"How reliable is the person who told you this?" Jarl asked.

"Very reliable. And I also heard other rumors that many of the prisoners simply disappeared. And I heard that, across the Greymist River from Ispwich, a farmer discovered fifty near-naked bodies hidden in a ditch. The Church said it was the work of robbers, but the locals say that no bandits have ever lived in the area."

Navee thought for a moment, then asked, "And who, with half a brain, would rob half-naked men just released from one of the Church's work camps?"

"And how could those men have gotten across the river?"

Navee continued, "I think it was smart that we decided to get off the road that day. I think the Church was looking for someone... maybe Jonson... I think the Church killed those men. And I think they transported the bodies across the river to hide their deed."

Jarl said nothing, but he remembered the prison guard who had stared at him, and not at Jonson. They talked on then about little things, but Jarl noticed that Navee never asked what he was going to do with the translated Bible.

Were his plans that obvious?

CHAPTER SEVENTEEN:

STORI AND JANIS

The next day, while the snow melted, Karl and company built a shed over the two printing presses, leaving enough room for a third press, which Levi intended to begin constructing the following day. Navee and Jarl went into Tyr, purchasing the promised clothes, boots, gloves, and coat, and placed more orders for paper, leather, and ink. The following morning brought yet another surprise. Jarl was writing in the back room—a tedious operation when using a quill pen and coarse paper—when Ali bustled into the room, clearly upset. Jarl dropped the pen and hurried into the front room, discovering the place empty.

Parked outside was a handsome carriage, new and built along the lines of his own Concord coaches, pulled by two matching teams of white horses. While an immaculate, uniformed driver held the reins, a servant—wearing a tall, feathered hat—stiffly dismounted from the driver's box. A third man stood beside the near lead horse, which wore a light saddle, holding the animal's head with a white gloved hand. Milling in front of and behind the lacquered coach were no less than four mounted guards, all well dressed and well armed, and all E'landota by their looks.

Ali was stammering, "They are High Ejliteta! Someone important!"

"No kidding!" Jarl groaned. He spent a few moments brushing himself off, then sent Ali back to tell Karl to tidy up the backyard. The young girl was not listening. Twice he repeated his request, finally he had to pinch her on the arm to get her attention. At that, Ali scurried toward the back of the house. Jarl tucked in his shirt tail a second time and, as the servant opened the carriage door, gave up waiting, opened the door of the house, and stepped outside.

The mounted guards took no notice of him. Through a thin layer of curtains, he could see several people inside the carriage. There was a brief glimpse of white lace, then a man with bushy brown eyebrows parted the curtains and stepped outside. The man could have knocked Jarl down with a feather—he was the tall man from the Church's quarry who had pardoned one fifth of the inmates.

The servant introduced the man in a loud voice, "The High Duke of Kamjar, Lord Hjas Gautrekson."

Jarl thrust out his right hand and said, "I'm Jarl Hawkins. I run the Elder Oak Printing Company." His breath was steamy in the cold air.

The Duke smiled, and his grip was strong as he shook Jarl's hand. His voice was a deep baritone, "I know. I have heard much about you." Noticing Jarl wore no jacket, he pointed to the open door to the house, "Shall we go inside?"

Ali met them at the door, her face still a pale white. Jarl allowed the Duke to enter first. For the first time, he was aware of how uncomfortable the front room of Karl's old house was. The old white paint on the walls was faded and flaking; the benches, displaying the various books of the Elder Oak Printing Company, were worn, stained, and cracked; the floor creaked; one table hid a hole in the floor; and the ceiling matched the walls, with ancient boards of yellow sycamore showing through wide gaps in the paint. The one window was covered with soot and the curtain in the interior doorway was torn and dirty.

Ten minutes ago—and three months of yesterdays—the room had been more than adequate for his small company's purposes. Now, in the presence of one Lord Hjas Gautrekson, the place had a worn, old, and filthy feeling. Jarl was embarrassed.

The Duke appeared not to notice. He bent over the first bench, examining the books. The first copy he opened was the blank paper handbook. The tall man straightened—his bearing was nothing if not dignified—and raised one of his bushy eyebrows in surprise. Jarl explained, "We sell these books so that other people can write their own text, figures, or whatever."

The Duke nodded, satisfied with the answer. Then he asked, "Does it sell well?"

Jarl had recently shaved off his beard, and he wondered if the tall man remembered him from that day at the Church's quarry. "No," he said, "Not as well as I would like."

The Duke now examined one of the publications of children's fairy tales, then the first reader, and finally the manuscript on the Battle at Burkes Station. This one he read for several seconds, complimenting Jarl on his style of writing. To one side, Ali stood, wringing her hands, her face still white. Jarl tried to relax, but could not.

The tall man straightened and said, "Interesting." He looked at the doorway and the dirty curtain. "That leads to the printing press?"

Jarl nodded, "Yes, would you like to see them?"

"Yes, I would. You have more than one?"

Jarl wanted to give an impression of honesty. He knew it would help later when he had something to hide. "We have two, and we are just constructing our third."

The single bushy eyebrow again arched upward, and the tall man smiled, obviously trying to put Jarl and Ali at ease. One of the E'landota opened the outside door and stuck his head inside, "Sir, your daughter would like to know if she can come in."

The Duke looked at Jarl, "Would you mind if my daughter joins us?"

Jarl was taken aback by the man's formality. He was equally polite, "Of course not."

Once more, Jarl stepped outside into the chill morning air. The Duke and Ali followed. The servant again opened the carriage door. This time, when the curtains parted, an ankle protruded. Then a hand was extended. Jarl took the hand, and the lady stepped down. For such a tall man, his daughter was no more than five feet tall, a little on the plump side, with bright green eyes and a charming smile. Still holding the woman's tiny hand, Jarl glanced back at the Duke and began, "Your daughter..."

The tall man's smile broadened and humor touched his hazel eyes, yet for a few seconds he did not answer, letting Jarl stand there, his face turning red, holding the hand. Then the man's deep baritone intervened, "No, this is my daughter's best friend, Pio Pipher. She is visiting us from the Southern Province."

Jarl felt foolish. On the steps in the open doorway, Ali's face abruptly turned from white to red.

Once again, the curtain parted and a second ankle appeared. Once more, Jarl took the hand that was offered to him. This time there was no mistaking the lady for the Duke's daughter—she was tall, with the same spark of amusement in her black eyes, which were the same color as her hair. And her face was familiar—it was the woman from the aid tent at the Battle of Burkes Ford!

Jarl searched his memory but could not remember the woman's name, but the Duke was speaking, "May I present my daughter, the Lady Rebecca Stori Hrafkel Gautrekson. I believe you know her as Stori."

Jarl looked up at the amused black eyes and stammered for a few seconds. Finally he exploded with one word: "Damn!"

The Duke laughed out loud. Then together, the four of them waded past Ali—who was still standing red-faced on the steps—and into the front room of the printing shop.

Jarl showed them all his books. He presented Stori with a copy of *The Battle of Burkes Ford*. The Duke bought a copy of everything, including the children's readers and six copies of the blank books, saying that he thought they were a good idea. Then they toured the back room and watched Sirota stitch a final copy on the sewing machine. Next was the backyard, where Pio and the two Gautreksons took delight in watching Karl print six pages of the second children's reader in less than a minute. Jarl showed them one of his maple laminated panels with the small lead characters resting on the narrow wooden slides, and Karl demonstrated his process for making the letters. The final stop was the third press, which Levi and Navee were beginning to construct. Between the Duke and his daughter, Jarl was asked more than a hundred questions.

They then retired to the back room, where Karl served tea and small cakes. For a while Stori spoke of the battle, and Jarl asked her to write an article on her version of it. Her reply was quick, "But you already have one."

"So... what's wrong with two?"

Stori stopped, thinking for a long moment. Then she asked, "Do you really want me to write an article?" Her voice was still like music.

"Yes."

The tall woman was thoughtful, taking the request seriously, but then she argued, "But most of your readers will be interested in the glory and the honor of battle, not in a mere woman's work in the aid tent." To one side, her father listened quietly, his eyes aglow.

"I do not agree," Jarl said. "And, I will tell you this: if you write it, I will print it. And I think people will be interested in your version of the battle."

The Duke interrupted, "What are your plans now?"

"Expand. Print more books. Continue the newspaper."

"What else can you, or will you, print?"

Jarl pretended to be thoughtful, but the question frightened him. "I haven't really thought much about it," he lied. "Maybe another volume of children's fairy tales. Perhaps a dictionary, or another collection of my Bumpkin Tales, which you saw as separate articles."

"It sounds as if you have thought a great deal about it," the Duke said. He paused, then added, "You know, the Church feels that this is a play toy... a passing fad..."

Jarl thought, 'How foolish.' But to the Duke he only shrugged and said nothing.

For a moment they talked of other things, the port, the Church, the weather. Then, somehow, he and Stori were discussing the great battle in Kettlewand once again. Jarl told how he had become sick and she described the days and nights spent in the aid station, after the battle was over. It had been close to three weeks before she finally left the battle site. Even while talking about it, her fatigue seemed to return. In the end, her father, who had been in Desjhan, had come and retrieved her. Together they had journeyed west, on the King's business, touring the gutted ruin of Orrin's Fort, which the Glasseys had burned during their retreat. Then they returned to Tyr, so that the Duke could report to the King.

Jarl turned to the elder Gautrekson, "It must take great courage to allow your daughter to be a battlefield nurse?"

The Duke rolled back his head and laughed. "No courage at all. She told me she was visiting Pio in Southern and I believed her." Stori blushed, hiding her mouth behind one hand. Jarl stared, fascinated by the feminine gesture. The tall man continued, "It was only when I bumped into Will James in Desjhan that I discovered she was in Kettle. A despicable wench...." He grinned at his daughter, "Just like her mother!"

Stori's black eyes flew open. It was obvious she was used to her father teasing—and that she enjoyed it. Her voice was musical laughter, "Oh, father!" The man chuckled, his smiling eyes meeting his daughter's.

Karl was trying to tip toe around them and serve them more tea and small cakes. The wide, two-meter-tall hunk of a man towering over them was making Jarl nervous, and he diverted the conversation to Will James, asking if he had survived.

Laughter again touched Stori's black eyes. "Oh, yes, he survived. After he left you... it must have been immediately after he left you... he joined a countercharge against the Glasseys. They said he was quite brave, capturing a Glassey standard and rallying a company of pikemen against the next attack. General von Rhinehart personally congratulated him afterwards, to both their mutual embarrassment."

Remembering Will James' fear after his first battle, Jarl could well imagine his chagrin at being singled out for bravery by his commander. "He was not wounded then? Will James, I mean..."

"Except for his hand, he escaped the battle quite unscathed."

"If you see him, tell him I would like to see him again."

Stori's black eyes laughed again, "I will do that. He lives in Tyr, and I am sure he would like to see you too."

The Duke suddenly realized Jarl's first customers were outside, being held back by his guards. The three High Ejliteta took their leave, bundled up against the cold morning air, picked up their merchandise, and hurried from Karl's house to their waiting carriage. Jarl bid them goodby and told them to come back, if they so pleased. With that, the first two customers—two elderly laddies, one who had yellow teeth and old, dirty lace hanging from each sleeve—entered the store, complaining about the uppity nature of the High Ejliteta. Somehow, Jarl enticed Ali to come down out of the clouds and wait on them. After a quick tour of the two presses and sewing machine, he sat back down to his writing. He discovered, much to his dismay, that now the words just would not come to him.

Two weeks later, with the third press running and business caught up, Jarl called everyone into the back room and outlined their winter's work, which included the construction of yet a fourth press.

Levi interrupted, "But we don't have enough work for three presses, much less four..."

Jarl shook his head no. Then, as calmly as possible, he told his few employees what he intended to print next. Their faces, especially Ali's, paled, and everyone soon wore a scared look. Jarl's words were quiet and solemn, "Tell no one what we are printing. Ali, you cannot even tell your parents."

Navee spoke, "I have two friends who can be trusted to help... and they can keep a secret." The little man looked directly at Jarl and said, "My friends will not be afraid of the danger." Jarl understood that Navee's friends were E'landota.

The next morning, Karl moved the heavy press, and they dug up the small sack of coins and the translated Bible. While Levi filled the hole, Navee and Jarl began to lay out the first pages. That morning set the pattern for the next month. First only one press printed the translated Bible, then—after the fourth press had been constructed—two machines printed the book. When they caught up on the stock Jarl calculated they would need in the spring, three of the massive wooden presses printed the Bible. It was cautious and frightening work, aggravated by everyone's strained nerves. And now, when they should have been most watchful, the two men who had spied on them all fall from the single tree to the south had disappeared.

Jarl hired Navee's two friends, Lannie and Sol, both of who were E'landota. Karl braced the upstairs floor with oak beams, and they carried the sewing operation upstairs and into a corner that faced both Tyr and onto the street. They rigged strings to that room and to the front room, so that either Sirota or Ali could ring an alarm bell in the backyard if there was danger. Jarl moved a chair and table into the attic. There, while writing, he searched the surrounding countryside for watchers or tracks in the snow.

Of course, it was winter and the cold weather had probably driven the spies home. Jarl purchased an old army tent to cover the backyard and two potbellied iron stoves to heat the tent, putting the enormous supply of firewood cut by Levi and Karl to good use. They left the south side of the tent open—that was their blind side—so that the printers could keep a watch in that direction. Toward the west, the steep side of the mountain protected them. Fortunately, none of Jarl's suppliers ran out of their respective products; in fact, Jarl was not even sure if they realized what was required to manufacture one book.

One press printed a thesis on hygiene for a week, while two printed the Bible, and the fourth printed his Bumpkin Tales, which Jarl intended to combine into one book in the spring. Never once did they miss publishing their weekly newspaper and never once did anyone report any suspicious person approaching or watching the house. Jarl was thankful that the main Tyr-Smyrna Road was well below the house—trying to watch that busy highway would have easily destroyed their nerves, even with the lesser numbers of people who traveled it in the winter.

One evening, an hour after dark, there was a sharp knock on the front door. Only Jarl and the three E'landota were living in Karl's old house. There was a general scramble for weapons. Then Jarl, his projectile pistol in his hand, slowly unlocked and eased the front door open. There were no moons and all he could see were two figures, one tall and one short, both hooded by dark cloaks. Then the tall figure reached up and dropped her cowl. It was Stori Gautrekson.

Jarl quickly pocketed his pistol, opened the door, and ushered both visitors into the warm kitchen. The shorter person then removed her hood. It was a frightened young girl, about fourteen, with long, dirty, stringy brown hair, who was clutching a small, black kitten tightly to her chest.

Stori was dressed for a fancy ball, and she told her tale in a hurry. "This girl has been accused by the Church of being a witch, which—as any idiot can see—is a charge that is completely unfounded and entirely ludicrous. The only thing she is guilty of is protecting her cat."

"Why did she need to protect her cat?" Jarl asked.

Stori's black eyes flashed with impatience and anger. "Black cats are a symbol of evil. One of the priests tried to catch it, to throw it onto a fire and release its soul. The man scared the cat and it ran to the girl, hiding behind her. The priest bent to grab the kitten and received a swift kick to his nose for his trouble. Pio witnessed it all. Her exact words were, 'The blood flowed like wine.'"

Jarl sucked in a quick breath. He knew that the rest of the story was not going to be good.

"The priest was infuriated and called for his guards. He called the girl a witch and wants her burned. Fortunately, the child was able to scoot under a wagon and outrun the heavily armed men. We allowed her to hide in my coach."

"What do you want me to do?" Jarl asked. He was deathly afraid, almost too frightened to breathe.

"I want you to hide her here at your printing company."

Jarl shook his head no. He did not want the Church to have any reason to search his premises. Legally, there was no way he could stop them.

Stori was insistent. "The child is a street urchin." Jarl's eyes and nose had led him to suspect as much. "She lives in the back alleys and has no one to turn to, no one to protect her from the Church."

The young girl's brown eyes were large and sorrowful. Jarl knelt and asked, "What's your name?"

He received no reply, but Stori answered, "Her name is Janis Eirik."

Jarl looked up, "Did any of the Church follow you here?"

Stori shook her head. Her voice, as always, was musical, "No. And I don't think they will be able to recognize her, especially once she is cleaned up." With anyone else, Jarl would have taken that statement with a grain of salt; but, with Stori, he suspected that, unless her luck had been very bad, then she had not been followed.

He made a quick decision, one that caused him a small amount of pain, "All right, there is a tub upstairs. We will bring some water. You clean her and cut her hair."

Stori shook her head, "I can't. I am supposed to be at a charity ball. It would look suspicious if I missed it."

Now Jarl shook his head, "Stori, there are four men here and no women. We can't bathe her. You have to stay."

"What about...?"

"Sirota is off visiting a sister, Ruth lives in town, and Ali lives at home with her parents."

Stori grimaced, but her decision was quick. "All right, show me the tub."

Jarl nodded to Navee. The little man led the two women upstairs. Jarl, Lannie, and Sol carried two buckets each of water up the stairs, cursing the idiot who had put the tub on the second floor—a situation that had not bothered Karl, who did not take many baths. There was no time to heat any water. Stori scrubbed, Navee cut hair, and Jarl found some cast-off clothing that Stori put on the young girl. Jarl bathed the kitten and handed it back to Janis. Stori said she would be back before daylight with proper clothes. Then, after Jarl had slid into his heavy sheepskin coat, he escorted the tall woman back across the Vilyur River bridge and into the city proper. They stopped next to the dark, recessed side door of a large house, which was surrounded by expensive coaches and waiting servants. Inside, amid bright lights, came the sounds of soft music and loud voices.

Stori touched Jarl's sleeve and whispered a soft, musical thanks.

"Will you be all right," he asked, "sneaking in like this?"

Stori grinned, and Jarl could feel the humor in her black eyes. "The gossip should be nothing serious." She kissed him lightly on the cheek and quickly ducked through the dark doorway. Jarl listened, making sure she had made it safely inside. Then, as he turned to leave, he tripped over an abandoned snow shovel. After climbing out of the snow drift, he walked home, silently crossing the wooden bridge.

The night was cold and quiet, and the dry snow squeaked underfoot. The kiss lingered warm on his cheek, but the painful memories of other such bitterly cold nights walked with him. When he arrived back at the printing company, after thinking of dead friends and other planets, his cheeks were tear-stained and covered with ice.

It was Navee who let him into the large house. The little man was nervous, glad to see that Jarl had safely returned. He said that Janis and her kitten were sleeping in his bed and that he would sleep in the kitchen. The next morning, more than an hour before daylight, Stori was good to her word, arriving with several dresses, blouses, and pants that the young girl could wear, as well as a narrow, long needle and a candle.

While Jarl watched, and with a determined expression on her face, the tall woman heated the needle and drove it once through each of Janis' earlobes. From each she hung a small earring, sure—she said—to set the Church on the wrong trail. Finally, Stori produced a pair of scissors and trimmed Janis' hair. Before the first light had begun to creep across the snow-covered plain to the east, the tall woman was gone, silently leaving through the backyard.

That morning, Jarl introduced Janis to the company's employees, telling everyone she was Navee's niece, who had just arrived from Nowell.

He told Ali to show the younger girl how to sell the books, then he climbed to his attic room to write.

But then, several hours later, Jarl had to run down the stairs to referee a fight. Two elderly ladies—dressed as High Ejliteta—had purchased four books. Ali had added up their total, but Janis had interrupted, telling the older girl her sum was incorrect and too little. One, then the other of the old women, had totaled the numbers, and somehow Karl had become involved. Everyone was agreeing with Ali.

Jarl ordered Karl back to the presses, and sent the women on their way, allowing them to pay what they felt was correct. He then explained to Janis that he did not want her upsetting the customers again.

The young girl's voice was weak and thin, almost impossible to hear. She apologized for the argument and said she would not let it happen again. Something in her small voice caught Jarl's attention, and it took him only a moment to retrieve the piece of scrap paper with the various calculations scribbled on it. Ali watched him, her expression smug with pride.

The older girl pointed to her own column of figures, four numbers and then a total. Beside it was a second set of figures, scrawled by one of the old women. That sum was the same as Ali's number. A third column equaled a totally fanciful number—someone had been playing for an audience. The fourth set of figures were neatly written, and equaled a higher number.

It took Jarl just a few seconds to add the numbers, doing so in his head. Then, he rocked back on his feet in surprise. The hard part was telling Ali that she had been wrong—he didn't want to hurt her feelings and have her run home to her parents. He then spent the remainder of the morning, not writing, but testing Janis with various math problems. Not only could the young girl do addition and subtraction, but she could multiply and divide, an ability unheard of, even in the nation's capital. But no matter how often he asked, Janis would not tell how she had come by her knowledge. Although, when tested, Janis could barely read, Jarl was not discouraged. He had a feeling that the young girl would prove to be a fast learner.

And he knew how she felt about the Church.

CHAPTER EIGHTEEN:

THE PRINCE!

When their warning system failed, it failed magnificently. It was a beautiful cold, clear day near the end of January. To the north, the buildings and homes of Tyr stood out with crystal clarity, appearing sugar-coated under their drapings of ice and snow. Thin trails of smoke drifted southward from the hundreds of chimneys, and the occasional sound of someone chopping wood carried up to the printing company. To the northwest, the tall waterfall had frozen into a single column of blue ice, dusted with tiny ledges of dry, powdery snow. Above the printing company's backyard, the cold, steep, beautiful peaks of the Sabre Mountains rose, with stark white cornices outlined against the clear blue sky. To the east, the flat coastal plain was a cold crystal fairyland, its few folds smoothed by the deep cover of snow. The smoke plumes and buildings of Ispwich were a dark smudge beside ice-rimmed Greymist River, on which floated a few broken ice floes. Further east, past Ispwich, the snow ended and the ground became a drab brown landscape, interrupted by the dark-green pattern of conifer forests.

In the backyard, between the two roaring wood stoves and under the old army tent, four men worked the levers on four presses, squeezing out sheets of paper lined with neat rows of small black letters. Karl was somehow threading his huge bulk between the presses, picking up the printed pages and delivering fresh paper. To one side, next to the large pile of snow-covered firewood, Levi and Navee were beginning to construct a fifth press.

Inside the shed, Janis was cleaning and rearranging the small lead blocks of letters into their respective sorting trays, so that they could be easily found when needed to prepare the next page. Beside her, in an empty tray, lay a contented black cat, its tail hanging lazily over the side. Ali, in the front room, had no customers; she was proofing the neat maple panel to be placed on one of the wooden presses. Jarl had recently dipped into his stagecoach money and purchased a second sewing machine, and upstairs—and in a brightly-lit front room—Ruth and Sirota were stitching the together leather bindings of several books. Jarl was above them in his attic room. In theory, he was either writing or searching the nearby roads for danger. In reality, he was watching two mountain goats negotiate a precipitous wall far above his head.

Then he noticed that the soft thump, thump, thump of the presses had stopped. In its place rose the excited commotion of many voices. Jarl set his pen aside, and after quickly negotiating the narrow stairway leading from the attic, ran down the wider stairs to the first floor, bumping into Sirota at the bottom and pushing Ali out of the open doorway and into the backyard. Work had stopped and everyone—except Navee, who was sitting quietly on the wood pile—was gathered in the open shed, where Janis had been working. As Jarl hurried across the frozen backyard, Karl stepped aside, and Jarl saw the tall figure of Stori Gautrekson standing in the middle of the milling confusion. Jarl's heart sank—by noon they could all be in one of the Church's many dungeons.

Jarl elbowed his way into the crowd. Stori was standing over one of the wooden trays, reading the backward lead figures. Karl, not wanting to touch a High Ejliteta, was waving his massive hands in the air, trying to shoo her away. When Jarl arrived, the tall woman looked up. As always, her black eyes were amused and there was music in her voice, but she was also sarcastic at the moment. "Why, Jarl Hawkins, whatever have you been up to?"

The woman was not stupid, the answer was obvious and Jarl's voice was cold, "You can see what we've been up to!"

Stori continued to rummage through the maple panels and the masses of printed sheets. Sirota and Ruth were jittering. Karl was wringing his hands. Lannie and Sol were stone-faced, their emotions hidden. Ali, still standing in the open doorway, appeared ready to faint. Even Janis, the hard street urchin, was pale under her tanned face. Jarl stepped in front of Stori, barring her from examining any more of the pages of the translated Bible.

For a few moments, they stood there, an outlander with cold brown eyes and a tall High Ejliteta with amused black eyes. It was Jarl who finally spoke, quietly and seriously, "What are you going to do now? If you tell the Church, we could all be dead by nightfall. You could give these people a head start, as little good as it will do."

Stori evaded his question with a question, "Why are you doing this?"

"A Church should be a place for people to worship, a place to help people with their spiritual needs. The Church here is nothing but a rich, power-hungry organization that wants to rule the land. The government—the King, if you will—should be that law, overseeing the courts, and running the prisons, not the Church. With a Bible that they can understand, I think the people will realize how badly the Church has been misusing its power and then—hopefully—some sorely needed changes will take place."

Jarl paused and took a very deep breath. Then he repeated his question, "What are you going to do?" His voice was not kind.

The tall woman said nothing. Karl, his face white and his voice a weak whine, asked, "Are you going to turn us in?"

Stori was thoughtful. When she spoke, she said, "I'm not going to turn you in." There were a half-dozen sighs of relief from the small group of employees. She continued, "You helped Janis when she needed it. What kind of a person would I be to turn you in?"

Jarl was not satisfied, "What are you going to do?" His eyes were still very hard.

The tall woman steepled her long fingers, still thinking. "Nothing. As you say, the Church has entirely too much power... and they abuse it." She hesitated, but Jarl had the feeling her pause was only for effect. "I will not tell the Church."

Jarl escorted the tall, black-eyed woman to the side gate. Again, he cautioned her to tell no one. Stori's eyes became full of fire, and her whisper was intense, "I said I will not tell the Church! I will not tell the Church!" With that, she turned and marched away along the path shoveled through the snow.

Jarl asked Karl what had happened. The big printer did not know. It was Navee who told the story. Ali had somehow missed the tall High Ejliteta when she had walked past the front window. Stori had come to the side gate, probably to visit Janis, for the first time since the dark, cold night she had left the young girl at the printing company. Stori had entered the backyard without knocking and had walked straight to Janis, working in the open shed. Once in the shed, it was only a few seconds until she noticed the printed pages of the Bible nearby.

Jarl interrupted, exasperated, "There were seven people between the fence and Janis. No one saw Stori?"

Navee's words were soft, "I saw her... but no one else did. She moved very quietly..."

"Why didn't you stop her?"

The E'landota shrugged. He clearly was not too concerned. Then he said, "I didn't see her as a threat."

Jarl waved his arms in the air. "Not a threat!!" he shouted. "Everyone is a threat, especially a High Ejliteta!"

It was close to noon before Jarl could coerce anyone back to work and then—because Levi, Ali, Sirota, and Ruth had all quit—they were short-handed. Jarl assigned Janis the job of putting the small lead characters into the laminated maple trays used for printing. Here her poor reading abilities were not that critical; all she had to do was simply imitate the letters on the translated Bible. Then he closed up the shop—it was too cold for any customers anyway—and he and Navee climbed into the upstairs front room, sat down at the sewing machines, and took over the job of the seamstresses. As he jammed a cold needle into his thumb, he looked at Navee again and growled, "Stori Gautrekson not dangerous? What jug of whiskey have you been drinking?"

The shop remained closed for the remainder of the week. Karl, Graff, Gary, Sol, and Lannie printed the Bibles and ran errands. Janis continued to compose the pages, sometimes helping with the book binding. Navee did most of the stitching, sewing the leather bindings around the heavy sheets of paper. Jarl was thankful they were only working on the Bumpkin Tales; he dreaded stitching the heavy Bible. Karl suggested that the company work all of Saturday, and since everyone was agreeable, they did so, then took the warm Sunday off. Jarl loafed around the printing shop and did some much-needed housekeeping.

Monday morning was cold again. Before they started work—as they were standing around a fire, drinking tea, and warming their ink—there was a series of sharp raps on the front door. The blood drained from Karl's face, but Jarl tried to remain calm, thinking that this was an odd time for the Church to come calling—they would instead choose the dead of night.

It was Stori and Ali. Jarl admitted them into the front room. Stori knocked the snow off her cloak and dropped the hood. Her black eyes were very serious. "I have come to help. Ali will take her job back, if you will have her."

Jarl said nothing.

"You do need help, don't you?"

"Yes. Badly."

"Well, I can read and write. Put me to work!"

Jarl stared into the woman's black, fiery eyes for a long time. When he spoke, his words were very soft, "The work will be dangerous."

The tall woman replied, "But important. You said so yourself!"

Jarl nodded, but he stood rooted in one spot, unsure if he should accept this woman's help.

Stori spoke again, "Yes or no, Bookwright?" She was becoming angry.

Jarl, one hand on his chin, thought he could at least keep an eye on her in the narrow confines of the shop. And they might be safer with a High Ejliteta present. He spoke one word, "Yes."

He tried to put Stori to work with Janis, but the black-haired woman would have none of it. She instead insisted on replacing Jarl as a seamstress, so that he could get back to his writing. In the end, he moved into the sewing room—it was heated by a stove below in the front room, which Ali kept stoked—and began writing, not more Bumpkin Tales, but a thesis on religious reform, to be distributed with the Bibles. As always, without a dictionary, the work went slowly.

On Wednesday, the pace at the printing company became even more normal, when Ruth, Levi, and Sirota arrived shortly after dawn, asking for their jobs back. Soon Levi and Navee were back next to the snow-covered wood pile, constructing the fifth press, almost as if their work had not been interrupted.

Stori was a godsend. For the first time, Jarl could completely trust someone else to do the proofreading. Her math was just as meticulous, although she became exasperated when Jarl asked her to do some calculations, saying that Janis was every bit as good. And no job was too tedious or too hard for the tall High Ejliteta. Some days she would work upstairs with the seamstresses, sewing the heavy bindings of the books and keeping a lookout for suspicious people on the street below. One long day, with ink all over her face and white apron, she inked and printed the pages of the translated Bible. Often Jarl would simply stop and watch her, enjoying both her beauty and her graceful feminine personality. He would pass her in the stairways, where she would be carrying large stacks of books upstairs or down and complaining, with her eternal good nature, about the idiot—always louder when Jarl was near—who had placed the two sewing machines on the second story of the house. The tall woman always arrived early in the cold morning, usually with Ali, in time for a hot cup of tea, and she was the last one to leave late at night. Often, she stayed to teach Ruth, Soirta, Levi, and Janis how to read.

Stori always dressed in old clothes—in effect, becoming the nurse Jarl had known at the Battle of Burkes Station—and would work in the small front room of the house, waiting on the few winter customers. She obviously took great pleasure in playing the part of a woman of Tyr's lower caste, and Jarl had to chuckle when watching her. The men and women who came to purchase the books and newspapers had no idea they were in the presence of one of Tyr's High Ejliteta, who rarely—if ever—rubbed elbows with the common folk of Vanir. And, of all of his employees—although since Stori took no money, she was technically not an employee—the tall, black-haired woman was the only person he could regularly trust to go into Tyr and return with an order and not be overcharged.

However, despite repeated efforts, neither Stori nor Jarl could entice Janis to admit where she had come by her learning of mathematics. And Janis was full of other surprises. Once Jarl caught her sitting on the wood pile, the little black cat on her lap, teaching division to Karl and Ali. The young girl's principal job was to put the small lead characters into the wide maple trays, which Jarl hoped would improve her limited reading skills. Often Jarl would stop and watch her sounding out the words with her lips, frowning at a word or pronunciation she did not know. And when Stori mentioned that Janis had already learned all the words in the second reader, Jarl quickly wrote and printed a third, presenting the first copy to the young girl.

Often, in the evenings, the small group of employees would gather in the kitchen or around one of the stoves in the backyard and Karl would tell a story from one of his endless supply of children's tales. Sometimes Stori would describe the fancy parties the High Ejliteta attended. The women were always fascinated, and with Stori's easy personality, they were seldom envious. Occasionally, Jarl would tell a camping or hunting story from his own childhood, never mentioning how far away that place now seemed.

Jarl finished a second thesis on hygiene and then one on more modern medical practices. Neither paper did much more than stress cleanliness and better sanitation. The next day he dumped his writing materials on the table in front of Stori. Soon he had her writing not only an account of her part of the Battle at Burkes Station, but of a hunting trip she had gone on as a child, high in the Sabre Mountains, near the King's hunting lodge in Smyrna.

Time seemed to fly, and even with everyone now working six days a week, it did not seem possible that enough Bibles would be printed by spring, especially with Jarl wanting to print 500 copies. Nevertheless, the small company was doing the best it could. Everyone was working hard, there were very few breakdowns, and their supplies of ink and paper were plentiful. And, as incredible as it seemed, the Church appeared to have lost all interest in the small printing company. Jarl wondered if they had a secret plan he could not guess. It was a terribly fearful time for him, knowing he was trying to change the very structure of Vanir's society. In six months, he—and all his employees—could well be dead, or serving life terms in one of the Church's many work prisons.

February came and went. With March came more snowstorms and fewer customers. One cold morning—there was a fresh layer of snow on the ground—Ali came running back into the backyard. Her face was white and her voice was a whisper. Jarl, who was stoking a fire, looked up. The girl was so fearful she could hardly talk. "This is it," he said to himself. "The Church is here." He sent the three E'landota scrambling for their weapons before he finally understood the two words Ali was mumbling over and over again. "The Prince, the Prince..."

Jarl was perplexed and impatient. "What about the Prince?" he demanded.

The young girl's voice was even lower. Karl was leaning forward, trying to catch her words, "He is in the front room..."

The backyard exploded into activity. Three or four people began to gather up the copies of the Bible, others began to clean the presses, Karl backed into a stove and jumped high into the air, shouting and knocking the stove over in the other direction. Jarl joined everyone in throwing snow onto the fire, but then Stori grabbed him and pushed him into the house. For a moment, he stood in the kitchen, composing himself and knocking the snow off his clothing. Stori watched, her arms crossed, impatiently tapping her foot on the floor.

With a funny feeling in his stomach, Jarl walked to the curtain leading to the front room. He opened it and was immediately confronted by a tall E'landota, a man with long white-blond hair, who had a long-barreled flintlock pistol tucked into the front of his waist sash and a samurai sword slung over his back. The man appraised Jarl with cool, competent gray eyes. A tiny, red-tipped feather hung from his right ear and a sharp-tipped shirvken was stuck down in the hat band of his wide-brimmed felt hat. For a moment Jarl hesitated, thinking the man was a Ghost Raider, but then he remembered the Vanir occasionally employed the nomads, calling them Tame Ghosts. Nothing about this man appeared tame.

The E'landota eased back against the wall, allowing Jarl passage. There was nothing threatening about his manner. Jarl stepped by, into the small front room. Another E'landota stood, his back against the side wall, watching Jarl as he entered. This man, although dressed similarly to the first bodyguard, had brown hair and brown eyes. Outside, through the front window, Jarl could see an ornate carriage and several more E'landota. The Prince, his cloak a deep, rich color of blue fringed with the hair of a white wolf, was leaning over the book table, his back to Jarl, thumbing though one of the many volumes there.

The E'landota at the front door made some small motion. The Prince straightened, looked at the man for a second, and then turned toward Jarl, smiling and thrusting out his right hand. The man was tall, young, had a pale face, and light reflected off his glasses. Even as Jarl stuck out his own right hand, his lower jaw fell toward the floor. It was Will James!

The younger man rushed forward, enthusiastically. He shook Jarl's hand, then pulled him close and hugged him. Jarl stood rooted in one place, a confused expression on his face. Will James chuckled and then laughed, and finally Jarl managed three weak, gasping words, "You're the Prince?"

Will James stepped back, bowed, and then straightened, his smile becoming larger. "Prince William James Lostkoth, son of King William Host Lostkoth and Queen Gretchen Bergelmire Lostkoth, heir to the High Throne of Vanir, and Hero of the Battle of Burkes Station. At your service, sir!" When Jarl continued to stare at him, his jaw still hanging, Will James continued, "Well, don't look so dumbfounded! I could have turned out to be a lot worse things."

Jarl shook his head. A smile slowly came to his lips. Then he muttered a single curse word under his breath. Behind him, the Tame Ghost was broadly grinning and Stori, her head stuck in through the door, had a small smile on her lips. Jarl looked over the tall woman and asked, "Did you know about this?"

"You said you wanted to meet him!"

Will James added, innocently, "I believe she might have mentioned it once or twice... just in passing, you understand."

Still shaking his head, Jarl looked back at Will James. "What happened to you after you left us on the last day on the ridge?"

Will James' smile faded only slightly. "I ran down and found myself in charge of a company of Pike whose commander had been killed. I led them in a counterattack, capturing a Glassey flag. Then we held the position against the next greencoat attack. We captured a large part of a Glassey company during that attack." The tall man shrugged, and then added, "In short, I got lucky."

Stori did not agree, and Jarl could easily see the admiration in her black eyes. "That's not true!" she said. "What you did was a very brave thing! General von Rhinehart personally awarded you the Croff la Medal for your courage."

"And it surprised him half to death when he discovered who I was." Will James looked back at Jarl. "But, anyway, not too bad for a scared city boy, eh?"

Jarl shook his head again, laughing at the thought of von Rhinehart's discovering the Prince of Vanir was posing as a lieutenant. "I'm glad to see that you lived," Jarl said honestly. "I was very concerned about you when you didn't reappear after the battle."

Will James quieted. "I had to see to the company of Pike. They had no commander. Then one of the men from that Kettle rifle unit said you'd been taken ill. Neither I nor von Rhinehart could figure out what had happened to you."

"I ended up at the Pepper Ford Station, just east of the battle site. They cared for me all winter."

Will James was concerned. "Are you recovered now?"

"Yes."

"You made me into quite a hero, you know, with your writings... holding the line in that first attack and then going with you high on the mountain, searching for the missing Rangers and Kvasir. It's funny, but I think a lot of people are more impressed that I went into the haunted mountains, trying to rescue the Rangers, than they are because of the actual battle."

Jarl was impressed with how much Will James had matured, and how he spoke and moved with much more confidence. "People know it was you in my story?" he asked.

"Oh yes, I am afraid my little escapade is well known by now, at least among the High Ejliteta. And your book only added to it."

Jarl snorted. "I can't call those few pages a book."

"Whatever. I thought it was really quite accurate too, and I was impressed with your ability to tell a story. You've done some writing before...?"

"Yes, back home. I used to write a bit. I'm glad you liked it... and I am glad you thought it honest. I take some pride in that."

The Prince reiterated, "Well, you do a good job, but it's not too honest. I noticed you left out our little conversation after that one Glassey attack."

"And my confrontation with the surgeon in the medical tent."

Will James chuckled, then he changed the subject. "Stori tells me you have quite a little factory here..."

"Would you like to see it?" Jarl asked, knowing Karl and Navee had had enough time to hide the Bible.

"Yes!"

As the Tame Ghost led the way into the kitchen, Jarl asked Will James, "So this is what you and Stori were discussing so secretly in the medical tent that day?"

Will James laughed again. "She had stolen away from her father, and I from mine. A High Ejliteta pretending to be nurse and the High Prince pretending to be a common soldier. I guess we both got caught... but..." Will James flashed a quick smile at Stori, "but neither one of us gave the other away."

"I never suspected anything anyway," Jarl admitted.

In the backyard, all the employees had nervously gathered into a single line. A third E'landota was standing next to the side gate. Ali's face was still extremely white, and Jarl wondered if she might faint. Karl was wringing his hands, a twisted expression on his face; Levi and Sirota were hunched over, as if they were in pain; and Janis was hiding in the back, clutching her black kitten.

It was Navee who Will James approached first. "So this is the famous Navee Odror, who I have heard so much about." At Jarl's questioning look, the Prince continued, laughing, "You didn't know you had such a famous person working for you? Navee is a renowned person in Tyr. He has had the distinct honor of punching the High Priest Killeap square in the nose. I wasn't there, but I have a friend who was, and she said that there was blood everywhere, which is not surprising for Old Balloon Nose." Will James again glanced at Stori, and the tall woman blushed, ever so slightly—it was clear she was the friend Will James spoke of. Jarl felt a sudden sharp pain of regret, and he knew that there was more between the Prince and Stori than a simple friendship.

Navee bowed, bending at the waist.

Will James continued, "I see you somehow managed to avoid the clutches of the Church. How is that?"

Navee answered, "I was pardoned on the first anniversary of the Battle of Burkes Station, Your Majesty." Jarl groaned inwardly, hoping he did not have to become so respectful, but also thankful Navee had not mentioned that he too had been imprisoned.

The Prince talked briefly to the other employees, asking Levi about his part in the same battle. Soon he had everyone, with the exception of Ali, at ease. One or two were even smiling. Then the Prince toured the small shop, commenting on the five presses, fingering the lead characters, and leafing through the finished pages that were waiting to be carried upstairs to be bound. Jarl was glad he did not realize how little work the five machines were producing.

Will James then asked to try one of the presses. Jarl quickly steered him to a press with an innocent piece of work in the maple panel. The Prince smudged his first attempts, but with Karl's enthusiastic assistance, he had soon printed no less than six sheets. He looked at his work, commenting on how easy it was.

Jarl started to speak, but he suddenly realized Will James was not listening. He was instead reading the sheet, realizing who had written it. He looked up at Stori, surprised, and complimented her on the work. The tall woman blushed, proud of his praise. Then she curtsied, quickly and just a bit.

Will James quickly read a second sheet. Jarl was impressed with how fast the man could read. Then he moved to a second press, staring at the panel of lead characters, resting in their maple tray. Jarl stepped forward, intending to knock the tray to the ground and scatter the lead pieces in the snow, but Will James caught his hand just as it touched the tray. For a moment they stood there, their eyes locked together, then Stori's dry words cut through the air, "He knows."

Jarl shivered, as if someone had dumped a pitcher of ice water down his back. He looked at Stori, "You said you weren't going to tell anyone!"

The woman's black eyes were defiant, "I said I wasn't going to tell the Church. The King and the Prince have no more love for the Church's power than do you."

"Damn." Jarl looked back at Will James. Once again his life and those of his employees was in someone else's hands. "How long have you known?"

Will James' eyes were smiling, "Longer than you think." His voice was very serious. "Stori is right, we have little love for the Church, not as they are now... And they clearly want to take over the entire country, as they have done in Glassitron.

"If this book," he waved his hand toward the tray of backwards letters, "helps take the Church out of the purses and courtrooms of my people and puts it back into their hearts and souls, then we will be forever in your debt." He paused, then asked, "How many have you printed?"

Jarl was hesitant, but—after a few moments—he motioned to Karl to uncover the printed pages of the translated Bible. The huge man was too upset to be of any use, and Lannie stepped forward and uncovered the printed pages and the leather-bound copy of the original Bible. Will James leafed through the printed sheets. He then opened the heavy, battered book, reverently turning the pages and reading the faded words. Finally, he nodded at some thought he kept to himself and turned back to Jarl, "How many copies are you printing?"

"500."

Will James whistled in amazement. "There will be fighting when this book is sold. Men will die. Have you thought of that?"

"Yes, but there will be fighting anyway. Many people are never going to accept the Church's dictatorship. And innocent people are dying every day in the Church's prisons."

Will James was quiet, thoughtful, "Yes, that is true."

"Do you think the Church knows of this yet?" Jarl asked.

"If they had even the slightest suspicion, they would have shut you down long ago. They have great power, you know."

"I know," Jarl said quietly.

"No, the Church has no idea what you are doing here. They think that your press is only a child's toy. And they believe you only have one printing machine. Two foolish ideas on their part. You were very smart to print the children's fairy tales first."

"I lucked into that. But if it has thrown the Church off our scent, then it is good on two accounts."

"How so?"

"Because in the spring, when we start selling the Bibles, there will be a few more people who can read a little bit better, because of the readers and the children's books."

"True." Will James abruptly changed the subject. "Are you planning the same reforms for the government?"

Jarl thought honesty was the best policy. "I intend on making some suggestions, but nothing nearly as drastic as this..." He waved a hand toward the Bibles. Still being honest, he continued, "I would like to discuss my political reforms with you before I print anything."

"That could be a good idea. I would like that."

Jarl sighed, looking back at the Bibles. "Of course, I am not changing the religion, I'm giving everyone a chance to understand it, not just the clergy."

"True." Will James changed the subject yet again. "Do you mind if I come back? Not as Prince Lostkoth, but as Will James."

Jarl was discovering that it was impossible to turn down Will James, no matter what name he used. "Of course, come back anytime."

Will James nodded. He said his goodbyes, first to Jarl, then to the remainder of the employees, and finally to Stori. He departed, using the side gate, boarded his carriage, and drove off into the cold morning.

It was well past lunchtime before the small printing company was able to resume anything like its normal routine.

CHAPTER NINETEEN:

MAY DAY

One week after his first visit, Will James returned, this time not in the robes of Vanir's only Prince, but as the modest son of a merchant family, accompanied by two E'landota guards. The tall young man later confided to Jarl that his father had not been so much upset at him for escaping off to Kettlewand to fight with the army as he had that his son had taken no bodyguards.

Will James was fascinated by everything, the five presses, the two sewing machines, and the already printed and bound books. Often, he would grab the nearest stick and draw outlines in the dirt, impractical designs of flying machines or the outlandish peoples and animals believed to live on a long-lost western continent. Jarl tried to turn the young man's head to plans of indoor plumbing and sewer and drinking-water systems, but these ideas left Will James frowning and he would soon scratch out Jarl's drawing and begin one of his own.

It took quite a while for the employees of the small printing company to be even remotely at ease in the presence of their ruler-to-be; a matter not helped by the fact that Will James only found the time to visit the house once or twice a week, and then only for part of the day; but the young man's willingness to carry books, sew, or work the printing presses for hours at a time—and his ability to laugh at his mistakes—finally brought a smile to even to dour Sirota, who said over and over, but never to Will James' face, that it was not proper that the Prince of Vanir should be stooping to such lowly work.

And work they did. Jarl, Levi, Karl, and Navee carried the two heavy sewing machines from the second floor to a hastily constructed porch built on the back of the house. They constructed four smaller wooden presses to squeeze the air out of the printed Bibles, so that they were not as thick, and they moved one of the iron pot-bellied stoves from the printing press area into the shed, where Ruth and Sirota began stitching the leather-bound Bibles, occasionally with the help of Jarl, Navee, Stori, and Ali. Often, one or two people would sew on the heavy machines until the wee hours of the morning. One person, who was not to be distracted by any other job, wandered the upper stories of the tall house, always on the lookout for spies from the Church. By mid-April, finished with the Bible, the five presses ran nothing but Jarl's theses on health, hygiene, and religious reform, as well as the two stories of the Battle of Burkes Station, the last of which was now combined in one bound volume and hand stitched by Navee and Stori.

After long discussions with Will James, Jarl was surprised to learn that the Vanir had no formal court system and that the King tried only a few select arguments at his leisure. The result was that the Church, with its so-called legal system, had become the *de facto* court system in the nation, and had been able to consolidate a great deal more power. Jarl described a system of courts and judges, appointed by the King, where each defendant would be allowed an attorney and have the right to be tried—not by the Judge—but by a picked jury of common men and women.

Will James found the idea interesting, and after considering it for most of a week, said that Jarl could publish a short essay on such a system, with one condition: he had to delete the parts about the juries and the defense attorneys, an ultimatum that made Jarl suspect that the Prince had cleared the idea with his father. After some thought—all of one second— Jarl decided to go for all or nothing, and argued to publish the essay unchanged. Much to his surprise, Will James allowed him to publish the unaltered article. Jarl never mentioned that he had written the final copy of the essay the night before and, even as they argued, Karl was printing the first copies.

April was heralded by the loud collapse of the frozen waterfall, and once again Tyr was graced with the white fury of the Vilyur River falling from the high mountain cirque. Now the small printing company was running two shifts on the sewing machines, stitching the heavy Bibles. The only other publication that required binding was the third children's reader, which Navee, Lannie, and Sol began to sew, hand-stitching them in the kitchen. In addition, after their day's work was finished, the three E'landota began to practice not only unarmed combat, but with split bamboo swords and long hickory poles. More than once, Will James' own E'landota—including a tall female Tame Ghost named Laufey—joined in the training. Because of the deft movements, the brutal power, and the ballet-like dancing, the training often brought all the work to a halt, as the mock combat was fascinating to watch.

The first day of of May was an ancient holiday among the Vanir, celebrated by a day-long festival along the Nanoo River. It was this day that Jarl decided to first sell the translated Bible.

However, a week before May Day, without explanation, Jarl purchased six small, wooden barrels and the same number of smaller metal buckets. The next morning, a Sunday, he, Navee, and Janis took Karl's rickety old wagon into the mountains and returned at noon with a load of wet, spring snow. Unexpectedly and full of innocence, Stori and Ali arrived with fresh strawberries, salt, sugar, and vanilla extract. Not more than a few minutes later, the entire Ahlum clan appeared at the door, carrying two large containers of cream. While he and Stori split the sugar and cream between the two metal buckets, Jarl had Levi and Navee drill a hole in two flat, wide pine slabs with a hand auger.

Then—he had to push Karl, overwhelmed with curiosity, out of the way—Jarl poured the strawberries into one pail and the vanilla extract into the other. The hard spring snow was dumped into two of the wooden barrels and a bucket was forced down into each barrel. More snow was piled around the sides of the buckets, salt was added to the snow, and a pine slab was placed over each bucket. Jarl produced two wooden paddles, which attached to two handles that he had Lannie make more than a month previously. Two people then held down each slab while another person turned the handle.

Karl—and now Janis—could hardly control themselves, and were continually asking what they were making. First the handles turned easily, but then over a period of twenty minutes, while more salt was added to the snow, the wooden handles turned harder and harder and slower and slower.

Finally only Karl could move the handles, and Jarl sent Ali, Janis, and Sunny scurrying into the house for bowls, promising not to crack the lids until the three giggling girls returned. Once they had returned, they opened the buckets with an almost religious silence. Inside was a creamy substance, colored white in one bucket and pink in the other. Then, using spoons that only Stori had remembered to bring, Jarl began to dip out huge helpings of the thick, creamy substance.

Sunny and Ali got the first scoops, but they poked at their bowls, attempting to figure out what it was without tasting it. Stori received the third serving, but she too was cautious, licking a near-empty spoon. Not so with Janis. When given the fourth bowl, she took a big spoonful and quickly popped it into her mouth. Her mouth slowly closed and her eyes opened wide. For a long second, she stood quietly, unable to decide what it was she was eating. Then, her eyes narrowed to a squint and a big smile replaced her thoughtful expression. Soon everyone was tasting both substances, with immense smiles. Jarl was greatly relieved with his first taste—the ice cream was good even by his Earth standards.

It seemed only a short time before they had finished both buckets. Then, Stori, Thir, and Sunny produced two cakes and five pies, which—along with the few remaining strawberries—were eaten with the same wild abandon and merriment. In the following week, with the exception of 250 promotional fliers, printing ceased altogether. Stori found a reliable supply of vanilla extract, chocolate, and sugar. Somehow she even discovered some dry blueberries, left over from the previous summer. Strawberries, of course, were no problem—they were in season. Jarl borrowed two wagons—one from the Ahlums—and the day before the big May Day celebration, while Levi, Graff, and Gary set up a wide booth on the fairground, Jarl, Navee, Karl, Janis, Lif, and Sunny rode and walked into the Sabre Mountains and brought back two full wagon loads of heavy spring snow.

Before daylight the next day, they loaded all three wagons with books, buckets, barrels, extra boards, and food. By dawn, the first wagon was crossing the congested Nanoo River bridge onto the wide coastal flat east of Tyr. After off-loading the snow onto a tarp and covering it with an old sail, Jarl and several his employees began setting up the long rows of their wares. Karl took the wagons and another crew of workers, and tried to return for a second load. At first they had trouble crossing the river, because most of the traffic was coming east, but, for a few pennies, Jarl hired two large young men to direct traffic, breaking the eastbound flow so that the few westbound vehicles could cross.

Within an hour, the three wagons returned with Navee and a second load of books. Most of these too were neatly stacked to one side, but some—in fact, a full wagon load—were secretly covered by the old sail. The three vehicles made one last trip, this time bringing Lannie and Sol. For the most part, these loads too were set aside. Laufey and her husband, Kyle, the brown-haired Ghost Raider who had accompanied Will James on his first visit to the printing shop, appeared, apparently off-duty. Stori and Janis had, for all of this time, been supervising the making of several kinds of ice cream—with any strong-armed labor they could recruit—and Jarl was now able to serve the two E'landota dishes of the creamy substance. The couple was happy to linger nearby, contented smiles on their faces.

Will James arrived, clothed as a rich commoner, with close to ten E'landota, most of who were dressed so as to remain unnoticed among the festival goers. The Prince's eyes were aglow and excited by the prospects of the day's activities. Three times he asked what Kyle was eating. But each time, the tall Tame Ghost remained quiet, his eyes laughing and his smile growing larger. Finally, exasperated, Will James turned and hurried to the book stand, almost knocking over Stori who was rushing to meet him with a bowl of strawberry ice cream.

Will James tasted the first bite tentatively. Slowly he tried to chew it. Then he swallowed and stood quietly for what seemed a very long time. Jarl looked at Karl. The big man was perplexed, and he dipped a finger into his serving, to see if there was something wrong with the taste. But then Will James' eyes popped open and his face became one big smile. Stori, also dressed as a commoner, led him from one bucket to the other, allowing him to sample the contents of each.

Jarl's original idea had been to give the ice cream away for free, as a promotional gimmick, but Karl had talked him out of it. Now they began selling the ice cream for a half-penny a board shingle. Jokingly, Jarl told Will James the cost of his six servings. The disguised Prince was only too happy to pay the small sum, and he placed the few coins on one of the plank tables. Jarl, remembering the long hours Will James had worked for free at the printing company, refused to take his money.

More than one set of eyebrows popped upward when Jarl grabbed the Prince, intending to stuff the coins in Will James' coat pocket. Will James dodged away, and Jarl gave chase, racing him completely around the stall before both men turned a corner too sharply and slipped and fell, laughing. As Jarl stumbled back to his feet, he saw Kyle standing to one side, frozen in time, one hand holding the plate of ice cream, the other on the butt of his flintlock pistol, an incredulous expression on his face. In the end, Will James gave the few pennies to one of the many charities that had set up booths on the fairground.

While Will James and Jarl had been involved in their shenanigans, Janis and Ali had already sold close to thirty books and an unknown number of single stories. Jarl had printed a special edition of the newspaper—mostly it was nothing more than advertisements from the local vendors—and it too was selling quickly, at a half-penny a copy. Karl, happily making more ice cream, wore a smile that matched even his own dimensions, contentedly envisioning himself rich before evening. And, as yet, no clergy nor their numerous guards had made an appearance.

A quick movement at the book stand caught Jarl's attention. Stori was laughing and flirting with an older, tall man. As she turned, Jarl saw the shaggy eyebrows of Hjas Gautrekson. The tall, black-haired woman raised an eyebrow, asking Jarl an unneeded question. Silently and discreetly, Jarl nodded yes. From under the tarp, Stori produced a Bible that she sold to her father. Two more High Ejliteta, one a frail little lady Jarl had noticed before in the store, stepped forward and bought one book and one book only—the translated Bible.

Before the day warmed, Jarl, Will James, Navee, Lif, and two of the Prince's bodyguards wandered the fairground, sampling the food, buying a small trinket here or there, and watching an array of jugglers, musicians, and magicians. Once Jarl caught an edge of a mindbeam, someone alerting a companion that the authorities were close by. It was the first mind message he had felt in more than a year, and carefully—without drawing attention to himself—he turned and attempted to locate the source of the telepathy. He was not successful.

A half-hour later, Lif, Jarl, and Navee wandered back to the book stall. They discovered that the books and ice cream were selling at a near hectic pace. Stori informed Jarl, in a hushed whisper, that they had sold three more copies of the Bible. As yet she had seen no priest or church guards, an observation that mirrored Jarl's own. To one side, Hjas sat at a special table, surrounded by E'landota, talking to some friends. Stori and Jarl had decided to sell the translated Bibles one at a time, from under the tarp. Now, because no one was buying this book, their largest production, Jarl paced the book stall like a caged cat trying to control his energy. Stori finally ordered him out of the booth, and he and Navee walked down to the Nanoo River and passed the time skipping small pebbles across the water's surface.

It was there that Jarl spotted the first red-robed priest, moving with the heavy traffic crossing the wooden bridge. Before the clergy and his guard had reached the middle of the bridge, a small, frail old woman approached the man and showed him an object, which judging by the size and shape, was one of the translated Bibles. The man opened the book, studied it for most of a minute, and then ran—with his guards in hot pursuit—west, back into Tyr. Jarl cursed. He had hoped the Church would not discover what he was selling before midday. But now, with less than ten Bibles sold, there was about to be trouble—serious trouble.

He hurried back to the book stall and told Stori to place a few copies of the Bible in plain view, so that if worse came to worst and everything was destroyed, perhaps a few more of the translated books could be placed in the hands of the Vanir people. Then he told Navee to take a one-word message to Will James.

The good-natured little man refused to go. He smiled and, in an easy voice, said, "I will stay here with you..."

Jarl's reply was short and to the point. Navee, surprised, sprinted to find the Prince, who by pre-arrangement, would send a squadron of riflemen to practice their weaponry on the hillside near Karl's house.

Fifteen long minutes later—during which they sold only one Bible—a gaggle of red- and yellow-robed priests and no less than two dozen of the green-armored guards marched down out of Tyr and across the Nanoo River bridge. They turned left at the bottom of the bridge and paced across the sandy flat to the book stall, pushing people out of their way. Five meters away, all but two of them stopped, forming a rough semi-circle around the long stall. Two bald priests stamped up to the booth, and the older man twisted his head this way and that, looking in vain for a translated Bible.

Finally, the younger man spotted one and, in a melodramatic gesture, pointed with one long, bony finger. "There's one!" he shouted, loud enough to be heard in all of Tyr.

The old priest picked up the Bible. He opened it and turned the pages. One finger shook as it crept down the long page, occasionally halting for a moment, while his lips mumbled the words. That quiet noise highlighted the solemn silence that now surrounded the booth. Ali and Karl both had white faces and their eyes were full of fear. Stori had stepped back from the two men, her expression unreadable. Navee, as always, seemed unconcerned. Janis, holding her black cat, was biting her lower lip. Jarl touched out with a short mindbeam and discovered, to his surprise, that the young girl was not frightened, but angry.

Finally, with a terrible expression, the old priest looked at Jarl and shouted, "This book is not written in the language of the Church!"

This man had almost unlimited power, and Jarl was frightened. "That is correct," he said quietly, but loud enough for everyone to hear. "The book costs two dollars if you want to purchase a copy."

The priest's face flushed, becoming beet red. "That is ridiculous," he sputtered.

Jarl's answer came easily, "True, the book is very inexpensive." He listened for someone to laugh, but all he heard from the crowd was a tense, oppressive silence.

The old priest stood rooted in one place for more than ten seconds, actually spitting with anger. The younger clergyman stood behind his colleague, his hands on his hips, his feet spread wide, his face flushed with arrogance. The old man slowly got himself under control, finally understanding what Jarl had said. Then he shouted, "It is ridiculous for anyone to sell the Church's Bible written in English! The people would not be able to understand it correctly! They need the Church to translate it and tell them what it says!" He spoke slowly, with great emphasis on each word, as if he believed Jarl was a simpleton who was also hard of hearing.

Jarl had folded his arms across his chest, more to keep his hands from shaking than to make an impression. He stood there, saying nothing.

The old priest shouted, "I forbid you to sell these books!"

Jarl only shook his head, maintaining a quiet calm, now trying to impress the crowd, "There is no law in Vanir that says what books we can or cannot sell."

"*I*," there was great emphasis on that one word, "order you to stop selling these illegal books!"

Jarl, his arms still crossed, spoke in a near normal voice, "You do not have that authority."

Once again, the old Priest began to sputter with anger. After several seconds, he began shouting again, "I order you to cease selling this... this... work of the Devil."

"It is not the work of the Devil. This is the word of God." The entire crowd seemed to be holding its breath, making the conversation seem even more intense.

The old Priest screamed, "Then I order you and your people arrested and your books—all your books—burned!" He waved a red-sleeved arm and his guards moved forward, led by their captain. Behind Jarl, someone coughed, somehow innocently and conspicuously enough that the captain turned and looked.

There stood Kyle, a slight smile on his face, both hands resting on the butt of his pistol, still tucked behind his wide, red sash. Beside him was Navee, an easy grin on his face. The captain stopped, his hand on the first Bible, recognizing Kyle for who he was, and counting off the E'landota around the table. On the other side of the two priests, another of the Church's guards upset one of the long board tables, knocking books to the ground and sending Karl, Lif, and Stori scrambling backwards out of the way.

Jarl stepped forward, rotated on his left foot and kicked the man hard in the center of his leather breastplate with the heel of his right foot. The man fell backward and onto the ground. He sat there for a brief second, his legs spread wide, while his astonishment turned to anger. Then, just as he began to launch himself to his feet to attack Jarl, he realized that the other Church guards were standing still, trying to square off against the E'landota emerging quietly from the crowd. Ever since their time in the Church's prison, Navee had repeatedly told Jarl that most of the Church's E'landota were bullies hired off the street and were not as good as the regular E'landota—and once he had added with a smile, "And they know it." Now Jarl could see, by the way the guards in their green leathers moved, that Navee had been right. They did know who was better in a fight. And at least a few of them could also count. The Church's guards were outnumbered.

The old priest was sputtering in anger. The younger priest was now pouting, his hands still on his hips.

It was a standoff for a few seconds more, then someone in the back of the crowd—someone with a strong voice, one used to command—shouted, "What is going on here?"

As if by magic, the crowd parted, and a small group of men walked through the opening. One was surprisingly short and gray-haired, wearing old fashioned robes, a long broadsword, and a bejeweled crown of silver. At the sight of him, everyone in the crowd bowed slightly on one knee, including the two priests, who also arranged their faces into happy smiles, expressions that any fool could see were false. Jarl quickly imitated the bow.

Beside the King was Will James, now dressed in his royal finery and—Jarl could not hold back a smile—Liebs Hisson and Enrick von Rhinehart. The King, once he was in the center of the crowd, loudly repeated his question. Jarl was surprised how round the man was—and bow-legged too, possibly from a long life on horseback.

The red-robed Priest spoke quickly, his voice most respectful. "Your Highness, this man here..." he gave Jarl a look most people reserved for slugs and spiders that they come upon unexpectedly, "is selling illegal books! I have ordered him to stop!"

Jarl spoke, "It is true, Your Majesty." Several people gasped and Jarl was suddenly terrified that 'Your Majesty' was not what people called this King. "I am selling books. But I am not selling any illegal books. I am selling Bibles and the Bible is not illegal." The old priest tried to interrupt, sputtering, but the King held up one hand. There was power in the glance he gave the red-robed man. Jarl continued, "There is no law in Vanir saying that any book is illegal."

The Priest spoke again, raising his voice against any interruption from Jarl. "That is not true, My Lord. These Bibles are written in English, and as you know, the selling and distribution of such publications is illegal and immoral."

There was a long, drawn-in breath from the crowd. The King, however, was not swayed. His voice boomed out, "I do not know that." He turned to his son, "William, you have studied a great deal of Vanir law. Have you anywhere, in your studies, seen any notation or references that any books, no matter their language, might be illegal?"

Will James pushed his glasses higher on his nose, "No, Father, I have not. No book in Vanir is illegal... According to my studies, that is."

The King turned back to the old priest, "Can you provide proof of a law stating that these books—your Bibles—are illegal?"

The clergyman sputtered, "Given time..."

The King waved his hand, cutting off the old man. "Given time, I am sure you can produce proof, probably dating back to the beginning of our colony. Given time, this man will lose the day's sales, something that he has probably been counting on all winter."

The old priest's face suddenly became red again. He was angry, for a second yelling at the King. Then, abruptly, he realized who he was talking to and got control of his emotions. His voice became smooth and soothing, "Your Majesty, this man was a prisoner of the Church. He should be returned to the prison from which he was so unfortunately and mistakenly released."

Von Rhinehart leaned down to the King and whispered something in his ear. The King's bushy eyebrows shot up and he stared up at the old priest. When he spoke again, and his voice was loud and authoritative. "This man was released on my explicit pardon. Are you saying that I made a mistake?"

"No, My Lord!" The old man was sputtering again. He took a step backward.

The King continued, with the same commanding voice, "He is also a hero of the Battle of Burkes Station. He personally commanded a part of the battle and prevented the Vanir line from breaking."

"No... Yes, My Lord." Another step backward.

"And you are preventing him from selling his wares! As is provided by Vanir law!"

"Yes... No, My Lord." The old man backed into one of his guards, who in turn was pressed against the crowd.

"Then let him sell his books. They are your Bibles... you should be happy to see them in the hands of your flock!"

"Yes, My Lord." The old Priest was clearly anything but happy.

The King stood there for a few seconds more, then he turned, and without so much as glancing toward Jarl, walked through another magically produced opening in the crowd. Von Rhinehart, Hisson, and Will James followed. For most of a minute the old Priest stood next to the book stall, sputtering and stamping his foot. Then, after giving Jarl a hateful stare, he turned and marched off. The younger Priest and the entourage of guards followed.

Jarl stood still for several moments, finally letting out a breath of air. His hands were shaking badly now, and he hooked them into his belt, so no one could see them. Stori and Janis began to rebuild the plank table and pick up the books on the ground. Jarl looked over at Karl; the big man's expression was one of pure misery. Jarl suddenly grinned, looking at the ice cream near the big man's feet. "You know, it's not that bad," he said.

"What's not that bad?"

"The melting ice cream!"

The gigantic printer looked down and shouted, "Oops!" He jumped back, as if the liquid goo was going to bite him. Jarl shouted to the crowd, "We are giving away the melting ice cream!" A dozen people quickly stepped forward, with Kyle in the front, a smile on his face, holding his wooden platter out. But he had to wait his turn, as three children darted in front of him, each holding out a dripping platter of their own.

For the remainder of the morning, they sold only one copy of the newspaper. Then Will James passed back by, still in his royal clothes, and bought a copy of the newspaper, a combined issue of the Battle of Burkes Station, a Bible, and two scoops of ice cream. After that, the crowds slowly began to drift back, buying mostly the ice cream, and in ever increasing numbers, more and more books, theses, and individual stories; but never copies of the translated Bible. By two in the afternoon, the Elder Oak Printing company was out of ice cream, but—nevertheless—the intermittent book sales continued. By four, Jarl was ready to call it quits and they packed up their wagons and began to haul the many unsold books back to their small store. They had sold only a dozen Bibles all day, far, far less than Jarl had hoped, and all three wagons had to make a second trip back to the fairgrounds.

After the wagons returned, they slowly loaded the remaining books—all Bibles—onto the three vehicles. On top of that load, they threw the few remaining boards and a barrel of trash. Then, as Fjlar led the horses away and the wagon started to roll forward, Tiger—Janis' black cat—hopped from her arms and ran toward one of the heavy wheels. The young girl was quick to chase it, catching it a mere breath away from the moving wheel. She scolded the animal, not verbally but in an easily understood mindbeam. Jarl, who had hopped off the wagon after Janis, heaved her back onto the wagon.

She had scared him—twice over. As soon as they were settled back on the heavily loaded wagon, Jarl beamed a tight message to the young girl, telling her not to use her telepathy so recklessly or the Church would condemn her as a witch. She looked up, suddenly scared, and Jarl wondered if anyone had ever communicated with her mentally before.

She stammered out a verbal whisper, "I won't."

He rubbed the top of her head, trying to let her know she had friends, then—using his mindvoice, again with the same tight control—he asked, *"Has Tiger ever answered you?"* He had never heard of anyone ever mindbeaming animals before.

The young girl's brown eyes were wide, and she shook her head no. Jarl put his arm around her, and she put her head on his shoulder. The black cat only purred.

Their easy relaxation did not last long. Six times on the way back to their shop, the wagons were stopped by people who wanted to purchase copies of the translated Bible. And all night long, people—old ladies and young girls, High Ejliteta and commoners, field hands and factory workers, even the captain of the Rifle company that was camped next door—rapped on the door of the house and asked to purchase a Bible. By morning, they had sold thirty-two additional copies.

For the next two weeks they sold their regular books by day and the Bibles by night, forcing Stori to move into the large house to help Ali and Janis with the continual work load. And, much to Jarl's exasperation, the two watchers returned to the spot beside the one lonely tree, just south of the printing company.

CHAPTER TWENTY

THE WAR OF THE BIBLES

The squadron of riflemen camped next to the printing company for only five nights, but its brief presence was a blunt statement to all of Tyr and Vanir that, although not officially, the King was supporting Jarl and the Elder Oak Printing Company. But, despite King William's patronage, the threat of the Church was there. Always two or more watchers sat under the single tree south of the house, and, more times than Jarl cared to remember, garbage and human feces were piled against the outside of Karl's old house during the night. Within a week after May Day, the front window had been broken three times. Jarl finally ordered it boarded up. And, during the first week in June, Ali arrived for work to discover that someone had set the corner of the house on fire. Despite their nightly guard, no one inside had noticed, and the fire had gone out on its own accord.

One warm summer morning, a bald-headed priest, dressed in lemon-yellow robes, stood in the middle of the road in front of the printing company and delivered a long, tedious sermon. When that failed to raise any action—from either the printing company or the heavens—the clergyman resorted to muttering and screaming threats, none of which were very imaginative. Jarl bet Navee a supper in town that the man would resort to obscenities before he finished, but he was wrong, and the next night Jarl had to treat Navee and Janis—who somehow tagged along—to a not-too-expensive supper in Tyr.

But, for each person who threw garbage at Jarl or the building, and for each person who called him an ugly name, it seemed that there were three who wanted to purchase the translated Bible. Stori's sole job became opening crudely written letters and sending the Bibles north, via the King's stage, into Nowell and Greenlands, east into Ringhorn and Garlands, south into Smyrna and Southern, and west into Atrobee and Kettlewand.

One morning a letter arrived from Marri Stephenson, saying that even her illiterate mother had purchased one of the translated books. Alfheim Vail told similar stories. One of the first westbound stages from Foord carrying the new Bibles had been halted by more than two dozen cloaked people, waving pitchforks and sharp corn knives. The stage driver had stopped, fearful for his life, and quickly met their demands: the confiscation of the holy books. The angry horde had immediately quieted. Then someone opened one of the massive books and began to read aloud, delaying the vehicle more than an hour. Finally, before the stage was allowed to leave, the tearful men and women gave the stage line the few processions and poultry they owned, including the very weapons they had just used to halt the stage, as payment for the Bibles. Alfheim said the stage line would be happy to deliver those few tools and treasures to Jarl if he wanted them, but he cautioned, with a chuckle, that the chickens had already been eaten.

Shortly after May Day, Levi and Karl, on their own initiative, began a second, time-consuming printing of the translated Bible. That, more than the company's profits, convinced Jarl to sell a part of the Elder Oak Printing Company to the two men. In the end, after several hours of deliberation, he drew up papers allowing Karl, Levi, and Stori each to purchase one-eighth of the company. The next morning, Jarl discovered Karl's copy of the agreement nailed to the trunk of the red oak tree. It took both him and Stori two days to convince the big man to take the document down and store it somewhere for safe keeping.

Founders Day, in mid-July, was the next Vanir holiday. Once again, Jarl's small company loaded three wagons and hauled their books and ice cream down to the flat east of the Nanoo River bridge. On this occasion, the Church had a well-thought-out plan. Although their guards did not bother the book vendors—there were still too many E'landota present— they began to harass those persons who were purchasing the translated Bibles. Jarl set a few Bibles at one end of the long booth. As long as no customers approached them, the Church's bullies left everyone alone. But when someone walked near that end of the books—even if they accidentally strolled by—the guards would jostle, shout taunts, and even throw garbage at the customer, Jarl, and his employees.

The strategy had some merit, and it began when the first wagon was unloaded. At the booth, only five Bibles were sold all day, on this, the Vanir birthday. But as well as the Church's plan worked, it had been started too early in the day. Many of Bibles were hauled to the fairgrounds by the wagons' second and third trips. When the commotion developed at the book booth, Jarl simply sent a message, via Lif, and no more Bibles were delivered to their booth. All day long, while the Church's people surrounded the long tables, Stori, Janis, Navee, and Lannie sold the Holy books off the tailgates of one of the wagons, on the far side of the fairground. In terms of sales, Founders Day was the best day yet for the Elder Oak Printing Company, and such was the Church's concentration on Jarl and the booth, that it was almost dusk before they realized they had been duped.

The Church was not happy. Already there were rumors of smaller, bootleg worship services being held in barns and abandoned houses throughout rural Kamjar. One night, an ancient, unused house was burned down in southern Tyr, just down the mountain from the printing company. The rumor Jarl heard later was that the building had been the site of clandestine church services. Three nights later, a beaten body was found floating in the Greymist River, reportedly the unordained minister of those nightly services.

The Church had lost a good deal of integrity on Founders Day, and the first attack on the little printing company came exactly one week later, in full daylight, early on a Saturday morning. That day, Lannie was cleaning one of the presses, and Levi and Navee were repairing a cracked leg of another of the massive wooden machines. Karl, Sol, and Graff were working the three remaining printing presses, Janis was placing the lead characters into the sorting trays, and Jarl was stoking one of the wood-burning stoves, in an attempt to take the chill off the morning air.

Stori was in the kitchen, figuring what publication had to be sent where. Gary was hidden in the third-floor attic, taking a break from printing and searching for the spies from the Church; Sirota and Ruth were sitting under the back porch, doing the worst job the company had to offer, stitching the heavy bindings; and Ali was in the front room, selling publications to two women, who—given the speed at which they disappeared—Jarl suspected of being in league with the Church.

The seven E'landota of the Church's small assault force, dressed in black and wearing hoods and masks, traveled south on the Tyr-Southern highway past the printing company. There, they climbed the steep hillside and, staying out of sight, waited at the single tree south of the printing company. The watchers had discovered that they could tell when the lookout was at the southern window of the third-floor attic. When Gary left that window, the seven men lunged to their feet and raced across the road to the single building, unseen by anyone in the printing company.

Jarl was never sure who spotted the raiders first. He first glimpsed one of the assailants, one hand on a post, vaulting the fence into the backyard. Two other E'landota ran up the wood pile and hurdled the fence. One man smashed, both feet first, into the small of Karl's back, knocking the big man into Navee, who fell to the ground. The printer then toppled into the press he had been working at, and both machine and man collapsed with a groan of breaking wood. The Church's E'landota fell backward and onto the ground. His companion landed on one foot and took a long step, swinging his samurai sword two-handed toward Jarl's face. Jarl shoved the piece of firewood he was holding directly at the man, trying to block the blow. Somehow, more through luck than design, the wood caught the fast-moving blade.

Navee spun onto the small of his back and attempted to tangle his feet around the legs of the E'landota who had vaulted the side gate. At the same time, he tried to block the man's sword with a long lever from the dismantled printing press. Levi, after throwing his hammer at the attackers, scurried back toward his wife. A shirvken spun through the air, its sharp, deadly blades flashing in the bright sunlight—but, somehow, Sol deflected it with a long hickory pole he produced from some hiding place.

Someone was screaming. The E'landota who had attacked Jarl dropped his now useless sword, which was wedged deep into the block of wood. Had the man attacked then, he probably could have killed Jarl, but instead the E'landota brought up both hands in a classic karate defense, right hand back for a hard thrust. Jarl quickly grabbed a second piece of firewood and heaved it toward the man's head.

From the man's left, a wooden tray of lead characters appeared, thrown by Janis. With a quick downward rotation of his arm, the E'landota blocked the tray, knocking it to the ground. Jarl saw the man's eyes shift—just for an instant—following the tray downward. Almost immediately, the man refocused on Jarl, but the piece of firewood hit him square in the forehead, knocking him backward and onto the ground. He did not get up; instead, he rolled onto his stomach and held his head, moaning.

Another of the Church's E'landota hurdled himself through the air, using the wood pile as a launching pad. As he landed, Sol moved in, wielding his long hickory pole in a series of violent, quick thrusts. Navee managed to block his assailant's sword, and then he hit his attacker full in the head with a heavy wooden mallet. That man collapsed, knocked unconscious. Karl was lying in a pile half under the broken press, moaning, clearly out of action. The E'landota who had attacked him rolled to his feet. Lannie, ink up to his elbows, moved forward, and before the Church's E'landota could fully regain his feet, began kicking the man, using short, powerful blows.

Two more E'landota vaulted the fence, and the third ran up the wood pile and jumped the fence, flying through the air in the manner of his companions, intending to kick Janis. The young girl dropped face-first onto the ground and all her assailant attacked was the printing press Lannie had been cleaning. Something snapped with the impact and, as the wood groaned, both the press and the E'landota sagged to the ground.

Jarl grabbed another piece of firewood. The remaining two E'landota moved toward him, weaving slow patterns in the air with the tips of their swords. A dull explosion came from the house, and the lead attacker lurched, grunted, and almost dropped his sword. Jarl hit him in the head with another piece of firewood. Navee was now on his feet, and he picked up a dropped sword and attacked the other E'landota. The man spun and parried the first blow. He then shouted a quick, one-word command and ran across the yard, past Levi. The dwarf-like man was frozen in place, holding a broom, trying to defend Sirota and Ruth, who were both screaming. The E'landota vaulted the back fence and sprinted away, running north toward town.

The assailant trying to fight Lannie—and who was only receiving a royal beating for his effort—somehow managed to launch himself into a flat dive over the fence. He scrambled on all fours along the side of the house and quickly ran across the road. Then he fell and rolled down the mountainside toward the main highway. The E'landota in front of Jarl dropped his sword and, clutching his side, spun around. He darted by Lannie and jumped the fence, and—with flailing arms and legs—imitated his comrade's mad four-legged scramble across the road.

Stori was framed in the back doorway, holding a tiny flintlock pistol. Blue smoke drifted up out of its barrel, and a cloud of smoke wafted across the backyard. For a moment everyone stood still, watching Sol swing first one end of his long stick and then the other end toward his adversary's head. Each time the Church's E'landota was able to block the fast-moving pole with his sword, but each time the brute power of Sol's blow forced the sword backward more and more. Then Sol pivoted, rotating a full 360 degrees on the ball of one foot. He struck the other E'landota on the side of the head with his other foot. This time, the man was far too slow with his parry, and he collapsed in a pile at Stori's feet. Sol swung his long pole one last time, hitting the prone man alongside the head with a resounding thump.

Stori, standing on the stone step above the fight, grimaced, clearly feeling the man's pain. Navee, watching from the middle of the backyard, let escape a soft, reverent "Ouch!"

A second later, with a loud groan, Karl pushed the massive printing press off of him. It fell to the side, with the crunch of more breaking wood. Likewise, toward the back shed, the remaining assassin did the same, rolling that press to one side.

That E'landota attempted to stand, stumbling toward Janis. One leg collapsed under him, and Jarl caught a glimpse of blood and perhaps the end of a broken bone. Janis reeled back, more from the sight of the ink-covered man than from fear. The E'landota's mask was gone, and his young face was white and tears were running down his face. Then, trying to escape Lannie, who was approaching from one side, the E'landota more fell than ran, knocking over the hot wood stove. He stumbled back to his feet and limped and stumbled, wincing in pain, openly sobbing, past Levi and his upraised broom. He then tumbled over the back fence on the other side of the house and, leaving a trail of blood, crawled away while dragging his broken leg behind him.

The attack had lasted less than a minute. Two more minutes passed before Ruth and Sirota ceased their awful screaming. Three of the Church's E'landota remained in the backyard, knocked unconscious. Scattered about the backyard where six swords and one shirvken, driven into the interior wall of one of the open sheds. A wood stove had been knocked over, three presses were now broken, and lead characters were scattered throughout the dirt. But, other than Karl's bruises, not one employee of the small printing company had been hurt.

Jarl and Sol, using the long hickory pole, quickly righted the upset stove. While Janis scrambled to pick up the lead characters, Lannie and Navee relieved the three remaining attackers of a dozen knives and shirvken. Then Navee, Jarl, and Sol carried one of the unconscious E'landota out of the backyard and across the road. Karl followed with the other two, carrying one in each hand, held by their belts. Then, in full view of the two watchers under the tree to the south, the four men rolled their three would-be assailants down the steep mountain toward the main highway.

By late the next morning, Levi and Navee had one of the disabled presses fixed, the one they had been working on when the attack began. The following afternoon, one more of the damaged presses was put back to work and the next morning, after repairs were completed on the third broken machine, all five presses were once again running. That night came the second of the Church's attacks.

This assault came in the wee hours of the morning and failed only because of pure luck. Jarl, his modern pistol in hand and without a light, had gotten up to use the outhouse. With his business attended to, he opened the door of the small building and stepped out, unseen by the five E'landota crouching on and near the back steps. Just as Jarl spotted the intruders, the first of the black-dressed E'landota eased open the back door and began to creep inside. Jarl raised his pistol, aimed, and squeezed off his a shot, firing at the second man in line. The E'landota crashed back against the house wall and began to slide to the ground. His second shot dropped a second man and shots three and four went into the group of dark figures.

The E'landota on the right spun around, hurdled the fence, skidded around the corner and disappeared, running for the road. The man on the left raced across the back porch, between the two sewing machines, and leaped over that fence, also running for Tyr. The two wounded men staggered back to their feet, then collided into each other as they started to run in opposite directions. They jumped back up, and one of the dark figures, hunched over in pain, sprinted to the right and ran into the fence, falling across it to the ground. The other ran between the two sewing machines and jumped that fence. Navee said the fifth man, who was in front of the group, ran across the darkened kitchen, tripped over Lannie, rolled across the floor into the front room and then tried to jump out the boarded window. He knocked one board free but fell back into the dark room. But before either Navee or Lannie could intervene, the Church's E'landota jumped to his feet and forced his way out the tiny opening, tearing his black shirt on a protruding nail and landing on the hard road beyond.

The next day, a Wednesday, Will James moved twenty riflemen into the meadow south of the printing company, supposedly on some extended training exercise. Jarl told Navee to find two more of his friends, as he intended to hire them to guard the premises. Then he went into town and bought four double-barreled flintlock shotguns. He attempted to teach Karl, Levi, Gary, and Graff to load and use these, but this did not work, and finally he and Janis, who quickly mastered the technique, loaded the weapons and distributed them around the house.

Jarl never hired the additional E'landota; he decided that the King's riflemen were protection enough. He instead employed a near-sighted, one-armed man whose face was scarred with the marks of smallpox. The man, known simply as Hjor, freely admitted to having been a priest at one time. Jarl assigned him the tedious job of compiling a dictionary. Hjor showed up for his first day on the job, collected a large, empty black book and left the shop, walking into Tyr to do his work there.

That night, Jarl and Navee visited Will James at the palace, meeting Kyle and Laufey at a side door and passing between a half score of armed guards. The two E'landota led Jarl through a maze of corridors, climbing a set of wide, polished steps. En route they encountered the Prince, Liebs Hisson, and Enrick von Rhinehart. For a few minutes they all stood in the hallway, quietly talking, then Will James led them into a wide corridor, flanked by old battle flags and portraits of the Vanir royalty. While the Prince rattled off his ancestors' names, Jarl looked at the paintings. He noticed the primitive clothing, weapons, and musical instruments, and he wondered how much of the Vanir heritage and technology had been lost.

The three E'landota disappeared elsewhere. Will James opened a wide door and he, Jarl, Hisson, and von Rhinehart entered a spacious room, where a large fire burned in a huge fireplace. The place was a man's room: a huge painting of an ancient cavalry battle hung above the mantel, old weapons ornamented the walls, a bear rug lay on the floor, and stuffed eagles, hawks, and cats were displayed along the walls. From a decanter hidden in one corner of the dark room, the Prince poured each man a not-so-tiny goblet of a red wine.

"That battle," Will James said, pointing at the painting, "took place 200 years ago... My great-grandfather turned back a Glassey invasion force that had landed near Horst." Then the tall Prince soured. "Unfortunately, my grandfather was not as successful."

Jarl approached what he thought was a large, stuffed mountain lion, one that had massive hindquarters. When he stepped in front of the animal, he almost dropped his drink on the expensive carpet. From the upper mouth hung two long incisors. The animal was a saber-toothed cat, extinct on Earth since the Pleistocene Epoch. He turned to Will James, and asked about the feline.

The young man grinned, always ready with an answer. "This particular cat was killed by my great-grandfather on a hunting trip in Smyrna. It is a particularly large and beautiful specimen, don't you think?"

Jarl nodded yes. "It is certainly the largest saber-toothed cat I have ever seen," he said honestly. "Are there many in Smyrna?"

"A few. There used to be a great many more, but each year there are fewer. I have only seen three."

"Do they live anywhere else other than Smyrna?"

Will James' mouth dropped open in surprise, and Jarl knew he had asked a stupid question. "Of course," the Prince said, "why do you think the mountains are named the Sabres?"

Jarl felt foolish. He camouflaged his embarrassment by holding out his empty glass. Will James was happy to refill it.

It was obvious that the three men wanted to pick Jarl's brain, and Jarl was all too happy to answer their many questions. First, they discussed old battles and campaigns, stratagems that had and had not worked. Jarl treated the three Vanir to the names and descriptions of such battles as Bushy Run, Brooklyn, Cowpens, Chancellorsville, Isandlwana and Rorke's Drift, and Cassell Hollow. Jarl, in turn, was told of many engagements that sounded strange to his ears: Orrin's Last Stand, Horst, Papaw, Walker's River, and Beer's Bend.

They then discussed the Battle of Burkes Station and the ill-lamented Sir Kevin Goran, who still had a great many friends and champions throughout Vanir.

Finally, the talk turned to Kvasir. Holding a fresh glass of wine, Will James told of his numerous, fruitless efforts to discover what had happened to his tutor after his capture. "I've searched everywhere for him," the young Prince explained. "I've bribed untold numbers of Glasseys. I've personally talked to the Glassitron ambassador, much to his pain, I might add. I've had countless Glassey prisoners questioned. I've had agents search Glassitron itself. I've had my men talk to ships' captains who might have transported him. I sent agents to Horst. I can't find him anywhere, either in Cimarron or Glassitron."

"Then what do you think happened to him?" von Rhinehart asked.

Will James drew in a long, sad breath. "I'm sorry." He looked at Jarl. "I think he is dead. I think the Glasseys murdered him secretly, and he never got back to Glassitron. Perhaps he never even got back to Cimarron."

Von Rhinehart raised his glass. "I'm truly sorry to hear that. I liked that old man. He was obstinate and sometimes an aggravation underfoot, but he was a good man in a fight. And he always gave his honest opinion, no matter what others thought of him."

Hisson too raised his glass. "He was one of the best swordsmen I've ever met. And one of the most clear-headed men in a crisis I've ever met."

Will James spoke, "I'll miss him. He made a real difference in my life, and—despite what my father thinks of him—the things Kvasir taught me have been very instrumental in the decisions I've had to make." The young Prince paused, for effect, and then added, "And he taught me the difference between moral and physical courage.

"Of which he had both," von Rhinehart quietly said.

Jarl hoped the three men were wrong about the old wizard and that he was not dead, but he was touched by their heartfelt statements. He too raised his glass. "Although I only knew Kvasir for a short time," he added, "I enjoyed his company and felt him to be a true friend."

They all brought their glasses together with a slight tinkle, then they drank their wine. Will James looked over the top of his glass at Jarl. "You only knew him for a short time?" he asked. "I thought all of you wizards have known each other forever?"

Jarl snorted, spitting wine all over von Rhinehart. "I'm not a wizard!" he said.

Will James laughed—it was clear he had been teasing Jarl. Even von Rhinehart, who was handed a cloth napkin by General Hisson, chuckled at the joke.

The talk then turned to different governments and economic systems. Jarl suggested a public school system and a military academy, not where students would be taught the arts of the E'landota, but where they could learn about tactics and strategies, mathematics, and the physical sciences. Will James silently shook his head no, then he said, "The Church will not approve of that. They will only allow schools that teach spiritual and moral disciplines." He paused, then added, "The translated Bibles are enough of a problem. Let's not fight the Church on two fronts."

From the depths of a deep, comfortable chair, Liebs Hisson said, "And why not? They're fighting us on many fronts, and a military academy sounds like a good idea to me."

"And," Jarl added, "without a system by which you can develop new ideas, your country is going to stagnate and wither on the vine. Look how many books you've lost in the past two generations. It is possible that your descendants will some day forget the things that you take for granted."

Will James attempted to turn the talk to a lighter subject, but somehow they found themselves discussing the manufacturing plants along the Nanoo River. Jarl was no less eloquent, telling of the near slave labor and how the owners were becoming richer and richer at the cost of their employees. "It's a top-heavy system," he said, "and sooner or later it will come crashing down. Step in now and pass laws to protect the employees. If not, you, or your son, are going to have some real problems down the road."

The evening ended on that sour subject, and Jarl—thinking that perhaps he had offended his friend—walked home in silence, not speaking to Navee. But the next morning, Will James invited him to visit a small shop shoved up against the mountains in the middle of Tyr. There, the two men observed a series of experiments utilizing large lead-acid batteries, built by a portly, bald craftsman named Mani Chevk. For most of the morning, the three men discussed possible electrical applications, and Jarl explained how to construct a crude electrical generator. Mani listened with a grave, intent expression, and although Will James acted almost comical, his attentions were no less serious.

That afternoon, Mani produced an ancient transit and the three men surveyed the streets that surrounded the small shop. Then, using a few simple trigonometric functions, Jarl drew their survey onto a scrap of paper. That night, when he returned home, he had another contract. Will James had offered to fund the calculation and printing of a complete set of trigonometric tables.

Will James allowed Jarl one day of rest and then literally dragged him out of the printing shop and down to the local military barracks, where a small group of junior officers were involved in a lively discussion on the theoretical use of rockets in warfare. Other midnight talks at the palace followed, occasionally with only Will James, but often with von Rhinehart and Hisson. Often the four men talked of potential campaigns that might be employed against the Glasseys and the Roomians, and they discussed the different ways to train the Vanir army.

Never once did Jarl meet the King, and—one morning at the printing shop—Stori whispered that he was in poor health.

One night, Will James unveiled a large map of his county. Now it was Jarl's turn to learn. First, he traced the route of the Greymist River east from Tyr to the large bird-foot delta formed by the river. On both sides of the river was the wide coastal plain, the agricultural heartland of the Provinces of Kamjar, Smyrna, and Ringhorn. To the south lay the Province of Southern, which—like Kamjar—backed up against the Sabre Mountains. Well north of Tyr, and on the interior of one large bay, formed by a river that was none other than the Snowy, was New Hope, the provincial capital of Ringhorn. North and east of that kingdom were the farmlands of the provinces of Garlands and Greenlands. The last formed the base of a northern peninsula that narrowed to become the Province of Freyr, a small but rich agricultural area that was across a narrow strait from the Dominion of Roomia.

"Freyr used to be a part of Vanir," Will James said sadly, "but was conquered by the Dominion of Roomia during my grandfather's reign." A range of coastal mountains, the Noatuas, extended from New Hope to the very tip of the Freyr Peninsula.

West of coastal Ringhorn was the Kettlewand Plateau, graced by the provinces of Nowell, Atrobee, Kettlewand, and Cimarron. To the south, the plateau became the high Sabre Mountains. Along the coast of the Western Ocean, well north of Cimarron, was a city that Jarl had heard little of, the legendary home of wizards and witches. Will James pointed to it with one finger and said, "This is Vor, which was once the provincial capital of Olympic."

"Now," said Liebs Hisson in his deep baritone, "that province has fallen onto hard times, its city is in near ruins, and its roads are in disrepair. Olympic is difficult to get to, hard to travel through, and a harsh place to live in, forgotten by most of the Vanir."

"But, I've heard that Vor's streets are lined with gold and it has tall towers," Jarl said.

Hisson snorted in disagreement, and then said, "That is a Kettlewand legend. But, in fact, no one has been to Vor in years."

East of Olympic, across the northern part of the Kettlewand Plateau, were the White Plains. It was a wide, open area on the map, and made up almost one third of all Vanir. The map showed the deep gorge of the Snowy River and, far to the northwest, against the Coldspray Ocean, was a roundish circle of low mountains called the Sulfur Hills, home—Jarl knew—to the barbaric Ghost Raiders.

Liebs Hisson offered another comment, "In ancient times, before the mutiny of the Ghost Raiders, the lands they live in were three Vanir provinces, Sulfur, Queis, and Jumar."

The entire southern portion of the Vanir nation was dominated by the Sabre Mountains. These were the mountains in Vanir, with occasional peaks over 5000 meters. Off the coast of these mountains, on the inland Cimarron Sea, were dozens of rugged islands, some large and some small. One of these, Will James said, was the home to a mysterious school of the E'landota.

The map showed nothing of the Roomians' land, only the narrow straits northeast of Freyr; however, south of the Cimarron Sea, the yellow parchment displayed nearly all of the Royal Empire of Glassitron. For the most part, this land appeared to be a hot, empty desert broken only by a small mountain range on the west and a southern continuation of the Sabres on the east. Before the Vanir had lost the White Plains to the Raiders, it had been the larger nation. Now, especially after the Empire had annexed Cimarron, Glassitron was larger.

Cimarron was an inland sea, with a wide opening to the Western Ocean. It was shaped like an oval, and was much larger in its middle. To the east, the Cimarron Sea was separated from the Aegonian Ocean by a narrow isthmus that was the border between the Southern Province of Vanir and the northeasternmost part of Glassitron. The Sabre Mountains formed the backbone of the isthmus and extended both northwest, along the western side of the Province of Southern, and southeast, to the Aegonian Ocean. It was here that Jarl's eyes kept returning—to the main cordillera west of Southern. High and rugged, with great inland basins, these mountains were more than 500 kilometers in breadth, becoming the lower—but still high—Blue Hills to the north.

The map was crudely drawn, but certain portions of it, such as the La Sinuosite, the carefully delineated coastlines around Vor, and the dozens of peaks within the Sabres that had precise elevations, gave Jarl the impression that the map was a copy of some earlier survey, perhaps even a copy of a copy. He voiced his question and Will James answered, "That is indeed the case, but some portions of the map, particularly a cluster of islands off the east coast of Glassitron, are inaccurate. In fact, those islands are not to be found."

All of Jarl's time was now spent at the printing company, at the palace, or—more and more—visiting with Mani Chevk. The last Sunday in July, he loaded half his employees and the four Ahlums into Fjlar's wagon and the small group journeyed up into the nearby mountains. Once there, they enjoyed a picnic near a stark alpine lake and a snowball fight on one of the nearby snowfields.

Afterwards, Navee, Stori, Lif, Sunny, Janis, and Jarl climbed a small granite peak. Tyr was directly under their feet, appearing to be a fairylike city from the great height. The printing company, the palace, and the black church could be clearly seen. Navee claimed he could see the Aegonian Ocean, but all Jarl could see was a dozen round hummocks, all east of Ispwich, which he knew to be eroded granite hills. Behind them, to the south and west, the higher horns and snowfields of the Sabres dominated their view. After long deliberation, they made plans to return and climb one of the more prominent peaks.

Twelve days later they returned. It was a happy occasion for Jarl—not only was he among good friends, but Lif had ridden to the printing company the Sunday before, a large grin on his face, mounted on a horse his father had just purchased from an unemployed E'landota: the dapple gray Jarl had inherited at the Battle of Burkes Ford. Jarl's loud shout brought most of his employees running into the street from the backyard. Lif rolled off the horse's back and handed the reins to Jarl, repeating his father's instructions that he was not to accept any money for the animal. Jarl was ecstatic. He mounted the gray and rode the horse up and down the street. That night he built an addition to the small shed were Karl kept his two swaybacked horses and the next day he took the wagon into town and returned with a load of grain, hay, and straw.

During the intervening week, Jarl had the dapple gray re-shoed and purchased a used saddle and bridle. Now, mounted on his horse, he was leading what could only be described as a small expedition into the Sabre Mountains. In addition to four servants of the Prince, there were Hjas and Stori Gautrekson; Will James, Kyle and Laufey; Sunny, Lif, and Fjlar Ahlum; Lannie, Navee, Janis, Ali, Levi, and Karl. They camped the night in the head of the high mountain meadow near their picnic spot.

The next day, with the exception of Karl, Ali, and the servants, everyone started out, on foot, to climb the designated high peak. They carried no ropes or climbing equipment, only a few weapons, lunch, and some winter clothing. For the first few hours they hiked up a gentle slope through a quiet, conifer forest. To one side was the inlet of a fast-flowing mountain stream. They left the forest behind, crossed a patch of hard summer snow, and climbed on through a long, grassy mountain meadow that was bright with many colorful flowers. Then, just as the slope became steep, they encountered that dreaded hazard to all mountain expeditions—ripe blueberries. It was close to an hour later before Jarl could coerce his small group to climb higher on the mountain, and even then, Stori, Will James, Hjas, Kyle, and Laufey remained behind.

A short time later, when it became necessary to crawl under a thick forest of stunted, wind-flagged evergreens, Jarl's party became even smaller. This time Sunny, Fjlar, Lannie, and Levi turned and started back down to their camp. Only four people continued on—and Navee immediately began wanted to turn around. Jarl took a quick vote, and the little E'landota lost his argument to democracy.

The day wore on and still the four continued up the mountain slope, scaring a tiny herd of mountain goats and ascending a hundred meters up a narrow, precipitous ravine of broken granite, where they were careful not to knock any loose rocks down on their companions. At the head of the gully, they climbed—gasping for air—out onto a high, wind-swept ridge, where they quickly pulled on their heavier clothes, buttoning them up tight against the sudden mountain cold. Behind them, far below, were the mountain meadow and the lesser peaks of the Sabre Mountains. To their left—east—their ridge quickly descended into a steep notch, beyond which was the sheer wall of another mountain. To the south, across a wide glacier gulf, higher, snow-covered peaks formed a massive wall they could not see over. To their right, a high alpine ridge ascended, a rocky road to the peak they hoped to climb.

By now it was early afternoon and Jarl was worried, as it was time to start down. But, instead the four of them continued upward, or at least they did until Navee balked at crossing a steep snowfield. Lif was also tired and the two men remained behind while Jarl and Janis climbed the last crest along the ridge. Once there, they could see the high peak, less than thirty meters above them and almost two hundred meters away, but across a narrow, rocky arête.

After a brief telepathic discussion—and in spite of Jarl's better judgement—the two climbed down onto the arête and, as best they could, walked and scrambled across to the high peak. Twice the high ridge narrowed, and with precipitous drops on both sides, they inched across the ridge on their hands and knees. Soon they were standing on top of the rock-covered summit.

Janis was overjoyed that they had been successful in their climb. She held onto the wide brim of her hat with both hands to prevent it from blowing away in the violent gusts of cold wind and grinned like the young girl she was. To the north, where there were many smaller peaks, the highland gradually became a plateau. To the east was the high valley where they were camped and the coastal plain beyond. South—across a wide, deep valley—was nothing but more mountains, more than a kilometer away and hundreds of meters higher. As they watched, an eagle, its shrill cry resounding among the peaks, flew below them, far down in the gulf, silhouetted against the dark valley. But the most incredible spectacle was to the west, where a long, U-shaped basin of azure-colored lakes and white snow fields was surrounded by precipitous horns and arêtes. The sky was a deep blue, matching the color of the lakes, and without a single cloud, broken only by the small, red moon of Mytos and the larger, bright, ringed moon of Kmir. For a long time the two stood, mesmerized, looking out across all the horizons; then, chilled by the cold mountain wind, the two of them turned, and carefully retraced their steps across the narrow arête.

Soon they were back at the snowfield. Lif was glad to see them, but Navee was clearly angry with Jarl for taking so long. However, the little E'landota was soon racing to keep up, because Jarl was clearly in his element and the two youngsters were very willing to follow. Jarl adjusted their line of travel and they descended a long, glaciated valley that was snow-covered on the eastern side. Squatting directly over their feet, the four slid down the mountainside, which was not that steep. Then Jarl left the snow and fought his way upwards through another forest of stunted trees. When they reached the top of the granite ridge to the east, the grassy mountain meadow lay before them.

A raven's sharp cry scared them and caused them to look up. Navee was tired, either from the mountain or from the altitude. Nevertheless, he followed as Jarl, Janis, and Lif ran, rolled, and laughed their way downward through the tall grass. Twice they scared marmots back into their holes and once Jarl had to run back and get Janis, who was picking fresh mountain flowers for her wide-brimmed hat.

The small group arrived at the conifer forest just before dusk. There they quieted. Driven on by the thoughts that these mountains were haunted and that they were late for supper, they hurried on silently through the forest. They encountered Hjas a hundred meters uphill of the camp. All the other parties had returned long since, supper had been eaten, and the older man was concerned for the stragglers' well being. In fact, Will James, Stori, Laufey, Kyle, and Lannie were even now readying themselves to come and search.

Jarl and the two youngsters apologized, over and over again, and then the five of them continued downhill. Soon they were back at the camp. There, as they walked into the light of the campfire, Jarl glanced over at Janis, and in a tight, controlled mindbeam, said, "*Good trip, eh?*"

Janis' good mood had soured when they had met the nervous Hjas Gautrekson, but now she grinned and mindbeamed back, "*Damn right!*"

On the opposite side of the fire, unnoticed by anyone else, Laufey—bent over a pack—suddenly chuckled to herself.

CHAPTER TWENTY-ONE:

MAKING PLANS

The second anniversary of the Battle of Burkes Station came and went. With it was the two-day holiday called Memorial Day, a remembrance of the Vanir's ancestors. Once more, the Elder Oak Printing Company set up their long stalls and once again, the Vanir Church sought to prevent them from selling the translated Bibles, this time by having their guards surround the book stall. But on this occasion, the Prince dispensed with his supposed neutrality in the Great War of the Bibles and ordered a full company of pikemen to guard the booth. For the duration of the festival at least, order was restored.

Jarl was unable to attend the Memorial Day festivities. Two days before the Friday it began, while painting the planks with which they would construct their booth, he suddenly became thirsty, a thirst no amount of water would ease. By nightfall, he was bedridden. For close to two weeks, while Janis, Navee, Sirota, and Stori brought him food and water, he remained in bed, with many of the same symptoms he had experienced at Pepper Ford Station, two years before. Finally, just after Karl completed the first few Bibles of the second printing, Jarl felt strong enough to venture into the backyard, but it was another week before he was capable of mounting the dapple gray to ride north to visit the Ahlum family.

The first snow fell in mid-October, but quickly melted the following day. That night, via an E'landota messenger, Will James invited Jarl to the palace. After he and Navee had completed their ritual of sneaking in through the side door, Jarl was again led upstairs to the room with the stuffed saber-tooth cat. Von Rhinehart was present, serving drinks from a tall, dark decanter of wine. That night and the following three evenings, the three men talked long into the wee hours of the morning, discussing potential military campaigns, legal and religious reforms, a military school, and an improved method of training the Vanir army.

The second night, while walking back to the printing company, just as Jarl and Navee reached the middle of the long wooden bridge over the Vilyur River, three black figures emerged from a hiding place south of the river. Jarl and Navee drew their weapons and began a slow retreat to the north—but in that direction, three more men silently detached themselves from the shadows. Jarl and Navee were trapped. On both sides of the river, the many lights of Tyr twinkled through a hundred unshuttered windows, but nowhere was another person in sight.

Jarl and Navee, now back to back, edged toward the upstream side of the bridge. Three meters below, the black rush of fast-moving water was hypnotizing, almost impossible not to watch. Downstream, the lower falls of the Vilyur blocked their way, preventing them from jumping into the river. The two groups of men came closer. All were E'landota, dressed in black, and each held a samurai sword. Jarl held his projectile pistol away from his body so that the three men on his side of the bridge could see it. Those E'landota stopped, waiting, facing Jarl.

Behind Jarl, the other three assailants silently stalked Navee. They held their swords two-handed and wove the tips of their blades in slow, mesmerizing circles. One of them feinted and a second assailant, his sword a white flash of light in the dark night, attacked, slicing downward with the point of his bright blade.

But Navee had not been distracted—and he moved faster. His sword was a quick blur of power, blocking the deadly thrust. The little E'landota twisted his blade and his opponent's sword flashed across the narrow width of the wooden bridge and fell into the dark water on the other side. Navee spun on one foot and kicked his now unarmed assailant in the chest. The man fell backward and into the river. Navee then, with short, powerful hacking strokes of his sword, attacked the remaining two of the Church's E'landota. For a few moments, the three men fought, their blades bright flashes of movement, the sound of their battle ringing out in the silent night.

Only one of the three E'landota at the north end of the bridge moved. Jarl raised his pistol, just a little, and the man—perhaps familiar with the weapon from another night—hesitated and stepped backward.

Navee's fight was short—soon one man turned and raced away. For the briefest of instants, the remaining E'landota withstood the little man's attacks, but then he threw his sword at Navee and sprinted after his companion. Navee took a long, deep breath and pivoted toward the other three men. For a long second the five men stared at each other, but when Navee took a step forward and Jarl simultaneously raised his weapon, the three assailants turned and ran away. Jarl and Navee now had the bridge to themselves.

Jarl walked to the upstream side of the bridge, where the Church's E'landota had been knocked into the water. He looked down into the black shadows, but saw nothing except for the dark rush of the water. He crossed the highway and then peered under the other, downstream side. There, looking more like a drowned rat than a trained warrior, was the man, clinging tightly to one of the oak bridge posts. Despite Navee's objections, Jarl lay belly-down on the bridge and reached down toward the bedraggled E'landota.

Several long seconds passed, but finally the man abruptly reached up and grabbed the outstretched arm. Jarl gave a great heave and pulled the E'landota up and onto the bridge. For another moment, the two of them stood there, unsure of what to do next, but then the Church's E'landota turned and sprinted for northern Tyr. Navee made a half-hearted swing at the man's rear end with his sword, but missed.

The next night, Lannie accompanied Jarl and Navee to the palace, and each man carried a double-barrel shotgun, loaded with buckshot. Again, they were attacked when returning to the printing company, in the exact same place. This time, when they reached the middle of the wooden bridge, a half-dozen men leaped onto the road behind them, firing black-powder weapons. No one was hit, and Jarl spun around and pulled both triggers on his shotgun, firing from his hip. One assailant yelped and abruptly sat down in the middle of the highway, and the remaining men turned and jumped back into the roadside ditch. They then scrambled up the bank on their hands and knees, leaving their wounded comrade behind.

Jarl, Navee, and Lannie all turned, so that they were facing the other, southern end of the bridge. From that side another small group of men appeared. Lannie dropped to one knee and fired his shotgun, but these men screamed battle cries and charged forward, firing back-powder weapons at the same time. A lead ball chewed a hole in the heavy floor of the wooden bridge nearby, and a shirvken flashed by, thrown by someone behind them, as Jarl dropped his empty shotgun and reached for his modern projectile pistol. Navee knelt and carefully aimed his shotgun at the charging men. He fired once, then again. One attacker fell and rolled off the bridge and into the river; another stumbled and almost fell, dropping his sword.

Lannie tossed his shotgun to one side and withdrew his sword, but the Church's E'landota, including the wounded man, now turned and ran back toward the safety of the southern end of the bridge. Navee was only a few steps behind them, screaming at the top of his voice. Lannie quickly scooped up his shotgun and sprinted after him, running through a cloud of dissipating smoke. Jarl grabbed his dropped shotgun and ran after his two bodyguards.

They chased the Church's E'landota southward for a quarter of a kilometer, between darkened houses, shouting and running as fast as they could. Their attackers raced left at one prominent intersection, staying on the main highway. Jarl, Lannie, and Navee all turned right and ran, at the best speed they could muster, up the hill to the printing company.

The following night, the three men discovered more dark figures on both sides of the long wooden bridge. But these men were not the Church's E'landota; they were instead the King's riflemen, all armed with muskets and long bayonets. They had no more trouble crossing the bridge.

One week later, Jarl returned to the palace during the day, carrying several sheets of paper, and asked to speak to the Prince. After a long wait, Will James appeared, dressed in an immaculate military uniform. Jarl presented his papers, which were not only an idea for a judicial system, where all the judges were appointed by the King, but also a written plan for religious and governmental reform. These described a government where everyone could worship the god of their choice and where the governing bodies would be organized into democratic congresses, who would draft legislation that the King could either approve or veto.

Will James listened attentively to Jarl's plans, then he asked, "Why should we do this? As I see it, the royal family gets nothing out of this."

Jarl spoke with a quiet intensity. "Listen to me," he said, "when your father dies, the Glasseys are going to try to take Kettlewand. You might be able to stop them, but—even if you do—the Roomians are going to come down the Freyr Peninsula and try to take Garlands and Greenlands. You don't have the strength to stop them both, and there's only one way you might have a chance of winning."

"How is that?" Will James asked suspiciously.

"You have to get the Raiders on your side!"

The Prince's eyes popped open in surprise. "The Raiders are our enemies. Why would they help us?"

"Because after Vanir falls, they are next!" Jarl said quickly.

He paused, then added, "And besides, they were at one time a part of Vanir. With a new legal system, one that is going to have to be just; and a new policy of religious freedom, one where the Raiders can worship as they please; and with equal representation in a parliament or congress—one that is set up not to advise, but to make laws—you might be able to coerce them back into your nation. This war of attrition is doing neither of you any good, and it is going to make it easier for either the Roomians or the Glasseys to take Vanir from you. You need the Raiders as your allies, just as they were in the past."

Will James snorted. His eyes were cold, and it was clear he wanted nothing more of this conversation.

Jarl realized he was losing his audience, and he continued quickly, "Please, what do you have to lose by sending an emissary to talk to the Raiders?"

"Only the life of the emissary," Will James said, his face a mask. He dismissed Jarl very quickly. It was a long walk home that day, with Navee and Lannie, and Jarl was afraid that he might have lost a good friend.

However, two mornings later, Hjas Gautrekson arrived unexpectedly at the printing shop in the early morning, bearing an invitation for Jarl to attend a formal party, thrown in honor of the Prince's birthday. The announcement sent the small shop into an uproar, and Stori, Janis, and Ali all began arranging his night. Stori talked Pio into being his evening companion. Hjas loaned Jarl an old suit and somehow, especially considering the height differences, Stori and Sirota made the necessary adjustments. Jarl rented a coach and a matched team of horses and finally, on the night of the party, with Lannie as a bodyguard and Navee as the driver, he picked up Pio at the Gautreksons.

By Jarl's standards, it was a tedious evening. Pio, obviously dressed in her finest clothing, was a roundish bubble of continual joy, full of small talk, gossip, and admiration for the food, furnishings, and people. They danced a dozen waltzes together, strange dances that Pio had to lead Jarl through while he tried his awkward best not to step on her toes. Will James was again dressed in his immaculate uniform, with many medals, white trousers, and tall, black boots. He danced with all the women, and especially with one short, blonde lady.

At one point in the night, the guests formed a long line and were formally introduced to both the Prince and his mother. The King was not present, and Pio whispered he was sick. "Diabetes," she said.

"Is he able to rule the country?" Jarl asked.

Pio rolled her large eyes heavenward and whispered, "No... not really."

"Then who...?" Jarl began.

Pio spoke in an even quieter voice, "The Prince... I thought you knew..."

This was the first occasion Jarl had met the Queen. He found her an extremely tall, bejeweled woman, who stared coldly down on him from a great height. Jarl was nervous after his recent argument with Will James, but when he presented him with a pen set, inlaid with gold and small diamonds, the tall man grinned and shook his hand as if nothing was wrong. The short, blond woman, who stood beside Will James with an empty smile on her face, allowed Jarl to kiss her hand.

That ordeal over, Jarl steered Pio toward a white-gloved waiter who was dispensing narrow, impossible-to-drink-from glasses of white wine. "Who is that woman at Will James' side?" Jarl asked.

Pio's eyes flew open and she came close to spilling her drink, "She is Gradwich Solym, Prince William's fiancée. I am surprised you don't know, especially being so close to Prince William and all. They've been betrothed since childhood."

Jarl's own eyes widened in surprise. Will James had never made any mention of this woman and he had been certain, after long watching

Will James with Stori, that the two shared some relationship. "When are they...?" he stammered out.

"They plan to marry next fall." Pio had no chance to comment further, because, giggling, she was spirited away by a handsome young cavalry captain, formal and polite in his uniform. Jarl was left with three half-empty wine glasses.

Jarl paused, catching his breath, and looked around the vast room, which was lit by a thousand candles. The floors and furniture were waxed to a high sheen; all manner of flags, banners, and tapestries hung along the stone walls; and on the wide dance floor, amid the flashing jewelry, close to one hundred couples danced, swirled, chattered, and laughed, all to the sound of a small orchestra, perched on a high balcony. To Jarl, it was as if he was in a dream, or was a part of a fairytale, one that was very far removed from what he considered his real life.

In the shadows, next to an open set of wide, glass doors, Jarl saw Hjas Gautrekson. He walked around the dance floor and joined the tall High Ejliteta. From nowhere, Enrick von Rhinehart appeared, also dressed in an immaculate uniform with many medals. The two men steered Jarl into a side room, and Hjas quietly closed the doors behind him.

Jarl set down his glasses, and von Rhinehart immediately produced a goblet of wine and three large glasses. Hjas, with a twinkle in his eyes, complimented Jarl on his suit. After they had each tasted the red liquid, von Rhinehart became serious, his voice quiet, "Prince William has shown us that very interesting document you gave him the other day." The man paused for several seconds. "Do you intend to print it?"

"No, I do not. That would serve no purpose," Jarl said. Then he added, "Did the Prince tell you what my reasons were for drafting such a document?"

Hjas answered, his voice very solemn, "Yes, he did. Do you really think it will be possible to get the Ghost Raiders to join our nation?"

"I don't know. But I think you should try. After all, at one time, they were a part of the Vanir nation, and more importantly—if you and the Raiders cannot work together, then either Glassitron or Roomia will conquer you both, piecemeal."

"It's been a long time since both the Vanir and the Raiders were one nation," Hjas said. "A lot of blood has been spilled since then."

"I agree, but I see nothing to be gained from the present war. The Raiders don't have the strength to defeat you or form an independent nation of their own. And you can't defeat them if you can't draw them into an open battle."

Von Rhinehart nodded in agreement. "The few times we've sent armies out onto the White Plains, the Raiders simply ran and harassed our flanks and supply lines. Our armies suffered many casualties and, as near as we could tell, inflicted no damage on the nomads."

Jarl looked up at the tall general. "Given their limited manpower, intimate knowledge of the terrain, and the considerable space of their homeland, that is exactly what I would have done in their situation... and you too, I would wager."

Von Rhinehart was hesitant and his eyes suddenly cold, but he again nodded his agreement.

Jarl continued his argument: "All I offered the Prince was a possible solution to the Raider and Glassey problems, and a chance to turn an enemy into an ally. But, whatever happens, the Ghost Raiders will not cooperate without some major concessions from the Vanir... some proof of intention that they'll be treated as an equal, with respect and honor, and I can think of no way to do that other than allowing them to have a voice—a strong voice—in the government."

Before Hjas and von Rhinehart could comment, someone opened the double doors leading to the dance floor. Hjas looked over Jarl's shoulder and his eyes suddenly twinkled with mischief. Long, thin feminine fingers took Jarl's arm and propelled him through the doors and onto the dance floor. There he danced not one or two, but three dances with the tall, black-haired beauty who he had long since decided was the most beautiful and most charming woman at the ball, Stori Gautrekson.

It was the highlight of Jarl's evening, minutes that blended together into a kaleidoscope of bright colors, music, and people talking in the background. Their last waltz was the final dance of the evening, and they joined the others in applauding the band. Jarl then collected Pio, Lannie, and Navee—who was grinning so broadly that Jarl suspected he was drunk—and returned to the Gautreksons' home. After more wine, Jarl drove the coach home with Lannie on the high seat beside him, and with Navee inside, sleeping or passed out.

Throughout the fall and winter, Jarl was invited more and more to the Gautreksons' home. Navee always accompanied him, often spending the evening sleeping in the warm kitchen. In front of the large fireplace in the family room, Hjas and Stori sounded Jarl out on his ideas, discussing at length his proposals and securing his repeated promises not to print any essays without the Prince's approval.

Hjas and Stori both asked Jarl to share their Thanksgiving dinner. On this occasion, a third High Ejliteta and his mother joined them. Stori, as graceful and witty as usual, introduced the man as David Soroka. He was a tall, thin young man, who, after the evening meal, produced an ancient brass altimeter and proceeded to show Jarl how to use it. Stori, gathering her skirts up under her, sat on the floor next to David, and described how the young man spent his summers high in the Sabre Mountains, wandering alone among the meadows and ridges, often climbing many of the snow- and rock-covered peaks, and measuring their heights with his instrument.

Jarl, always the bookwright, immediately asked David for a series of articles. The young Ejliteta was surprised at the question, and the moment was made more awkward by Stori's quiet laughter, but he quickly agreed. For a long time, they talked of the nearby mountains, and David told of his adventures and the things he had seen.

Jarl accompanied David to his coach that evening, and promised that he would go with the young man on one of his excursions. Then, he asked the one question that had somehow slipped his attention during the evening. "Have you ever seen anything to indicate those mountains are haunted?"

David was already inside the coach, swinging the door closed. "No, but then I've only traveled in Smyrna and Kamjar. I've heard tales of witches and wizards in other parts of the Sabres, particularly in the Forests of Atrobee." The man paused, thinking. The door closed with a click. The coachman clucked and the horses began to walk away. David spoke again, "I think one of them was supposed to be a sister of that old wizard who tutored Prince William."

Jarl was quick to arrange a second meeting with David and, a few days later, he, the young man, and the Gautreksons all met in an expensive restaurant in Tyr. There, in spite of the strange looks dispensed by the other customers, the four of them compared David's altimeter with an instrument Jarl had borrowed from Mani Chevk, and adjusted them so that they showed the same elevation. In the spring, David planned to visit relatives in New Hope. While there, Jarl suggested he calibrate his instrument at the ocean's edge. "You should do this on your last day in New Hope, even on the morning you leave. Then you should travel as fast as possible to Tyr."

David cautioned, "It will be a slow trip. I will be with my mother."

"Well, travel to Tyr as fast as politely possible. Then, once you are here, set this other instrument to the same altitude. Then all summer, Stori can take readings each day while you are in the mountains, and you can subtract or add the difference from what you know is the correct Tyr elevation to your readings. That way you will obtain a more accurate reading of the mountains you climb."

The young man was amazed at the suggestion. He thought about it for several moments, then he nodded his understanding and agreement.

Hjas was confused. "Wait," he said. "Why can't you read the other altimeter?"

Jarl sucked in a long breath. "I am thinking about returning to Kettlewand and visiting my friends there."

Stori's black eyes flew open in surprise. "And who is going to run the printing company?" she asked.

"You are!"

"But..."

Jarl silenced the tall woman with a wave of his hand, and then—for a few minutes—they talked of the small printing company and bookstore. Jarl, with considerable assistance from Hjas, finally convinced Stori that, together with Karl, she could run the printing business for the summer while Jarl was away.

Then, looking back at David, Jarl bluntly asked, "Tell me everything you know about this witch in Atrobee, the sister of the wizard who was the Prince's tutor."

David was embarrassed. "I'm afraid I know very little and all I have heard are stories and vague rumors... The witch is supposed to live along a branch of the Locust River."

Hjas frowned, "That's somewhere above Henlopen, isn't it?"

David answered slowly, "I think so. But I don't really know that much about that area. It's reputed to be very wild country, and I believe one story mentioned the name of a town or village. Sprite, I think... No. Spice." He turned back toward Jarl, an apologetic expression on his face. "Sorry. That's all I know."

"And who did you hear this from?" Stori asked. "I thought that no one lived in the Sabre Mountains."

"Oh, there are a few people who live there. And occasionally, I've met other travelers."

Hjas interrupted, "I hope you're careful... Some of those people can be dangerous."

"Yes. I carry a pistol... sometimes..." David paused, thinking and looking at Jarl. "I've heard the story of that witch two... no, three times. Once was down here in Tyr. The other two times were up in the mountains, both from other travelers." He again paused, then said slowly, "I'm sorry, but I'm not very confident in those sources. Campfire gossip, you know."

Jarl was hopeful—perhaps too hopeful. "Campfire gossip can provide very accurate information sometimes," he said. "Was there anything else?"

David thought for several long moments. "No, there was nothing else. And everyone said so little that it is hard to tell you anything at about the witch." He thought for a few more moments. "I do remember the name Spice though."

"Was there any description of the witch?"

"Yes. She's reportedly very old. Ancient, in fact. Stooped, with white hair and a long, hooked nose."

Hjas laughed out loud, and said, "Sounds like your typical description of your average witch. Should be no trouble at all to locate." The tall man scrutinized Jarl and asked, "Are you thinking about going there? To Spice?"

Jarl was noncommittal, "I don't know... I'm just collecting information."

Within the week, Will James invited Jarl back to the palace. On this occasion only Hjas Gautrekson was present. The three men talked for a long time, sipping wine in front of a roaring fire. Will James had news from Kettlewand, but it was not what Jarl was expecting. "A religious leader has surfaced in Atwa," the Prince said. "He is evidently a poor man, who is calling for massive reforms in the Church, including a more open-door policy, and the use of the new translated Bibles. And he wants to incorporate singing into the services..."

"That's something I promoted in one of my theses," Jarl said.

"I know," Will James said, leaning back in his chair.

"And there is something else," Hjas said, very seriously.

"What's that?" Jarl asked.

"I've told the Prince that you plan to visit Kettlewand, and he's going to send some company with you. E'landota company."

"Who?"

"Kyle and Laufey."

"That may not be good. They're Ghost Raiders, and I'm going to Kettlewand, where they won't be welcome."

"Their destination isn't the Kettlewand Plateau. It's the White Plains." Hjas grinned, and then added, "They're going home to try to arrange some kind of preliminary peace or treaty with the Raiders."

Jarl's eyes widened in surprise, and he looked at Will James to see if it was true. The young Prince smiled and nodded, then Jarl asked, "What do Kyle and Laufey think of the idea?"

The Prince's eyes narrowed and his smile disappeared. "They don't think the Raiders will listen; however, I've still written out an agreement that I hope the Raiders will at least consider. It contains some of your suggestions."

"Which ones?" Jarl asked.

"That," Will James continued coldly, "is between me and the Raiders." He then changed the subject, "Now, what is this you're asking about Kvasir's sister?"

Jarl repeated all of what David had told him, and the Prince quickly produced his ancient map of Vanir. Soon the three men were leaning over the old yellow parchment, tracing out the route of the October and Locust Rivers and attempting to locate Henlopen and Spice. Neither village was shown on the old map, but Hjas had asked someone in his employment and he pointed to a fork in the Locust River where he thought Henlopen might be located.

Jarl asked Will James, "Did Kvasir ever mention having a sister?"

"No," the young Prince said, "Never. In fact, I have no idea if he had any family at all."

"Did you ever see Kvasir do any magic?"

Will James was thoughtful, "No, I never did."

Hjas spoke, "After thinking about it, I have to admit I've never seen anyone, Kvasir included, do anything I would consider magic."

"So what is a wizard then?" Jarl asked. "What is sorcery?"

"Things like shape changing, making cows go dry, changing the weather, and making people sick."

"I've heard that before. But no one seems to have ever seen any kind of sorcery for sure."

"What are you getting at?" Will James asked.

"Did you know, that in some places, being left-handed is a sign that a person is a sorcerer?"

"I didn't know that," Will James said quietly. Unlike Hjas and Jarl, he was left-handed.

Jarl leaned forward, staring into the younger man's brown eyes, keenly aware that Hjas was sitting quietly to one side. "How many of your subjects have been burned to death when they've been no more guilty of magic than you and I are? You for being left-handed and I for having a strange coat and strange weapons. But they're not the High Prince or the Bookwright of Vanir, so the Church has their way with them."

Will James was thoughtful. "What do you want me to do?" he asked. "Being left-handed is not a crime in Vanir."

"Not yet..." Jarl said slowly. "But everyone should have the right to a fair and just trial, no matter what they are accused of. In fact, good witches and wizards could be very useful, if they exist."

"They exist," Will James flatly declared.

"But no one, it seems, has ever seen one. Did they ever exist?"

"Yes, and that's why sorcery is illegal. Long ago, sorcerers used their powers to destroy armies and navies."

"And no doubt they used to command and overthrow kingdoms too...?"

"Yes, that is true," Will James said.

"Is there any written documentation of this? Are there any oral stories that says such-and-such wizard did such-and-such magic at such-and-such place?"

Neither Hjas nor Will James had an answer, and Jarl continued, "Where I come from, a witch hunt is a search for something that doesn't really exist. Have you ever stopped to think about that? That the Church is burning all these witches and wizards at the stake, and there may not be any such thing as a real sorcerer?"

"But Kvasir was a wizard," Will James said weakly.

"But nobody has ever seen him do any magic..."

Will James spoke again, "But at Vor..."

Jarl threw up his hands in exasperation. "Has anybody ever been to Vor? Do you even know anybody who has been to Vor?"

Both Hjas and Will James said the same name at the same time, "Kvasir."

That answer caused all three of them to laugh. Hjas, being a diplomat, said, "I think this conversation has come full circle." Then he filled their wine glasses, and no one pursued the subject further.

It took Jarl more than a month to settle his affairs at the printing company. He celebrated the mid-winter holiday at the shop, having a small quiet meal with most of his employees. He ordered a special-made rifle from Mani Chevk and purchased a flintlock pistol from a shop in Tyr. Mani was extremely proud of the rifle, and walked out to the printing company to deliver it in person. The weapon was relatively short, especially compared to the long rifles of the Kettle Rangers. It had a single barrel, was rifled, and was fired by a flintlock. However, instead of having to ram each charge down the barrel, Jarl had designed the rifle so that it could be opened at the breach, using a rotating crank under the stock, and allowing the paper charges to be inserted there. And, from a deep pocket, Mani produced a brass telescope, a gift that he snapped open with a theatrical gesture. Everyone passed the instrument around, surprised when they first placed it to their eyes, examining Ispwich, nearby Tyr, and the high peaks above the shop.

All of his employees were sad to see Jarl return to Kettle, even for a visit. Both Navee and Lannie insisted on accompanying him, so he had to hire two more E'landota to protect the shop. Stori and Hjas promised to look after the printing business. Karl and Levi would be in charge of the presses. Janis cried, hugging Jarl for a long time. Jarl genuinely regretted leaving the young girl, who, to his pride, was now managing and writing much of the weekly newspaper. In private, he cautioned her to be very discreet with her mindbeaming. With Stori, he outlined his plans for the next few months. He gave her several more of his articles and theses to print, and he got her promise to encourage both Janis and David to write articles for the company. Finally, he showed her the formulas for calculating the elevations utilizing the altimeters, and he reminded the tall woman that somewhere—sight unseen in Tyr—Hjor was compiling a dictionary.

Jarl had one more conversation with Will James, during a midday lunch on a green hillside near Ispwich, after an unsuccessful rabbit hunt with a handful of High Ejliteta falconers. Jarl promised a dozen times to return to Tyr before mid-summer, and then, with much fanfare, Will James presented him with a short-barreled flintlock pistol, inlaid with silver and engraved along the length of the barrel. Jarl accepted the gift, but he had to laugh, confessing that he had already bought a similar weapon—although one of far less quality. After mounting his gray, he paused, looking down at his tall friend. They were silent for a moment or two, then Jarl asked, "Do you intend on marrying Gradwich Solym?" He was blunt, and despite his best efforts, the words came out sounding cold.

Will James' brown eyes popped open. He frowned and, after a few seconds, said, "Our parents arranged the marriage when Gradwich and I were babies."

Jarl continued to be honest, hoping his friend would not be offended. "We have talked a lot about reforms. Here is another one for you. Marry a woman you care for and one who cares for you. Don't marry a woman just because your parents say that you should."

"But Gradwich and I care for each other a lot."

"Care, but not love. A lifetime is a long time. Spend it with someone you can love and can respect ten years down the road, no matter what your mother and father say."

"But we respect each other, and my parents are the King and Queen. Their word is the law." Behind his glasses, Will James' eyes were wild, almost afraid.

"Someday, you will be King. Are you going to arrange the marriages of your children?"

Will James had been resting one of his hands on the dapple gray's mane. He held a falcon on his other arm. Now the sensitive bird began to mimic his nervous mood, softly ringing its hunting bells. The young

Prince stepped back, stroking the falcon's head, trying to calm it. It gave him time to think. "I hadn't really thought about it, but it's the way things have been done, ever since there was a king and queen."

"You'll grow tired of Gradwich, and sooner or later you'll take a mistress. That woman loves you, you know?"

"Gradwich?"

"Stori!"

"Stori? How did we get on the subject of Stori?"

"Stori! And I think she's going to spend her entire life waiting on you."

"But I'm promised to..."

"Someday you will be King. Then you can marry who you want. Just think about it."

Will James threw back his head and laughed. He spit out one loud curse word and laughed again. Then he shouted, "I always get into trouble when you say that!" With that—and despite the high-strung bird on his arm—he swatted the rear end of the gray, sending the horse off at a gallop. When Jarl turned and looked back at his friend, Will James was standing on the hillside, two dozen paces in front his servants and the other High Ejliteta, still laughing, still holding the fidgeting bird, and waving goodby.

CHAPTER TWENTY-TWO:

KETTLEWAND

It was at dawn on a cold morning near the middle of January when Jarl, Lannie, Navee, Laufey, and Kyle rode through the empty, snow-covered streets of Tyr, traveling north toward the Foord Road. Beside them, mounted on one of Karl's swaybacked mares, was Janis, who was wearing Jarl's old sheepskin coat and her floppy, wide-brimmed hat with the dried mountain flowers still hanging in the hatband. Twice, near the black church, the tiny group skirted small parties of richly dressed clergy and their ever-present guards, their green leather armor now hidden by heavy robes of wool.

Then, near the Soo-Hoo tavern, they encountered a small, dirty, unorganized mob carrying long poles and pitchforks. This situation was unusual, for although Jarl and his friends had often been forced to endure many threats, taunts, and curses, seldom, except during the attacks by the Church's E'landota, had they been fearful for their lives. Once they spotted Jarl, the tangled cluster of excited men ran down the long hill, waving their crude weapons. At their head was a ragged old man who had a dirty beard that touched his chest. Jarl reined in the gray and sat there for a moment, watching, and letting the mob approach.

Then, suddenly, Jarl recognized the unwashed creature at the head of the group. It was Jonson Baeldaeg, the rogue Priest who had hidden the translated Bibles. He was shouting, over and over, "You took the books! You took the books!" Jarl, as the small group got closer, turned his horse away and rode back toward the center of Tyr. Once the horsemen had begun their retreat, the excited mob rushed forward in a quick sprint, but they were too slow—the travelers, urging their animals forward at a fast walk, had already turned a corner and were gone.

Jarl led his small group downhill, through snow-covered alleys, toward the bridge across the Nanoo River. Soon, the horses were crossing the structure unopposed, their hoofs making dull, hollow sounds on the heavy wooden planks. To their right, the harbor was devoid of life and the stark masts of the sailing ships were outlined against the early morning sky. The travelers turned in the opposite direction, and rode through the now empty fairground, with the wide river on their left. It was ice-rimmed, but the muddy water flowed on, unimpeded by the cold and the season.

Janis rode with them almost three kilometers. When their sad farewell took place, Jarl and Janis touched hands and then each turned to travel their respective roads. Three times, Jarl turned in the saddle and watched the tiny figure become smaller, dwarfed by the snow-covered city, the high, steep mountains, and the silver streak of the tall, frozen waterfall.

The day slowly warmed, but the road remained frozen. There was little snow, except along the edges of the highway, and the five travelers—although slowed by four packhorses—made good time. All day long, the road wound across the flat coastal plain. It was a pleasant land, with large farms and extensive conifer forests. Rarely were they out of sight of at least one group of farm buildings, and the friendly residents waved at the travelers as they tended to their daily chores. To the west, the sharp, precipitous peaks of the Sabre Mountains rose majestically in the winter air, their every gully and ridge outlined by the bright snow and their wind-shaped cornices stark against the blue sky. Winding unseen between them and the high, snow-covered mountains was the wide, muddy Nanoo River.

The party took two weeks to reach Foord, again crossing the Nanoo River and climbing onto the plateau from the east. Once outside of Tyr, no Vanir recognized Jarl as the clever bookwright who had so changed their lives, and for the first time he could travel without fear of flying snowballs or equally painful sneers and curses. But, on the other side of the coin, neither did people stop or touch him, showing a quiet respect, or thanking him for giving them a Bible that they could understand.

The five travelers spent two days in Foord, warming themselves and bathing, and at the same time waiting out a small snowstorm in a large tavern on the west side of the city. The third morning, when they attempted to leave Foord, a tiny squadron of pikemen at the western gate closed in around them and would not let them depart. A lieutenant asked Jarl his name, and a mounted courier was dispatched back into town.

Jarl was nervous. He rested his right hand on the butt of one of his flintlock pistols, and wondered aloud to Navee if they would be arrested. The little E'landota seemed disinterested, and the smile he usually wore had been replaced by a thin-lipped scowl.

The courier soon returned and, despite Jarl's arguments, the lieutenant led them and the entire contingent of pikemen back along the main road to the prominent military barracks, situated near the center of the city. There, a captain approached them and saluted, apologizing for the delay. His squadron of two dozen cavalrymen was being ordered to western Kettlewand and, at the Prince's request, they planned to escort Jarl and his four companions to the Pepper Ford Station. Jarl spent a long hour arguing with the insistent officer—none of the E'landota were of any help—and finally, with the horsemen in tow, they once again rode out of Foord, this time passing through the gate with no trouble.

With their escort, the journey was slower. After spending another four days in eastern Atrobee, sharing a barn and waiting for another snowstorm to abate, they required close to one month to travel to Desjhan, on the Kettlewand border. It took another two weeks to reach Judy Station, and they first had to cross the flat, snow-covered Rhombus, where the horsemen kept a nervous lookout for sorcerers only they could see. They arrived at Judy Station in the early afternoon, after a long, miserable day of traveling in the cold, never-ending wind of the White Plains and watching nervously for the sudden appearances of wild Ghost Raiders.

The group of travelers spent a night in Judy at the military barracks, and Jarl visited with the sheriff and his family. The next morning, as they again started west along the road, Kyle and Laufey turned north and rode out onto the White Plains, taking one of the packhorses with them. No one, other than Jarl, seemed sorry to see them go, and he rode a short distance with them and wished them luck in their mission for the Prince.

The day wore on, the road was long, and the afternoon became cold. As always on the plateau, the wind buffeted them, and the cavalrymen and two E'landota did nothing but complain. They had long since passed the eastbound stage when they spotted another, smaller group of horsemen far to the west. The cavalrymen readied weapons and Jarl checked the load in his rifle, but gradually, as they approached the other riders, who had stopped and were waiting, it became obvious they were Kettlewand Rangers. Many had familiar faces and there was no doubt who their leader was; she leaned back in her saddle, chuckled and hooted, and then—in a loud voice—debased the ancestry of everyone within earshot, shouting her joy at seeing Jarl. The Rangers and Jarl joined Mylea's obnoxious laugher, but the cavalrymen and the two E'landota became hard-faced and would not speak. "You'd think they had never heard good honest cussing before," Mylea later told Jarl.

Jarl shook a dozen hands, then amid loud chattering and talking, the combined group walked their horses west along the snow-covered road. Mylea was full of news. Everyone was safe and Chad had not burned down any more chicken houses. And, for the second year in a row, there had been relatively few skirmishes with the Ghost Raiders. In fact, the woman added, there had been only two fights, and both had been running affairs where few shots were fired and no Rangers were injured. "Probably," Mylea added, "no Raiders were hurt either."

As Jarl rattled off names one by one, Mylea told how each person was doing. Jorm was showing no interest in his studies; Chad, Molly, Marri, and Iajore all were still learning to read and write using the many books Jarl had sent to the Station; Kevin had grown a new mustache; and Aaron was well. Jarl glanced slyly at the woman and asked how many children she and the Ranger captain now had.

Mylea, leaning back in her saddle, shouted a loud, "None!" Then, just for the briefest of moments, the girth of her saddle slipped. Her eyes and mouth popped open and, as one leg flew skyward, she grabbed for the horse's mane. As Mylea righted herself and her saddle, the other Rangers— no respecters of rank—all howled with laugher and booted their horses into a run, leaving their leader behind. For close to two kilometers, despite the cold weather, they cantered west along the road, laughing at Mylea, who was once again exercising her fine repertoire of curse words.

At long last, Roundbottom Hill edged into sight. As they once again began walking their horses, Jarl asked about Otis. Mylea sobered and a moment of sadness touched her eyes, but then her smile returned and she stammered, "He is all right now."

"What happened?" Jarl asked, worried.

Mylea told the story slowly. "After you left, things were quiet for about a week. Orr, for lack of someone better to aggravate, began to pick at Otis, taunting him every time they met. That lasted about a week, then Aaron, at Kevin's request, told Orr to leave. A half dozen of those cavalrymen sided with Orr and for a couple of minutes I thought we were going to have a genuine old-fashioned fist fight, but the cavalry lieutenant had a rare moment of intelligence and ordered his men elsewhere. There was a bunch more threats, and then Aaron and a couple of the men threw Orr off the property. The cavalrymen were ordered home about a week later, and things finally settled down and back to normal."

"And?"

"It remained that way until this January, when the same cavalry unit returned to the Station on the way to Atwa. Orr was with them. He is a private now, and wearing a wooden leg. The horse soldiers spent one night at the Station, camping out in the forest well back from the main buildings. Late that night, four of those boys jumped Otis on the trail between the barracks and the Station. They had two clubs and they beat him pretty bad."

Mylea stopped speaking, and it was clear she was remembering that evening.

Finally Jarl asked, "What happened then? How bad is Otis hurt?"

"What happened?" The thin woman looked up, surprised. "They left him lying on the ground and began to walk away. Otis got up and, as badly beaten as he was, took one of the clubs off those boys and proceeded to give them the thrashing of a lifetime." Mylea stopped again, her eyes wide and frightened.

"They had to take all of them back to Judy," she continued. "That old man broke four arms, two legs, god knows how many ribs, and a couple of those boys are singing soprano now. Orr tried to kick Otis with his wooden peg leg, but somehow Otis got that leg off Orr and bounced it off Orr's head a couple of times. Orr has a cracked skull. For a while that old witch at Judy was afraid he would die."

"How's Otis?"

"He's banged up something fierce. He has a lot of bruises, but... he is really pretty much about the same..."

They rode on quietly, until they came to the base of Roundbottom Hill. There, as they rounded the turn, leaving the White Plains behind them, a black animal burst from the undergrowth on the left side of the road.

Cavalry horses danced in every direction. Navee spurred his horse, jumping his gelding into a position between Jarl and the charging animal. Someone shouted, "Raiders!" Someone else shouted, "Bull!" Mylea was cursing. Jarl caught a glimpse of a young bull, running in sheer terror.

As the bull cleared the forest, one small figure, who had been trying to hang onto the tail, let go and fell into the snow. A young man held onto one end of a rope, the other end of which was wrapped or tied around the bull's neck. That person ran as quick as he could through the snow, staying beside the terrified animal.

Mylea, shouting at the top of her voice, rammed her horse into one of the cavalryman's horses—the soldier had been earing back the hammer of his carbine. The weapon exploded, pointed skyward, and black smoke engulfed Jarl. Then he heard Mylea, wheeling her dancing horse, her face mere centimeters from the cavalryman, shout, "You stupid idiot! It's only a bull!"

Somehow the large group of horsemen parted and the bull and the young man—it was Chad—went flying through the opening, quickly crossing the road and jumping into the snow on the opposite side of the highway. More than four meters of rope separated Chad and the bull, and as the animal ran on one side of a tree, Chad—still holding the rope—ran on the other side. The middle of the rope caught on the trunk of the tree and both Chad and the bull swung together. Chad quickly ducked under the rope, and wrapped the rope around the trunk. The bull, although small, weighted a good deal more than Chad. It tossed its head, knocking Chad into the snow. He bounced back to his feet, grabbed the rope and tried to tie it. Once again the bull butted him, but this time Chad wrapped an arm around the animal's neck and hung on.

The snowfield between the tree and the road became a sea of flying wet, heavy snow, as a dozen Rangers, Jarl included, spurred their horses to Chad's aid. Grayson got there first, and more fell than jumped onto the small bull's back, knocking its hindquarters to the ground. Chad jumped to one side, rolling clear of the bull and Grayson. Someone tried to grab a hoof and almost got kicked. Someone else fell on top of Chad. Mylea and Jarl both jumped off their horses and grabbed the rope, trying to pull the animal closer to the tree. The young bull charged, as best it could, knocking both of them down. Jarl was thankful it had no horns. He landed in Mylea's lap, and loud cursing erupted in his ear.

Navee pulled his sword from its sheath and the bright blade flashed high, as the little E'landota prepared to kill the bull. Jarl caught a glimpse of Molly, standing knee-deep in the heavy snow, her hands to her mouth, her brown eyes wide with fright. Then a Ranger shouted a loud "No!" and knocked Navee into the snow.

The bull twisted on the rope, trying to kick his tormentors and throwing snow into the blue sky. One cavalryman, then a second, fell off his horse. Several people were now laughing; others were cursing. Mylea pushed Jarl back up onto his feet. He grabbed the rope and, with her help, pulled the bull closer to the tree. But then the rope broke, sending Jarl flying back again into Mylea's lap. This time the woman laughed loudly in his ear.

Grayson wrapped an arm around the young bull's neck and grabbed its ear with his other hand. The animal gathered itself in the snow, preparing to throw the man off. Another Ranger was hanging onto its tail. From above Jarl's head, a lasso floated down and settled over the bull's head, narrowly missing Grayson. Jarl, again with Mylea's help, jumped to his feet and grabbed the new rope. This time, using more luck than savvy, six or seven people hauled the bull up against the tree and tied it there. For a moment, they stood there, congratulating themselves. Then the animal began a sudden, renewed effort of kicking, and everyone scrambled back through the trampled snow, getting clear of the flying hoofs.

Jarl tripped over a fallen body and abruptly sat down again. That someone cursed and struggled to his feet. To one side, Navee was muttering similar oaths, trying to untangle himself from underneath a pile of bodies. Lannie was still on his horse, holding his rifle skyward. The cavalry captain was also mounted, shouting orders that everyone was ignoring.

Chad tried to apologize. Molly had disappeared. Mylea collapsed into a pile of laughter. Grayson rolled his eyes and looked at Jarl apologetically. Most of the Rangers then begin to smile and laugh. Some rubbed bruises where they had been kicked by the young bull or by their own companions.

On the nearby road, most of the cavalrymen still sat on their horses, silent and unamused.

Grayson explained this was Kevin's prized bull, which had escaped the previous week after knocking down a fence post. Jarl was for leaving the animal where it was, tied to the tree, but Grayson produced a second rope that he secured around the young animal's neck. He then mounted his horse. After the bull was untied from the tree, Grayson and English began to walk the young animal back to the Station, holding it between their two horses.

Jarl mounted his gray and was about to offer Chad a ride when, amid a loud crash of brush and more raised rifles, a pony dashed out of the forest. This animal raced straight toward Chad and for a moment Jarl thought it was going to run him down. Then it skidded to a stop, throwing wet snow into the air. Chad reached up and grabbed the arm of the young girl riding the pony bareback. Without speaking, he swung up onto the pony's back behind Molly and—before he had pulled himself into position behind her—the girl booted the animal and went chasing after Grayson, English, and the bull. Mylea was laughing. "That," she said, "is Chad's pony, Scottfree."

The remainder of the journey back to the Station was uneventful. Marri met them in the courtyard, hugging Jarl after he dismounted. Iajore ran down the porch, almost crushing Jarl with her embrace. As the Rangers and the cavalry dismounted, Jarl shook hands with Kevin, who was sporting a handsome handlebar mustache, then with Hjad and Aaron, who muttered, "Good to see you again."

On the porch, Jarl caught a glimpse of a tall, old man, who limped to the top step. Jarl stepped back and looked up at the Ranger, who had a bruise on his forehead and a second one on the side of his chin. Then the man smiled and spit. Jarl grinned and said, "I heard you had some trouble..."

Otis' eyes were bright. "Wasn't nothin'. I heard you had a run in with the Church."

Jarl nodded, and quickly told the short, abridged version of that story. After introductions and after Kevin had doled over his newly arrived bull, Jarl distributed the books that had required one packhorse to carry. They then stabled their horses and a dozen people entered the large Pepper Ford

Station house to have a long and lengthy supper, while everyone asked more questions and told more stories. Chad asked a hundred questions about the mountains; Marri was fascinated by stories of the Prince and the one ball Jarl had attended; Iajore wanted to hear about Tyr, Jorm asked over and over about the two fairs; and Molly just sat silently and listened, her big brown eyes wide with excitement.

Jarl spent the remainder of the winter at the Station, quickly discovering, much to his chagrin, that the cavalry captain carried orders from the Prince forbidding him to patrol with the Rangers. During the day, Jarl resumed his teachings, and was impressed with the progress that the children and Iajore had made in the past two years. The cavalry unit hung about the Station, not patrolling, and scaring themselves silly with stories of Raiders' atrocities. It was obvious that they had been sent to Kettlewand for one purpose and one purpose only—to guard Jarl.

And Lannie and Navee became more and more bothersome. Not only were they always close by and watching, but seldom could he even enjoy a conversation without their presence. Once, on a hunting trip up Getout Run, Jarl enticed Lannie and Navee to field-dress one of two elk they had killed, while he and Otis worked on the other. The two men talked in quiet sentences, well aware of how far their voices could carry across the quiet mountainside. Finally, disgusted by the sloppy job the two E'landota were doing, Jarl turned his back on them. Otis then grinned and teased Jarl that he could not even go to the outhouse without one of the E'landota nearby. "Or maybe...," the old man said, "Frontier outhouses are just more dangerous than those in Tyr."

Jarl laughed and was soon in a better mood. He told Otis about the prison, and what a good companion Navee had been there.

The old man's eyes twinkled. He described his fight with Orr and his three companions, not making light of his beating, as he often did at the Station. "You watch out for that Orr," the old man cautioned, "there's murder in that man's heart."

Jarl spoke, "You know, it's strange, but during my so-called trial by the Church, I had the feeling I wasn't being tried so much for killing the sheriff of Glad, but for using what they called a 'witch-weapon' to do it. And the Church was upset that I used the weapon at the Battle of Burkes

Ford. You'd have thought they'd have been more understanding, as I was fighting for the Vanir."

Otis was thoughtful. "That's not surprising, that they were more concerned over what they called sorcery rather then whose side you were on. Leastwise to my way of thinking. What happened to your weapons?"

"They're gone, taken by the Church. Thir saved my coat and a couple of my knives, and Fjlar had found my horse and returned it, without any thought of money."

Otis nodded his approval. "That sounds like Thir and Fjlar. They're good folks."

The subject then turned to Kvasir and his sister, the Locust River, Henlopen, and Spice. "I don't know none of Kvasir's kin," Otis said. "In fact, I ain't even sure where he hailed from, but I always thought it was somewhere in Kamjar."

"How about Spice and Henlopen?" Jarl asked. "Have you ever heard of those places?"

Otis considered the two questions for most of a minute, then drawled, "I've never heard of Spice, but Henlopen is south of Desjhan, a day or two into the Forests of Atrobee. It is at the mouth of the Locust River."

Now it was Jarl's turn to be thoughtful. "Those forests are supposed to be haunted, aren't they?"

The old man shrugged, then he said, "I've only been there once, but yea, those forests are supposed to be haunted. But then so's the Blue Hills and the Sabre Mountains."

"So..." Jarl added, "they might not be haunted at all."

"Maybe... But who knows for sure..."

On another hunting trip, one that included Chad and Molly, Jarl asked about saber-tooth cats. Otis had only seen two in his life, and one of those had been far out on the White Plains, when he was a young man. The old Ranger grinned with his usual dry humor, and said, "Still got the scars!"

Somehow the subject turned to mastodons, and Chad piped up, describing how a small herd had come as far south as the Foord Road.

"When?" Jarl asked.

"About a week before you arrived."

"Oh darn! I would have liked to have seen them!"

That day, the six of them climbed higher and higher into the Blue Hills. The trip gave Jarl the chance to test Navee and Lannie in the deep woods, and it gave Otis the opportunity to show Jarl some of the high country, to compare it to the Forests of Atrobee. Just as Jarl expected, both E'landota became nervous, with Navee being the worst of the two. Finally, at the insistence of his two bodyguards, they returned to the Station, without meat for the pot. Still, the day had been very enjoyable. Never, even on his patrols with Aaron, had Jarl climbed so high, and Chad, Molly, and Otis were all excellent companions. But there was one final sour note—at dusk, as they rode out of the forest and into the small clearing next to the Rangers' barracks, the cavalry captain was impatiently waiting, slapping his gloves against his leg, searching the woods for some sign of their return. Behind him, a full squadron of soldiers were saddling horses, readying themselves for a night search.

The remainder of March and then April passed all too quickly. Once more, Jarl found it time to say goodbye to his friends at the Station, and once again he found it painful. The Kettlewand Rangers, Otis included, had left for the Cimarron border four days before, and today, bolstered by the numerous books he had left as presents, the occasion was somewhat less sad. Everyone knew that Jarl would again return and, with the King's troops for protection, there was little chance danger might befall him, unless it was from being trampled by his many bodyguards.

Jarl and his escort left the Pepper Ford Station late that morning, after a relaxing and enjoyable breakfast. They spent that night at Judy Station—the cavalry and Lannie in the barracks, and Jarl and Navee with the sheriff and his family.

With the coming of spring, the wind from the Plains was now less bitter, but the road had turned to mud and travel was slow. On the Rhombus, the ruts seemed deeper than elsewhere. Jarl dismounted twice to search the gullies and ditches for some sign of the haunted caves, but with a cast of many—who, with each step he took from the highway, produced all manner of weapons and pointed them in every direction—Jarl finally opted to do his investigating from horseback along the road. There, at least, he thought there was less chance of his guards accidentally shooting each other.

Desjhan was Desjhan—full of red mud and obnoxious smells. Of all the Vanir cities Jarl had visited, it somehow seemed the most loathsome, although many people, Otis included, described it as a very popular place in the summer. That night, Jarl, Lannie, and Navee spent the night in the same boarding house Jarl had stayed at on his previous journey east, a wooden tavern and inn built around the massive roots of three long-dead walnut trees. The cavalry stayed in the nearby military barracks. Once again, as had been their habit, the twenty-some men had a leisurely breakfast and, late in the morning, mounted their horses and rode east.

They spent the first night in Atrobee in another of the Stage's inns, while the cavalry detachment slept in the nearby military barracks. The next morning, at first light, Jarl woke Navee and Lannie. Despite their protests, he rushed them downstairs for a hurried breakfast and then outside to where their four horses stood, fed, watered, and saddled, waiting in the pre-dawn light.

Both Lannie and Navee complained and dragged their feet. Lannie asked if he should go and wake the cavalry. Jarl said that the soldiers could catch up to them later in the day. Navee stated he had forgotten some belonging. The little man was in the process of entering the inn when Jarl replied that he too could catch up. Navee looked sorrowful, next observing his horse was throwing a shoe. The innkeeper stood to one side, amused. Lannie told the man to go and wake the cavalry, but the man continued to stand in one place, watching and briefly smiling. Jarl, after overpaying the innkeeper to saddle and feed the horses, knew the man would not obey Lannie's orders.

Jarl swung onto the back of the gray and led their one packhorse across the young spring grass. Belatedly, Navee and Lannie mounted and hurriedly followed. All together, they left four sets of obvious tracks on the tavern's lawn. They joined the highway at an angle and followed the Foord Road east for two kilometers, passing two groups of merchants. Then, as the highway climbed around a low hill, Jarl turned right, down a narrow overgrown road. Navee and Lannie balked, complaining and asking where he was going, but finally both raced after Jarl. When they caught him, they again asked where they were going.

Jarl said only one word, "Spice!" He hurried the gray onward, away from the main highway. The two disgruntled E'landota followed.

CHAPTER TWENTY-THREE:

ATROBEE

The narrow, high-banked road wandered along the side of the hill for less than a kilometer, then it crossed a narrow creek. It had been a long time since the ford had been used and no tracks marred the greasy, black mud near the water's edge. The gray quickly jumped across, splashing mud on Jarl and the packhorse, then the two animals resumed their fast westward walk along the unused highway. They were traveling through a dark, old forest, where gnarled trees overhung the road, almost as if they were ancient beings from another, earlier age, with a long-forgotten history dating back to the very beginning of time.

Reluctantly, Lannie and Navee followed. Jarl had gambled that the two E'landota would make two mistakes. They could have left a mark or a message at their turnoff, or worse, one of them could have returned for the cavalry. Jarl hoped that, between the tracks across the tavern's lawn and the innkeeper's directions, the horsemen would soon be racing east. Or at least they would be whenever they woke and checked the inn, which might be for several hours yet, considering the leisurely mornings the small party had been enjoying. And given the early-morning traffic on the Foord Road, plus the fact he had never seen so much as one of the cavalrymen study a single horse track, Jarl was fairly certain that they would overlook the side road and continue east.

The big unknown was Navee and Lannie. Obviously, because they were such poor mountain travelers, he could not take them deep into the Forests of Atrobee, but neither did he feel it wise to leave them behind—yet.

Otis had explained it to him. "You leave all your bodyguards, especially all at once, then you're going to anger the Prince. And with the Church mad as hot bricks at you, you don't want to be in hot water with the Prince. That will be the death of you. And I mean that literally!" So, Jarl and Otis had formulated a plan where Jarl would lose his guards in stages, at the same time sending a letter to Will James.

That letter, and a letter to Stori, were already traveling by stage to Tyr. Both were sincere, because Jarl honestly missed the company of Will James and the people in his printing company, but he felt he had to try to find Kvasir. After all, the old wizard was his only link to the spaceships orbiting the planet and his only hope of ever getting home.

His letter to Will James had been especially heartfelt and he hoped—fervently hoped—that the Prince would not be angry with him. "You are my friend," that letter had said, "and I hope you will always be my friend, but I must find Kvasir, because he too is my friend, and it is he who holds the key to my past.

"Please forgive me for leaving my bodyguards and the E'landota behind, and thank you for your help and protection these past months, as the Church would have long ago had me killed and my printing company destroyed." The letter ended by saying he expected to be back in Tyr about a month later than he had originally planned.

A little before noon, the three men rejoined the main highway several kilometers west of the inn where they had spent the night. The overgrown path they had traveled had, in fact, been nothing less than the old Foord-Atwa Road, disused for years and known only to a few old campaigners, such as Otis. By mid-afternoon, with the red banks of Desjhan within sight, Jarl turned off on another side road. This path led south, toward the Blue Hills. Lannie and Navee, both wearing dour expressions, followed, saying nothing.

That night, under the red moon of Mytos, the three men camped in a meadow next to the October River and suffered through a quiet meal of venison, potatoes, and onions. At dusk, the two E'landota approached Jarl and said they would allow him a brief search up the Locust River. Jarl said nothing. In truth, he was happy they had not tied him up, thrown him over his horse, and hauled him bodily north to the Foord Road, where he was certain the cavalry was now backtracking, racing toward Henlopen. At least, Jarl assumed they were backtracking—but then, perhaps no one had told the young captain of his interest in the Locust River area.

The next day, Jarl, Navee, and Lannie followed the October River upstream to Henlopen. Late the following day, they walked their horses down the only street of the small town, arriving two hours after dark. They roomed in one of the taverns the Vanir seemed to enjoy, constructed half-buried in the ground around the base of three ancient sycamore trees, whose intricate root systems formed two walls of the building. During supper, Jarl asked several people about the way to Spice. One man seemed to be the most informed person—or perhaps just the loudest—and he directed Jarl's party up a small river that joined the October River at Henlopen. When Jarl asked the name of the tributary, the man said, "It's the Locust."

Before first light the next morning, the three men began traveling upstream along the Locust River. Jarl often cantered the gray, hurrying toward his unknown destination. After a cold, snowy night, they continued their journey, which became more and more muddy as the snow melted. By early afternoon, they arrived at a long plank building, with three outhouses in the back, set next to the narrow path. Here they dismounted, tied their horses, and stiffly climbed the short steps, entering the weathered structure.

A middle-aged bald man tended bar inside. The room was dirty, with only two tables. Through an open door, Jarl could see into the one back room, where there was an unmade bed. He ordered the local drink and the special of the day, which proved to be a homemade whiskey and venison stew. After eating, he asked about Spice.

The bald man, his expression sour, replied, "This is Spice."

Jarl moved to the bar and ordered another glass of whiskey. Navee and Lannie, glum beyond all hope, remained silent, sitting at one of the tables.

For a long time Jarl and the bartender talked, leaning on the plank bar, while the man drew a crude map in spilled water. Afterwards, an hour before dusk, Jarl, Navee, and Lannie led their horses across the road and into a meadow of tall grass, where they camped for the night. That evening, Jarl and Navee returned to the building in an attempt to learn something about any witches living nearby. Despite what Jarl hoped were subtle questions, the bartender would say nothing at all on the subject.

The next day, the three men rode far up the narrow and ill-maintained road, looking over the country. Far up the valley, a snow-covered highland glittered. They saw no human tracks, recent or otherwise, and trees had occasionally fallen across the road, attesting to its lack of use. Jarl was despondent, thinking he could never find one old woman in this immense wilderness. And for the first of a hundred times, he wished Otis was with him, instead of two city-bred warriors, anxious only to race back to the lowlands.

Although the junction was not obvious, Spice was situated near the confluence of two valleys, the East and West Forks of the Locust River. The road continued up the wider bottom of the East Fork; then—according to the bartender—it climbed a low mountain to the east and followed another stream downstream and back to the more settled portions of Atrobee. The mouth of the narrow West Fork river was just west of Spice in a place that was pinched together by two hills. That region was wild, and the trees were gigantic and old, ancient beyond all reckoning. Their twisted limbs reached skyward in all directions, and it was easy to see why the forest had the reputation of being haunted.

The three men spent one more full day upstream of Spice, under threatening rain clouds, exploring the East Fork, riding well past the point where the path-like road climbed the mountain. Although they discovered several inhabitants who lived further up the valley, they learned nothing new and heard no tales of witches. That afternoon, as they rode back downstream, Navee and Lannie told Jarl they would search one more day, then they would return to Desjhan.

"All three of us will return?" Jarl asked innocently.

There was a long, long silence. Finally, Navee turned to Jarl and gave him a dark look. His words were solemn and left no room for argument, "All three of us."

"Well then," Jarl said, "Let's ride up this track tomorrow, across the mountain, and descend the stream valley to the east."

Navee's hard expression did not change, "No. We will return to the main highway by way of Henlopen."

That evening, before supper, three men, a young boy, and an ancient woman arrived at the tavern. Jarl was not hopeful, but he and the two E'landota trooped across to the one building after sunset. As they crossed the wide ditch next to the road, Lannie slipped. There was a sharp snap and the man collapsed. Jarl and Navee picked up their companion and carried him up and onto the porch of the tavern. Jarl felt Lannie's ankle, while the man groaned in pain, but he could detect no broken bones, swelling, or broken skin. The one local had come out on the porch, investigating the commotion. For lack of any other medication, Jarl ordered drinks for all three men and then for the entire house, including the owner.

A half dollar later, everyone, the E'landota included, still wore their sour expressions and sat unmoving at their tables. Jarl had never seen a party get less off the ground. All of his questions about sorcerers had gone unanswered and, finally, two hours after they had arrived, Jarl and Navee carried Lannie back to their campsite and leaned him gently on his saddle. The E'landota still complained of pain, and Jarl again went through the motions of examining the leg, but he was convinced Lannie was not hurt. That night, while Navee remained awake, supposedly guarding their camp against the boisterous mob across the way, Jarl attempted to sleep, thinking only of the next day. He was tired and lonely for good company, and he now wished he had left the two E'landota on the main highway.

A cold, spring drizzle woke them the next morning. Navee and Jarl slowly cleaned up their camp and carried Lannie—whose ankle was still not swollen—to his horse, and then helped him to mount. Then, from downstream, two horsemen rode up the road, startling Jarl, who was expecting their long-overdue cavalry detachment. As the rain increased, and the two riders dismounted and entered the lone building. Navee mounted his own horse and led Lannie's horse across the road to the tavern, jumping the water-filled ditch. There the two men dismounted, and Navee somehow carried Lannie up and onto the porch.

Jarl pulled his hat low and stood in the rain, leaning against a tree, disillusioned with the whole situation. His original plan—to spend at least two weeks looking for Kvasir's sister—was rapidly turning sour.

The rain slackened and increased again. Then, as it once again lessened, the gray snorted and Jarl turned. Behind him was the boy who was traveling with the small group across the way. His hand was on the horse's reins.

Jarl spoke quietly, "Going somewhere?"

The boy, who was no more than fourteen, was startled. Clearly he had not seen Jarl next to the tree. He froze, and his rain-wet face was suddenly white. He dropped the reins. Jarl could see that he was trembling, either from the cold, nervousness, or outright fear. Jarl's face was dark under the wide brim of his hat, and he had a rifle nestled in his arms. The butt of a pistol protruded from his belt and to one side was a long knife, a gift from Mylea. For a long time, the two stared at each other, the boy shaking, and Jarl unsmiling.

Finally Jarl said, "Go on. Leave. I'm not going to hurt you."

The would-be horse thief stood silent for a few more seconds, then he slowly started to back away, toward the hillside, which was the way he had come. He moved silently and like he was born in the mountains, and Jarl asked, "Do you live around here?"

The boy stopped, again too scared to move.

Jarl repeated the question, this time telepathically.

The boy answered, in the same manner, "*Why do you want to know?*" His mindbeaming was strong and clear.

"*Just asking...*"

The boy slowly turned and nodded yes. His face was still white with fear.

Jarl spoke aloud, "A friend of mine has gotten himself in trouble. Bad trouble." He paused, then said, "The only way I can help him is with the help of a witch, a witch who is supposed to live near here. The witch I was asking about last night."

The boy did not speak.

Jarl spoke again, "I don't want to see my friend die, even if it means finding a witch." He again paused. "I was hopeful that someone could tell me where she lives."

The cold rain increased its tempo again. The boy said nothing.

Jarl again resorted to telepathy: "*I could have shot you for trying to steal my horse.*"

This time the boy spoke aloud, with a heavy mountain twang, "Are you going to?"

Jarl stood quiet for a long moment, listening to the drum of the rain onto his hat. "No. Go."

The boy took one slow, silent step, and then another. Soon he was in the woods. There he stopped again, and mindbeamed, "*Are you from the mountains?*"

"*Yes,*" Jarl answered. "*But not these mountains. I'm from others, far away.*"

"*Jacob says that witch lives up the West Fork.*"

"*How far?*"

"*Don't know.*"

"*Where's Jacob?*"

"*He got killed in the war.*"

"*Sorry to hear that.*" Jarl paused, then asked, "*Do you know anything more about her?*"

"*No,*" the boy mindbeamed back. "*But Jacob said he saw her twice.*" The boy then turned and started to creep deeper toward the forest. When Jarl called out a low thanks, the boy stopped and looked back. After a moment's hesitation, he mindbeamed again, "*Jacob also said there was a big bear that lives up that hollow.*"

"*Black bear or grizzly?*"

"*Grizzly.*"

Jarl nodded—that was something to consider. As the boy disappeared into the forest, Jarl turned back toward the tavern. There was no one on the porch, nor did he see any sign of his two-man escort. Still, Jarl could feel their eyes on him, almost like a physical presence.

He walked over to his horse. After brushing most of the water from the saddle, he swung up onto the animal's back. Taking up the reins and the packhorse's lead rope, he walked the gray slowly toward the trees, down the valley and away from Spice. Twice he ducked under low branches, knocking water down onto his hat. Just as he turned onto the road, Navee stepped out onto the wide porch. Jarl waved and pointed north along the rain-wet track. Then he turned the gray in that direction. Navee ran back inside.

Jarl walked his horses slowly up the road, and, as he rounded a slight bend, he saw three men come running out of the building, hurrying toward their horses. When he calculated the packhorse was out of their sight, he booted the gray and cantered up the narrow track, crossing a small, muddy, rain-swollen creek and leaving obvious tracks up the opposite bank. Then, just beyond, he left the road, and walked the horses across a wide, flat sandstone rock and down into the creek.

He soon found a tributary stream that he followed upstream for a few score meters. There, hidden by the trees and the shadows between the narrow banks, he waited until his pursuers had raced by, splashing across the ford. Although it was hard to tell, it seemed there were four horses on the road, not two. As the noise of the horses continued down the mountain valley, Jarl walked his two horses back down to the ford. There he climbed back onto the road.

Still holding his rifle in the nook of his arm, Jarl cantered his horses back toward Spice. He crossed a meadow behind the town's one building, splashed across the narrow East Fork of the Locust River, and climbed a steep, rocky slope into the trees beyond. It was a dark conifer forest, the only one around. He stopped just inside the forest and looked back, his eyes searching for Navee and Lannie. Of them there was no sign, but the man who owned Spice's one building was standing in his back door, watching Jarl.

Jarl turned the gray into the woods and followed a wide bench to another narrow river. He had purposely not explored the West Fork for the past two days, hoping to use it as a hiding place against his two companions' unrelenting vigilance. No road or path led up this river bottom and it was possible, although not likely, that the two E'landota had overlooked the little valley completely, despite the fact they had virtually lived beside its mouth for two entire days.

Jarl knew he should have been counting his blessings, happy that his luck had been good, but—as his two horses walked silently under the rain-soaked trees—he was cold, nervous, and outright scared. He was also dejected. Not only was his escape from his E'landota and the cavalry going to upset Will James, his friend and the one person who he had come to depend on in the past year for protection, but a devious plan had been required to escape from a man, who a year ago, Jarl would have easily counted as his best friend.

For the first time in two years, since he had met Navee Odror in the Church's prison, he was totally alone, and he was in a wild, ancient forest, a dark and spooky place that was reported to be haunted and home to a large grizzly.

And it was likely—despite his best hopes—that no witch lived here, much less a sister of Kvasir.